PRIYA'S CHOICE

PAUL BOUCHARD

PRIYA'S CHOICE

This is a work of fiction. All of the characters, names, incidents, organizations, and dialogue in this novel are either the products of the author's imagination or are used fictitiously.

iUniverse books may be ordered through booksellers or by contacting:

iUniverse
1663 Liberty Drive
Bloomington, IN 47403
www.iuniverse.com
844-349-9409

ISBN: 978-1-5320-9653-2 (sc)
ISBN: 978-1-5320-9652-5 (e)

Library of Congress Control Number: 2020909665

Print information available on the last page.

iUniverse rev. date: 08/14/2020

The human race divides politically into those who want people to be controlled and those who have no such desire.
—Robert A. Heinlein

OPPORTUNITY

Priya Kumar, twenty-five, was walking inside the skyway connector linking the Malaysian airliner (Flight 831) to the LAX terminal. Her flight had originated twenty-two hours earlier in her home city of Chennai, India, whereby she flew to Singapore, had a four-hour wait, and then boarded Flight 831. Her final destination was El Paso, Texas, and to get there, she would have to take another connecting flight, one from Southwest Airlines, but for now, her focus was getting a cup of hot tea, for she felt the onset of a lack-of-caffeine headache coming her way.

Wide awake and walking briskly, jet lag had not set in yet. (Priya had slept comfortably for a good portion of the Singapore leg of her flight. The Southwest Airlines connecting flight was not a concern because that was four hours away, and her baggage—two suitcases containing clothes and shoes and small gifts for her two sisters—was not a concern either, for her luggage would automatically be transferred between the two airlines.

Petite at five feet four and 105 pounds, Priya was wearing dark blue jeans, a blue blouse, a thin brown sweater, and gray Nike running shoes. Her jet-black hair was cropped short, and her thick, dark eyebrows were expertly trimmed. Her face, light brown in color, resembled that of the famous actress Halle Berry. And over her right shoulder was her brown leather purse, which held some personal items, including her iPhone.

She exited the skyway connector—walking felt good after the long flight—and immediately felt the cool and pleasant air-conditioning of the airport's interior.

Priya's decision to be a graduate student at New Mexico State University's newly enacted one-year business administration /

fine arts degree program had begun more than a year earlier in her native Chennai, India's fourth largest city. Back then, she was an editorial assistant with the *Chennai Times* (English version), mostly covering local politics and business news, with the occasional crime story added on as one of her beats. Her life's ambition was to be a novelist, but her novel, *Money Matters*, about a wealthy British industrialist and his difficulties in expanding his auto parts business in India, was, as of yet, unpublished, and the constant flood of publisher rejection slips she kept receiving wasn't changing that any time soon.

The Kumars consisted of her father, Govin Kumar, age sixty, a financial officer for a large hotel in Abu Dhabi—like so many Indian expats, he sent most of his earnings back home; Priya's mother, Aarna, age fifty-eight, a homemaker who helped manage the small, three-story apartment building the family owned, lived in, and rented out; Janni, age thirty-four, the oldest of the quartet of Kumar sisters—she lived with her mother and shared in the property management duties. And then there were Rani and Deepika, both doctoral candidates at NMSU in Las Cruces, New Mexico. Rani, thirty-one, who had two years left for her PhD in accounting, moonlighted for McKinsey & Company in nearby El Paso (a forty-minute drive from Las Cruces), while Deepika, twenty-eight, majored in microbiology and was also two years shy of completing her studies.

It was Rani, nearly two years ago, who had recommended NMSU's recently enacted joint MBA/MFA program to the youngest of the Kumars.

"Why don't you come here to study in America?" she had said back in early 2017 during a telephone conversation with Priya. "I don't think you'll have a hard time obtaining a foreign student visa. Your TOEFL scores are excellent, and the fact that me and Deepika are already here at NMSU will no doubt help your chances of getting accepted at this university. You can live with us here, in our apartment, free of charge. With an MBA/

MFA degree, you can go back to the *Chennai Times* and enter the management ranks."

"But how will I pay for the classes, Rani?"

"Well, your expenses will be zero as far as rent and food while you live with us. There are always opportunities to edit college students' papers, which can bring you some money. Besides, Deepika and I, as PhD students, are teaching assistants, so we make some money, and we can help you out. And my pay at McKinsey is quite good, so that too will help."

Priya thought about Rani's recommendation and decided to run it by her editorial manager, Ram Mehta, a thin man of fifty-four who, when he was younger, had studied in Manchester, England; Vancouver, Canada; and Pittsburg, United States of America.

"I think it is a most interesting and proper suggestion," Mehta had told his young editorial assistant that Friday afternoon when Priya asked him to weigh in on the matter. "Some of my most cherished memories are from when I studied overseas. And, if I may say, an MFA degree is nice to have, and an MBA degree is well valued here. This I tell you: an MBA degree may place you in management here, which, as you know, brings with it a higher salary." He added enthusiastically, "I could use an assistant managerial editor."

"Are you saying, sir, that if I obtain this dual degree in America, then I will get a better job here at the *Times*?"

"The gods willing and the stars lining up, yes. I will put in a good word for you with the Desai family, the owners of this fine newspaper."

The thought of better employment prospects and a higher salary weighed heavily on Priya and, in the end, was the impetus for her to apply for and pursue that dual degree at NMSU. She promised herself she would never give up on her dream of becoming a novelist and getting *Money Matters* published. She also told herself she could always pursue her writing dreams on the side; more money for herself and her family made sense.

On her last day of work at the *Chennai Times*, while she was packing up her personal items, Mr. Mehta came to Priya's cubicle and said, "You've made the right decision, Ms. Kumar. You will not regret studying in the West."

"Thank you, sir," Priya had said politely. "It is only for a year. The program starts this summer and ends in the summer of 2019. A summer session, a fall session, a spring session, then the final summer session. Then it will be the graduation, and I will be back here at the *Chennai Times*."

"Most exciting, Ms. Kumar. I wish you good success. And do remember one thing as you pursue your studies in America."

Priya looked at him quizzically.

"Remember, when in Rome, do as the Romans. So when you are in America, do as the Americans. Learn all you can about America and its ways. I will see you back here upon your graduation."

Priya stepped out of the women's bathroom at LAX and immediately started looking for a place where she could buy a cup of hot tea. She wasn't in a rush or concerned about time, for she had plenty of it, four hours to be exact; four hours till her Southwest Airlines connecting flight would depart.

She turned to the right and started walking down the wide and shiny airport aisle. Her first impression was unmistakable: just how *big* things were. Everywhere she looked, things were big— big, wide aisles; big windows; big seats for people to sit in. Even the female bathroom stall and toilet seat she had just occupied were big. And the people—they were big too, and so different. In a span of walking for some three minutes, Priya passed by an older gentleman who looked like a banker or some sort of professional, because he was wearing a dark blue suit, starched white shirt, bright red tie, and shiny black shoes. Behind this professional-looking man was a much younger man who was wearing a yellow tank top, baggy white shorts, and a blue baseball cap on his head, the cap's "LA" white letters prominently featured. This younger man's feet were comforted by beige sandals, and his bare left shoulder and upper arm featured a tattoo of the Christian cross. Priya inferred that the lady next to this man was his wife, for she was standing very close to him and was similarly dressed: tank top, shorts, sandals, and also a tattoo, hers being two roses above her partially revealed left breast. The woman had clearly dyed her hair blonde, because Priya could see the small remnants of black roots at the base. And to the right of the woman was a small girl, also in shorts, sipping some orange-pink drink from a thick, clear straw that was anchored by a humongous cup that Priya felt could pass for a small bucket.

Incredible diversity, she thought as she kept walking and looking for some place that sold hot tea. Out in the distance, toward where the aisle curved to the left, she saw the slanted boards next to the ceiling tiles that announced the arriving and departing flights, and beyond the air flight boards was a food court, where she noticed a McDonald's and Domino's Pizza, two brands she was familiar with, for both had franchises in Chennai.

Good, she thought. *I can get a tea at McDonald's, and the board will tell me the gate for my connecting flight.*

She looked at the time on her iPhone, a gift she had received from Rani three months earlier, and then continued walking toward the flight board and food court. Suddenly she noticed many people talking on their cell phones, some folks not talking into the cell phone but rather just talking to themselves, an earpiece encircling one of their ears.

The earpiece must be how they can follow the conversation, she thought. *Must be a new technology I do not know about.*

She noticed white people, black people, Hispanics, Asians,

and young and old people. Whites and Hispanics dominated, but there was a fair number of blacks and Asians. Some five paces from her was a young couple, hugging and kissing, with the husband saying as the couple separated, "Have a safe flight, honey. Text me when you get to Sacramento."

Priya was maybe fifty feet from the flight display boards when she took an abrupt right to hug the far-right side of the aisle, because directly in front of her previous path was a young, blonde lady heading her way, and next to the lady's left leg was a big dog, yellow-beige in color. Priya was afraid of dogs. She reminded herself, *In India, all dogs are stray and wild, and they're never inside buildings or homes, let alone airports.* Thankfully, this big dog was on a leash, and the lady and her dog passed by Priya quickly.

Priya walked another twenty feet or so and stopped at the flight board, where she quickly found her El Paso flight slated to depart at 6:00 p.m. She turned to the right and started heading toward the food court, and in no time she noticed so many eating establishments announcing their brands with bright, big signs. Before, from a fair distance, she had only noticed McDonald's and Domino's Pizza, but now she saw so many places to eat and drink, some (Subway, KFC, Pizza Hut) she was familiar with, but most she didn't recognize (like Menchie's Frozen Yogurt, Dairy Queen, Cold Stone Creamery, Sea Legs Wine Bar, and Shake Shack). To the side of the food court, she noticed a sign that read Starbucks. The line was long there, but that's where she wanted to go. Though she had never been to a Starbucks (Mumbai had one, but Chennai did not), she had heard of the brand, thanks to Rani and Deepika, who were both fans of the coffee chain and often frequented it, especially the one located next to their apartment complex across the street from NMSU.

Priya made her way to the back of the long line of Starbucks patrons and stood behind a tall young man who she thought was talking to himself until Priya noticed a white earpiece around his right ear.

"Yes, I do love you, honey, but I just need some time to think things over. You know, take it down a notch," the man said. "Anyway, I'll call you from Andrew's apartment tonight. Okay? We're watching the fight on pay-per-view. Guys night out. I'll call and text you. Later, babe."

Wide awake and anxious to try a Starbucks tea (maybe she'd try coffee too?), Priya was absorbing it all—the people, the signs, the products, the sounds, and the smells, especially the coffee smell. In twenty minutes she would have her tea (black Earl Grey; she passed on coffee), and then she would call Rani and Deepika, informing them she had landed in Los Angles and would arrive in El Paso at the scheduled time. She was excited about being in America, this big country with big things, and she was particularly excited about living with her two sisters and starting that intensive one-year dual degree graduate studies program.

Little did she know just how much her life would change in a year.

Priya's first week in America consisted of setting up her room in Rani and Deepika's apartment (she would share a room with Rani); cooking for herself and her two sisters (mostly vegetable biryani for her sisters, who were strict vegetarians, and chicken biryani for herself—Priya ate chicken and fish but never beef nor pork); visiting the nearby NMSU campus; and signing up for her courses online.

On a Wednesday afternoon during that first week, Priya was sipping tea with her sisters in the apartment they shared. Rani, at one point, asked enthusiastically, "So what are your impressions of Las Cruces and America thus far?"

"Well, it's so different than Chennai, as you know," Priya said. Chennai is buildings everywhere, mostly white in color, and we have the ocean with the Bay of Bengal. But Las Cruces is in the middle of the desert. Here, the landscape is so vast; one can see for such long distances."

"Yes, that's so true," Rani replied. Deepika nodded in approval.

"The Franklin Mountains are beautiful—rocky and jagged. I like the mountains," Priya said. "And the Spanish architecture here is nice. Beige stucco homes with red tile roofs. The adobe style. And the yards filled with gray, crushed rocks are interesting. No grass."

"Yes, I agree," Deepika said as she took a sip of tea. Rani also agreed.

"And what has been your biggest surprise so far, Priya?" Deepika asked.

Priya took a sip of tea, thought for a moment, then said, "I'm not sure. The Walmart where we shopped is so impressive. They have everything—food, clothes, shoes, everything for bedrooms and bathrooms. Toys. Everything. The aisles are so big, and everything is well placed and shelved. Everything is so big and plentiful around here. To have seventeen different types of cheeses and twenty-five flavors of ice cream is most amazing."

Rani and Deepika laughed.

"The weather of course is a surprise. So very hot here but yet very dry. It is ninety-five degrees every day. And the sun here stays up late and only sets around eight o'clock."

Priya took another sip of tea. "You know, when I really think about it, the biggest surprise this week has been signing up for my entire coursework for the one-year program and doing so all online. And having choices about it. I'm so surprised that I can actually choose many of the classes for the program."

"Yes, that is different than the university system in Chennai," Rani said. "Education in Chennai is more structured. I too can select some of my accounting courses for my PhD program."

"Yes, me too," Deepika interjected. "My PhD program in microbiology is structured, but we can choose so many electives."

"And online registration is very efficient," Priya said. She had been able to see all the courses on her laptop, and once she had made her selections, she received course confirmation numbers. She had also been assigned a student number. On her desk, in the room she shared with Rani, she had the printed page of her entire one-year coursework:

2018 Summer Session
MBA—Internet Marketing and Why It Matters
MFA—Independent Study (one-year project)

2018 Fall Session
MBA—Supply Chain Management
MBA—International Finance
MFA—Independent Study (continuation of one-year project)
MFA—Fiction Craft and Workshop
MFA—Focused Poetry Workshop

2019 Spring Session
MBA—Applied Statistics
MBA—Operations Management
MFA—Independent Study (continuation of one-year project)
MFA—Long-Form Narrative Journalism
MFA—Focused Script-Writing Workshop

2019 Summer Session
MBA—Cost Accounting for Business Leaders
MFA—Independent Study (with reading presentation of one-year project)
MFA—Memoir Chapter Workshop

Classes would begin in five days, on Monday.

"Good morning, class," said the tall, middle-aged man at the front of the small classroom. He was wearing faded jeans, brown shoes, and a blue, collared, short-sleeve shirt, and his nose supported thick-frame glasses. Bald except for grayish hair on the sides, his hair was pulled back into a short ponytail.

"My name is Mark Martin, and I'll be with you for the next year as part of your master's in fine arts program here at NMSU. The class is entitled Independent Study, and I've been teaching it for going on three years now."

Standing, Martin turned and headed toward the large desk situated in the front left corner of the small classroom. Instead of sitting in the chair behind the desk, he causally sat on the front edge of the desk itself, his long legs hanging out, his feet firmly touching the tiled floor.

"The requirement in this course is to write a fifty-page paper that you will read to the class during next year's final summer session. I have to approve your paper topic, and the goal is to have that topic approved by next week's class, on Wednesday. You will be able to work on your paper during some classes here, but a good portion of our classes will entail you discussing your progress on your paper to the class. By the end of this summer session, the first ten pages of your paper will be due. By the end of the fall semester, the first twenty pages will be due. And so on. This is a seminar course that meets once a week on Wednesdays. Today, a Monday, is the only non-Wednesday when we'll meet."

Martin stood up and walked to the front of the class.

"I like this class size—typical and perfect. Eight students. This is a fun course. My best advice to you all is to pick a paper topic that you enjoy, because you will be working on it a lot."

Martin placed his right hand in his right front pocket, then started slowly pacing in front of the class, first to his left, next to the desk, and then to his right.

"This is an interactive course where your classmates will

share their opinions about your paper during our class discussions. Class participation will constitute 30 percent of your grade each semester—summer, fall, spring, and summer—so you have to speak up in this class and offer your opinions."

Priya, sitting in the middle of the second row, thought, *Opinions, discussions, speaking up. I'm not used to that.*

"This is an eight-credit course," Martin added, speaking fast. "You receive two credits for each semester. So with that, let's introduce ourselves to one another. I'll kick it off. I'm Mark Martin. I'm fifty-six years old. I'm on my third marriage. I have two grown boys and a nine-year-old stepdaughter. I'm from Connecticut originally. My father worked for General Electric for thirty-five years, and my mother was an elementary school teacher. I have two older brothers and a younger sister. At eighteen, I joined the navy and served for three years. I then went on to college at San Diego State University—go, Aztecs. Upon graduating, I worked for a marketing company. On the side, I also got my real estate license. I then worked for an advertising agency for eight years. All throughout this time, I did some freelance journalism and taught some English courses at night. When I was thirty-four, I enrolled in the fine arts program at Arizona State University. In the past two decades, I've held various teaching positions at universities. Six years ago, I joined the staff here at New Mexico State, and I've been teaching this course for three years. For hobbies, I enjoy brewing my own beer, and practicing tae kwon do. I'm on my brown belt; not sure if I'll go for the black belt because I'm maybe a bit too old for that. I also enjoy working on my supped-up Bronco. My wife and I like four-wheeling on the weekends. I have two dogs, Cooper and Rocky. Cooper is a German shepherd, and Rocky is a Belgian Malinois. We also have two cats, Whitey and Moe. I like reading. All writers are readers. My favorite writer is a toss-up between Jack London and William Faulkner. I also like Hemingway and Steinbeck."

He stood up. "Okay, let's go around the class and introduce yourself to your classmates."

Priya slid down in her chair. She was nervous.

"Let's start with you, sir. No need to stand up. Just tell us about yourself."

Priya quickly figured she was the sixth of eight students in the class based on the order of chairs and desks. Before her, there was Bob, a seventy-year-old Vietnam veteran who spent the better part of his working life as a certified mechanic at Walmart. Bob, who had three kids and five grandkids, enjoyed hunting and fishing and motorcycling. Five years ago, he married a woman thirty years his junior. Bob's favorite writer was Tom Clancy.

Next to Bob sat Carlos, a twenty-year-old NMSU college student majoring in business. Carlos, who grew up in Las Cruces, loved soccer and had detailed plans of opening up a Tex-Mex sports bar named, what else, Carlos's. Carlos's favorite writer was Gabriel Garcia Marquez.

Then there was Geneva, also from Las Cruces and also twenty years old. Geneva was a music major; her instrument was piano. Geneva also took voice lessons and acting classes. Her plan was to move to Los Angeles and break into the movie business or modeling. She told the class, "I think I may be too short for modeling, but I'd love to give it a go." Geneva's favorite writer was a coin flip between J.K. Rowling and Anne Rice.

Sitting next to Geneva was Jose, twenty-seven, a manager of a Buffalo Wild Wings restaurant in El Paso. Jose was married with two kids. He was a part-time student at NMSU studying marketing and film. His goal was to be a screenwriter. An avid *Game of Thrones* fan, Jose's favorite writer was George R.R. Martin, the famous writer who created the series and lived around New Mexico's capital, Santa Fe.

And sitting behind Jose was Brenda, age forty-nine, a retired schoolteacher and also a mother and grandmother. Brenda enjoyed wine tasting, cooking (she had once trained as a pastry chef), and traveling once a year with her husband of thirty years to Italy. Brenda told the class, "Twenty-five years of teaching was enough for me. I want to be a food writer. If that doesn't work out, my husband and I can always open up a café, and I'll make my favorite pastries." Brenda said she didn't have a favorite writer but that she enjoyed watching all the cooking shows on TV.

Priya was next. She cleared her throat. She felt her heart pounding. "My name is Priya Kumar. I am twenty-five years old. I am from Chennai, India. I live with two of my sisters here in Las Cruces. Both of my sisters are doctoral candidates here at this university. I have enrolled in NMSU's joint MBA/MFA degree program."

As she spoke, she relaxed some. Her voice, at first shy and shaky, grew smoother and more confident. "In Chennai, which used to be called Madras, I was an editorial assistant at the *Chennai Times*. I would like to be a writer someday. I have written a novel, but it is unpublished as of yet. My thinking is this dual degree program will help me obtain better job prospects at the *Chennai Times*. I do not have a favorite writer, but I enjoy the works of Jhumpa Lahiri, Salman Rushdie, J.K. Rowling, and E.M. Forster."

"Very well. Always great to have a foreign student in class," Martin said. "Tell us, what is the title of your novel?"

Priya proudly replied, "*Money Matters*. It's about a rich British entrepreneur and his difficulties of expanding his business in India."

"Very interesting," Martin said. "And your name is Priya. Am I pronouncing it correctly, Pree-yah?"

"Yes, sir. That is correct; good pronunciation."

"Call me Mark," Martin insisted. "By the way, gang, I forgot to mention that we're all on a first-name basis in this class. We'll be together for a year. Get to know each other because every one of you will critique each other's papers. Remember, a lot of your grade is class participation."

Martin stood up and looked at the two young men sitting to the left of Priya. "All right, let's hear from our final classmates."

There was Brian Robinson, twenty-four, a first lieutenant in the New Mexico National Guard who had graduated two years ago from NMSU with a degree in finance. Brian was an MBA student whose studies had been interrupted last year because of his nine-month deployment to Afghanistan. He had signed up for the class because he wanted to write a fictional account about his experiences downrange. Brian worked part-time for Junk King, a franchised garbage-hauling service. His goal was to move up the ladder in his military unit and get into real estate development in Las Cruces. When asked if he had a favorite writer, he said that he didn't but that he liked the works of the great screenwriter Aaron Sorkin, especially since it was Sorkin who wrote the screenplay of his favorite movie, *A Few Good Men*.

And the last student in the class was Anthony Cantu, who announced in a loud voice, "Call me Tony." Cantu was thirty-nine, married with two kids, and a part-time substitute teacher and full-time bartender in Las Cruces. His dream job was to be a screenwriter. Tony had plans of writing a movie script based on the drug cartels battling it out in nearby Juarez, Mexico.

"Great," Martin said as he stood up. "Very interesting class. We're gonna have a great year, gang."

He sat back down again on his desk and said, "Let's take a ten-minute break. After the break, if you want to meet with me one-on-one to discuss your paper topic, then please do so. I'd be happy to meet with you. If not, then I'll see everyone next Wednesday. Remember, you have to have your paper topic selected by next week and approved by me."

After the break, the students returned to their desks, but half of them—Carlos, Geneva, Brenda, and Jose—picked up their belongings and left the classroom, with Jose saying, "Mark, I'll have my topic ironed out next week. I know I want to write something like a spin-off of *Game of Thrones.*"

Martin replied, "That'll work. A fiction-fantasy piece. I've seen those papers in this class before."

Bob, Tony, Priya, and Brian stayed back. They were at their desks, and Martin said, "All right. Let's discuss paper topics. We can meet one-on-one or we can discuss it in an open forum. It's up to you guys."

"Open forum works for me," Bob said. "I know I want to write about Vietnam. I'm thinking about a work of fiction—a soldier in his platoon, combat, crap that's going on back home."

"That's fine," Martin said, sitting at his desk. "Are you thinking memoir here but fictionalized?"

"Yeah, sort of," Bob said. "Semiautobiographical but fictionalized."

"That's fine," Martin said. "I should have said earlier in class today, but I'll be sure to mention it next week, that the reason I have to approve your paper topic is when I first started teaching this course, I was getting some pretty good paper topics but also, on occasion, some weird ones as well. One time I had a student who wanted his entire paper to be cartoon images. I'm okay with graphic novels, but it can't just be all images; there has to be dialogue among the characters. Another time, I had a student who wanted to write a paper about Jesus Christ, but her whole paper ended up being why everyone needs to be a Christian or else they'll burn in hell. It ended up being a religious-conversion project for her. I also once had a student who ended up being a racist, and I told him he couldn't continue writing his paper as is. He ended up quitting this course. Anyway, that explains that. Bob, your paper topic is fine. The Vietnam War is always great material."

Bob picked up his belongings and headed for the exit, and Tony went next.

"Well, Mark, as I mentioned just a while ago, I want to write about the drug cartels in Juarez."

Priya was listening in and still had a hard time processing the fact that students and the professor—at least in this course—were on a first-name basis. *That would never happen in India,* she thought.

"I think that's a great subject, Tony," Martin said, smiling. "I know you eventually want to write a screenplay about that topic, but I see you writing a good, solid academic paper about the cartel wars. There's been some good journalism and good reporting on that subject. You'll have plenty of material."

"Thank you, Mark."

"You bet," he said. "It's an interesting topic and so close to us here in El Paso / Las Cruces."

Priya quickly glanced at Brian, not sure who would go next. He smiled at her and she decided to discuss her paper topic.

"Oh, sir. My interest is to write about America."

"Please, Priya, call me Mark."

"Yes, sir … oh, I mean Mark. Uh, in many ways, I came to America not only to study certain courses but to also learn about the country itself."

Martin thought for a moment. "I think writing a paper about America is way cool and a great subject," he said. Brian, smiling, nodded in approval. "I have an idea for you, Priya."

"Oh, yes, thank you, sir," she said, smiling, a bit relieved. Then she caught herself. "I mean, thank you, Mark."

Martin smiled. "You know what would make a good paper? It is generally accepted that the very best book on America is Alexis de Tocqueville's two-volume *Democracy in America*. Tocqueville visited America in the 1830s and wrote about his experiences and observations. His book—the two volumes are in one book—is not an easy read, but so many of his arguments can be analyzed today and still seem to hold relevancy. Priya, I recommend you write a paper like Tocqueville's. In fact, I would outline his arguments, and then you can comment on them. See if you agree with him or not and interject your own opinions on the particular matter. I think that would make for a great paper."

"Oh, thank you, sir," Priya replied. Martin looked at her smiling. "Remember, Priya, it's Mark."

"Oh, yes, Mark. Thank you." She then asked, "This book, it is titled *Democracy in America*?"

"Yes, that's correct."

"And the author is The-tok-ville?" she asked, not sure of the pronunciation. How do you spell that, sir ... I mean, Mark?"

"I know his first name is Alexis—A-l-e-x-i-s," Martin said, pronouncing each letter. "His last name is small d and small e, for de, the French word for *of*. He was a French aristocrat. His last name, I'm pretty sure, is spelled T-o-c-q-u-e-v-i-l-l-e," he said, again pronouncing each letter.

Priya was writing his every word and letter in one of her five-subject notebooks and when she was finished, she stood up, gathered her belongings, and said, "Thank you, Mark."

"Sure," he said. "I think it's a great topic." And then he said, "And last but not least. Our young military officer. Brian, what do you have for us?"

"India," Brian said in a loud clear voice. Priya, nearly halfway to the door, stopped dead in her tracks, turned around, and looked quizzically and directly at Brian, who was smiling.

"Like Priya is writing about America, I want to write about her home country," Brian said, still smiling. He thought, *I actually wanted to write about my experiences in Afghanistan, but I can do that some other time, maybe in some other course.* "I want to learn about and write about India."

"Cool," Martin said. "I don't know too much about India. I know it has a large population and that its economy is growing fast. I've heard about Gandhi of course. But I think that's a great

17

paper topic. Maybe you can get with Priya and have her give you some suggestions."

Exactly, Brian thought.

Brian exited the classroom and caught up with Priya, who was a few steps ahead of him in the hallway.

"Well, Priya, any tips for my paper topic?"

Priya, still walking and looking straight ahead, said, "A lot has been written about my country. I'm sure you can research it."

"Yes," said Brian, "but do you have any suggestions?"

Priya looked at him while still walking down the hallway. "Well, Mr. Robinson, this I tell you. Maybe you can do the opposite of what I'm doing. I'm looking at America through Indian eyes. Perhaps you can read all you can about India and offer your opinions about certain observations through American eyes. Of course, I have the advantage of being here in America. Best if you could visit India and observe things for yourself, but for now, I'd recommend reading all you can about India and interjecting your American perspective where appropriate."

"Please, call me Brian."

"Okay," she said. "If that is your wish."

They continued to walk down the building's hallway. "Can I call you Priya?"

Priya, without looking at him, said, "It depends. Context is important, at least in my culture. With that, you can call me Priya when we are in the class of Professor Martin, for that's how he wants it. And you can call me Priya if we are somehow alone, like presently—one-on-one as you Americans like to say. But, should we find ourselves with a group of people, call me Ms. Kumar."

"Okay, fair enough," Brian said. He opened the large exit door for her.

"Thank you," she said, this time looking at him. They stepped outside the classroom but avoided the sun by standing in the shade.

"Listen," Brian said. "It's lunchtime. Are you up for lunch? My treat. I'd like to discuss my paper with you. I know some great places here on campus."

"Actually," Priya said, "I'm meeting my two sisters for lunch in fifteen minutes."

"Oh," Brian said.

An awkward silence followed.

"You can join us for lunch if you like."

The restaurant was named Bombay Palace, and it wasn't located on the NMSU campus but rather right across from it on East University Avenue, near Telshor Street. Brian was familiar with the nearby FedEx-Kinko's store and the Starbucks, but he had never eaten at this restaurant.

Priya and Brian entered the restaurant as a line of patrons was already forming up. Brian counted twelve patrons ahead of him, with only one other Caucasian; all the others were Indians, and all were young college students.

"My sisters will arrive shortly," Priya said as she stood in line ahead of Brian. "They're on their way; they just texted me."

The line kept moving forward, slowly.

"Have you ever had Indian food, Brian?" Priya asked as she grabbed some utensils and napkins from the first of three buffet tables.

"Just once," Brian replied, "but it was a long time ago."

Priya then smiled and said, "Oh, I see Rani and Deepika."

Brian looked behind and saw two young Indian women walking side by side. They were both wearing blue jeans and long-sleeved blouses, one rose colored, the other dark blue.

Priya waved to her sisters and said, "Get a table, Rani. That booth in the corner would be great." Brian then saw the two sisters sit at the corner booth, waiting for them.

Priya started loading her plate with food items—white rice

in the middle, then naan bread and vegetable biryani to the side, a cauliflower dish also to the side, then yellow lentils next to the naan. Brian was relieved when he saw name cards before each buffet item. Rice was the first food item, but he selected the fried rice instead of the white rice Priya had chosen. Next came the naan bread, which Brian selected a few slices of. Then there were various meat dishes that looked appetizing—chicken curry, chicken tikka masala, peppered chicken, and lamb curry. Brian selected a bit of each. Priya, still ahead of him, selected a tall white paper cup filled with an orange liquid, about which Brian asked, "What is that drink, Ms. Kumar?"

"Mango lassi," she replied. "And you can call me Priya in here."

He picked up a cup of mango lassi and followed Priya to their booth.

"Rani, Deepika, this is Brian Robinson, a classmate from the Independent Study course," Priya said as she and Brian sat next to each other, opposite in the booth to Priya's sisters. Both of the sisters were petite and beautiful like Priya.

"Hi. I'm Brian." He shook hands across the table with the two sisters. "Nice to meet you both."

They replied, "Nice meeting you."

"We'll get our food," Rani said as she stood up. "Priya, look after our purses, okay? Please, go ahead. Start your meals. We'll be back shortly."

Rani and Deepika headed toward the buffet line while Priya and Brian started eating.

"This place is popular with Indian students," Priya said, "especially during lunchtime."

"I see that," Brian said.

"My sisters and I plan to have lunch here every Wednesday to fit my schedule."

"Oh, that's interesting," Brian said.

The next ten minutes were filled with Brian asking culinary questions of Priya. He learned she wasn't a strict vegetarian in that she did eat chicken and fish on occasion, but she wasn't in the mood for those food items today. He also learned the doughy, triangle-looking pastry she started her meal with was called a samosa and wasn't a pastry at all but rather a dough ball filled with mashed potatoes and peas. "Would you want to try a piece?" Priya asked.

"Sure," Brian said. He took a small bite and quite liked it.

When Rani and Deepika arrived with their buffet plates, the conversation shifted to their majors—Rani, accounting, and Deepika, biology with a focus on plant sciences. Both were doctoral candidates not interested in academic careers but rather desiring to work in the private sector. Brian further learned Rani was a strict vegetarian and was the only family member who had a driver's license, the sisters' car being a thirteen-year-old Honda Accord with high mileage. Like Rani, Deepika too was a strict vegetarian. She actually tended a small garden on the NMSU farming acreage on the campus, where she grew lettuce, tomatoes, cucumbers, and peas for herself and her sisters.

While the conversation was flowing, Brian noticed the Kumar sisters sometimes ate without the use of utensils. He observed the naan bread did the trick: they would pick up a piece of naan between their thumb and index finger, then fold the bread in such a way as to leave the open side as a grabbing mechanism to pick up the food items on their plates, like rice and lentils and vegetable dishes. *What the hell?* he thought. *Let me give it a try.* He copied the technique and liked it, for every bite came with bread, a combination he enjoyed.

Another thing Brian noticed was the sisters all ate from one another's plates, as if the plates were communal. Rani freely ate some of the cauliflower dish on Priya's plate while Priya freely took naan from Deepika's plate, and Deepika took swipes at Priya's rice and Rani's okra selection. Everything was being shared, except Brian was not in on it; the sisters didn't take any items from his plate. *Maybe they didn't like my selections, or maybe they figured I wasn't used to eating this way and wouldn't approve it.*

When lunch ended, Brian offered to pay for the meals, to which Rani resisted, insisting she pay. They finally agreed to split the bill.

As the foursome exited the restaurant, Brian said, "I can offer you all a ride back to your apartment. My car is not too far away on the NMSU campus."

"Oh, that's okay, Brian," Priya said. "We live right across the street, behind the Starbucks there."

"Oh, okay," Brian said. The word *Starbucks* made him say, "Anyone up for coffee?"

"We're not coffee drinkers," Deepika said, smiling. "However, this I tell you: I could go for tea. We love Starbucks because they have good tea there. And good cookies."

"Tea and cookies it is," Brian said, and the quartet walked no more than two hundred feet to the corner Starbucks, where the conversation included discussions about Indian cuisine, Rani's coursework, Deepika's garden vegetables, Priya's paper on America, and Brian's paper on India. Upon leaving the Starbucks some thirty minutes after entering it, Brian said, "Thank you all for a very pleasant lunch. And Priya, I'll see you next Wednesday for class."

"Yes," she said, smiling. "See you next week. And good luck with your research on India."

Brian entered his apartment. His roommate, Charles "Chuck" Landon, twenty-three, was stretched out on the couch playing video games. The flat-screen TV directly across from the couch was on one of the ESPN channels, the audio muted. A square glass table in front of Chuck supported an open Papa John's cardboard pizza box, with one slice of pepperoni in it. Next to the pizza box was a bottle of Corona half-full.

"What up, dude?" Chuck said. Standing five feet ten inches tall, the muscular Chuck was barefoot and wearing loose shorts and an NMSU T-shirt. He had the beginnings of a goatee around his chin. "How was the first day of classes? Learn anything?"

"Dude. Great day. Met this beautiful chick in my Independent Study class."

"You don't say."

"Yeah. She's from India, man. Real sweet girl. I think I'm falling for her."

"Nice. Going exotic, huh? The Asian sensation."

"I think so, buddy."

Chuck Landon had graduated from NMSU last year with a degree in management. He had met Brian a couple of years back when they were both taking business classes. Like Brian, Chuck worked part-time for Junk King—(the two of them often did hauling jobs together). Chuck also did a fair amount of construction work, for he was a skilled finish carpenter commanding twenty-two bucks an hour for his know-how. Two weeks ago, he had obtained his New Mexico real estate license, and his game plan was to get into real estate development, specifically, house flipping with his roommate as a partner. All the pair lacked was that all-important start-up capital.

"Dude, you hungry? Help yourself to the last pizza slice."

"Nah, I just ate. Indian buffet in fact. Pretty good actually."

"Already had a first date, heh? Lunch date—way to go. What's the chick's name?"

"Priya. Priya is her name. And it wasn't really a date. Her sisters showed up for lunch too. They're cool."

"Nice. How many sisters does she have? Maybe I need to go on the exotic side too, with me and Lisa always riding the on-again, off-again roller coaster. I could use some stability. Maybe I need to date an Asian."

"Priya has two sisters, both beautiful, both PhD candidates."

"Sweet," Chuck said. Then he switched gears. "Hey, we've got a Junk King hauling job at four o'clock. Are you up for it?"

"Sure. I can always use some money."

"Right," Chuck said. "Hey, by the way, there's a good poker tournament this weekend at the Inn of the Mountain Gods. What do you say? Are you in?"

Poker was a passion the roommates shared.

"Afraid I can't," Brian said as he headed to his room. "I've got military drill this weekend and also a lot of schoolwork."

"Schoolwork? Dude, it's a summer session. You're only taking two classes."

"Yeah," Brian said. "But I've got to learn all I can about India."

During that first week of classes, Priya had ordered Tocqueville's *Democracy in America, The Complete and Unabridged Volumes I and II,* through Amazon. Two days later, the book appeared on her apartment footsteps, just as ordered. *American efficiency,* she thought when the book arrived. She immediately began reading the 926-page paperback, and as she read, Priya took copious notes about Tocqueville's arguments and also her observations of America thus far. The book's arguments, her notes, and her observations were handwritten in one of her five-subject notebooks she titled "*Democracy in America,* Thoughts and Observations," and her daily regime consisted of the following: thirty minutes of prayer and meditation; reading and outlining the textbook for her other weekly summer course, Internet Marketing and Why It Matters; lunch with Rani and Deepika, now slated for Wednesdays so Brian could join the trio (she needed to pick his brain about America for her paper); thirty minutes of walking for exercise; reading the

New York Times and the *Wall Street Journal* at the nearby Starbucks; and a full hour of carefully reading Tocqueville's book. She also chipped in with her fair share of cleaning the two-bedroom apartment and cooking for herself and her sisters.

On this last topic of cooking and cleaning, it had been Rani, through a telephone call to Priya soon before Priya's flight to the United States, who had informed her youngest sister, "America is a lot different than India. Brace yourself for many changes. Labor is not cheap in the United States, so few families have maids to do the cleaning and cooking. We do our own here. You'll have to help us out with the chores." (In Chennai, the Kumars had a cleaning lady who did cleaning, laundry, and a bit of cooking four times a week.)

At night, Priya would go over her handwritten notes for her Independent Study class and summarize them by typing the notes into a word document on her laptop.

During that first week, she had written then typed the following:

Tocqueville's arguments, verbatim:

> Equality of Condition.
> Love of comfort has become the dominant national taste.
> I know of no country, indeed, where the love of money has taken stronger hold on the affections of men.
> In America, most of the rich men were formally poor.
> The citizen of the United States is taught from his earliest infancy to rely upon his own exertions in order to resist the evils and the difficulties of life; he looks up upon social authority with an eye of mistrust and anxiety ...

The Americans, therefore, change their means of gaining a livelihood very readily; and they suit their occupations to the exigencies of the moment, in the manner most profitable to themselves.

Men are to be met with who have successfully been barristers, farmers, merchants, ministers of the gospel, and physicians.

My comments and observations:

Equality of condition—very true. Think of patrons at a Starbucks where a man is dressed in a nice business suit, and behind him is a woman in shorts and T-shirt and sandals, and she's covered in tattoos, and her jean shorts have tears in them, and behind her is a well-dressed lady in professional attire. All the patrons get the same service, no matter their station in life.

Yes, Americans chase money—"comfort is the national taste."

Americans can change job, profession—very true. Think of classmates in our Independent Study class. Bob, seventy years old, a retired mechanic, and now he's back to school. Same with Brenda, who is almost fifty. She's a retired teacher with plans of becoming a food writer, and if that doesn't work out, she'll start a restaurant with her husband. Old people going back to school is not possible in India, because education is structured. In India, there is national testing, and a student only has one opportunity at taking a test to get the right scores to get into the top schools. Here in America, I've heard students can retake the SAT exam, and students can retry and also reinvent themselves. Part-time school or evening classes are also available, and there is no age limit. Americans can and do reinvent themselves.

In America, students borrow money to go to school. (Tocqueville quote: "They rely upon his [their] own exertions in order to resist the evils and the difficulties of life.")

Entrepreneurship is very strong in America. Brian wants to get into real estate development; Carlos wants to open a sports bar; Brenda will open a café if she's not successful as a food writer.

I have read about the American dream. Jose in class wants to be a screenwriter while Geneva wants to be an actress. Americans can be very creative and resourceful, and they borrow money if they have to.

Big. So many things are big in America. The people are generally big. The cars and trucks are big. The roads are wide. The stores are big. The aisles are big. The boxes are big. The television screens are big. The chairs are big. The glasses and cups and food portions are all big.

Freedom/individualism/choices. Students can choose their courses at times, certainly their electives. This individualism starts young, for children can discuss matters with their parents as if they are adults themselves, and children can argue and talk back to their parents if they so wish. I witnessed a young boy of maybe twelve years old telling his mother, "No, Mommy, I disagree. I think Wendy's has the best hamburgers." Children in India do not debate with their parents.

Much abundance, more choices. To order a coffee in America is complicated. "Do you want a short or medium or Venti?" (This is Starbucks.) "Cream or milk?" And if milk, "Is it regular milk or half-and-half or skim or cream?"

Functionality. Things work in America. There are no power outages (I've heard thunderstorms can bring power outages but not for long). The rooms are lit, and the rooms are well acclimatized with air-conditioning. The mail gets delivered. Amazon has two-day shipping—very efficient, right at your doorstep.

Openness. Americans are very open with their personal affairs. Strangers can hear their conversations. And holding hands and kissing in public is not frowned upon. And the people are often laid-back. Many people refer to themselves by their first names— no sir or miss. Even strangers refer to one another by their first name—think Professor Martin in class, "Call me Mark."

Brian started reading about India during the evening hours of his National Guard drill, for he knew "writing about India" was way too broad of a topic for his Independent Study class, but it was a starting point. He had looked up India on Wikipedia and printed out its contents. His drill time was in nearby Fort Bliss, in El Paso, where he and his fellow unit members were housed in a modern, redbrick barracks building. As an officer, Brian had a small room to himself. He was sitting at the small desk, sipping a coffee, and highlighting the following:

Second most populous country (with more than 1.2 billion people) and the most populous democracy in the world.

Indus Valley civilization of the third millennium BCE. In the following millennium, the oldest scriptures associated with Hinduism began to be composed.

Social stratification, based on caste, emerged in the first millennium.

In 2017, the Indian economy was the world's sixth largest.

One of the fastest growing major economies. However, it continues to face challenges of poverty, corruption, malnutrition, and inadequate public health care.

A nuclear weapon state and regional power.

Consists of twenty-nine states and seven union territories.

Official languages are Hindi and English.

Religion: 79.8 percent Hinduism, 14.2 percent Islam, 2.3 percent Christianity, 1.7 percent Sikhism, .7 percent Buddhism, .4 percent Jainism, .9 percent others.

The name India is derived from Indus, which originates from the old Persian word Hindu.

Eighteenth-century East India Company.

Indian rebellion of 1857. Although the rebellion was suppressed by 1858, it led to the dissolution of the East India Company and the direct administration of India by the British government.

After World War I, beginnings of a nonviolent movement of noncooperation, of which Mohandas Karamchand Gandhi would become the leader and enduring symbol.

Independence in 1947. Partition of India into two states: India and Pakistan.

World's most populous democracy ... Parliamentary republic ... Seven recognized national parties ... More than forty regional parties ... Parliamentary system governed under the Constitution of India.

States were reorganized on a linguistic basis.

Tense relations with neighboring Pakistan.

First nuclear weapons test in 1974.

As of 2012, India is the world's largest arms importer.

Major agricultural products include rice, wheat, oilseed, cotton, tea, sugarcane, and potatoes.

Seven of the world's top fifteen information technology outsourcing companies are based in India.

Telecommunications, car manufacturing, pharmaceuticals—major industries.

Largest number of people living below poverty line.

Fifteen percent of population is undernourished.

There are 940 females per one thousand males.

Life expectancy in India is at sixty-eight years, with life expectancy for women at 69.6 years, and for men it's 67.3.

The literacy rate in 2011 was 74.04 percent.

Brian took a sip of coffee and highlighted some more facts. He quickly read over the Wikipedia sections on art and architecture, literature, performing arts, motion pictures, and television.

The Indian film industry produces the world's most-watched cinema.

The Indian caste system embodies much of the social stratification in many of the social restrictions found in the Indian subcontinent.

An overwhelming majority of Indians, with their consent, have their marriages arranged by their parents or other elders in the family.

Marriage is thought to be for life, and the divorce rate is extremely low.

Female infanticide has caused a discrepancy in the sex ratio.

The payment of dowry, although illegal, remains widespread across class lines.

Cricket is, by far, the most popular sport in India.

Brian took another sip from his coffee cup. He looked up to the ceiling and thought, *What am I going to write about? India's caste system? Its military and foreign policy? Its economy?* He remembered that Professor Martin had said he didn't know much about India, just that its economy was growing and that it produced Gandhi.

On the far left corner of the desk was his laptop. His right hand was holding his coffee cup, and with his left hand, he grabbed his laptop and slid it across the desk, placing it in front of him. He flipped open the screen and pressed the start button. After entering his password, MASELCNU (Uncle Sam spelled backward), he double-clicked on Google Chrome, typed "Gandhi India" in the Google search option, and started reading about Mahatma Gandhi.

"Okay, folks," Professor Martin said to the class of eight students that second week of the first summer session. "We need to finalize our paper topics by the end of class. I've met with you all, and I think we're good to go. Bob, you're writing a semiautobiographical fictional account about a soldier in Vietnam."

"Roger that, Mark," Bob said.

"Good," Mark said. "And, Carlos, I've got you down for some sort of paper where food will factor heavily."

"That's correct," Carlos said. "My paper is titled 'Beating Bobby Flay: A Step-by-Step Guide on How to Beat a Master at His Own Game.' The paper will be a fictional account of me facing off against Bobby Flay on his cooking show. I'll first be a chef from New York, with Flay picking the secret food ingredient for the first competitive round. The secret ingredient will be tomatoes. I'll make the best tomato bisque and side of bruschetta to win that round. Then I'll face off against Flay and get to pick the competitive dish. I'll pick fish tacos and win it all."

"Very creative," Mark said.

Brenda, the trained pastry chef / retired teacher, added, "Yes, very creative, Carlos. I'm anxious to hear more about your paper."

Mark, wearing jeans and a short-sleeved green shirt, then asked, "Geneva, you're writing a memoir type of paper?"

"That's right, Mark. Like Bob, semiautobiographical, except I haven't lived it out yet, but it's how I imagine things will go for me when I move to Los Angeles and break into the movie business. I think the title of my paper will be 'Geneva Moves to Hollywood.'"

"Great," said Mark as he walked over to his desk and leaned against it, his feet firmly on the floor. "Jose, what about you? I know you want to write something like George R. R. Martin's *Game of Thrones.*"

"Yes, that's right. My story will be set in 2035 when Elon Musk establishes a thriving settlement on Mars. The settlement is called Muskia. In Muskia, people are not identified by race or religion or gender but by a way of thinking. The governing rule among Muskians will be that everything you do to a person or with a person has to be consensual; you have to get permission from the person affected. Muskia is very successful, and Muskians see Earth as a big mess, so a large group of Muskians decide to invade earth and teach us humans about Muskian ways."

"All righty then," Mark said, smiling. "Muskia it is." He crossed his arms. "And, Brenda, what about your paper?"

"My paper is titled 'Anthony Bourdain RIP: A Farewell to a Pioneer Culinary Traveler.'"

"That's great, Brenda. An academic paper?"

"Yes, Mark. A straightforward account of Bourdain's food travels."

"Very good. Oh and, gang. With academic papers, I expect correct citations, footnotes, and a bibliography." He stood up. "And Priya, I know you're critically looking at Tocqueville's *Democracy in America* and interjecting your own thoughts and observations."

"Yes, sir. My paper is titled 'Democracy in America: A Critical Look at Tocqueville's Work from an Indian's Point of View.'"

"Very well," Mark said. "And Priya, please don't call me sir." He was smiling.

"Oh yes, sir." A few students laughed, and she corrected herself. "My apologies. I mean Mark, not sir."

"And, Tony, you're writing about the drug cartels in Juarez. Correct?"

"Yes, that's correct. At first I was thinking of a true account, academic paper, but I now want to write about the cartels in a fictional way. It will be about a guy named Jorge who has family in Juarez and also in El Paso and how the drug wars are affecting his relatives on both sides of the border."

"Very well," Mark said. "Good stuff." He paused for a couple of seconds. "And finally, what have you got for us, Brian? I know you want to write about India, Priya's home country. What will your paper be about specifically?"

"My paper is titled 'Gandhi and Why He Still Matters.' There was so much to that great man's life. I think he's still relevant."

The rest of the class period was filled with Professor Martin discussing writing tips with his students, such as, "Writers must show, not tell. Read as much as you can because all writers are readers. Develop a daily writing routine, like committing to writing three hundred words each day." He ended the class by saying, "And remember, gang, the important words of the great Anne Rice, who said, 'Go where the pain is; go where the pleasure is.' Basically, folks, pain or pleasure provide for great writing material and great writing. Brenda, think and feel the pain and pleasure of Anthony Bourdain when writing your paper. Bob, I don't think I have to remind you of this, but here it goes: think of the pain and pleasure of your Vietnam War experience when writing your paper. All of you, remember, go where the pain and pleasure is."

"How is the summer class going, Brian?" Rani asked. She, Deepika, and Priya were with Brian at Bombay Palace for lunch. "We see Priya reading the *Democracy in America* book every night. How is your paper coming along?"

Priya enthusiastically chimed in with, "Dear sisters, I have an announcement to make. I learned about an hour ago that Brian has decided to write about the great Gandhi, the father of our nation."

"How wonderful, Brian," Deepika said.

Rani agreed, saying, "That's awesome."

"Yeah, I was reading about India in general," Brian said, "and then I stumbled upon Gandhi and decided to read about him. What a fascinating life he had. I didn't know he spent so much time in South Africa, and his time there shaped his views immensely. Did you know he was thirteen when he got married? Thirteen years old. His wife was fourteen."

"Yes, he was a great man," Priya said. "I knew he lived in South Africa, and he was a lawyer. But no, I didn't know he was so young when he married."

"Yep," said Brian. "Of course, that was in the 1880s. Gandhi was born in 1869. Things were different back then, I'm sure."

The conversation continued as the foursome ate their lunches, the sisters once again sharing the food among themselves, freely taking items from one another's plates. Brian, working on a samosa, asked, "So tell me, what's the biggest thing that stands out for you all here in America?"

Priya, eating lentils and naan in combination, started thinking, and Deepika, eating rice with naan, also pondered the general question. Rani, who was eating an okra dish, said, "For me, I think the biggest difference is how people in America handle themselves. Here, this is an Indian restaurant, and they have adopted some American ways but not fully. Let's say we were at an IHOP restaurant. I've been there before. The waiter or waitress would come to us and sit us down and hand us menus and introduce themselves—like 'Hi, I'm Lisa, and I'll be serving you today. Our special today is ...' And so on. Lisa introduces herself by her first name. And she brings water right away without the patrons asking for water. In India, you have to ask for water if you want water. And there are much fewer waitresses. In India, it's waiters; it's a man's profession. And waiters in India do not reveal their names, including their first names. Here in America, the waiter or waitress tells you their first name, and they often have their first name on their uniform in the form of a name tag. This, to me, is a big difference. In America, many things seem to be out in the open."

"Yes, that is so true, Rani," Priya said. "Brian knows that in our Independent Study class, the professor insists—he actually mandates—that we call him by his first name. You will not find a professor in India doing that."

"I agree," Deepika said. "In one of my biology classes, the professor wants us to call him by his first name also. It's not in all my classes, but I see it now and then. This, I tell you, would not happen in India."

"There are many differences between our cultures," Priya said. "For example, in this country, people can carry guns. At least in this state they do. I believe there's a law on it. I forget. It's something about carrying."

"You mean the open-carry laws we have here in New Mexico?" Brian asked.

"Yes, that's it. Open-carry laws. The other day, I saw a man with a handgun in his holster around his waist. Just like you would see in cowboy movies. Gun rights, as you put it, the right to bear arms, is a big thing in the United States. I don't think there are many countries that have such laws. Another big difference is children. I have noticed this at Walmart and other public places where parents are with their children. It seems the children are treated as equals to their parents, especially once they reach the age of a young teenager. Yesterday, I saw a woman and her daughter at Starbucks, and the daughter—I am estimating she was around twelve years old—was disagreeing with her mother about some television show. It was not a heated argument, but the daughter kept stressing her point, making her argument, and disagreeing with her mother. Such a conversation would not happen in India. Can you imagine us disagreeing with mother or father when we were growing up in Chennai?"

Deepika and Rani both laughed, as did Priya. "No way," Rani said, smiling. "We would never talk back to our parents or disagree with them. Mother and Father would not tolerate it."

After lunch, the four stood in the parking lot between Bombay Palace and Starbucks. They said farewells, and Rani and Deepika started walking toward their nearby apartment complex.

"It was nice seeing you and your sisters for lunch," Brian said to Priya.

"Thank you, Brian."

Brian then took a chance at asking something he had wanted to ask for a week. "Priya. I'm just wondering if I could have your phone number?" He stuck to his game plan by following up with, "I'm of course reading a lot about Gandhi, and there are things I will probably want to run by you. I know our class will include student critiques, but I would prefer going through you first." It was a bit awkward, but he got it out. He felt relieved.

Priya smiled and said, "Sure, Brian," and she gave him her phone number, which he entered in his iPhone.

That night, back at his apartment, Brian was reading about Gandhi and stumbled upon a sentence that seemed to encapsulate what Gandhi was all about. The sentence read: "Gandhi captured the imagination of the people of his heritage with his ideas about winning 'hate with love.'" *Nice*, thought Brian. Now armed with Priya's phone number, he decided to call her and discuss. *Priya, what do you think about Gandhi's strategy of winning hate with love?*

Chuck suddenly walked by him as he was heading to the refrigerator.

"What up, dude?" he said as he opened the refrigerator door and grabbed a bottle of Corona. "How goes it with Mr. Gandhi?"

"Very well, thank you. And oh, by the way, now that I've got Priya's phone number, I'm going to give her a call to further discuss the importance of Mr. Gandhi."

"Cool, dude." They high-fived. "Congrats. Got the phone number of the Asian sensation, heh?"

"You betcha. Number already programmed into my high-speed iPhone here."

"Nice. Well, let me slide away and give you two Gandhi students some privacy while I partake in my good buddy Corona here."

Brian pulled out his smartphone. He was sitting at the kitchen table, his Gandhi papers and laptop in front of him. He cleared his throat, selected his phone icon on the phone screen, and pressed the contact option. He scrolled down, found Priya's entry, and pressed her number.

One ring, then a second ring, and then the line picked up. "Hello," said the receiving person. Brian immediately recognized it as Rani's voice.

Dammit, he thought, but he moved forward with, "Oh, hi, Rani. Is Priya there? This is Brian. I want to run something by her about Gandhi."

"Oh sure, Brian," said Rani. "Let me get her."

Crap, he thought. *She gave me her apartment phone number. Oh well.*

Priya got on the line, and Brian talked about his paper and asked her about her thoughts on winning hate with love. The two talked for about fifteen minutes straight on the subject, whereupon Brian asked, "And how is your paper coming along, Priya?"

"The book *Democracy in America* is not easy to read, but it is interesting. I am taking notes." Then she said, "I marked something this evening. Let me go get it."

In less than a minute, she came back with, "Brian, tell me, what do you think of the following passage by Tocqueville: 'In the United States the citizens have no sort of preeminence over each other'?" That generated another fifteen-minute discussion by the pair.

During their discussions about their papers, Brian glanced at the white refrigerator, where something caught his eye. It was the bright, printed monthly poker tournament schedule of the Inn of the Mountain Gods Casino, and on the margins were Chuck's handwritten notes in red magic marker, circling when the best tournaments were going to be held. A thought hit Brian.

"Hey, listen, Priya. I'm just wondering if you would be interested in visiting a casino with me, not this weekend but the following weekend. It's only about a three-hour drive. It's on an Indian reservation and—"

"An Indian reservation?" she said in a perplexed tone.

"Oh, yes … uh, I mean a Native American reservation. You know, the native tribes before Europeans discovered America. The geography up there at the casino is totally different than here. There are trees and a lake. The temperature is at least ten degrees cooler there, maybe fifteen degrees."

"Oh, I see," Priya said. "In two weekends, correct? Let me check with my sisters. Just a minute please."

Brian rolled his eyes and thought, *These Indians are all about family. Lunch with her sisters. Now a casino trip, but her sisters are tagging along. I can't get her alone. So it goes … Her sisters are thankfully nice. That's cool.*

Priya got back on the line. "Oh, Brian. Yes. My sisters and I are interested in visiting this casino. Thank you for inviting us."

It was a late Saturday morning, and Brian was driving his eleven-year-old, four-door red GMC pickup, a truck he had bought from his dad as a hand-me-down for $5,000. Priya was in the front passenger seat, her two sisters in the back seats. The destination—the Inn of the Mountain Gods Casino and Hotel in Mescalero, New Mexico, was a three-hour drive north of Las Cruces.

"Sorry, ladies, but my old Honda Civic is still in the shop for some repairs," Brian said as he shifted lanes to pass a slower vehicle. "But this here pickup truck is very reliable."

"Yes, this is a comfortable vehicle," Priya said. "And spacious." Her comment made her think back to Chennai and her parents' car, a small, old white Suzuki sedan that no one in the family knew how to drive. (The family hired a young local driver when needed). And the Kumars were fortunate to have a car, for few families owned cars in Chennai. The principal means of transportation is motorcycles or motor scooters. *Here in America,* Priya thought, *everything is big and wide and spacious. The vehicles are big and comfortable.*

"And you bought this truck from your father?" Priya asked, curious.

"Yeah," Brian said. "For five g's—five thousand dollars. That was the blue book value. Square deal with my dad."

"What is blue book value?"

"It's this book that comes out every year. It has a blue cover, thus the name. The book lists the various values of vehicles based on the vehicle's year, make, model, mileage, and wear and tear."

"Oh, I see," Priya said.

The foursome continued heading north, and Priya was enjoying the scenery of dessert plains with mountains to both sides. It was a bright, sunny morning, and Priya was able to see forever with such a vast landscape. Aside from the few homes, there was the occasional farmland and very little traffic. Brian, scoping the landscape while driving, suddenly said, "Ladies, look to the left. See that coyote out in the desert?"

"Yes, yes, there it is," Rani said, and her sisters saw what she was pointing at.

"The coyote is out hunting for a late breakfast," Brian said.

"What do they eat?" Priya asked.

"Mostly rabbits."

Midway to their destination, Brian stopped at a large, bright gas station with twelve gas pumps. "Good time for a bathroom break," he said as he pulled next to one of the pumps. "Plus, I gotta fill up this truck with some gasoline."

The Kumar sisters exited the pickup and entered the gas station. All of them were wearing jeans, tunics (purple for Priya, blue for Rani and Deepika), and comfortable sneakers. Deepika headed to the restroom, and Rani decided to check the snacks, where she would eventually buy a bag of pecans. Priya, curious, decided to simply go around the aisles and check things out.

In one of the aisles, she saw a tall man wearing a large black cowboy hat, light blue jeans, a beige, long-sleeve shirt, and brown cowboy boots. A handgun in a brown leather holster was snug against his right hip. Directly to the right of this man was his young son, dressed identically and sporting a shiny toy gun in a plastic holster off his right hip. Priya glanced to her right and noticed a small restaurant that was part of the gas station. There were a fair number of patrons, mostly men, many of them also wearing cowboy hats. She walked to the restaurant section to check out the displayed menu.

Steak, eggs, hash browns, corn beef hash, sausage, pancakes, French toast, grits, oatmeal. Some of the items she recognized, some she didn't. *What is corn beef hash? What are grits?* She made a mental note to Google these food items later that night.

She turned around and headed to the cash register to link up with Rani, who was in line.

Back on the road heading north, the quartet continued to view the landscape. Brian, chewing gum—he had bought a pack of

Juicy Fruit at the gas station—offered the sisters sticks of the sugary treat, but they all politely refused, Priya explaining, "We find gum to be so sweet, so sugary."

Brian smiled and then laughed. "Too sugary?"

"Yes," Priya said. "Very sugary. Chewing bubble gum is not common in India. Nor is soda. Some people drink it, but we don't. We find it too sweet. And I'd never heard of iced tea until I arrived here in America. Tea is a hot beverage. It should be hot when drinking it."

"Absolutely," Deepika said.

Rani replied, "I agree."

Fifteen minutes later, with Brian rolling at an eighty-mile-an-hour clip, Priya began to notice the shrubbery getting larger and the sand dunes getting smaller. Small trees began to appear, and the terrain became hilly—no more flat landscapes. The straight stretches of road were replaced by frequent curves. As Brian kept driving north, the trees got bigger, as did the hills. Priya also occasionally noticed horses in peoples fenced-in yards.

Brian parked the GMC pickup in the parking lot to the left of the small casino.

"Oh wow," Rani said as she exited the pickup. "Look at the tall mountain there, with so many trees on it. And the small lake in the back of the casino. So beautiful. You're right, Brian. This is like Canada. I've seen photos of Canada and movies that took place in Canada, and this resembles it. And the temperature—it's a lot cooler here than in Las Cruces."

Brian smiled. "Let's go inside, ladies." He led the way as he looked at his watch—11:15 a.m. "We can do an early lunch. They have nice restaurants in the casino and also a full buffet."

They entered the front main entrance of the casino, and Priya marveled at the building's beautiful interior. The tiled floor was immaculate and shiny. Out to the sides were large picture windows, and there was artwork and paintings hanging on the walls, some of the artwork made of shiny twisted copper and other metals.

"I recommend we walk to the left," Brian said. "We'll pass the buffet restaurant. It's very good, but I recommend the sports bar restaurant. It's got good food. Plus, I want to show you guys something."

The sisters followed Brian's lead. They passed the buffet restaurant and came to a curve and a small open area. To the right was a fancier restaurant with a huge fireplace. Glass tables and couches occupied the front of the fireplace, but there were just two patrons at this restaurant.

Brian noticed a small crowd of patrons to the right, taking photos of an Apache woman, a young woman dressed in her native attire of a long brown dress with blue trim, numerous necklaces, high moccasin boots, and black-and-white feathers in the back of her head. Her long black hair ended at the small of her back.

"Let's take photos," Rani said, excited. In seconds, Brian discovered from a patron who had just taken her photo with the Indian that this Mescalero Apache had just won a local beauty contest. The young woman was indeed very beautiful, with high cheekbones and big brown eyes. Brian estimated her age at eighteen, no more than twenty, and her height to be around five feet four inches.

Priya looked at the beautiful young woman. *I don't know too much about Native Americans*, she thought, *but I definitely recognize the Asian strain in this girl. The black hair, the high cheekbones, the light brown skin, the slightly slanted eyes.* She had once read that the natives originated from Asia and had crossed the Bering Strait between Russia and Alaska in pursuit of large game.

Brian and the Kumar sisters lined up next to the Apache beauty queen, who spoke English. "Welcome. Photo for you four?" she said, smiling.

"Yes," Brian said. "Thank you." He handed his iPhone to a nearby middle-aged lady, who snapped a few photos.

The four entered the sports bar and were led by a waitress named Tina to a round, wooden table toward the midsection of the restaurant. "Table for four?" she asked as she led the way.

Brian said, "My roommate will be joining us later, so it'll be for five."

"Sure thing," the waitress said, leading them to the wooden table.

Once they were seated, Tina inquired about the drinks. Brian ordered a Bud Lite, and Rani said, "Just water for three. No ice please."

"Sure thing," waitress Tina said.

"I noticed you guys don't drink your water with ice," Brian said, smiling. "And I noticed the waiters at Bombay Palace back in Las Cruces never serve water with ice. Why no ice with water?"

"Too cold," Priya said. "This I tell you: in India, we don't drink water with ice. We're not used to water with ice. It's so cold."

"I see," Brian said. "That's interesting—no ice." Then he switched topics. "What do you guys think of the walls?" The walls were filled with mounted heads of deer and elk and preserved dead birds.

"Oh, we are not used to such displays," Priya said as she scanned the walls. "Heads of dead animals on walls? What are these animals?"

"The smaller ones are deer. The larger ones are elk, which are also in the deer family. The birds are obvious."

"I see," said Priya. "These animals are hunted? Is that correct?"

"Yes, they're hunted."

"Hunted for their meat?"

"Correct. But some hunters mount the heads of the game they kill on walls. For display. I guess you can say it's like a trophy."

"Oh, and look—there are photos on the walls. Over there," Deepika said excitedly. She pointed to the back wall. "Let's go check those out." Priya and Rani followed her to the back wall while Brian stayed back. He had seen the photos before. The photos were of hunters, draped in bright orange vests and bright orange hats. They were posing with their killed prey of deer and elk. There were a couple of photos of small brown bears midway up a large pine tree, their claws and paws supporting them by hugging the thick tree trunk.

Lunch was ordered and consisted—for the Kumar sisters—of nachos with cheese and jalapeno peppers, with the guacamole and sour cream on the side. Brian ordered a burger and fries and another Bud Lite beer. Early on during the lunch, he had texted his roommate: "we're in the sports bar restaurant with the mounted animals." Chuck joined the group about half an hour later after the text was sent.

"Hello, everyone. Name's Charles Langton. Call me Chuck." He was wearing jeans, a blue hoodie with the hood not over his head, and an Arizona Diamondbacks sweatshirt. "I'm Brian's better half." He took the seat next to Deepika. "I'm his trusted roommate."

"So how's the action on the green felt?" Brian asked. "Are you up?"

"Down actually," his roommate said just as he ordered a chicken sandwich and fries and a Corona beer. "I was up around three Ben Franklins, but then I got involved in a big pot where I hit my set on the flop. I bet big, protecting my hand, and it ended up heads-up, but the guy hit his ace low straight on the river. So it goes." He took a sip from his Corona beer. "As you can see, Brian and I love poker. I try to come here once a month if I can. I got here last night and started playing the two five-game. And—"

"What's the two five-game?" Priya asked as she picked up a nacho smothered in cheese.

"It's a cash game version of poker. Two dollars is the small blind, and five dollars is the big blind. I bought in for five hundred dollars. I had more than doubled my money but lost it all in that big pot." He took another sip of beer. "Up and down, up and down. Last month, I made four hundred dollars, but today—last night and this morning—I lost three hundred. So it goes. Maybe Brian and I can teach you poker some time."

Priya replied with, "Oh, I don't know. I don't know anything about gambling."

After lunch, the five moved to the adjacent upscale restaurant with the fireplace. To the right of the fireplace was a bar, and Brian and Chuck both ordered Coronas while Priya and her sisters ordered hot tea.

They all sat at the nearby couch-sofas and looked through the immense picture window showcasing the small lake in front of the casino. To the right of the lake was a small beige tepee, and beyond the lake were the beautiful wooded hills that doubled up as a reflection off the lake's dark blue waters.

"The views here are so beautiful," Priya said as she took a sip of tea. "Thank you for bringing us here, Brian."

"Sure thing," he replied. Then he pulled out his iPhone and Googled "zip line at the Inn of the Mountain Gods Casino." He had heard about the zip line and wanted to know more about it, thinking it would be a fun thing to do this afternoon. Unfortunately, the Google search resulted in "The zip line is closed for two weeks for necessary repairs."

The group continued to sip from their drinks, relax, and enjoy the views. The conversations consisted of an array of subjects, like shopping at Amazon versus Walmart, more about hunting in America, and—"Is hunting common? Is it popular? How much does it cost? Is it year-round? Who cooks the animals? …

How beautiful is the state to the north, Colorado? We have seen pictures of Colorado." ... The popularity of cooking shows on TV and how much cars cost in the United States. Classes at NMSU and the popular Netflix show *Breaking Bad*, filmed in not too far away Albuquerque.

"Hope you guys had fun today," Brian said when he parked his pickup truck at the Kumar sisters' apartment.

"Oh, thank you, Brian," Rani said. "Thank you so much. I've lived in Las Cruces for going on three years now, and I didn't know about the nice lake and forest just three hours from here."

"Yes, thank you so much, Brian," added Priya. "The casino is very nice. Lovely in fact."

Deepika said, "This I tell you, Brian. We all had a most excellent afternoon. We thank you once again."

Just as he was getting ready to pull out of the parking lot, Brian said, "And I'll see you Wednesday for class, Priya."

"Yes, Wednesday it is. See you then."

Rani, who was just getting out of the pickup truck, said, "Oh, Brian. Two weekends from now, we are going to the Hindu temple in El Paso. Would you like to join us?"

"Sure," Brian said. "I'd love to."

That night, Priya decided to skim sections of Tocqueville's *Democracy in America* in search for the passages he had written about America's natives. She typed the following on her laptop for her Independent Study paper:

Tocqueville:

> [Indian] he loves his savage life as the distinguishing mark of his race, and he repels every advance to civilization.

The Indians will not live as Europeans live, and yet they can neither subsist without them.

[Indians] consider labor not merely as an evil, but as a disgrace; so that their pride prevents them from becoming civilized[.]

War and hunting are the only pursuits which appeal to him worthy to be the occupation of man.

The Europeans have not been able to metamorphose the character of the Indians; and though they have had power to destroy them, they have never been able to make them submit to the rules of civilized society.

Below that, Priya typed the following:

My personal notes on Tocqueville's arguments:

Tocqueville observed the Spanish sometimes married Indian women and had children with them, and the French did this also, but not the Anglo-Saxons. The Anglo-Saxons traded with the Indians, but they did not marry their women, at least not in large numbers. Some of the French in America went out and lived with the Indians and wanted to live like them.

Read more about America's Indians. Living on reservations—have they assimilated into American culture? Is Tocqueville correct about America's natives?

She then tapped the *enter* key three times to create spaces as she was changing topic.

Brian bought a truck from his father for $5,000. This would never happen in India—business transactions between parent and child. And the price is determined by a blue book value. Law and order and structure are part of the American way of life. Such a commercial transaction does not seem to be subject to too much negotiation; the value can be found in a book.

"Food for the short trip to El Paso?" Brian asked Deepika as he was squeezing into the back seat of Rani's old Honda Accord. He had volunteered to drive to the Hindu temple, but Rani insisted on driving. As he squeezed into his seat, he noticed Deepika was in the front seat, holding a white plastic bag filled with a brown coconut and a batch of yellow bananas. The contents in the bag prompted his question.

"Oh no, Brian," Deepika said, smiling. "These are offerings for the temple."

"Oh. Should I have brought food items for an offering?"

"Oh, it's okay," Priya said. "No problem at all, Brian. There's no need for you to bring an offering. We have it."

The night before, Brian figured he'd read up on Hinduism as much as possible as preparation for this trip to the temple. He had Googled certain subject areas and taken notes. Now, sharing the back seat with Priya, he was trying to remember what he had written down for notes the previous night:

Hinduism does not have a founder.

The four aims of life are called *purusharthas*— ethics, prosperity/work, desires, and liberation/ salvation.

Hinduism does not have a leader, no governing body, no prophets, no one holy book.

Hindus believe all living beings have a soul; they believe in reincarnation.

Yoga and vegetarianism have roots in Hinduism.

Karma is a big belief, the laws of cause and effect.

Some Hindus believe in one god, but god has many manifestations, many avatars.

All life is interconnected.

Varnas, the four classes of people. This is the caste
system.

Cows are unselfish caregivers.

Rani took a few turns and headed toward I-10 East. "I think
the ride will be no more than thirty minutes, Brian. The temple
is on the edge of New Mexico and Texas. It's El Paso's first exit."

"Oh cool," Brian said. "How often do you all go to this
temple?"

"No set schedule," Priya said. "This will be my second time
visiting this temple. Rani and Deepika have gone more times of
course."

In a few minutes, Rani was on I-10 East cruising at a seventy-
mile-an-hour clip. It was almost eleven o'clock, a bright, sunny
morning with the temperature in the low nineties. To the left
were the jagged Franklin Mountains, and to the right was desert
and farmland and a small, green, low valley filled with beautifully
lined pecan trees.

Out in the distance, to the right, Brian saw immense cattle-
feeding fields with the feeding stalls, hay bales, and heads of cattle
too numerous to count. He was familiar with this stretch of I-10
and its unfortunate stench.

Cattle, he thought. *I think they're basically considered holy in
Hinduism.*

"What's that smell?" Priya suddenly said. "It smells terribly
awful." Rani and Deepika agreed, both commenting on the
smell.

"It's those cattle fields to our right," Brian said.

There was an awkward silence.

"Cattle do not smell that bad in India," Rani said. "We take
milk from them, but otherwise we leave them alone. They are
such a giving animal."

Priya looked at the countless cows and then asked Brian,
"Are these cows used for meat or for milk? Do you know? I

know Americans eat a lot of meat, especially beef. And I know Americans drink a lot of milk."

"I don't know," Brian answered truthfully.

Fifteen minutes later, Rani took a right on El Paso's first westside exit. A Rudy's Barbecue with a packed parking lot was to the right, and across the street from Rudy's was a Shell gas station, also doing brisk business.

Five minutes after the exit, Rani parked the car in the temple's parking lot. To the right, on the east side, were two metal barns and a large pasture where a handful of horses were grazing. And off to the north were the red Franklin Mountains.

The temple was small and expertly maintained. The walls, made of stone, were a shade of pink while the top of the temple—the second story—was white. The parking lot was L shaped and hugged two of the temple's walls while the exterior of the other two walls featured colorful flower gardens. Brian counted roughly a dozen cars in the parking lot.

"Wow. This is impressive," he said, marveling at the temple. "The structure is so solid. This building will last for a long time."

"Yes," Priya said. "Temples are built to last. They are expensive, and it takes a long time to build them."

The four walked to the arched entrance. To the right was an elevated, small, stone pool filled with water, the stone black in color, and next to the pool was a short, bare-chested man of middle age, wearing a white toga skirt over his legs. His head was completely shaven except for a small patch of his black hair at the rear of his head, which was woven into a two-foot-long, slim ponytail. Barefoot and inspecting the small pool, he saw Brian and the Kumar sisters, placed his hands together in prayer, and bowed.

Priya and her sisters did the same—hands together, fingers pointed up, hands about waist high. They said, "Namaste."

Brian gave the "Namaste" respect greeting too, seconds behind them.

Rani, the first in the group, turned around and opened the massive brown metal door, and they all entered the temple. To the left was a pile of shoes neatly spread out in matching pairs on the beige tile floor. The sisters walked there and began removing their shoes, and Brian did the same while marveling at the scenery: polished tile floors; bright, high ceilings; the smell of incense permeating everywhere. There were shrines made of stone with intricate carvings, and worshipers were bowing and praying before them. There were priests standing next to most of the shrines, barefoot, bare chested, white skirts over their lower halves. Brian, standing next to Priya, removed his shoes. He noticed there was no structure to the worshiping. Some small children ran around aimlessly while other children followed their parents to individual shrines. Off to the left, there was a big red square carpet, and some children were sitting there, their legs folded Indian style. Some patrons were giving a few dollars or bananas or coconuts in a small metal bowl situated before each shrine. There was no reading from a holy text, and the priest did not lead a congregation in prayer.

Brian noticed only priests were allowed inside the small stone shrines and that some priests walked around holding gold metal plates, small fires burning in the center of the plate. He observed priests placing the plates in front of patrons, the patrons then placing their cupped hands above the small flames. Worshipers walking in circles around the shrines—that too caught Brian's eye. He saw older women dressed in saris (the Kumar sisters wore jeans) and the men wearing shirts and pants. Everyone was barefoot or in socks.

Deepika placed the coconut and bananas in front of a shrine. Next to the bananas were bright yellow and red flower garnishments that were a previous offering. Brian saw that inside the shrine was a statue of a human figure, blue in color, with four arms. The sisters began walking around the shrine in the clockwise direction. Brian walked directly behind Priya.

After an hour of walking around shrines, Brian and the Kumar sisters put on their shoes and headed outside toward the back of the temple where the parking lot extended.

"Let's eat," Rani said, leading the group to a shaded area adjacent to the temple. "They have good food here at cheap prices."

There were metal picnic tables and a line of patrons paying for food served on white paper plates, supported on brown, plastic trays. An older lady with streaks of gray in her long black hair was behind the first table. She was taking money from patrons and making change. Brian noticed every patron paid in cash—no credit cards.

Rani ordered a rice and lentil dish called sambar rice, fried bread, and a cup of mango lassi.

"Gang, let me pay for lunch please," Brian said. "It's the least I can do since Rani drove."

"No," Rani said. "This is on us."

"Okay, if you insist," Brian said. Then he ordered what Rani had ordered and picked up his tray, and the foursome found a nearby picnic table to sit at. To his left, on a portion of the outdoor temple wall, Brian saw a large beige corkboard filled with flyers announcing yoga sessions, music classes, and dance lessons. In the middle of the corkboard was a large poster advertising SAT prep courses, and below that poster was an even larger poster with the words *Find Your Way—Find Your Path* in bright blue cardboard letters, with pictures of what looked like five religious leaders. The only picture Brian recognized was that of Jesus, who occupied the picture to the far left.

Later that afternoon, during the thirty-minute drive back to Las Cruces, Brian asked Priya, "What was the shrine with the blue humanlike figure in it? The one that Deepika brought the coconut and bananas to?"

"Oh, that is Vishnu," Priya answered from a back passenger seat. "Vishnu is the second god of the triumvirate. There is Brahma the creator, then Vishnu the preserver, then Shiva the destroyer. Vishnu protects people and brings order to the world."

"And what about the priests carrying the small gold plate with a burning flame in the middle?" Brian asked. "People were placing their hands over the flame, then placing their warm hands on their foreheads."

Priya replied, "The fire gives positive energy and is a way to cleanse oneself."

"All right, gang, last day of the summer session. Overall, I'm pleased with all your papers," Martin said. He was wearing black pants, a light purple shirt, and a purple tie. "Grades were in the A to B range." He started walking around the class, handing out each paper to its respective author. "Everyone is doing well."

He headed to the front of the class and leaned against his large desk. To his right, on the desk itself, was a yellow legal notepad with his notes about each student's paper. He picked up the notepad.

"Bob, solid paper. I like the title of your paper: 'The Suck Called Vietnam.' I particularly liked the fact you incorporated song lyrics in the narrative. Can you read that portion of your paper?"

"Sure," said Bob, who looked at the second page of his paper and saw he had received an A. He was wearing a black T-shirt, the back side of which read, in white lettering: I Stand for the Anthem, and I Kneel before the Cross. Next to the word *cross* was a white cross with the crucified Jesus. He turned to the page of his paper where he had incorporated a song into the story.

"The protagonist in my paper is one John Clark, nineteen

years old, from a small Texas town. It's 1968, and he's in the jungle in Vietnam with his unit. Yesterday, there was heavy fighting, and he lost one of his battle buddies, a guy named Ryan. Like John, Ryan was drafted into the war effort. John is squatting down, Indian style, with other members of his platoon, cleaning his weapon. He's thinking about Ryan. Then he thinks of the lyrics of that Creedence Clearwater Revival song, 'Fortunate Son.'"

Bob cleared his throat and sang the following:

> Some folks are born made to wave the flag
> Oh they're red, white and blue
> And when the band plays Hail to the Chief
> Oh, they point the cannon at you, Lord
> It ain't me, it ain't me
> I ain't no senator's son, son
> It ain't me, it ain't me
> I ain't no fortunate one, no.

"Thank you, Bob," Martin said. He looked down at his notepad. "And, Carlos, good paper thus far. I know you're not facing off against Bobby Flay just yet because you have to beat the first chef in the first competition. Heck, maybe I'll try that tomato bisque recipe of yours sometime."

"Sure, Mark," Carlos said, smiling. "I got the recipe from my grandmother." Carlos received a B-plus for the summer session.

"And, Geneva. Good work," Martin said, looking at his notepad. "Good detail. I can see why your paper is written in the first person."

"Thank you," Geneva said. Her grade, also written in the top right-hand corner of her paper's second page, was an A-minus.

"And 'Muskia Will Save the World.' Good work, Jose."

"Thank you, Mark."

Jose received a B-plus for his efforts.

"Brenda, well done," Martin said. "Good backstory. I didn't

know Anthony Bourdain had written some crime fiction books in his younger days."

"Thank you," said Brenda. Her grade was an A.

"And, Priya, very good work."

"Thank you, sir."

"Remember, it's Mark."

"Oh yes, Mark."

"Tocqueville's argument about the equality of condition is one you agree with. I liked what you wrote on page 4 of your paper. Can you read us what I underlined on that page?"

"Yes, of course," Priya said as she flipped to the page.

"Tocqueville wrote 'In the United States the citizens have no sort of preeminence over each other.' He also wrote, 'In democratic countries even poor men entertain a lofty notion of their personal importance.'

"I believe Tocqueville's arguments are still very much alive in the American fabric today, for America stands for opportunity," Priya told the class. "Tocqueville's equality of condition does not mean everyone has the same size house or the same amount of money in their bank account, but rather that everyone is treated the same, and everyone has a chance at improving their lot in life. It's also about people who are working class and middle class feeling good about themselves, and people who make a lot of money and are upper middle class mingling with the working classes and middle classes and not feeling superior to them."

"Thank you, Priya."

"You're welcome," she said. She received an A-minus for her ten-page paper.

"And, Tony," Martin said, "like Geneva, I fully understand why you are writing in the first person. Jorge, your main character, has an interesting family background."

"Yeah, that's right," Tony said. "He grew up in El Paso, but he has a lot of relatives in Juarez. Very typical actually."

"And I like the fact that his brother is a US Border Patrol agent."

"Thank you, Mark," Tony said. His grade was a B-plus.

Martin stood up. "And last but not least, Brian. Good work on Gandhi."

"Thank you," Brian said. His grade was a B-plus.

"Brian, can you read us that portion of page 9 that I underlined?"

"Yeah, sure," he said, and he read the following, quoting two Gandhi scholars.

"The general image of Gandhi has been reinvented since his assassination as if he was always a saint, when in reality his life was more complex, contained inconvenient truths, and was one that evolved over time."

"Thank you," Martin said.

"Let us begin our service by greeting our brothers and sisters," said the bald priest at the head of the altar. He was in his midsixties, sporting a thick and long white beard, and his nose supported wire-frame eyeglasses. His attire was a priestly white robe over a thin black one, and around his neck was a bright green stole adorned with embroidered Latin crosses.

Brian, Priya, Rani, and Deepika occupied one of the middle wooden pews that was stained dark brown, the seats upholstered with long green cushions. A week earlier, during a lunch at Bombay Palace, the Kumar sisters had invited Brian to the Hindu temple, and now it was only proper that Brian invite them to a Catholic Mass; they accepted his offer.

Priya noticed the parishioners—numbering maybe two hundred—shaking hands with their neighbors and introducing themselves. Brian turned to Priya and said, "God bless you, Priya." In an attempt to impress her, he added "Namaste." He then shook hands with Priya's sisters and also with the older couple sitting behind them, a couple who also shook hands with the Kumar sisters.

"Let us pray," the priest said. Priya noticed the parishioners all bowed their heads, so she did the same. "Heavenly Father, we thank you for your continued blessings," the priest prayed into the short microphone on the altar. "We ask for your continued help and support in guiding us to what is right, to what is good, and to what is just. We ask for your forgiveness of our sins. We ask this in your holy name. Amen."

"Amen," the parishioners said.

Priya took in the interior of our Lady of Angels Catholic Church. High ceilings, beautifully crafted stained windows, solid wooden pews, polished tile floors centered with wide green carpeting.

At one point during the Mass, a tall gentleman dressed in a dark suit walked up to the big wooden podium to the left of the altar. He adjusted the microphone to suit his height, and then he said, "Today's reading is from the first letter of Saint Paul to the Corinthians." Priya, like Brian and her sisters, was standing and holding the missalette, and following the reading:

> Thus says Yahweh: Make fair judgment your concern, act with justice, pursuing my salvation will come in my saving justice be manifest. As for foreigners who adhere to Yahweh to serve him, to love Yahweh's name and become his servants, all who observe the Sabbath, not profaning it, and cling to my continent; These I shall lead to my holy mountain and make them joyful in my house of prayer. Their burnt offerings and sacrifices will be accepted on my altar, for my house will be called a house of prayer for all peoples.

The tall reader then picked up the Bible he was reading from and said, "The Word of the Lord."

The congregation responded in unison, "Thanks be to God."

The tall reader stepped down from the podium and returned to his pew. The priest walked up to the same podium and delivered a fifteen-minute sermon about fairness and justice and the importance of being kind to everyone, for the Lord said, "My house will be called a house of prayer for all peoples."

Toward the end of Mass, the priest directed, "Let us now offer each other a sign of peace," and the parishioners shook hands with one another.

"Peace be with you," Brian said to Priya, offering his hand to shake hers. They shook hands, and as they did, he said, "And namaste."

She smiled at him, holding his hand, and said, "Namaste."

Brian shook hands and offered peace to Priya's sisters and the parishioners standing next to them, and Priya and her sisters did the same, shaking hands with nearby parishioners.

After Mass, Brian treated the Kumar sisters to a cuisine they all enjoyed—Thai food, and during dinner at the Thai restaurant (they had attended the 4:30 p.m. Saturday-afternoon Mass), Brian answered the many questions the Kumar sisters had about the religious service they had just taken part in.

"And when the people lined up and ate the bread, that is called Communion?" Priya asked.

"Yes," Brian said. "Communion is the body of Christ. The bread, the white wafer, is called the Eucharist. By partaking in the Eucharist, you accept Christ and his teachings in your life. It also means you are in communion with the Church."

"And only Catholics can receive Communion?" Priya asked as she was sharing a noodle dish with Deepika.

"Yes, that's correct," Brian said. "At Catholic Mass, only Catholics can receive Communion."

"And who are the young girls and young boys who were dressed like the priest? They were holding candles," Rani said.

"They are called altar girls and altar boys," Brian answered. "They are basically servants who help the priest at Mass."

Priya took a sip of water out of a straw and said, "And, Brian, tell me. There are usually two donations? Is that correct? I noticed the gentleman came by twice with a basket at the end of a pole, and the people were placing money in the basket."

"Yes, that's right," Brian said as he was working on a chicken curry dish. "The person going from pew to pew with the offerings basket at the end of a wooden pole is called an usher. And yes, there are usually two collections. The first is for the maintenance of the church and expenses, the second for some charitable cause."

"That was interesting," Rani added. "I noticed the second collection was to help build houses for the poor, and I chipped in with a dollar."

"Yeah, I noticed you gave some money, Rani," Brian said. "The church does a lot of good things. Nice of you to help out."

"Well, as you can tell, Brian, today's church service was all new to us," Rani said as she finished up some rice. "It was a lovely experience." She then added, "You know, there are Christians, including Catholics, in India."

"Yes, I know," Brian said. "There are Christians who do missionary work there, like Mother Teresa did."

"That's right," Rani said. "And in Chennai, where we're from, there is a shrine in a church for Saint Thomas."

"Saint Thomas Aquinas?" Brian asked.

"No," Deepika said. "Thomas. I believe he was with Jesus. Christians call him Doubting Thomas. He was martyred in Madras, which is now called Chennai."

"The apostle Thomas?" Brian asked.

"Yes, I believe that's him. Christians revere him in India."

Brian drove the sisters to their apartment after dinner, and they all thanked him for a lovely day. And before Priya exited Brian's old Honda Civic, she said, "Oh, Brian, I have a favor to ask of you."

"Sure. Anything. What is it?"

"Could I have your phone number? My classes are going well

thus far, and I know I'll be discussing America with you for our Independent Study course. But I think I will need some assistance with my upcoming International Finance class. Your degree from an NMSU is in finance, is it not?"

"Yes, that's right," Brian said. He was still in the driver seat, the car parked in front of Priya's apartment complex.

"The professor is hard. He's an Indian. Professor Gupta is his name."

"Oh," Brian said. "I don't know Professor Gupta—never had him or her. But sure, Priya, no worries. Call me anytime," and he gave her his cell phone number. Priya programmed it into her iPhone.

"Thank you, Brian," she said as she exited the car.

"Sure. Anytime."

"Oh and one more thing," she said, just as she was about to shut the front passenger door. "If you want to discuss Gandhi, you can call me on my iPhone," and she gave him her personal cell phone number.

That night, Brian made it a point to do some Google research on the apostle Thomas, and sure enough, what Rani had said was spot-on and previously unknown to him: Thomas the apostle, who at first had doubted the resurrection of Jesus, had moved to the east and converted the people there. He died on July 3 in the year 72 in Mylapore, Chennai, Tamil Nadu, India. The Google entry went on to state, "The Saint Thomas Basilica Mylapore, Chennai, Tamil Nadu, India, presently located at the tomb was first built in the sixteenth century by the Portuguese and rebuilt in the nineteenth century. Saint Thomas Mount has been a revered site by Hindus, Muslims, and Christians since at least the sixteenth century. Saint Thomas is often regarded as the patron saint of India, and the name Thomas remains quite popular among Christians of India."

That same night, Priya read sections of *Democracy in America* where Tocqueville had written about religion. She took notes and wrote the following Tocqueville arguments in her notebook (later she would type those notes in her laptop computer):

Tocqueville:

There is no country in the whole world in which the Christian religion retains a greater influence over the souls of men than in America.

Religion in America takes no direct part in the government of society.

The Americans combined the notions of Christianity and of liberty so intimately in their minds.

[The Americans are] very proud for the last fifty years no pains have been spared to convince the inhabitants of the United States that they constitute the only religious, and landed, and free people; ... Hence they conceive an overwhelming opinion of their superiority ...

Religious insanity is very common in the United States.

Priya was settling into her fall semester routine of classes; homework; Bombay Palace lunches with her sisters and Brian after her Independent Study class; some walking, meditation, yoga; and chipping in with her share of cooking and apartment cleaning. Her schoolwork was demanding but presented no concerns, except for her International Finance class. She found herself texting and calling Brian for assistance when necessary, normally once or twice a week, and phone calls often diverted to discussing their favorite course—Professor Martin's Independent Study class—with Priya mentioning Tocqueville's argument of equality of condition and religiosity, and Brian sharing his thoughts about Gandhi. But inevitably, the conversation would eventually turn back to International Finance, with Brian offering assistance, guidance, and reassuring encouragement. "You're doing well, Priya. Trust me. You get this stuff. You received a B-plus on your first test, and the class average was more like a C-plus. You've got this."

One addition to the weekly routine occurred in late September in the form of a suggestion mentioned by Rani when the three sisters and Brian were having lunch at Bombay Palace.

"Brian, we are thinking of starting a movie night at our apartment," Rani had said as she was sharing a rice dish with Deepika. "Please join us. And Chuck can come too. Friday nights as movie nights."

"Sure," Brian had said. "That's a great idea. What time should I come?"

"Seven o'clock," Rani had said.

"And I can bring pizza and wings or whatever you guys like," Brian added. "And popcorn. I can bring popcorn."

"Oh, you don't have to bring anything, Brian," Rani had replied. "Well, maybe popcorn. We like popcorn."

Brian, prompt as always, arrived just a tad early for the first movie night at Priya's apartment. Chuck, who originally had committed to coming as well, had to bail at the last minute. "Got to patch things up with Lisa again."

Brian knocked on the door and was immediately greeted by Priya.

"Welcome, welcome, Brian. Come in please."

Brian entered the apartment and noticed the sisters were all barefoot, their shoes on a mat next to the door entrance. Rani was in the kitchen cooking away, and Deepika was sitting at the kitchen table looking at her laptop screen.

Priya said, "Please remove your shoes, Brian, and let me take the popcorn bag from you," and she proceeded to place the bag of popcorn on the kitchen counter. "Let me show you our apartment."

Priya showed him the small living room and two bedrooms. Books and papers and notebooks occupied most of the floor space in the bedroom shared by Priya and Rani, and Deepika's bedroom also had its fair share of books, papers, and notebooks. In one of the corners of Deepika's room, he noticed small gold dishes and incense sticks, small Ganesha and Buddha statues, and a black framed picture of Vishnu, the blue humanlike god.

"I noticed the picture of Vishnu," Brian said when he saw the neat display on the carpet floor.

"Oh yes. That is our puja," replied Priya. "In India, it would be an entire room, a puja room, but here we do not have the space for an entire puja room, our prayer room. So we make do with that corner."

"I see," Brian said. "It's very nice. I love the smell of the incense."

"Thank you," Priya said, and she led him to the kitchen.

In a few minutes, Rani proclaimed, "Dinner is ready," and she placed several dishes on the kitchen table. "Please help yourselves."

There was a plate of naan bread, and next to it was a small plastic container of red pepper hummus. Two rice dishes—plain white rice and yellow lemon rice—occupied the center of the small square table, and next to the rice dishes were plates filled with chickpeas and string beans. A cauliflower dish and an eggplant dish that included okra were the last food items.

The sisters helped themselves to the dishes and took samples of all the offerings. Brian followed, serving himself food with the use of large wooden spoons placed in each dish.

"We only drink water here," Rani said. "No soda, no milk,

except just a little bit of milk for our teas. We drink tea of course, but that's after the meal. Is that okay, Brian?"

"Sure," he said.

Rani poured a glass of water for Brian, and the four began to eat. Brian helped himself to some naan and hummus, and then he helped himself to a forkful of the eggplant-okra dish. He started chewing and swallowing and immediately felt the back of his throat burn.

He took a gulp of water—it was so relieving—but then he felt his entire mouth heat up. His eyes began to water. He quickly downed half his glass of water.

"Are you okay, Brian?" Priya asked, concerned. She noticed his face was reddening. Brian felt his lips puffing up.

"I'm sorry," he managed to say, his mouth and face burning. "It's just the food is hot. I need something cold," and then he drank the rest of his water. The water helped, but the burning sensation resumed.

"Do you have beer?" he asked.

"No, we don't drink alcohol," Rani said.

"Do you have ice cream?" Brian asked, this time squinting.

"No, we don't eat ice cream. We're lactose intolerant, but … but we do have yogurt!" Rani said loudly. "Do you want some yogurt?"

Brian, his mouth burning, gave Rani the thumbs-up.

Rani hurried to the refrigerator and retrieved a container of plain white yogurt, and at the same time, Priya poured Brian another glass of water, which he drank quickly.

When the yogurt arrived, Brian ate four spoonfuls of it and drank two more full glasses of water. In a few minutes, he felt relieved enough to continue with the meal.

"Sorry, gang," he said as he started eating some of the yellow lemon rice. "There was something in the eggplant dish that was just too hot for me. My apologies."

"Oh, no need to apologize, Brian," Rani said. "I am the one

who should apologize. I did add red chilis and red chili pepper powder to the dish. Sorry if it was too hot; we like spicy food."

"Man, I don't know," Brian said as he ate some more hummus, which also had a soothing effect on his mouth. "I can eat pretty hot, and I'm from New Mexico of all places, the land of chilis. But I'm sorry, the dish was just too hot for me."

After dinner, the foursome ate popcorn and watched an Adam Sandler comedy on Netflix in the living room. Brian thanked the Kumar sisters for a lovely evening, and Rani apologized once again for her eggplant-okra dish.

"Oh, that's okay," Brian said. "Everything was great."

That night, once he got back to his apartment, Brian texted the following to Priya: "Thank you for a lovely evening. I love the idea of Friday nights as movie nights. I unfortunately won't be able to make every movie night, as I sometimes have National Guard drills to attend, which sometimes includes Friday nights. Thank you for explaining the puja room. Maybe some Friday nights we can do movie night here at my apartment. Just a thought. You're doing great in your classes, including International Finance, and I enjoy your Tocqueville paper. Namaste."

Priya, lying down on her bed and reviewing her notes on her laptop, texted back: "Thanks for coming to our apartment. Sorry again for the too-hot dish—we will go mild next time. My sisters and I would like to do some movie nights at your apartment. Thanks for your help and encouragement, especially in an International Finance. Namaste. Priya."

Wednesday morning, Professor Martin was with the students discussing their papers. Bob's "The Suck Called Vietnam" zeroed in on the racial tensions not only back in 1968 America but also

Paul Bouchard

in the jungles of Vietnam between white and black American soldiers. So many soldiers had been drafted into military service, something, Bob argued, that contributed to the tensions.

I ain't no rich boy, John Clark thought to himself in "The Suck Called Vietnam" when he was on the shittiest of all details, hauling and burning the soldiers' excrements. Then Bob's reading fast-forwarded to the present, where Clark, now seventy, thought back to his combat tour.

"No education deferments for this boy. Shit man, former SECDEF Cheney—he got so many deferments for his drunken-DUI-college days, partying it up. And the current POTUS, the orange-haired orangutan bully currently occupying the White House. Some funky, lame-ass heel spurs got him out of Nam. And the dude has the audacity to criticize Senator John McCain. A draft dodger criticizing a war hero, a prisoner-of-war hero at that. That shit don't fly, man. No fucking way."

Priya loved Bob's paper thus far, and 1968 seemed to be such a pivotal year in American history: LBJ didn't rerun for the presidency; MLK was shot and killed; RFK met the same fate. Priya wasn't familiar with Robert Kennedy and his presidential hopes washed away by an assassin's bullet, but she did know about Dr. Martin Luther King Jr., for Gandhi was a well-known inspiration of his. When Bob was talking about the draft, Priya recalled what Tocqueville had written on the matter: "In America the use of conscription is unknown, and men are induced to enlist by bounties."

Conscription, in the form of a draft, had indeed occurred during America's Vietnam War, but Tocqueville's point seemed to resonate in these times, for as Brian would explain to her later during lunch at Bombay Palace, "We haven't had a draft since the Vietnam War; it's an all- volunteer military now. If the government needs more service members, the pay and/or education benefits or money bonuses go up."

Priya loved Bob's paper on so many different levels but

66

principally because it seemed to be so heartfelt. She also enjoyed Carlos's paper, particularly the level of deep detail Carlos used to describe his fish taco recipe—what type of fish, cooked at a specific temperature for a specific time; the spices; how to make the winning *pico de gallo*; and the tacos, the details of making great tacos.

At one point in that morning class, Geneva said of her "Geneva Moves to Hollywood" paper, "And Geneva was pursuing her American dream," a comment that really got Priya thinking. *I know of no other country that has a dream. There is no Indian dream or British dream or French dream or Japanese dream. The very fact that there is such a concept in America speaks volumes about this country and what it's all about.*

Jose followed Geneva with his "Muskia Will Save the World." *Very creative,* Priya thought. *Science fiction and fantasy-ish.* And Jose was really digging into the complex subject of consent. When exactly did consent start? At what age should consent be allowed?

Then there was Brenda and her tribute to Anthony Bourdain. Indeed, the combination of food and travel made for an interesting life, and Bourdain certainly had that. Priya was convinced there was no way Brenda wouldn't get an A for this yearlong course, for her class participation was so on point. Brenda was smart, so knowledgeable about so many things; the sheer depth and breadth of her knowledge was most impressive. Politics, food, 1968, music—you name it, Brenda knew about it. Priya was extremely impressed with this retired schoolteacher.

As for Tony's paper, it was building some interesting drama, for Jorge, the main character, was suspecting—for good reasons— that his older brother, Armando, a US Border Patrol agent, might be on the take of one of Juarez's cartels.

And finally, Brian's paper on Gandhi. Priya was learning so much about India's sacred national hero, things all new to her, especially since Gandhi perhaps wasn't always the saint history had portrayed him to be. For example, during that Wednesday class, Brian had read the following about Gandhi's time in South Africa:

"Gandhi wrote a legal brief arguing for voting rights for Indians in South Africa that read in part, 'Anglo-Saxons and Indians are sprung from the same area in stock or rather the Indo-European peoples,' which was central to his argument that Indians should not be grouped with Africans. So, in essence, Gandhi not only recognized the separation of some races but advocated for such separation."

When it was Priya's turn to discuss her paper, Professor Martin asked her to discuss a portion of her own observations about Tocqueville's themes of equality of condition and "I know of no country, indeed, where the love of money has taken stronger hold on the affections of men."

"This I tell you," Priya said, referring to portions of her paper on these themes, "things work in America. Hot water when you want it, cold water when you want it too, and it is drinkable out of the tap. There are no power outages in America, except for the occasional short ones caused by Mother Nature and her thunderstorms. You want something or you need something, you can find it at Walmart, which is open twenty-four hours a day every day. Or you can find it at Amazon, and it will find you on your doorstep in forty-eight hours, delivered courtesy of a few clicks from a computer mouse. You're hungry? Many McDonald's and other fast-food franchises are open all day every day, so you can do drive-through and get your french fries at three in the morning. Or you can go to IHOP and eat pancakes at any time. Amazingly, in America, if you buy a product and are not satisfied with it, you can return it to the store you bought it from and obtain a refund. Returning products after purchase is unknown in many countries but not in America. America works because of what Tocqueville observed: so many Americans are chasing money to better their lives. This leads to tremendous consumerism and entrepreneurship. America, indeed, is not lacking in both of these endeavors, for so many things seem to be commercialized in this big country. Take television programs, for example. Shows like *Shark Tank,* where prospective entrepreneurs pitch their business ideas to famous investors; a show called *Blue-Collar Millionaires,* where folks in the blue-collar trades turn their work into successful businesses; *How I Made My Millions,* a show about how folks become millionaires (hint—they don't win the lottery; they become merchants/businesspeople); advertisements on television at all hours by plumbers and electricians and air-conditioning contractors explaining their services, or sales reps pitching vacuum cleaners or jewelry items or skin-care products. I agree with Tocqueville when he observed, 'I know of no country, indeed, where the love of money has taken stronger hold on the affections of men.'"

Friday night, and Priya and her sisters were watching *Slumdog Millionaire* at Brian's apartment. Brian and Chuck, who incidentally had never seen the movie but had heard of its popular and critical acclaim, had spent two full hours cleaning their apartment, scrubbing and wiping and vacuuming and spraying healthy doses of Febreze to ensure the place was up to snuff. The Kumar sisters had previously seen the hit movie, but they were enjoying it for a second time. The cuisine for the evening's viewing was take-out Indian from Bombay Palace (ordered and paid for by Brian), popcorn, and a treat Brian recently discovered was a Kumar sisters' favorite—peanut butter cups. (He had bought a dozen.)

"Is this movie an accurate portrayal of India?" Chuck asked to no one in particular when the movie ended and the credits were rolling. "I'm wondering about those poor street kids. Are they really kidnapped and subjected to permanent blindness and begging because their kidnapper pours acid on their eyes and now collects their daily hauls from panhandling?"

"Sadly, yes," Priya said as she was finishing her last peanut butter cup. "Yes, those bad things do sometimes occur."

That evening, after he dropped off the Kumar sisters at their apartment and returned to his, Brian drank a Corona beer in bed and fell asleep with the television still on but muted. He dreamed a combination of *Slumdog Millionaire* scenes and Gandhi readings, sometimes with Gandhi in the movie scenes, rescuing the street kids or at other times giving speeches about living a pure and simple life.

Two miles away, Priya too was in bed, also dreaming, hers also about *Slumdog Millionaire* but interspersed with a diminutive French aristocrat named Tocqueville traveling through a mixture of 1830s and present-day America. Tocqueville at times was in a buggy being pulled by a horse, observing, at one point, folks collectively building a barn for a neighbor farmer. Then he saw a plantation with that awful institution of slavery, an institution he surmised this young nation would go to war over, because slavery would not last, for the nation was too Christian, and Christianity would eventually not allow slavery. Then, in Priya's dream, Tocqueville, dressed in a black suit in the style of the 1830s, was in present-day America, driving an SUV and observing billboards that read ...

Slip and Fall? Call Paul. Defending accident victims for more than 20 years. Call 1-800-and-Paul (1-800-263-7285).

Visit First Baptist Church. John 3:16. Believe
in Him and Have Eternal Life.

On bumper stickers, Tocqueville read: "Trump—Making America Great Again," followed by another bumper sticker: "Democracy Lost—Hilary Got More Votes."

After the bumper stickers, Priya's dream shifted to scenes in

Slumdog Millionaire, especially where the patrons of the TV show laugh at the poor, humble contestant. And then, in another shift, Priya began to dream about the broad-shouldered army officer she sat next to in their Independent Study class, First Lieutenant Brian Robinson.

Late October, it was a Saturday evening in the large parking lot of El Paso's Hindu temple. "Diwali is the Hindu festival of lights. It symbolizes a triumph of good over evil, truth over falsehood, light over darkness, and peace and goodwill." That's how Priya had described the meaning of the then-upcoming celebration, and when she added, "Brian, you must join us for this important celebration at the temple. Chuck can come too," it was an offer Brian felt obliged to accept. Plus, he was curious, and Chuck decided to tag along.

The five—the three Kumar sisters and the roommates—spent most of their time that unusually mild Saturday evening in the northwest corner of the temple's parking lot next to one of the last and many kiosks, kiosks that were displaying Indian food, beverages, jewelry (mostly made of gold), framed paintings of Buddha, Ganesha bronze statues, and saris—tons and tons of saris.

Carrying a white paper plate filled with two samosas and sambar rice, Brian was enjoying the food and the views of couples—not always of the husband-wife variety but young children or adults of the same sex, paired up—dancing with thick wooden sticks that were no more than eighteen inches in length. The duos would move their feet slightly to the left and right, but most of the action was displaying one's stick in front of one's partner, at about the height of the partner's upper chest, the stick always parallel to its holder and always at a forty-five-degree angle in the opposite direction of the partner's stick, thus creating an X when the sticks met. The meeting of the sticks created a soft but audible tap sound that was well paired with the high-pitch

Hindi music that was coming out of four large black speakers. Tap-and-tap-and-tap, all throughout a song, sometimes lasting around ten minutes. Brian counted nearly three hundred taps from one team—what looked like a husband and wife team—during one of the many songs. It was toward the tail end of that song when Brian noticed he and Chuck, out of what had to be a crowd of about three hundred people, constituted two of only a handful of Caucasians.

During the drive back to Las Cruces, a drive that started at around nine forty-five that night, Rani, dressed in a green sari and situated behind the steering wheel, for she was driving the old Honda Accord, opened up the conversation by asking, "So what was the best part of Diwali, gang?"

Chuck gave the answer, "The fireworks show," and all were in agreement, Rani included. Brian was particularly impressed with the ninety-minute fireworks display and how it lit up the reddish-purple Franklin Mountains in the background from his vantage point.

Everyone liked the food, all the Kumar sisters bought a few bangles, and the stick dancing was fun to watch, but nothing topped the fireworks. "It was by far and without question the best fireworks show I've ever seen," Brian said.

The only negative comment about the whole Diwali celebration came from Chuck, who, in his tactful and diplomatic way, said, "Awesome experience; fun times. Too bad there wasn't any alcohol."

In late November, Brian and Priya were at Bombay Palace with Rani and Deepika for lunch. Gone were the spring and summer temperatures hovering around the century mark or the high nineties, now replaced by cooler ones that necessitated Priya adding sweaters, sweatshirts, long-sleeve blouses, one overcoat, and a pair of leather gloves to her small wardrobe, clothing items she had never seen, bought, or worn. Light snow or cool rains were not uncommon this time of year, with the former at times heaving its deposits on the jagged surrounding mountains, giving them their white-capped look. Indeed, three days ago, when southern New Mexico had experienced its first snowfall (a light one measuring half an inch), Priya, who was with Deepika at the time at the local Starbucks, proclaimed excitedly, "Look, it's snow! Let's go outside, and you take a photo of me please, with the snow in the photo. I'll email the photos back home to Chennai!"

The snow of seventy-two hours ago had promptly melted the following day, and today's temperature hovered in the high fifties, low sixties. Brian was working on his mulligatawny lentil soup when he figured now was as good a time to go ahead with his proposal.

"Thanksgiving is next week. Do you guys have any plans? If not, I'm inviting you all to a traditional Thanksgiving meal with my family in Albuquerque."

"Yes, Mom, a twenty pounder will do," Brian told his mother over the phone in preparation for the Thanksgiving festivities. He was flipping channels on the muted flat-screen TV in his apartment. "Actually, Mom, these friends of mine are basically vegetarian, but a couple of them eat chicken, so I'm sure they'll like turkey."

"Vegetarian? Oh, okay," Mrs. Robinson said. She was sitting at the kitchen table, looking over some bills. "That's interesting. Well, I'll have mashed potatoes and string beans and sweet potatoes and cranberries of course. And your dad will make his usual pecan pie for dessert. You think they'll like turkey?"

"Yes, Mom. They'll like turkey."

"And my gravy is meat based. Will they be okay with the gravy? All guys love gravy, right?"

"Let's go gravy on the side, Mom," Brian said. "And actually, Mom, these friends of mine are not guys. They're girls. Sisters actually."

"Sisters?" Mrs. Robinson said. "Well, that's interesting. How did you meet them? Are you dating one of them? You know, your father and I talk about Susan from time to time. Such a sweet girl. Too bad she moved to Seattle." Susan was Brian's former girlfriend from his NMSU college days. During his deployment to Afghanistan, he had received the Dear John letter, also called the Jody letter, from her, informing him she was transferring to the University of Washington in Seattle, tagging along over there with Mike Crenshaw, a second-string NMSU defensive back. *Sweet. Girlfriend found herself another man, a teammate no less. Go fucking figure.*

"No, Mom, I'm not dating any one of them—just friends. They're really nice. I know you'll like them."

"Well, what are their names?"

Brian cleared his throat and said, "Their names are Priya, Rani, and Deepika. They're originally from India, Mom."

Silence.

"India. India," she repeated. More silence. "That's interesting, dear. I don't think we've ever had Indians over before. Dr. Patel and his family live at the end of the street. They're such nice people, such a nice family. Dr. Patel helped your dad with his back issues. We've invited the Patels over a few times, but Dr. Patel is so busy. I swear he must work eighty hours a week. You know the Patels purchased a summer cottage in Michigan two years ago. Mrs. Patel told me they hardly go there because they're so busy, but they rent it out at a hefty profit."

"That's interesting, Mom," Brian said. "Send my best to the Patels."

"Oh yes, I will. And you remember Siddhartha, their son,

right? He's nineteen and studying premed at UCLA. How lovely. Such a nice boy." She then said, "Well, how did you meet these Indian sisters? This is exciting."

"I'm in a class with one of the sisters, Mom. Priya. The Independent Study course I'm taking. Priya is in that class."

"Oh, how nice, dear."

"You'll like them, Mom. Rani and Deepika are both PhD candidates at NMSU, and Priya already has a master's degree from India. She's a writer."

"Oh, how lovely. Indians are so smart. I'll tell your father we're having the sisters over for Thanksgiving. I'm so excited."

John Robinson, fifty-eight, grew up in Midland, Texas, the second son of an oil field worker and homemaker. After high school, he followed in his father's footsteps and began working in the oil fields, a career choice opposed by both his parents, for it had always been their aspiration their second son would attend college and avoid the backbreaking physical demands of his father's livelihood. John toughed it out for two years in the fields. Then, in part out of curiosity and in part to appease his loving parents, he tried college, enrolling at Midland College and signing up for business classes. That too lasted two years, the end result being an associate's degree in management, a degree that helped him land an entry-level loan officer position with a local bank. Boy, were his parents proud of him—"The first Robinson to attend college. Our son has a desk job and in a nice air-conditioned building."

But John wasn't happy—desk, building, and climate control aside. It's not that he was miserable—he liked his coworkers and clients—but he knew he had always wanted to be his own boss. And he didn't mind working with his hands and working outdoors. Listening to his true desires and looking for some other opportunity, change for John Robinson came in the form of a full circle back to the oil fields—this time not with him standing in the windy, dusty fields changing drill pipes but rather sitting comfortably in the cab of a big truck, now involved in transporting the black gold instead of drilling for it. After quitting his loan officer job and going to a four-week truck-driving school (paid for by his future oil-hauling employer), John became a self-employed truck driver on contract with an oil-service company.

The first year as an oil field truck driver brought further happiness to the rugged John Robinson (he stood five feet, eleven inches and tipped the scales at 210 pounds). It was that year, 1985, that the then twenty-three-year-old proposed to his girlfriend, the only girlfriend he ever had, Sandra O'Brien, an attractive brunette, the third daughter of a Midland Walmart manager.

What an incredible team John and Sandra made, not only as a loyal, loving, married couple but as business partners, for after slightly more than a year as a truck driver, the twosome struck out on their own with J & S Trucking Inc., an oil transportation company with two trucks (John driving one of them, the other driven by hired help), and the engaging Sandra doing the dispatching. In no time, the young company was not only hauling oil but moving pipes and pumps and other machinery to West Texas oil fields, the two-truck start-up eventually building to a twelve-truck fleet. Along the way, John and Sandra had Brian, now twenty-four, an NMSU grad, current MBA student there, and an Army National Guard field artillery officer. Then came Ann-Marie, now twenty, an attractive and athletic brunette (she played soccer) and a sophomore at Colorado State, currently studying biology.

Starting in the fall of 2000, John and Sandra's business expanded to neighboring New Mexico with its growing oil and gas industry. Eight years later, with the real estate crash from the Great Recession, the successful couple decided to sell their company at a hefty profit (real estate prices may have collapsed but not the value of their trucks and warehouses) and settle down in

Albuquerque, where, with rock-bottom housing prices, they not only purchased a relatively new five-bedroom, 5,500-square-foot home but also numerous smaller houses and two large apartment complexes.

"We decided to become real estate investors," John would later tell a business acquaintance. "The oil business is a great business, but it's a boom-or-bust industry, all dependent on oil and gas prices. The real estate crash presented a tremendous buying opportunity. And Sandra and I wanted to slow down. Flipping houses and managing rentals ain't easy, but it's easier than the ups and downs of trucking for the oil industry. Plus, we don't carry debt, and I have a great contractor to flip houses and some good property managers to look over the apartments we rent out. We made very good money in trucking, but we were constantly in debt, growing our business. It's easier now."

John and Sandra, despite their business success, lived modestly, their 5,500-square-foot home being the only sign of their financial success. Brian and Anne-Marie attended public schools and were raised middle class—not upper middle or upper class. The Robinsons did not golf, and they weren't members of a country club. They could afford Manhattan or LA or San Francisco or Aspen, but that wasn't them; Albuquerque suited them just fine. And posh vacations, including to Europe or Asia, weren't their thing either, for Robinson vacations—normally an annual event—took the family of four to destinations like Branson, Missouri, Orlando, or Vegas, always with stays at modest hotels like Holiday Inn or plain Marriott brands. One exception: three years ago, John took the family to Rome (the Robinsons were practicing Catholics) to visit the main sites, including hearing the Angelus Prayer from Pope Francis in Saint Peter's Square. As for vehicles, John drove a seven-year-old GMC pickup, and Sandra's car was a nine-year-old white Cadillac.

John and Sandra made it clear to their two children: "We will always be there for you, but Daddy and I are not writing checks. We will pay for your educations, and that's it." John once emphasized, "Brian, regarding your goal of flipping houses and being a real estate developer, I think you and Chuck will make great business partners, but you know I won't lend you a dime or cosign a loan to help you guys flip your first house. There is no experience like direct experience. You guys are going to have to figure things out as you go."

The drive from Las Cruces to Albuquerque was pleasant and took three-and-a-half hours. Brian, behind the wheel of the old four-door GMC hand-me-down, talked about his family and answered the Kumar sisters' questions:

"So what do your parents do?"

Answer: "They are real estate investors. They used to own a trucking company that catered to oil companies."

"And your sister?"

Answer: "Anne-Marie is twenty years old and studies biology at Colorado State in Fort Collins. She plays soccer too. Anne-Marie's a lesbian. Actually, I think my dear sister is bisexual, but anyway, right now she has a partner, Sheila Patterson. I hope you all don't have any quarrels about homosexuality, lesbianism," Brian said matter-of-factly.

Rani responded, "Not at all. It is what it is. We just don't know too many homosexuals. It's not something that's out in the open in India. Personally, I didn't know any homosexuals until I came to the United States. My boss at work, he's gay."

Both Priya and Deepika also said they had no problem with the issue of sexual preference.

"Well, it took a while for my parents to come around on the idea that their daughter is a lesbian," Brian said. "You'll like my sister. And her partner is cool too."

The conversation about Brian's family weaved itself into a discussion about Brian's uncle, Ron Robinson, for yesterday evening, while Brian was on the phone with his mother, she had informed him, "We're all set for a wonderful Thanksgiving, dear, and we're so anxious to meet your Indian friends. Oh, and by the way, we have a new addition to the guest list. Your uncle Ron will be attending. Your father invited him. I just hope he behaves himself."

Ron Robinson, age sixty-three, had not found the success of his younger sibling, John. Like his dad and younger brother, Ron worked the West Texas oil fields, but then, in the early nineties, duty called in the form of his National Guard unit getting activated and shipped out to protect Saudi Arabia (Desert Shield) and liberate Kuwait (Desert Storm). Ron, a truck driver and refueler in his unit, was part of Storm'in Norman's forces that crushed Saddam's defenses and brought a quick and decisive victory to America and its allies.

But the quick big-picture victory ended up being a long, personal defeat for the then-married father of two. Headaches, joint and muscle pain, fatigue and sleep disturbances—hell, maybe there was something to the Gulf War syndrome. Ron surely had spent plenty of time around the burning garbage pits and burning oil fields. Upon returning stateside, his best friend became alcohol, a friendship that cost him a marriage, two DUIs (he would never find work as a truck driver again, even with his successful younger brother), unsteady employment, and grown kids who rarely spoke to him. Now, partly drawing on disability, Ron found side jobs as a handyman in Lubbock, Texas. "At least with Uncle Ron, he's a happy drunk," Brian told the Kumar sisters on the northerly drive to Albuquerque. "He has a loud voice and a loud laugh. He's actually a good guy and funny. I just wish he could find more steady work."

They arrived at the Robinson home, and Brian parked the four-door pickup in the horseshoe- shaped paved driveway. "Here we are," he said. Everyone got out of the vehicle.

Priya took in the surroundings on this lovely, crisp autumn day. *This house is so beautiful. And huge! Beautiful beige stucco siding with immense windows. A gorgeous, red tile roof of the Spanish style. An expertly manicured front lawn with four aspen trees. And a three-door garage facing the large, curved driveway.*

"This place is gorgeous, Brian," she said, marveling at the house and the gorgeous street lined with similar homes.

"And you said there's a pool in the back, Brian?" Rani asked. She too was marveling at the scenery.

"Yes, there's a pool in the back of the house. Dad closed it in early September for the fall and winter. He opens it up in the spring, in late May."

The four walked together to the front door, and before Brian could ring the doorbell, his mother opened the door with a beaming smile and said, "Oh, welcome, welcome." She hugged and kissed her son, and then she hugged each of the Kumar sisters. "Oh, and you brought a dish. How kind of you. And what is your name, dear? Brian told me the names, but I forget easy."

"I'm Priya," Priya said, smiling as she entered the home.

"Oh, how lovely. And it's a beautiful rice dish, I see. Please, come in. It's cold outside."

Everyone entered the home, the sisters started taking off their shoes, and Mrs. Robinson, dressed in white slacks, a red blouse, and a white apron tied around her waist, said, "Let me take your coats, dear. You don't have to take off your shoes, but if you want to, that's all right too." She turned to the right and opened the door of a huge closet. "Oh, and I love what you all are wearing," she said, smiling. "So beautiful, so colorful. What is it called?"

"We're wearing salwar kameez, traditional pants and shirt," Rani said as she continued to remove her shoes. Her combination was blue, Deepika's was maroon, and Priya wore loose, dark red pants with a lighter red top.

Suddenly, two small white dogs excitedly came from a hallway and went straight for the three strangers. Deepika turned toward

Rani and hugged her for protection while Priya stepped back and yelled, "Oh!" while still holding her chicken biryani dish. She too turned to Rani for protection.

"Oh, don't worry about them," Mrs. Robinson said. "They don't bite. Curly and Fritz, say hi to our new guests, the Kumar sisters."

"Sorry, Mrs. Robinson," Rani said nervously as Curly and Fritz, canine sister and brother, stood on their hind legs with their front paws on Rani's shins, their small tails wagging. "We are not used to dogs—or pets actually."

Brian laughed and said, "Curly and Fritz, come here," and the pair shifted their attention to Brian, who started petting them.

"Don't worry, dear," Mrs. Robinson told Rani as she left the large closet. "They're harmless. Like I said, they don't bite. They just want to be petted."

Mrs. Robinson led everyone to the kitchen and adjacent dining room. Priya was completely taken over by what she saw: high ceilings, beautiful crown molding, gorgeous hardwood floors, a stunning dining room with a large wooden hutch holding beautiful plates and crystal, a table expertly set—white linen and all—with candles and polished silverware for utensils. The kitchen—more than half the size of the sisters' two-bedroom apartment—had black granite countertops, modern appliances, a huge island (also with black granite), cooking utensils hanging from a polished metal frame, and large white cabinets.

"Please have a seat at the short bar," Mrs. Robinson said. "The table is almost set." She placed Priya's dish on the huge island next to many other dishes.

The Kumar sisters sat on the solid, high barstools across from the kitchen sink area. Curly and Fritz soon reached up with their front paws to the first rung of Deepika's chair, wagging their tails, wanting her attention.

Mrs. Robinson opened up a huge, modern oven. "Can I

offer you all anything to drink? We have wine, beer, fruit juices. Anything?"

"Oh, Mom, the Kumar sisters don't drink alcohol," Brian said. "I'll get them water."

"They don't drink alcohol? Ain't that a shame," said a loud voice.

"Oh, hi, Uncle Ron," Brian said as he was heading to the cabinets to get some glasses.

Ron Robinson, wearing dark jeans and a green collared shirt, was holding a Miller Genuine Draft bottle of beer in his left hand. He entered the kitchen area from the living room. "Hey, how's my favorite nephew and the finest field artillery first lieutenant in America's army?" They shook hands and touched chests simultaneously.

"Fine, Uncle Ron. Everything's fine."

"That's great," Ron said. "And who are these fine ladies who don't drink alcohol?"

"Uncle Ron, these are the Kumar sisters. We're all students at NMSU."

"That's great." He went over to each sister and shook hands with them individually.

"Name's Ron Robinson. Persian Gulf veteran. Pleasure to meet y'all." He took a gulp of beer. "Good that you all don't drink. Don't start. Hey, what's that red dot y'all are wearing on your foreheads?"

"Ron, dear, don't ask so many questions," Mrs. Robinson said as she pulled a steaming pumpkin pie from the oven.

"I'm just asking, Sandra. I think they're cool-looking actually." He gulped down the last of his bottle. "Hey, can I help myself to a re-spill? I mean a refill?"

"Yes, Ron," Mrs. Robinson said. She sighed. "The beer is downstairs in the wet bar. And you're staying with us tonight. You're not driving."

"Yes, ma'am. Roger that," he said loudly.

He started heading for the downstairs finished basement when Rani said, "What we have on our foreheads are called bindis. They are often worn by married woman, but single women wear them also. It is linked to the third eye of *ajna* chakra, a site of wisdom and power."

"Oh, how lovely," Mrs. Robertson said.

"Cool beans," Ron said. "So are y'all single or married?"

"Their students, Ron. PhD and graduate students," Mrs. Robinson said firmly as the Kumar sisters were giggling. "Go get your beer."

"I'm just asking," Ron said. He gave a military salute to the sisters, then turned on his heel and headed downstairs.

Brian started filling the glasses with water, and just then, the front door opened.

"Oh, that must be John and Anne-Marie and Sheila," Mrs. Robinson said. "Your dad had to pick them up at the airport." She headed to the front door to greet them.

Everyone was seated at the dinner table. Earlier, John Robinson had introduced himself to the Kumar sisters, and so did Anne-Marie and her partner, Sheila. A fit and younger version of her dirty-blonde-haired mother, Anne-Marie had complimented the Kumar sisters on their "lovely and colorful clothing. So beautiful, so nice." Sheila, a tall, fit brunette who also played soccer at Colorado State, also complimented the Kumar sisters' attire.

"Ann-Marie, dear. Why don't you say grace for us?" John said.

"Sure, Dad." Everyone bowed their heads, the Kumar sisters doing the same.

"Heavenly Father. We thank you for all your blessings. We thank you for continued good health, we thank you for our lovely home, and we thank you for this wonderful food we are about to eat. We have so much to be thankful for, and it is all through you, Lord. At this Thanksgiving, we are especially thankful for seeing Uncle Ron and meeting the lovely Kumar sisters. We ask that you protect them always. We ask this in your name. Amen."

Everyone repeated "Amen," with Ron's being the loudest.

Once all the food was passed around, John started carving the turkey, asking each person, "White or dark meat?" The Kumar sisters, unfamiliar with turkey, asked what the difference was between the meat variations.

"White meat is very good, but it is drier, while the dark meat is tastier and moist," Mrs. Robinson said.

Priya went first and ordered dark meat. Then Mr. Robinson had an idea: "Why don't I give you all both a sample of white and dark meat, and you guys can decide what you like best when we do the second helpings."

With that, he placed a bit of white and dark meat on Priya's plate and started to do the same for Rani, but she politely said, "My apologies, sir, but I do not eat meat. My sister Deepika also does not eat meat."

"Oh, okay," John said. "That's not a problem."

After the various food selections were served, John, who was wearing khakis and a white collared shirt under a red sweater, said, "Let's raise our glasses for toasts. Be sure your glasses are filled." He himself was drinking bourbon while his wife and daughter were drinking a Pinot Noir, and his son and brother were drinking Miller Genuine Drafts. Brian, seeing that Uncle Ron's bottle was nearly empty, poured some of his beer in the wineglass in front of him.

"Here you go, Uncle Ron. Some beer for a toast." He did the same for himself, pouring beer in a wineglass.

Priya, sitting to Brian's left, leaned in toward him and softly said, "What do we do, Brian? We don't drink alcohol."

"Don't worry," he said reassuringly. "Just pour water from your water glass into the wineglass in front of you. Here, let me help you." He took her glass of water and poured some of its contents into her wineglass. Rani and Deepika caught on and also filled their wineglasses with water.

"Anyone want to propose a toast?" John asked enthusiastically.

"Oh, why don't you start it off, honey," Mrs. Robinson said, smiling.

"Okay," her husband said. He raised his glass. "To a special Thanksgiving."

Everyone repeated, "To a special Thanksgiving," and they all touched glasses.

Priya smiled when she touched glasses with Brian. She said, "This is interesting, a toast, touching glasses."

"It's a tradition," Brian said. "Quite popular actually."

Suddenly, Ron said loudly, "To President Trump," and he raised his glass high above his head. "May he *make America great again.*"

John and Brian laughed, and Mrs. Robinson quickly said, "Oh, Ron, cut the politics please."

John gathered himself and said, "Well, Trump cut taxes. That's good. I'll toast to that," and he raised his glass toward Ron, the only two with raised glasses.

"To love and understanding throughout the world," Brian then said, and he raised his glass.

Everyone repeated, "To love and understanding throughout the world," and they touched glasses.

The ride back to Albuquerque took three-and-a-half hours, with Brian dropping off the Kumar sisters at their apartment right at 11:15 p.m. During the ride, Priya's mind was racing, thinking of the numerous pleasant experiences she and her sisters had just witnessed with *this holiday Americans call Thanksgiving. To give thanks for what one has—how nice, how appropriate. This country is so rich, everything so plentiful.* Her thoughts kept racing, for there was so much going on. *Brian's family, his parents and sister, very nice people. And what a home, an amazing house and property. And Brian's parents—husband and wife but also business partners. Equal in all things, it seemed. Mrs. Robinson not only could ask things of her husband but also direct him to do things: "Honey, get us more wine please. Honey, we need more napkins." Mrs. Robinson did all the cooking and the cleaning of that large home, and Mr. Robinson told us he took care of that huge yard—the trees, bushes, picking the weeds out of the rock portions of the yard, mowing the grass sections, and maintaining that huge pool. He did all that. No way this would occur in India. Inconceivable when I think about it. In India, a couple with that large of a house, a home with that big of a yard and with that big of a swimming pool, well, there would be servants all over the place, doing the work. The cooking, the cleaning, the laundry, the yard, the pool, even the driving around to do errands like groceries. This would all be done by servants, by hired help. For me and Rani and Deepika, we only learned to do laundry and cleaning when we arrived here in America, because here in America, so many of the people are do-it-yourselfers. I remember Brian discussing purchasing supplies at the big wonderful store called Home Depot. He was talking to Chuck, and he was saying how packed the store was, not only with contractors but with regular homeowners, these do-it-yourselfers. These things do not exist in India—homeowners buying tools and supplies and working on their residences.*

Priya's racing thoughts during that three-hour-plus drive at times redirected her to Tocqueville and his prescient observations of America, observations that became intertwined with her thoughts. *The equality of condition. How true, how so very true. Brian's family, with the parents and the two siblings, they are all equal and treat each other as equals. Mrs. Robinson's conversations with her daughter are like colleagues, adult female friends talking to each other. Same with Brian and his father—equals, treated like colleagues. Love of comfort has become the dominant national taste. Tocqueville observed that, and it still holds true today. The Robinsons are definitely comfortable. Very comfortable in fact. But there are no airs about them. They remain a simple people.*

"Thank you so much for a lovely day, Brian," Priya said when Brian dropped her and her sisters off at their apartment.

"Sure. Absolutely. Thanks for coming. Glad you liked it," Brian replied, smiling.

"Yes, Brian, thank you so much," Rani added as she got out of the pickup truck. "And thank you for teaching us American football. It was a fun game to watch. Six points when the ball crosses the end zone. Three points when the ball is kicked between the two yellow posts."

"Yeah, sure. Any time," Brian said, smiling.

"But it's only worth one point when the ball is kicked between the posts after the six-point down," Priya added, confident.

"Right you are," Brian said as he looked at Priya. "After a touchdown, the kick is for an extra point. Glad you all enjoyed the game. And Thanksgiving."

That night, as she was sipping Earl Grey hot tea, Priya thought some more about the lovely day she had spent with her sisters and with Brian and his family. With her notebook open and her thoughts still racing, she jotted down thoughts about Tocqueville's equality of condition argument and about the Robinsons lovely home:

> Tocqueville—perhaps there is no country in the world where fewer idle men are to be met with than in America, or where all who work are more eager to promote their own welfare.
>
> Food—Thanksgiving meal: turkey, I tried it even though I eat very little meat. It was so-so.
>
> Cranberry—too sweet. Pumpkin pie—I liked the crust, but the filling is too sweet. Stuffing in turkey—a strange taste with a strange texture. Gravy—meat base, and I tried just a little. It was okay. Mashed potatoes—very good; I enjoyed the potatoes

very much. Toasts with wineglasses—I participated in the toast without drinking alcohol.

"Okay, gang, great job by you all this past semester."

Professor Martin, dressed in black pants, a white shirt, and brown cowboy boots, was handing out the graded Independent Study papers for the fall 2018 semester. Classes, which normally convened on Wednesdays, met on Friday this time, on account of the rescheduling brought about by finals week. "Excellent work. Great progress with themes, and thoughts, and characters," he said as he kept walking and passing out the graded papers. "My apologies in advance, but I have to cut today's class short on account of I've got a flight out of El Paso that leaves in about two-and-a-half hours. My wife wants to spend Christmas in Vegas. Call it early holiday wishes from me to you all."

"Thank you, Mark," Brenda said as he was about to hand her paper to her.

A few more thank yous followed, and then Mark, pacing quickly in front of the class, said, "I look forward to seeing you all next year in three weeks. And I have two quick admin announcements. One concerns Tony's paper about the drug cartels' footprint in this region. Tony made a big addition this semester. He decided to add to the fictional story he's creating by incorporating the themes, plot, and characters of the popular Netflix series *Breaking Bad* into his work. I okayed this add-on and find it to be a great vehicle to show an entertaining story. So the main takeaway is you can always add to your papers, and develop new angles, and see me for my thoughts on these matters."

Priya was listening to what Professor Martin was saying, but at the same time she was glancing at his written marks on her paper: "Great use of Tocqueville's argument about religion in America interwoven with modern-day examples that support his position; excellent explanation of Tocqueville's point about chasing comfort and how this still applies today." She received an A-minus for the semester.

Martin walked behind his desk and sat in his swivel chair. "And the second and final thing I want to cover today, before we call it a day and a semester, is I'd like Bob to read a passage from his semester's work. I think it fits well with our tips about 'write what you know and know what you write.' I don't mean to put you on the spot, Bob, but if you don't mind, please read for us the page I highlighted in your paper."

Bob, wearing faded blue jeans and an NMSU Aggie football sweatshirt, said, "Sure thing, Mark." He stayed seated and flipped his paper to pages 23–24.

"Here I am in this rumble in the jungle called Vietnam, and not by choice, mind you. Talking draft. Uncle Sam's got my ass all right, just like so many of my battle buddies here. No draft dodging or college deferments for us suckers. While we're here catching bullets, 'em preppy deferments sorts are having themselves a grand old time on 'em college campuses. Listening to Hendrix, smoking weed, probably getting laid by some of the babes who left us. Just last week, Tom Matheson, one of our squad leaders, a big country boy out of Michigan, got the Dear John letter from his supposed-to-be fiancée who called off their engagement. That's the big suck.

"John Clark, now seventy, was sitting in his rocking chair on the front porch of his Denver bungalow, sipping his bourbon, his thoughts shifting from his tour in Nam to the present day. Slick Willie Clinton, SECDEF Cheney, our current Prez Trump himself—all deferment pukes. Clinton cut loose from his ROTC scholarship, Cheney going to school and boozing it up, and POTUS Trump apparently had foot spurs. At least with George Bush the son, he signed up with the National Guard. Just like the veep, for his old man, one Dan Quayle. Word is the Guard was a way to sidestep the suck called Vietnam. But shit, man, at least they served in some capacity.

"Clark thought back to the spring/summer time frame of 1968. Dr. King had been assassinated, and the black GIs in Nam couldn't have been more pissed off. Understandably so. Race riots broke out, not just in the good old US of A but right in Nam, man. There were some seven brothers in our platoon. I always got along with them. But I'd be lying if I told y'all I wasn't scared some. Not like I didn't have enough worrying and staying focused on the Vietnamese communists and the Vietcong. Now I had to worry about the brothers in our platoon and whether they'd decide to pop one of us white boys."

"Thank you, Bob," Mark said. "That was great. Thanks for sharing it with us." He then stood up and started pacing back and forth—left to right, then right to left—in front of his desk.

"Remember team: show, don't tell. Telling can be effective, but intersperse telling the story by showing actions and thoughts and beliefs. And don't forget the wonderful advice by the great novelist Anne Rice, who said, 'Go where the pain is; go where the pleasure is.'"

Priya, taking it all in with interest, wrote the following in the right-hand margin of the first page of her semester paper:

> Pain—?
> Pleasure—Brian and the Robinson family. My sisters too.

After the Independent Study class, Priya and Brian met up with Rani and Deepika at Bombay Palace for lunch, and after that, the four of them decided to warm up with some coffee and tea at the nearby Starbucks.

"So what are your plans for Christmas and New Year's?" Rani asked as she was working on her chai tea. Brian, who was nursing a short pumpkin spice latte, was sitting to the left of Priya, who, like Deepika, bought a short Earl Grey hot tea. Priya had also purchased the *Wall Street Journal*, but she hadn't read it yet; she was attentively looking at Brian, anxious to discover his holiday plans.

"Well, I'll be spending Christmas at my folks'," he said. "That's the family tradition. Mom will cook her great food, and then we'll exchange gifts. And then—drumroll please"—he tapped the table rapidly—"Chuck and I will head to Vegas to try our luck at the poker tables."

"Oh, that's interesting," Rani said.

Priya said, "Yes, that sounds great, Brian."

"Yeah, there's a great tournament at the Rio All Suites Hotel right after Christmas. Chuck and I did the same thing last year. We've saved up six thousand dollars for this. We have an agreement to split any earnings fifty-fifty. Chuck will use two thousand dollars and take his chances at the cash tables while I'll do my best in the twenty-five hundred buy-in tournament. The rest of our money is for expenses. How about you guys? What are your plans for the holidays?"

"We will go to the Hindu temple in El Paso around Christmas," Rani said. "And we will also exchange gifts."

Priya and Deepika looked on, and then Priya said, "Unfortunately, we don't have enough money to visit our family back in Chennai, India, but we will be sure to call them over the phone and wish them blessings for the new year."

"Cool," Brian said as he sipped some of his pumpkin latte. For the last couple of nights, Brian had actually thought of inviting Priya and her sisters over to his parents' home for the holidays, but every which way he looked at it, he always came to the same conclusion. *It would be awkward, and certain expectations would kick in, and what gifts to buy and exchange, and my parents and sisters would feel the necessity to entertain, and Chuck and I have been planning and saving for this trip to Vegas for so many months now, and the whole thing, no matter how I slice it and dice it, just doesn't add up.*

The next thirty minutes were spent discussing how relieved

everyone was that finals week was at last finally over. At one point, Priya said in a heartfelt tone, "Whatever my grade will be in International Finance, I want to personally thank you once again, Brian, for helping me in that challenging course."

"Anytime, Priya. I bet you did well on the final exam. You're smart, and you understand the material."

The foursome left the Starbucks, and the cold breeze hit them immediately. Brian, with his hands in his jean pockets to keep them warm, said, "Well, I wish you all a lovely holiday season and a happy new year. I'll see you guys in less than three weeks."

"Same to you, Brian," Rani said.

Deepika added, "Yes, merry Christmas to you and your family, Brian. And we wish you all a safe and prosperous 2019."

"Thanks," Brian said. "Same to you all."

And then Priya said, "Have fun in Las Vegas, Brian, and good luck. Do send us photos, please. You can send them by text to me."

"Sure thing," he said.

Minutes into the drive back home, Brian heard a text on his iPhone. He quickly glanced to notice it was from Priya. Concentrating on the road and the moderate traffic, he decided to call her when he arrived at his apartment, a destination he figured he'd reach within five minutes.

"What up, dude?" Chuck said, as Brian stepped inside the bachelor pad.

Brian looked at his iPhone and read Priya's "CALL ME ASAP!!!" text, the all caps and three exclamation points being out of character from her normal texting style.

"Hanging," Brian said. "Glad finals are over. I need something cold and alcoholic. Gotta call Priya too. Something's up."

He quickly walked to the kitchen and opened the refrigerator, then grabbed himself a tall yellow Corona and tapped Priya's programmed cell phone number.

"Oh, Brian. Thank you. Thank you for calling," Priya said in a quick, excited voice. "I had to send you a text. I have the most wonderful, auspicious news."

"Sure," Brian said as he placed the bottle cap of the Corona in the bolted bottle opener on the nearby drawer. He pushed down, removing the bottle's cap, and held the removed cap in his right hand. He took a quick gulp of the cold beer. "What's up?"

"The most wonderful news. This I tell you, Brian. We give thanks to Ganesha and God Vishnu and also to Jesus. It is so wonderful."

"Okay. Well ... that's great, Priya. What's this great news?" He took another gulp of beer.

"What a country, the United States. How grateful we are for this land of plenty, for the abundance and generosity one finds in this great country."

"Cool. So ... what's this all about?"

"Oh, I could tell you, Brian, but I rather you come to our apartment. My sisters and I are so excited. Please come here. This I tell you—you will not be disappointed."

"Okay," Brian said, and he placed his Corona beer bottle on the kitchen counter. "I guess I'll head over now."

"Yes. Please do."

Brian started walking toward the door, and Chuck said, "Leaving so soon? What gives?"

"Don't know," Brian said. "Priya wants me to go over to see her and her sisters. They're all excited about something."

"Tell them I say hi."

"Sure thing," Brian said, and he headed out the door.

He knocked three times on Priya's apartment door, and Priya immediately opened the door and pulled him inside.

"This is most exciting, Brian," she said rapidly. "Please, take off your shoes and come in."

Brian took off his shoes and noticed Deepika slicing ginger on the kitchen countertop while Rani was checking on the boiling water for the upcoming hot tea. He had noticed this before: the Kumar sisters never used a microwave to heat tea water, and they only drank two brands—PG Tips and Earl Grey. Tonight, it would be PG Tips, and the boiling water also included ginger slices. Brian noticed Deepika and Rani were both smiling, excitement written all over them.

"Brian, please, come, come, have a seat," Priya said, leading him to the tiny living room.

Deepika, all smiles and slicing away, said, "Oh, Brian, wait till you hear about our incredible luck. My sisters and I thank Ganesha and Vishnu and all the positive karma."

Rani, sporting a beaming smile, added, "This is a most auspicious moment."

Brian, curious to find out what this was all about, took a seat on the small sofa, and it was then that Priya headed to the kitchen. Soon she was holding something behind her back, and she reentered the living room and proclaimed, "Ta-dah!" She placed a stiff, colorful flyer in front of her so Brian could read it.

"Isn't it great, Brian?"

Brian stared at the bright and busy 8.5 x 11 flyer three feet from him. Its main caption read: "You Won a New Car!" Smaller print read: "Pick up the car of your choice and get top dollar for a trade-in!"

He did his best to keep a poker face. A flyer from the biggest car dealer in Las Cruces, El Paso, and Albuquerque—Smith Nissan, Honda, and Mazda. Bright yellow flyer, huge red lettering, exclamation points a plenty, even the little fake key taped to the advertisement. He observed Deepika jumping up and down in excitement, Rani raising her right fist and jabbing it to the sky in praise, and Priya—all smiles—tilting the flyer to the left and then to the right, back and forth, to highlight its importance.

"We won a new car, Brian!" Priya exclaimed, her sisters now clapping their hands rapidly. "Oh what a country, this I tell you. This notice says the dealership will close at eleven o'clock tonight and that they'll also hand out free coffee. We don't drink coffee, and maybe they'll have tea there. We're getting our own tea ready right now, but I think we will need a lot of time tonight to decide which new car to select. How exciting! We of course called you right away, Brian. Rani is the one who picked up this wonderful notice in our mailbox."

"That's right, oh yeah," Rani said excitedly, pumping her right fist to the sky.

"We will pick up our new car this evening," Priya said, all enthused, "and then we will call our dear parents in India and inform them of this most auspicious of occasions."

Brian, silent and stiff, cleared his throat and started to say, "Uh ... well ... uh ... car dealerships send out such notices just to get customers in their stores and—"

"We won a new car, Brian!" Priya repeated.

Then Rani said, "I've been in this great country for going on three years now, and I've never seen such a great announcement in the mail. How wonderful."

"Well, you see, businesses just want prospective buyers in their stores," Brian said calmly. "See, if you read the small print at the bottom of this flyer, it says—"

"Brian, we called you to inform you of this wonderful news," Priya said, still smiling, "and we also request your assistance and expertise in helping us select our new car."

"But the small print says, 'Visit our dealership to get a chance of winning a new car. Some restrictions apply.'"

"Oh, Brian, my apologies in advance," Priya said, "but this is not a time to think of negative energy, negative karma, now is it? We won a new car, and we request your assistance. The announcement even has the key to our new car. I wonder if the key works on any car we choose."

"It's not a real key, Priya. See, this is all a ploy to—"

"Oh, Brian, dear you," Priya said in a serious tone. "I'm a bit surprised here. I thought you'd be just as joyous as we are for—"

"But it's not true, Priya. This is false advertising to get you all to visit the dealership, where a salesman will talk you into trading in your old vehicle to buy a new one and—"

"Oh, Brian, hush, my American friend," Priya said, all business. "This is a land of plenty, and the stars have lined up for us. We won a new car, and we have the notice of it and the key for it. Dear Rani will soon be driving a new car, this evening in fact, and we will send beautiful photos of this great winning to our family in India. Come now. We are going to Smith Nissan, Honda, and Mazda to claim our prize."

Twenty-five minutes later, Rani, driving her old Honda Accord, pulled into the front parking lot of the dealership. Bright-colored balloons, strewn between the service garage and the main front entrance, were blowing side to side on this windy evening. Brian, sitting next to Priya in the back seat, peered through the huge front window of the dealership that showcased a large, brightly lit showroom. He couldn't miss seeing the tall, pudgy, older gentleman, sporting the white hair, white goatee, and black Stetson, standing in the center of the showroom, passing out foam coffee cups from a tray and talking it up to the many prospective buyers.

Harry Smith. There he is, Brian thought. He had seen the running ads on television. He noticed tons of customers, most of them lined up inside but some trickling in from outside the dealership. *Suckers*, he thought. He got out of the car, and soon he and the Kumar sisters were huddled outside in a queue near the front entrance.

"Come on in and make yourselves cozy," they heard in a beaming, loud, southern voice as they entered the dealership. "We've got free coffee for y'alls" the elder Smith proclaimed. "Helps keep y'all warm on a cool night."

Brian and the sisters slowly moved forward, following the crowd. Priya, directly one person ahead of Brian, turned to face him and said, "This is amazing. Did all these people win a new car?"

Brian, looking directly at her, said, "I'm telling you, Priya. It's a tactic just to bring people to the dealership."

"And boy do we have the best deals on cars and trucks going, folks," Smith said. "One of our sales associates will be with y'all shortly."

A few minutes passed, and the line kept creeping forward. "Oh that Honda crossover is just splendid," Rani said, all enthused. "That's the one I want. Such a nice blue color."

A heavyset man, wearing chinos and the familiar light blue Smith Nissan, Honda, and Mazda shirt, approached Priya and said, "I take it you fine folks are one party. As my name tag reads, I'm Armando. Welcome to our dealership."

The sisters politely said hello while Brian chose to keep quiet.

"I see you brought our flyer. Congratulations on your winning."

"Oh, thank you, kind sir," Rani said, smiling. "We're excited about getting a new car."

"Well, now you're talking my language. You've come to the right place, ma'am. And we're closing late this evening, so there's plenty of time to get the car you want."

The Kumar sisters clapped their hands rapidly in excitement.

Armando led the sisters and Brian to one of the manned tables to the right, where salespersons and customers were filling out paperwork.

"Right here we have Janice," Armando said, leading them to one such table. "She'll take care of you. Can I get you all some coffee? We had doughnuts earlier, but we ran out real quick."

"Oh, thank you, sir," Priya said. "We're fine. Actually, we don't drink coffee."

Janice, who was sitting behind the table, had a cup of coffee to her right, a stack of flyers also to her right, and a black Hewlett-Packard laptop in front of her.

"Howdy, folks. Welcome to our dealership," she said. Along with the dealership shirt, she also had the Smith Dealership cap atop her raven hair. "I see you have the flyer. Can I have it please?"

"Sure," Rani said, and she handed her the flyer.

"Okay, let's get started," Janice said as she placed the flyer to her left. "Can I have your name and email address?"

Rani's smile evaporated while Brian's smile commenced. "Excuse me?" Rani asked.

"Your name and email address, ma'am. I need it for you to claim your prize."

"We typically do not give our name and email addresses," Rani said bluntly. "We came here to get our new car."

"Yes, I understand that," Janice said. "That's why I'm asking you for your name and email address. I need this information for you to claim your prize."

"Why do I need to give you my name and email address? We came here to get a new car. In fact, I want that one—there. That nice blue Honda crossover."

"Well, ma'am, I understand that, but I need the information for you to claim your prize."

"The prize I want is that new car over there," Rani said, pointing again. "The flyer has a key Scotch-taped to it. We want that new car."

Brian decided to interject. "Ma'am, why doesn't a fine

salesperson such as yourself level with us. Can you please tell my friends here that they didn't win a new car?"

"Well, sir, that's not exactly true. Your lovely friends here may have won a new car. I just need to—"

"*May have*," Brian said. "Why don't you tell them their prize is behind that tiny, great scratch-off at the bottom of the flyer. Isn't that right?"

"Well, yes, that's correct," Janice said. "But if the nice lady here gives me her name and email address, she'll be in our database, and I'll send her periodic reminders about our specials. And her name will enter a pool of customers, and there will be a drawing in the future, and whoever's name gets picked will win a new car."

"And when will that drawing raffle thingamajig take place?" Brian asked. He crossed his arms over his chest and smiled.

"Down the road … I'm not exactly sure."

Brian said, "Isn't it true that the only prize these lovely ladies here won tonight is behind that scratch patch on that flyer?"

"Well, yes, but—"

Brian took the flyer and scratched the small patch with the fingernail of his right thumb.

"Says here ten dollars off your next purchase at this dealership. Minimum purchase one hundred dollars required." He looked at the Kumar sisters and said, "Let's go."

The sisters, stunned and speechless, followed Brian toward the door.

"Hey, what type of vehicle do you drive, ma'am?" Janice said loudly. "We're running great deals on trade-ins."

It was pin-drop quiet during the ride back to the Kumar sisters' apartment. Thoughts were pouring into Brian's mind, but he wasn't sure what to say; it was awkward.

I hate to remind you that I told you so, but I told you so.

Listen to me next time.

If it sounds too good to be true, chances are it is.

Ain't no such thing as free; everything costs something or comes with a catch.

A thought suddenly hit him. *Tocqueville.* Priya was writing a lot about Tocqueville's observations of America, and quite a few of those observations involved money: how Americans are commercially oriented and hardworking and entrepreneurial and enterprising, that "Love of comfort has become the national taste."

A perfect comment to break the ice. "Well, Priya, I know you're working hard on that Independent Study class of ours," Brian said in the back seat of Rani's car. "Tocqueville's commentary was so true then, and it still rings true today. 'Love of comfort has become the national taste.' Everybody's out to make a buck. One has to be cautious of sales pitches."

"A lesson we learned the hard way," Rani said, her eyes zeroed in on the road ahead.

"Sorry, Brian," Priya said. "We just thought that—"

"No need to apologize," Brian said, cutting her off. "There's a lot of scams out there, especially when businesses call you over the phone or send you stuff in the mail."

"But there were a lot of folks out there tonight, Brian," Deepika said in a perplexed tone. "Were they all fooled?"

"No, not all of them. People will travel a fair distance for free coffee and free doughnuts and 10 percent discounts. Plus, people are often looking to trade in their older cars, so they like looking for deals. And lots of people have no problem giving their name and email address to enter a raffle to win a new car."

"I see," Priya said.

Rani added, "We don't give out our names and personal information to strangers. Bad karma."

It was Christmas Day, nine o'clock in the morning, and the Kumar sisters were in their apartment, sitting Indian style around a short Christmas tree Rani had purchased at Home Depot. The sisters were sipping hot tea and anxiously awaiting the opening of presents. Each sister had two gifts next to them in the form of a card. Rani, sporting a big smile, got straight to the point that was in the back of all their minds: "Well, I guess we all got each other gift cards this Christmas," and the sisters laughed together.

"This is the land of consumer-driven shopping," Priya added. "We might as well exploit this opportunity."

The sisters decided to open the presents based on seniority, on age, with Rani going first, Deepika second, and Priya, as the youngest, going last. Rani opened up her first gift card, the one from Deepika. It was an Amazon gift card, good for seventy-five dollars, the agreed-to monetary gift limit for the Kumar sisters for Christmas 2018.

"Thank you, thank you, Deepika," Rani said. "Just what I love. I love Amazon. I will put this to good use."

"Glad you like it, Rani," Deepika said. Rani then opened her second gift card, this one from Priya. She unwrapped the green gift paper and pulled out the card.

"Oh, thank you, Priya. Thank you so much. A seventy-five-dollar gift card from Williams-Sonoma. Great. I want to buy more cooking items. In the tradition of the Americans, I raise my tea cup and thank you both. I couldn't ask for better sisters or better roommates."

"Okay, here I go," Deepika suddenly said. She reached under the short green Christmas tree and grabbed the first gift naming her. She opened the first card, this one from Rani. She pulled out a gift card—Amazon, good for seventy-five dollars.

The sisters burst out laughing. Priya, trying to hold back, finally managed to say, "You two cancel each other out," and more laughs followed.

"I think Amazon is great," Deepika said. "I love that company too. Thank you, dear sister."

"You're welcome," Rani said. "And besides, there's nothing wrong with thinking alike."

Deepika reached under the Christmas tree, next to its tiny trunk, the size of a medium twig. She opened the second card, which was from Priya.

"Oh, thank you, Priya. A gift card from Home Depot. Seventy-five dollars. How nice. How practical. When the weather warms up, I'll get a bigger plot of land at NMSU. This I tell you, come spring of 2019, I will be growing the finest cucumbers and eggplants and tomatoes for our home cooking. I need garden tools, so, Home Depot, here I come."

"Okay, Priya, now it's your turn," Rani said. "Let's see what the great Santa brought you."

Priya reached under the tree and opened a green card, and inside she saw a Starbucks gift card good for seventy-five dollars.

"Oh, thank you so much, Deepika. I'm at the Starbucks almost every day, drinking tea and reading the newspapers. So nice. What a thoughtful gift, Deepika."

"You're welcome," Deepika said, just after taking a sip of tea.

Priya then reached for the last card under the tree, its wrapping paper a shiny, dark blue. "Let's see what the great Santa Rani gave me for Christmas." She opened the envelope and pulled out a Costco card.

"Oh, thank you, Rani. Costco is probably my favorite store. This is absolutely great. How wonderful."

The sisters touched teacups and spent the next forty-five minutes eating a late breakfast of microwaved naan bread, assorted jams, and orange slices. After breakfast and the cleanup of dishes, the sisters decided to call their parents and Janni in Chennai, ten and a half hours away, to wish them all a merry Christmas and to see if they had received the cheeses, chocolates, and peanut butter the sisters had sent them by request.

Yes, they had received the beautiful cheese varieties, chocolate assortments, and peanut butter jars (crunchy style), and yes, how lovely and delicious these food items from America were. During the twenty-minute phone call, both parents reminded their daughters to get adequate sleep and to study very hard. "That is how one obtains a high-paying career."

After the Chennai phone call, Deepika decided to retire to her room to relax by surfing the net and watching videos on YouTube while Rani checked out vegetarian pizza recipes on her laptop. Priya, ready for one last cup of tea, decided to text Brian and wish him and his wonderful family a merry Christmas. She sat at the kitchen table, poured herself a hot cup of tea, and texted the following: "Greetings Gandhi. My sisters and I wish you and your family a most wonderful Christmas. May this holiday season bring you all great health, great wealth, and much happiness. Best wishes from Las Cruces. Priya, Rani, and Deepika. PS: I hope I did okay in International Finance. I checked online for the grades, but they are not posted yet. Thank you once again for your kind assistance in this challenging course of mine."

Brian, relaxing with his father and Uncle Ron over beers, texted back: "Hi Tocqueville. Thank you for the well wishes. My family and I send our hellos and well wishes. Don't sweat the international finance course—you're all over it; I'm sure you'll surprise yourself. Best. Gandhi."

For the next fifteen minutes, the two graduate students texted back and forth about a range of topics: the holidays, their course schedule for the upcoming semester, the dinners they had eaten last night (roasted chicken, meat pies, and garlic potatoes for Brian; vegetable biryani, naan with red chili hummus, and mango yogurt for Priya), and the presents they had received that very morning (Brian too had, like Deepika, received a Home Depot gift card, which he planned to spend on a new electric drill).

Priya's last text to Brian was "Good luck with your upcoming poker tournament. Send our best to Chuck. May the poker gods bring you great cards and great wealth."

Brian replied: "Many thanks. Oh, and I forgot to mention my last Christmas card I just discovered an hour ago. I got this flyer in the mail from a local car dealer informing me I JUST WON A BRAND-NEW PICKUP TRUCK!!! Dad, Uncle Ron, and I are picking it up later this evening. The dealership is open today for this special prize giveaway. They'll also have free coffee and donuts. Want to join us? Namaste. Gandhi."

Priya, smiling and shaking her head, texted back: "Very funny, Gandhi. No, I think I've learned my lesson, thank you. I'm always learning about America; nothing free as they say. Have fun in Las Vegas. Namaste. Tocqueville."

Brian was in the seventh seat at the poker table, the cutoff position, and he faced a three-blind bet from the number four seat. His hand was seven-eight suited, hearts. He decided to call. The button also called, as did the blind positions. It was level five of the first day of the $2,500 buy-in Ring in the New Year Tournament at the Rio All Suites Hotel. Chuck, in an adjacent poker room, was taking his chances at a five-ten no-limit cash table.

Brian loved poker, a game he learned to play when he was fifteen. His dad had been his teacher and had learned it from his dad. Chuck too loved the game, and the roommates had a pact: pool money together and split any winnings fifty-fifty. For all of 2018, that meant combined winnings just shy of $4,000. It was less than a month ago when the pair decided to risk their bankroll, come to Sin City, and have Brian enter a $2,500 tournament while Chuck would grind it out at the cash tables.

The flop came ace, ten, six, rainbow, giving Brian a gutshot straight draw. The fourth position player made it $5,000 to call. Brian, with a stack of nearly thirty-three thousand chips, made the call, as did the button player, but the two blind positions folded. The dealer, a short, middle-aged Vietnamese lady, burned a card and then flipped over a harmless four of clubs. The player in the fourth position—a heavyset, cowboy-hat-wearing, gray-haired, middle-aged guy from Oklahoma named Mitch—made it $15,000 to stay in the pot.

Crap, Brian thought, disappointed. He did his best to keep a poker face. *Too expensive to stay in.* He was wearing jeans, an NMSU sweatshirt, and aviator sunglasses. *Maybe if I was double-ended, I'd just give it a go, but not with just a gutshot draw.* He mucked his hand. The button player thought for a few seconds and then said, "I'm all in."

A couple of players said, "Good luck, All In," and then the dealer burned a card and then flipped over the river card, the nine of hearts.

Brian, stiff on the exterior, was burning inside. *Dammit. I would have made my straight. And this is a massive pot.*

No longer in the hand, he reached in his front right pocket and pulled out his iPhone. As long as a player wasn't in the hand, texting was allowed. He looked at his screen. Chuck, five minutes ago, had texted, "Up 400 Ben Franklins. Grinding it out."

Mitch, the Oklahoma cowboy, was thinking about his hand. Huge pot, pot committed, it would make no sense to fold at this point, which meant he had two moves—call or fold. He scratched his chin. "I call," and he flipped over Jack-nine.

"Nice hand," the button player said, flipping over pocket tens for a set. He stood up and started walking away, now busted out of the tournament.

Phew, thought Brian, relieved. *I avoided trouble there. My ten-high straight would have lost to the higher straight.* He texted Chuck: "Just dodged a massive bullet; glad I got out of a big pot."

During the poker dinner break, Brian hit the restaurant Hash House A Go Go and ordered corn beef hash with a waffle. He was sitting at a middle table, going over his inventory. With a stack just shy of forty thousand poker chips, he wasn't a short stack, but he wasn't in the best position either, as he had about thirty-five big blinds—some wiggle room but not that much considering the blind structure. The reality was cowboy Mitch was the big dog at the table with well over a hundred thousand in chips, and there were four other players at the table who out-chipped him.

All I can do is my best, he thought as he poured some maple syrup over his waffle. *I'm not in desperation mode, but I gotta keep pace with the action and take stabs at pots.* He decided to text Chuck. "On dinner break at Hash House. Level ten in 40 minutes. Hope you're up. Join me if you've got the time."

Chuck soon texted, "Running good. Up 1200 bucks. Good action. I'll see you in about 15 minutes for a caffeine break. I'm running low on my five-hour energy supply."

Brian, working on his dinner, then decided to text Priya: "Tocqueville, hope you and your sisters are having a nice holiday. Chuck and I are enjoying the poker action here. Just chilling now. Happy New Year in advance. Namaste. Gandhi."

Three minutes later, he saw the following text on his screen: "Glad you and Chuck are enjoying the poker. My sisters and I are enjoying our time off. I'm drinking lots of hot tea and enjoying the best-selling book *Hillbilly Elegy* by JD Vance. Happy New Year to you also in advance. Wishing you good health and prosperity. Namaste. Tocqueville. PS: Sorry it is chilly in Las Vegas. Can't you wear a sweater to warm up?"

Brian, chuckling, texted back: "Chilling means I'm just hanging out, relaxing. I'm actually on dinner break right now. It's not cold here—great climate control. Great you're enjoying the book. Gandhi."

Priya immediately texted back: "Sorry, Brian. I'm always learning American English. If chilling means just relaxing, hanging out, then I'm drinking tea and chilling. I highly recommend the book *Hillbilly Elegy*. It's a powerful memoir and another look into a slice of Americana. Tocqueville."

Priya was indeed enjoying Vance's best seller, a true account of his upbringing in Appalachia, Kentucky/Ohio. Halfway through the book, she decided to take notes about Vance's growing-up years, notes she placed in a section of her Tocqueville notebook. After texting Brian, she went to the kitchen to get a cup of mango-flavored yogurt, and then she went to her room and picked up her Tocqueville notebook and flipped to the *Hillbilly Elegy* section. She then returned to the living room with that notebook and began reading her notes:

> Broken family.
> Mother had many men; marriages/relationships that did not last long.
> Brother and sister often spend time at grandparents.
> Grandparents themselves are divorced and don't live together, although they live close to each other.
> Violent. The people are violent.
> Lazy. The people often don't have ambition.
> His uncle moves to California and is successful in the construction business. He is an exception.
> Mother has substance-abuse problems.
> Kids have a hard time concentrating at school because of the chaos at home.
> Vance says problem is not money; his mother is smart and a well-paid nurse. Problem is drugs and wasting money on cars and not caring.

Priya had a small scoop of the mango yogurt. Then she grabbed her mechanical pencil and wrote the following:

> This is different than what Tocqueville saw in America. Vance writes about another slice of America. His argument, at its core, is that values matter, and to change human behavior, the values and attitudes

of the people must change. In India, the problem is poverty; for some Americans, the problem is attitude.

It was a bit past one in the morning when Brian entered the hotel room. Chuck was already sound asleep in his separate bed. The TV was on Fox Sports 1, showing UFC highlights, the sound on mute. Brian had survived day one of the two-day tournament. Exhausted, he decided to open the small refrigerator and have a beer; Chuck had packed it with Coronas. He popped open a bottle and plopped down on his bed.

Some eight hundred players in all, two million bucks guaranteed, he thought as he sipped from his beer. *Poker tournaments are about survival. Gotta grind it out tomorrow. Action kicks off at eleven. We're around two hundred players left. Top eighty players are in the money. I'm nursing a short stack of less than a hundred and fifty thousand chips. Ain't got too many moves.*

He finished his beer and watched some UFC highlights. Though exhausted, he was anxious and excited and constantly thinking about tomorrow's poker. With that, sleep was difficult and only came at 2:30 a.m.

Sunday, December 30, Brian found himself down to a hundred and thirty thousand chips and all in with pocket nines preflop. Two other players were in the pot.

"Player five is all in. You can show your cards, sir," said the dealer, a tall, older gentleman with a white goatee.

Brian showed his middle pair of nines.

"Two other players in the pot," the dealer said. Then the flop came seven, jack, three, rainbow. The first player checked, as did the second player. Brian, still sitting, his right hand in his pocket with his index and middle fingers crossed, thought, *I hope my Wayne Gretzkys hold up. Either way, though, it's been a fun tournament.*

The dealer flopped the turn card, an eight of diamonds.

Cool, thought Brian. *More outs. Got a gutshot draw.* The two other players checked it down.

The dealer burned a card and then flipped the river card, a ten of hearts.

Brian was elated. *Yes*, he thought. *Jack high straight. Hope this takes it down.*

"Okay, players, let's see them," the dealer said, and the first player showed pocket eights for a set while player two showed big slick, ace-king.

"Nines take it. Straight," the dealer said, shoving the more than four hundred thousand chips to Brian.

Five minutes later, when he wasn't involved in the pot, Brian texted Chuck: "Recently took down a 400 K+ pot with an all in. Back to 35 BB. Got some breathing room. How goes you?"

Chuck texted, "Was down 500 but took down a massive pot. Up 1500 for this weekend. Greed is good, especially in poker."

While Brian was deciding to call, raise, or fold, Priya had decided to use her Costco membership at the Las Cruces Costco. She was there with her sisters, pushing a large cart and filling it up with her traditional favorites: red pepper hummus, jasmine rice, sugar, black pepper, garlic, naan (both plain and garlic), tomatoes, peppers, lemons, and chicken. And then there were her recently discovered American favorites: peanut butter (chunky style), croissants, salmon, provolone and mozzarella cheese, peanuts, dark chocolates, and Reese's peanut butter cups.

The sisters walked through every aisle (Rani explained Costco didn't have aisle signs so that customers would walk around more, searching products—a good business strategy). The sisters picked up necessities—water, Kleenex, toilet paper, paper towels, soaps, shampoos, and toothpaste, Priya marveling throughout the shopping process. *What abundance, what prosperity, so many options, so many selections. And free sample tastings at the end of some aisles—how clever.* She remembered the Tocqueville line verbatim: "Love of comfort has become the dominant national taste."

At 6:00 p.m., the players were just about to get ready for the dinner break, with one more hand to play. The cards were dealt, and Brian, down to roughly 375,000 chips (he was up and down all afternoon, at one point up almost 600,000, then down to 250,000), peeked at his hand, saw jack of clubs, three of spades, and mucked it. He looked at the player board and saw the total number of players remaining in the tournament—eighty-five. He took out his iPhone and texted Chuck:

"Last hand before one-hour dinner break. Have 375K in chips. Five from the bubble. I'll play tight and at least get in the money. Join me at Hash House if you can. How goes it?"

Chuck soon texted back with "Lots of action. Unfortunately down 600 bucks, but hope to make it back up and then some later this evening. See you in about 15 minutes."

At Hash House, Brian was working on a spinach and feta omelet and drinking coffee. He scrolled through his text messages and discovered that some two hours earlier, Priya had texted him with "A most splendid day here in Las Cruces. Sisters and I went shopping at Costco. What an experience, what a lovely store. Very impressive. Great selections, great prices. And free samples at the end of many aisles. Hope your day is going well, that you are making money, and, most of all, that you and Chuck are having fun. Tocqueville. PS: Tonight, I've decided for the fun of it to research famous and successful Indian Americans."

Brian texted back "Glad you liked Costco. Whenever I go there, I end up spending more money than I originally planned. Chuck and are doing well; win or lose, poker is always fun. Enjoy researching Indian Americans. Who knows, maybe someday you'll be one of them. Best. Gandhi."

At 9:00 p.m., Brian had around five hundred thousand in chips, the result of jabbing at a few pots, hitting a set in a good-sized pot, getting a flush to take down another good-sized pot, and having his ace queen beat ace king (a queen came out on the turn). The player board showed fifty-four players remaining, with the number constantly descending, as numerous players were forced to go all in, many of them busting out.

Seven hundred miles away, Priya was sipping tea in her apartment, her laptop on the kitchen table, her recent Google search being of famous Indian Americans:

Sundar Pichai, CEO of Google;
Indra Nooyi, chairman and CEO of PepsiCo;
Satya Nadella, CEO of Microsoft;
Nina Davuluri, Miss America 2014;
M. Night Shyamalan, director, filmmaker;
Kal Penn, actor;
Farid Zakaria, journalist;
Dinesh D'Souza, political commentator, author, filmmaker;
Ramesh Ponnuru, senior editor, *National Review* magazine;
Ajay Banga, CEO of MasterCard;
Ajit Jain, president of Berkshire Hathaway Reinsurance Group;
Shananu Narayen, CEO of Adobe Systems;
Salman Rushdie, author;
Nikki Haley, US ambassador to the United Nations;
Bobby Jindal, politician;
Preet Bharara, former US attorney for the Southern District of New York;
Padma Lakshmi, author, actress, model.

Priya, sitting Indian style in her chair at the kitchen table, took a sip of tea and then thought, *Absolutely amazing*. *Business leaders and writers, politicians and a beauty pageant winner, filmmakers and actors*. She moved her mouse to scroll over the list once more. *The other way around is inconceivable. There is no way an American can go to India and head an Indian company—no way at all. As an actor or filmmaker—maybe. As a writer—also a maybe. But not as a CEO and not as a politician. And a foreigner winning a beauty pageant—never.*

The writers and filmmakers interested her, so she decided to look at their Wikipedia entries. Salman Rushdie she recognized; he was famous and popular in India, and she had heard of M. Night Shyamalan, for he too was famous. But Farid Zakaria, Dinesh D'Souza, and Ramesh Ponnuru were all new names to her. She clicked on the Farid Zakaria entry and sipped some more tea.

Chuck texted Brian: "Dude, I'm punching out. It's 11 PM, a good time to call it a night. I'm up 17 Ben Franklins. Leaving to cheer you on. What poker room and table r u at?"

Brian felt his iPhone vibrate. He wasn't in the hand, so he removed his iPhone from his pocket and looked at the screen. He read Chuck's text and texted back "Congrats on the 17 BFFs, good job. 33 players left and almost at 700 K in chips. Brazil Room, Table 57, Seat Four. I'm exhausted. Can u bring me some five-hour energy?"

Twenty minutes later, Chuck found his roommate and handed him a small bottle of five-hour energy. "Dude, you da man. Deep in a major tourney." He scanned for the player board and found it near the ceiling to his far left. *Twenty-seven players left. Payout right now is a bit over twelve thousand dollars. You're doing great.* They did a knuckle touch. "I gotta watch from the sidelines. Rules are rules."

"Thanks, bud," Brian said. "I'm having a blast, but boy am I exhausted." He twisted open the bottle and took a swig. "Hope this does the trick."

At midnight, Brian was down to 450,000 in chips, the second smallest short stack at his table. With twenty players left on two full tables, he was down to less than twenty blinds. *I really have just one move—to shove.* He was two players from the cutoff position, and he peeked at his hand. Pocket sixes. The under-the-gun player—the one first to act—made a standard three-blind bet, and then the action folded to Brian.

"All in," he said confidently, shoving his chips toward the center of the table. *Win or lose, it's been a fun ride,* he told himself. *I hope I don't get too many calls.*

The action folded to the button player, who said, "I call."

The blinds folded, and the dealer said, "Three players in the pot, one player all in." The player sitting to the right of Brian, a young, skinny guy who was wearing a gray hoodie and sporting a thin goatee, said, "Good luck, All In."

"Thanks," Brian said.

The flop came queen, ten, seven, rainbow. The under-the-gun player checked, and the button player raised the pot by one million chips.

"Too expensive for me," said the under-the-gun first position player. "You boys have fun."

"Okay, gentlemen, let's see 'em," the dealer said.

Brian showed his pocket pair, and the button player showed ace-jack of hearts. The dealer burned a card and flipped the turn—a nine of clubs, giving both players straight draws.

"No king, dealer," Brian said as he stood up. "The eight would give me a straight, but he would get a higher straight. No ace or jack either. My sixes are going to hold up, man."

The dealer, a heavyset Asian man with a long, thin ponytail, burned a card and then flipped the river.

A harmless four of diamonds.

"Phew," Brian said as he sat down while the dealer shoved

the chips his way. "More breathing room." He looked at Chuck, who gave him a thumbs-up.

At one in the morning, the action was down to ten players, all seated at one table, the final table. The floor manager, a tall forty-something-year-old wearing a navy suit, white shirt, and dark blue tie, stood next to the seated dealer. "Good luck to all the players. Dealer, shuffle up and deal."

Brian, sitting in the eighth seat with just a little over a million in chips, was the second smallest short stack at the table. He scanned the table and assessed the chip inventories. Three of the players were from the previous table, where he had played against them for the better part of three hours. They all had average stacks. The smallest stack was the player in the fifth seat. The other players were also average stacks, except for the position three player and the position nine player, the latter the sole woman at the table, a slim, middle-aged brunette wearing dark sunglasses, a black cowboy hat, and a low-cut black shirt displaying ample cleavage. The top of her uncovered portion of her left breast revealed the tattooed words "Big Pair," while the top of the uncovered portion of her right breast revealed the words "All In."

The first hand was dealt. Brian saw his hole cards, king-jack, unsuited. He was two from the under-the-gun player and decided to muck his decent hand.

The action was four-way, with the shortest stack committed to risking all his chips. Five minutes later, when the action was over, he busted out in tenth place, losing to the Big Pair, All In cowgirl who held pocket fives.

Brian, now the shortest stack at the table, nursed his chips and didn't play any pots for the first twenty minutes of final table action until he woke up with pocket queens.

"All in," he said when the action turned to him. Three players called, including the second largest stack (the Big Pair, All In cowgirl had the most chips at the table). The second big dog at the table was a young, skinny Asian guy sporting a flashy gold watch and a thick gold necklace.

The flop came six, eight, king, rainbow. The second big dog bet big, and the two players folded, making it a heads-up showdown.

"Okay, let's see the cards, gentlemen," the dealer said.

Brian showed his ladies, pocket queens, and the young Asian showed big slick, ace-king, unsuited.

The turn card came out—a harmless two of diamonds.

Nice, Brian thought. He said, "No ace, no king, dealer. You're doing great." He stood up.

Chuck said from the rail, "All you, Brian. You got this."

The dealer burned a card, then flipped fifth street, the king of spades.

Brian, his hands over his head in disgust, tapped the table's green felt three times and said, "It's been great, folks. Good luck to you all."

He turned and headed toward Chuck, who was sipping a Corona by the rail. He glanced at the player leaderboard. Ninth place—good for $62,000. It was by far his largest poker cash.

Back in the hotel room, in the early hours of New Year's Eve, Brian and Chuck sipped their beers and periodically marveled at the sight of the $62,000 check. They were both exhausted but also too excited—too pumped—to sleep.

"That's thirty-one thousand each," Brian said as the muted TV was on ESPN college basketball reruns. "My dad says we can do our first house flip for about forty grand. I say we keep our eyes open, buy a small, run-down house for around forty K, put in ten K for the redo, and split the profits fifty-fifty."

"That's what I'm talking about," Chuck said. They touched bottles.

Sleep would come a few minutes shy of four in the morning for Brian. He promised himself to text his folks, sister, and Priya first thing in the morning and tell them all about his biggest poker score.

He awoke minutes shy of ten o'clock, Monday morning, New Year's Eve. He yawned, rubbed his eyes, then noticed Chuck was up, sipping coffee, and clicking his computer mouse as he stared at his laptop. The TV was still muted on ESPN.

"Morning, poker shark," Chuck said as he kept staring at the monitor screen. "Made some coffee. Help yourself. I'm looking over low-cost, older houses in Las Cruces. Decent inventory for potential flips."

"Cool," Brian said as he poured some coffee into a hotel brown paper cup. He was wearing blue boxers and an NMSU T-shirt.

"Uh, by the way, I checked who won the tourney earlier this morning," Chuck said. "Results already posted online. Big Pair, All In cowgirl took it down."

"Nice," Brian said. "Good for her."

"Yep. A cool six hundred fifty grand. Nice work for two days."

"Sure is."

"And in ninth place, the one and only, soon-to-be king of the Las Cruces flips ... drum roll please ... Brian Da Man Robinson."

"Thanks, dude. It was a blast. 'Bout time I go deep in a tourney."

"Oh, and Lisa says congrats. I texted her this morning. She and her girlfriends are having fun skiing in Utah."

"Great. Tell her thanks."

Brian walked toward the room's bathroom. He splashed some water on his face, urinated, brushed his teeth, then unplugged his charging cell phone and lay down on his unmade queen-size bed. He texted his parents and his sister with the great news about his poker winnings, and he immediately received a phone call from his father, who said, "Congratulations, son. Well done."

His mom, who took the cell phone from her husband, added, "Oh, this is great news, Brian. What a beautiful way to kick off the new year. Your father and I will tell our friends at tonight's New Year's party at the Hyatt Center."

"Thanks, Mom. Thanks, Dad," Brian said to his parents. "It was a lot of fun. Chuck and I head back tomorrow. I'll be home for New Year's."

Brian propped up another pillow and began flipping channels on the muted television.

"Dude, two-bedroom, two-bathroom house for forty-eight K," Chuck said.

"Garage?" Brian asked.

"Nope. Carport."

"Square footage?"

"Just twelve hundred."

"Make a folder," Brian said, "and save it on your laptop. We could do upgrades on a small house like that and sell it for around sixty-five K."

"On it," Chuck said.

Brian settled on the TV show *Dangerous Catches*. His iPhone was in his left hand, and his game plan was to follow Chuck's example and surf the net for prospective houses in Las Cruces, but before any of that, he decided to text Priya with the following: "Happy New Year, Tocqueville, to you and your sisters. This has been an incredible trip and a profitable one as well. I came in 9th place in the tournament! Won $62,000 for my efforts. Just planning on chilling here today. I'll probably play some small poker cash games later. Chuck and I fly back tomorrow. Wishing you and your sisters a happy and healthy 2019. Best. Gandhi."

Priya was at the Starbucks next to her apartment when she received Brian's text. She was drinking Earl Grey tea (she had tried coffee a few times, including this morning, but found it too strong, too bitter), and she was reading the *Wall Street Journal* and the *New York Times* as a break from Googling famous Indian Americans. She read Brian's text and texted back: "Congratulations, Gandhi. My sisters and I are very happy for you and your recent monetary winnings. The risk reward dichotomy worked in your favor. Well done. How auspicious. I look forward to hearing all about it upon your return. May 2019 bring you happiness in all that you wish for. Best. Tocqueville."

Priya placed the newspapers to the side of the small table. She was truly happy for Brian and couldn't help but think about $62,000. *What a windfall. Life-changing perhaps. Sixty-two thousand dollars in rupees is … Let's see …*

She pressed the calculator button on her iPhone.

The exchange rate is seventy rupees for one US dollar. She punched in the numbers: 62,000 × 70. It showed 4,340,000 rupees.

She took a quick sip of tea and thought, *In India, making the equivalent of US five thousand dollars in a year is a good salary. Brian just won more than twelve years' worth of those good annual salaries.*

She glanced at the line of patrons waiting for their orders, then looked at the cashier busily making change and the baristas brewing and pouring the coffees and mixing the drinks.

There is so much abundance in this country, she thought. *Many of the Starbucks drinks cost four, five, or six dollars. Good for Brian. Sixty-two thousand dollars is a lot of money, especially in India.*

It was two in the afternoon, and Priya had just finished reading both newspapers. She was still at the Starbucks enjoying her New Year's Eve (the later plan for dinner was for Deepika to make vegetable biryani and Rani to make vegetarian pizzas with four different types of cheeses). Priya, wanting to relax and read, had decided it was best for her to stay out of the busy kitchen and do her reading at the nearby Starbucks. Besides, she had agreed to buy cookies to complement tonight's New Year's Eve celebration at their apartment, and those favorite cookies of theirs were at Starbucks, Rani's favorite being the chocolate chip variety while Priya and Deepika favored the large peanut butter cookies with chocolate chips inside.

Feeling a bit hungry, Priya decided to buy herself a pumpkin muffin (it was on special) and another hot tea. She glanced inside the glass casing to see that the cookies (both chocolate chip and peanut butter) were quickly disappearing—only three of each left. With that, she decided to purchase tonight's dessert and a pumpkin muffin right then and there.

Minutes later, while sitting at her table, Priya placed the bag of cookies next to her Tocqueville notebook and the stack of just-read issues of the *Wall Street Journal* and the *New York Times*. She took a bite from her warmed-up pumpkin muffin.

The inside is nice, very good, but the top is too sweet, too sugary, she thought. She peeled the white, sugary layer off the top of the muffin and took another bite of the muffin's interior. Then she looked at her list of famous Indian Americans. The technology and industry leaders like Sundar Pichai of Google, Indra Nooyi of Pepsi, and Satya Nadella of Microsoft didn't interest her as far as reading more about them, though she once again looked at her notebook and noted there was no way an American could go to India and end up heading one of India's largest corporations. Indeed, it was the Indian American writers that piqued her interest. She looked at her list: Salman Rushdie, Fareed Zakaria, Dinesh D'Souza, and Ramesh Ponnuru. She took out her iPhone from her coat pocket, took a quick sip of hot tea, and began Googling these writers.

Two hours later, while working on a peanut butter cookie (she had cheated and removed the cookie from the bag and started eating it), she looked at the notes she had written in a separate notebook about each writer.

> Salman Rushdie. I have read him before. *Midnight's Children* was his best. Has both United Kingdom and United States citizenship. Had fatwa placed on him because of his book *The Satanic Verses*. Lives in the US since 2000. Was married to Padma Lakshmi for a few years.
> Ramesh Ponnuru. Born in Kansas. Conservative political pundit. Princeton graduate. Critic of President Trump. Converted to Roman Catholicism.

She took a small bite from her peanut butter cookie and then sipped some hot tea. She then read her final entry.

> Dinesh D'Souza. Born in Bombay. Came to the United States with $500. Graduate of Dartmouth. Conservative writer and filmmaker. Pled guilty to using straw donors in a political campaign. Was prosecuted for the crime by another Indian American, Preet Bharara, former US attorney for the Southern District of New York. D'Souza was pardoned by President Trump.

She decided to Google if there were any videos by and on these writers, and if so, she would take notes. To her delight, there were many such videos.

For Rushdie, she wrote the following:

> There's a video of him where he asks if there are universal values. Human rights? Different cultures have different priorities, he says. People want freedoms. He argues there are universal rights. Rushdie: the internet is a tool—like an ax. You can use an ax to chop a tree or chop someone's head off. Overall, the

internet is good. You can't get Facebook in China. Who controls the story? Liberty? Freedom? It boils down to who has the right to tell the story. The ability to have the argument is freedom. Writers and artists have the ability to challenge the official narrative. You do not end unpleasant thinking by banning its expression.

She then Googled Ramesh Ponnuru and wrote the following, quoting him:

> "There are 330 million people in America, and there are two main political parties. Not everyone fits well into politicized parties."

Next, she Googled Dinesh D'Souza and saw that he had, in comparison, considerably more videos about him than the other writers: debates on religion where he faced off against Christopher Hitchens; a video about his pardon from President Trump; a video of him on C-SPAN discussing his books; a video where he discusses immigration policy; D'Souza on the history of fascism; and numerous videos of D'Souza speaking at college campuses. She selected the video titled *A World without America* and quoted the following in her notebook:

> "The immigrant is a walking refutation of the dogma of cultural relativism which is the idea that all cultures are equal. The immigrant refutes this because he votes with his feet. He moved away from his country, which is not easy—leaving family and friends. Why did he leave? Because he believes life is better in America. One cannot become an Indian because being an Indian is a function of race and blood. It is derived at birth. But not America—one can become an American, because being an American is a function of assimilating to a way of life.

"What is the American Dream? Throughout world history, it was shown that wealth was derived by conquest, taking land from someone. But the American founders had a different recipe, one of wealth creation. The idea you can make money. So the prosperity dream is part of the American Dream, but it is not the main part of the American Dream. The core of the American Dream is the idea that your destiny is not given to you but is constructed by you. That you are the architect of your own future. That you are in the driver seat of your own life. The decisions of where to live, who to love, who to marry, what to believe, who to become—these are your decisions, your choices. The American Dream is about the self-directed life. The immigrant comes to America to make his own life."

The video would continue for another hour, but Priya had to cut it short on account of a low cell phone battery. She sipped some more tea, finished her peanut butter cookie, and kept reading, and in some instances rereading, some of D'Souza's passages.

Immigrant values are at the core of the American Dream ... To make your own life ... To be the architect of your own future ... Who to love and marry, and where to live, and what to believe, and who to become—your choices.

Later that sunny, cold winter afternoon, she would buy another peanut butter cookie at Starbucks, and then she would return to her apartment to share a New Year's Eve dinner of vegetarian pizzas and vegetable biryani with Rani and Deepika. Midway into the dinner, as Priya was finishing up her vegetable biryani and garlic naan, Rani said, "And the tradition here in the United States is to make a New Year's resolution. Have you both made a New Year's resolution?"

Deepika said, "Yes. Yes I have. My New Year's resolution is to grow the best tomatoes in Las Cruces. There's even a competition for this in June. Once I get my garden going, I want to win the best tomato competition."

"For my resolution," Rani said, "I've decided to work out more. I'm either going to walk more around here to do errands or join a gym in Las Cruces."

"Cool," Deepika said as she sipped some mango lassi.

"And what about you, Priya?" Rani asked. "Have you made your New Year's resolution yet?"

Priya, now working on a slice of vegetarian-cheese pizza, said, "Not really, no. If I have to do one, it would be eating more fruits."

Deepika immediately replied, "Do you know that a tomato is a fruit? You'll have all the fruit you need once I get my larger garden plot at NMSU."

Dinner would last for another hour or so, topped off by desserts of rice pudding and the cookies Priya had bought from Starbucks. Then the sisters watched television and later called their parents and older sister, Janni, ten-and-a-half hours away to wish them a happy and prosperous 2019.

In her bedroom later that night, after reading a few pages of Tocqueville's *Democracy in America*, Priya pulled out her personal notebook and wrote the following:

> 2019 New Year's Resolution.
> The American dream. To be the architect of your own future.
> Choices, America.

CHOICES

"Well, good morning to you all," Professor Martin said to his attentive students. "And a happy New Year to everyone." It was early January, the start of the new year and the spring 2019 semester. Martin, wearing expensive jeans and a thick, navy blue sweater, carried a white coffee mug with the San Diego Padres logo on it in his right hand. "Sad news, folks. I'll get right down to it. Class is canceled today. I'm not my regular self." He sat behind his desk and rubbed his chin with his left hand. "Just two days ago, one of my beloved dogs, Rocky, our Belgian Malinois, passed away due to old age. My wife and I think he was fifteen years old, an educated guess. His breed usually lives between ten to twelve years, so he had a great run. But I'm devastated, and my wife even more so. Anyway, we're making funeral arrangements today, and I'm canceling class. We'll make it up sometime—if not this semester, then the final summer session."

There was silence, then Bob, sitting in the front left seat, said, "Sorry for your loss, Mark."

Carlos and Brenda said similar condolences, and then Professor Martin said, "Thank you, all." He coughed and was visibly shaken up. "I'll see you guys next week, and I promise to be in better spirits."

Fifteen minutes later, Priya and Brian were walking to Bombay Palace to meet Rani and Deepika for lunch.

"Brian, I cannot thank you enough for your assistance with last semester's International Finance class," Priya said, her breath visible when she spoke into the slightly below-freezing air. "Of all my grades, that A-minus is my proudest achievement, and I'm forever grateful for your assistance."

"Don't mention it," Brian said. Both of them were wearing winter coats, winter hats, and gloves. "It was all you. You worked hard and did well."

The two continued walking at a fast pace, and suddenly Priya said, "You know, Brian, this I tell you. This morning's class cancellation is a unique event for me. Such an occurrence would never happen in my home country. India does not have a pet culture. We simply don't. There are dogs and cats, but they are all stray, and they make their way in life on their own, without the care and attention of humans. That's just how it is. And to have a professor cancel a college class because his pet dog will have a funeral is not only unheard of, it is simply unimaginable. Crazy, quite frankly."

"Is that right? No pets?"

"Correct. No pets. And no funerals for them either."

The two continued walking, and Priya said, "Brian, I have a suggestion. Since class was canceled, why don't we go to the nearby Starbucks and have some hot tea to warm ourselves. From the Starbucks, we will be able to see when Rani and Deepika arrive at Bombay Palace, and then we can join them."

"That's a good plan."

It was a Friday night, and the first week of the spring 2019 semester had ended. Priya, Rani, and Deepika were at Brian and Chuck's apartment. As was the custom, it was movie night, and the plan was to start watching Vince Gilligan's hit Netflix TV series, *Breaking Bad*. Brian and Chuck had seen a few episodes of the show and were thoroughly hooked, and they had decided to introduce the show to the Kumar sisters, starting with the first episode of the first season. The two roommates were enjoying the viewing fun while working on their Coronas and munching on popcorn while the Kumar sisters enjoyed hot tea, the popcorn, and the peanut butter cups.

After the first episode, Brian said, "Okay, break time, gang. Chuck, you need another brewski?" Chuck flashed a thumbs-up. "And, ladies, more tea? I know you all like Earl Grey, and I made it a point to buy that brand while grocery shopping at Walmart."

"Sure," Rani said. "We'll have more tea. And we like the popcorn too. Any chance we can get more popcorn?"

"There's plenty of popcorn," Brian said. "Coming right up." He headed to the small kitchen.

Priya, sitting Indian style on the carpeted floor next to the sofa, said, "This *Breaking Bad* show is amazing. Quite addictive, I think. It is violent, but it has a way of keeping one wanting to see what will happen next. Very suspenseful."

"Agreed," Chuck said. "Totally addictive. Great cast, great acting."

Deepika, also sitting Indian style and next to Priya, said, "This is a dynamic show. For me, it is about fearlessness. Walter White, fifty years old and with cancer, and the world did not recognize his talents. And now he does not care. He will provide for his family. He is fearless. It is a most brilliant show."

Last semester's grades, which had all been posted online during the week, were next discussed. Priya had received three As (Supply Chain Management, Focused Poetry Workshop, and the Fiction Craft Workshop, the latter being her easiest class, for she had just fine-tuned her unpublished novel, *Money Matters*). She also received two A-minuses, one in International Finance, and the other in Professor Martin's Independent Study class.

Minutes later, the five were watching another episode of *Breaking Bad*; they would view four episodes that night. And in the late evening hours, right before midnight, when Brian had dropped her and her sisters off at their apartment, Priya went to her bedroom, pulled out her personal notebook, and wrote: "2019. Fearlessness. Like Walter White, be fearless."

Brian returned to his apartment at 12:10. Chuck was on the couch, staring at the television screen and playing video games, a half-empty Corona bottle next to him. Not tired, Brian decided to go to his bedroom, sip some beer, and read about Gandhi.

He opened up his folder that contained his notes on Gandhi. He also had Wikipedia clippings, an article from the *Economist*, and a *New Yorker* piece about the civil rights leader. He decided to read the *New Yorker* piece dated October 22, 2018.

He powered up his laptop, opened up his desktop Word document containing Gandhi notes, and began reading and typing:

> Gandhi lived in South Africa from 1893 to 1914.
>
> Some say he did not unequivocally condemn the Hindu caste system. They called him the "saint of the status quo."
>
> He returned to India at forty-five and became an anti-imperialist.
>
> In 1930, he achieved international fame with the Salt March; he was against the British tax on salt.
>
> Gandhi wrote, "We will never all think alike and we shall always see truth in fragments and from different angles and vision."
>
> Gandhi said industrialization is exploitation but that Asia and Africa would catch up and the West will decline. He wrote, "I do not believe in the doctrine of the greatest good of the greatest number. The only real, dignified, human doctrine is the greatest good of all, and this can be achieved by uttermost self-sacrifice." He said, "Just as one must learn the art of killing in the training for violence, so one must learn the art of dying in the training for nonviolence."
>
> Gandhi had "Learned from my illiterate but wise mother that all rights to be deserved and preserved came from duty well done ... The very right to live

127

accrues to us only when we do the duty of citizenship of the world."

Churchill said Gandhi was "a faker of a type well known in the East."

The last quote, the one from Churchill, prompted Brian to look through his folder of clippings. *I know I got a clipping about Gandhi's thoughts on Churchill. Where is it?* He looked through his folder. He knew he had come across Churchill and Gandhi before. There—he found it. He brought the clipping closer to his eyes. It was a piece in the *Wall Street Journal*, an article by Ferdinand Mount, in the weekend edition of November 3 and 4, 2018. Brian saw his handwriting: "Gandhi on Churchill: 'Mr. Churchill … Understands only the gospel of force.'"

Brian reached in his desk drawer and found some Scotch tape. He taped the last entry next to Churchill's "faker" quote and went back to reading the *New Yorker* piece and typing entries where he felt it was warranted.

Pope John Paul II said Gandhi was "Much more of a Christian than many people who say they are Christians."

Brian's last entry was from the *Wall Street Journal*:

Gandhi never won the Nobel Peace Prize, but he was profoundly admired by many—Dalai Lama, Archbishop Desmond, MLK, Nelson Mandela.

Six hours later, at 8:30 a.m., Priya woke up. She rubbed her eyes and got out of bed. When she exited her bedroom, she noticed Rani in the kitchen making tea. She started walking to the left to go to the bathroom.

"Good morning, Priya. Would you like some tea?" Rani asked.

"Yes, of course. Thanks, Rani."

Priya entered the small bathroom, turned on the water faucet, and started brushing her teeth. She knew she had dreamed during the night, and she remembered she was in a *Breaking Bad* episode helping Walt and Jesse cook meth. Walt was in charge, directing tasks. Priya was mostly cleaning up and placing equipment, then Walt said he and Jesse had to go to Home Depot to get some supplies, and that's when Walt ordered her, "Watch shop while we're out. We'll be back within an hour."

"Yes, sir," Priya had replied.

In another dream, Priya was with the Apache Indians hunting elk. She had never hunted before. Alexis de Tocqueville was part of the group, observing things, taking notes. Priya did not fire a weapon, but she did help mount a huge elk head, antlers and all, on the wall at one of the restaurants at the Inn of the Mountain Gods Casino. Tocqueville asked her, "Do you like this lifestyle, hunting with the natives?" and Priya had said, "Sometimes. Yes."

Brushing her teeth, Priya thought some more about her dreams of the previous night. Her thoughts were fuzzy, events coming to her in bits and pieces. She remembered a nice big car. A car was in her dreams. It was a big blue car, brand-new. She didn't know anything about cars, but she was curious. In her dream, she had won the new car at a dealership raffle event. Brian and her sisters were with her, cheering her on, saying, "This time it's for real, Priya. No fraud. It's real. You won."

She finished brushing her teeth, and the final thought of winning a car in last night's dream refreshed her memory about her upcoming plan.

She rinsed her toothbrush, then entered the kitchen, and Rani handed her a cup of tea.

"Thank you," Priya said as she sat down at the kitchen table.

She was wearing loose gray sweatpants and a pink T-shirt. *Fearless.* She thought of Walter White and the *Breaking Bad* series. *Fearless.*

"Rani, I'm thinking of getting my driver's license. With a license, I can then help you with the driving, especially getting the groceries." She paused for just a moment. "How did you get your driver's license?"

Rani, with a tea cup in her right hand, said, "I received my driver's license … Let's see. About a year and half ago. I took driving lessons here in Las Cruces. Smith's Driving School. I did it over the summer."

"I see. Did it cost a lot of money?"

"I can help you out, Priya. But are you sure you need a driver's license? Your plans are to leave after the summer. There's no need for you to have a driver's license."

"Yes, that's true. But I want to do it, Rani." She took a sip of tea. "Cars and driving seem to be such a part of the American culture. I want to experience it. When in Rome, do as the Romans, as the saying goes. Plus, I can help with the driving duties."

"I see. Well, I can call the driving school. They'll probably start you in a week or two."

"Oh, thank you, Rani. And you'll help me when possible? You can teach me with your car?"

"Yes, of course. Learn everything you can. The driver's test is not easy. I was so nervous. I had a good teacher. Thank God."

A half hour later, Priya texted Brian with her new plan and a request for a favor. Sitting on the couch in her apartment, she texted: "Good morning, Gandhi. Thank you once again for a wonderful Friday movie night. I want to inform you of a decision I've made. I have decided to take part in a big aspect of American culture and obtain my driver's license. With a driver's license, I will help Rani with the driving duties. What do you think?

Rani and I just called the Smith Driving School, and I start next Saturday. Will you help me learn to drive the car if you have the time? Also, my tough class this semester is Applied Statistics. It's going well thus far, but I may request your assistance if necessary. Is this okay? Hope you have a good weekend. Say hello to Chuck. Best. Tocqueville."

Brian and Chuck were doing a junk-hauling job in central Las Cruces. "All these boxes have to go," instructed Dr. Kevin Ross, a seventy-year-old psychiatrist in private practice. "Those boxes are from clients of mine from three decades ago. I had all the patient records digitized on CD discs. These paper records take up so much space."

"Sure thing, Dr. Ross," Brian said as he suddenly felt his iPhone vibrate. He quickly placed a box on the floor, and then he pulled out his iPhone from his jacket pocket. It was a text from Priya. "We got it, Dr. Ross. We'll be done here in no time, and then we'll bring the boxes to the shredding company."

Chuck and Brian stacked up four boxes each on two trolleys and push-rolled their loads to the truck outside. Once at the truck, Brian said to Chuck, "Got a text here from Priya. Lemme take this. I'll load the truck and catch up with you inside."

"Sure thing, dude," Chuck said.

After reading her text, Brian pressed the text icon of his iPhone and typed the following: "That's great news. A driver's license is always handy. That way, when you win a car at the local dealership, you'll be able to drive it legally. No worries about the Applied Statistics. It's not easy, but I had Professor Cohen, who is really good."

Brian took a pause. The chilly outdoor air felt good compared to the heated and stuffy doctor's office. He thought for a moment and continued his text: "Say, would you and your sisters like to go snowshoeing? Not next weekend but the weekend after. It's in Albuquerque, just a 3.5-hour drive. Sandia Crest. Tons of fun. Let me know. Gandhi."

He headed back inside Dr. Ross's office and again felt his cell phone vibrate. It was a text from Priya. He read: "What is snowshoeing?"

It was a Saturday morning, nine o'clock, and Priya was at the Smith Driving School in downtown Las Cruces. Her instructor was a tall, older man named Joe Ryan.

"Please read this book and email me if you have any questions," he said as he handed her a thick book. "My business card, which is paper clipped to the first page, includes my email address. Our school has a high first-time passage rate. Our goal is to have you obtain your driver's license on the first attempt. We'll do six classes, every Saturday morning. I'll give you assessments and let you know when I think you're ready to take the driver's test. Any questions?"

"No, sir," Priya said nervously.

Ryan, a sixty-eight-year-old, six foot two, retired truck driver and Vietnam War veteran, politely said, "Don't call me sir. I work for a living." He smiled at Priya. "Call me Joe."

"Okay," Priya said.

"The book will instruct you on the rules of the road that you have to know. Most students don't have a problem with the written portion of the driver's test. The actual driving test is the hard part, with the key skills being parking on an incline and parallel parking. Okay, let's head out to the parking lot and drive a bit. Any questions?"

"No, sir—I mean no, Joe."

Joe led Priya to the parking lot outside the small driving school office. In his left hand, he carried car keys, and in his right hand, he held a large foam cup of Dunkin' Donuts coffee.

"Our student car is right here," he said, walking toward a newer-model Ford Taurus sedan. "Before we begin driving, let's talk about cars a bit."

He proceeded to open the hood and discuss auto parts. "Coolant goes here ... Here's the dip stick for the oil ... This is the battery ... Air filter ... Window washer fluid." He then opened the trunk and discussed booster cables, the spare tire, and the tools to change a flat tire. After that, he opened the front passenger door, flipped open the glove compartment, and showed Priya where the owner's manual was located.

"Okay, so how much driving experience do you have, young lady?"

"None, sir ... I mean, none, Joe."

"All right then. Let me drive first, and listen to what I say and observe what I do. We'll go to a large parking lot I know and practice there."

Joe got into the driver's seat and instructed Priya to sit in the front passenger seat.

"Be sure to always have your seat belt fastened," he told her. "Both as a driver and as a front-seat passenger. It's the law in New Mexico and I think in virtually every state."

"Okay," Priya said. She was already in the process of fastening her seat belt.

Joe placed his large, foam coffee cup in the placeholder next to the automatic stick shift. He proceeded to discuss the accelerator and brake pedals, the steering wheel, what the letters P and D near the automatic stick shift meant, the importance of mirrors and how to set them, and the features on the turn signal lever, including the cruise control feature and the windshield wiper. He turned the ignition, shifted to drive, and pulled out of the parking lot, and in the next ten minutes, he explained driving skills to Priya: the importance of turn signals to let other drivers know one's intentions; how to come to a complete stop; the importance of driving your car in the center of the driving lane; hands on the steering wheel at the ten and two positions; using one's mirrors to ensure lanes are clear; and how to take proper wide turns. He ended by parking the student car in a huge, nearly empty parking lot where older stores were being renovated. The construction crews were off today, a perfect no-traffic spot to practice with a novice driver.

"Okay, Miss Priya. Now it's your turn." With the car parked, Joe Ryan turned off the ignition, grabbed his coffee cup and the keys, and stepped out of the car. He then walked to Priya's seat and handed her the keys.

Priya walked around the back of the car and opened the door to the driver's seat. She sat down, not sure what to do.

"Step number one, Priya, is what?" Joe asked.

"Oh ... I need to start the car."

"Yes, yes, that's true. But before that, isn't there an earlier step?"

"I'm not sure, sir."

"Call me Joe, right?"

"Oh yes. I'm not sure, Mr. Joe."

"Joe is fine, Priya. No need to call me Mr. Joe." He took a sip of coffee. "First and foremost, you need to fasten your seat belt."

"Oh yes," Priya said, and with her right hand, she reached over her body, grabbed the seat belt, and fastened it. The car's keys were in her left hand, and she placed them in her right hand, then started placing the bigger key in the ignition.

"Isn't there a step you're forgetting, young lady?" Joe asked, smiling.

Priya, unsure of the next step, said, "I'm not sure, sir ... I mean, I'm not sure, Joe."

"Step number two," Joe said, "is always make sure any front passenger has his or her seat belt on. I deliberately didn't fasten my seat belt to ensure you knew this step. Come test day, the grader will be in the front passenger seat, and graders test students on this. Some graders will not have their seat belt on. They can fail a student if the student doesn't ensure the grader has fastened his or her seat belt."

"I see," Priya said.

"With that, just say, 'Sir, please fasten your seat belt.' It's the only time I'll let you call me sir. Say the same to the grader if he doesn't have a seat belt on."

"Okay," Priya said.

Joe took a sip of coffee and looked at her. "Well, Ms. Priya? Do you have anything to tell me?"

"Yes," she said firmly. "Sir, please fasten your seat belt."

"Thank you, Priya. Well done." He proceeded to fasten his seat belt.

Priya adjusted the mirror, then she placed the larger of the two keys in the ignition, fumbling around with it for just a second, but she got it in there. The car started, and then Joe said, "Okay, now press on the brake pedal to disengage the stick shift and change it from P to D, from parking to drive."

"Yes. Which one is the brake pedal?"

"The foot pedal to the left," Joe said. "And I don't want you to use your left foot at all. This is not a standard transmission. Your right foot is either on the brake pedal or on the accelerator pedal. Okay?"

"Yes, Joe," Priya said. She pressed on the brake pedal.

"Very good," Joe said. "Now shift from park to drive, P to D."

"Okay," Priya said, and with her right foot still pressing on the brake pedal, she took hold of the gearshift and started to pull it, trying to shift, but the shift selector would not move.

"I cannot shift, Joe," she said in frustration.

"That's because you have to press the top button of the stick as you shift. You can't shift if you don't press the button with your right thumb."

Priya pressed the button and pulled on the shift selector.

"It is not shifting, Joe."

"That's because you probably took your right foot off the brake pedal. To shift, you have to press the brake with your right foot, press the shift button with your right thumb, and then shift."

"Oh, okay," Priya said, and she proceeded to do as instructed and shifted to the D drive position.

"Very good," Joe said. "Now ease up on the brake, and the car will move forward as you press the accelerator a bit. Let's drive around the parking lot."

"Okay," Priya said, nervous.

The car began to move forward slowly. "You can press on the accelerator a bit to go faster," Joe said, and Priya did as instructed. The car moved forward for some two hundred feet. "Very good. You're doing well. When we come to the end of the parking lot, I want you to stop and turn left. Remember to use your turn signal."

"Yes, sir—oh, I mean, yes, Joe," Priya said, her eyes glued in front of her.

The car approached the end of the parking lot, and Joe said, "Now brake and come to a complete stop."

Priya did as instructed, and the car came to a stop. "Now use your turn signal to indicate you're turning left," Joe said.

"What is the turn signal?"

Joe took a quick sip of coffee and pointed to the turn signal.

Priya pushed the turn signal down.

"Not down, Priya. See the blinker on your screen? It shows you want to turn to the right. I want you to turn to the left, so gently push the turn signal up for left."

Priya pushed the turn signal up, and Joe said, "Very good. Now press on the accelerator to get this car moving and turn left." Priya pressed on the accelerator, and the car quickly turned to the left. "Jesus!" Joe yelled as some of his coffee spilled on his pants. "Press gently and slowly, Priya. You went too fast with that turn."

"Sorry," she said.

One week later, on a Saturday afternoon in late January, Brian and the Kumar sisters were dressed in heavy winter clothes and snowshoeing in Albuquerque's Sandia Crest. Early in the morning, Priya had her second driving class with Joe—more parking lot driving but with a short stint of highway driving—and she was, in Joe's words, "showing lots of improvement." After Priya's driving session, Brian had picked up the sisters for the planned snowshoeing trip, and in less than four hours, they were in Albuquerque, renting snowshoes and going up the Sandia Tramway to find some trails.

The foursome did nearly three hours of snowshoeing and in the process enjoyed the spectacular views of Duke City, the Rio Grande, and especially the Turco's Trail. Priya was especially impressed with the immense landscapes. At their altitude on that bright, sunny, cold day, they could see for miles and miles.

There were some firsts for the Kumar sisters that afternoon. Snowshoeing was an obvious one, as they had never experienced the winter activity. The sisters also were the victims of their first runny noses. All of them complained of this, and Brian had to explain it was due to the cold and that they had to blow their noses to clear them.

"How do you blow your nose?" Priya had asked when Brian offered the solution.

At first surprised by the question, Brian realized that Priya was serious. "Well," he said, "be sure to close your mouth. Then blow out through your nose so that your nose clears. You can blow into a handkerchief or Kleenex," he said, and he reached into one of his jacket pockets and handed each sister a Kleenex.

Another Kumar sister first was drinking hot chocolate back at Brian's parents' home after the snowshoeing. The sisters were tired, and their legs were sore, but their bellies were full of the chicken and rice dishes Mrs. Robinson had made for them. After a round of hot tea after dinner, Mrs. Robinson brought out a tray of cups filled with the hot chocolates.

"What is the white foam on top of the drink?" Rani had

asked when she politely accepted one of the cups from Mrs. Robinson.

"Dear, why, that is marshmallow," Mrs. Robinson said.

The sisters drank their new chocolate drinks, but they found them too sweet. Out of politeness, they drank them completely, never complaining.

"Lieutenant Robinson, I'll need the slide deck in thirty mikes. Briefing's in two hours, stud."

"Roger, sir," Brian said to the battalion executive officer. "PowerPoint slides are complete. I'll save it to the master folder in the G drive."

"Great. Good work, LT."

Brian was at his monthly weekend National Guard drill at White Sands Missile Range. He had completed his PowerPoint slide deck on his unit's personnel numbers (last physical test date and scores, marital status, deployable status, shot records, online training status) twenty minutes ago. Sitting at an old office deck, his issued laptop open and on, he maneuvered the mouse to place the cursor over the personnel file document on his desktop screen and dragged it over into the G drive master folder. Mission accomplished, he went back to reviewing his notes on Gandhi.

> Gandhi promoted unity among Hindus and Muslims.
> Theme: nonviolent resistance, vegetarianism, meditation, celibacy.
> Emphasized the dignity of manual labor.
> Emphasized duty.
> Sacrifice of oneself over others.

And from an old article he had clipped from a July issue of the *Economist*, he read portions of an article titled "How India Fails Its Women."

The female employment rate is lower [in India] then in any big economy bar Saudi Arabia, and falling.

The unrealized contribution of women is one reason India remains so poor. Why? Number one, women stay in school longer. Number two, as households become richer, they prefer women to stop working outside the home. Social standing increases if women stay at home.

"Lieutenant Robinson," yelled Captain Koss, the company commander. "We need you in the motor pool ASAP. Time to unload a deuce-and-a-half truck."

"Roger, sir. En route." He logged off his laptop, grabbed his hat, and headed out of the office.

"Another brewski, dude, as we pause for the next episode?"

"Sure, Chuck. I'll have another," Brian said as he passed a bowl of popcorn to Rani and Deepika.

Chuck headed to the kitchen to get the beer. It was a Friday night—movie night—at Brian and Chuck's apartment. Chuck's girlfriend, Lisa, was over too, also enjoying the viewing pleasure of *Breaking Bad* on Netflix.

"Oh, Chuck, while you're at it, I'll have another glass of Pinot Noir when you get a chance."

"Sure thing, Lisa. Glass of Pinot Noir coming right up."

During the earlier break, about an hour ago, Brian had led a discussion as to who was smarter, who was more cunning, Walter White, the high school chemistry teacher, or the big honcho drug kingpin, Gus? Six people (the Kumar sisters, Brian, Chuck, and Lisa) weighed in on the matter, and Brian, attempting to resolve the ultimate decision, suggested a vote, taken by a show of hands. The result was an even three votes for Walt offset by three votes for Gus.

"Walt is by far the smartest character," Brian said after he orchestrated his democratic plan. "He's always a step ahead of everyone, including Jesse, his brother-in-law, Hank, and Gus himself. He's super intelligent and manipulates events to meet his needs."

"I absolutely agree," Priya said as she was eating some popcorn.

Chuck, after sipping a Corona, said, "But they all work for Gus. Somebody has to be the boss, and it's Gus. He runs the operation. And the Albuquerque Police Department and the DEA, they think he's just the nicest guy and a local philanthropist generous to the law enforcement community."

Lisa, sitting with Chuck in the big armchair, took a quick sip of wine, then switched topics. "Priya, I hear you're going for your driver's license. How exciting. How's that going?"

"Oh, it is going well. I have so much to learn though—all the rules. Driving cars is not as common in India as it is here. Thank God Rani has her license. That's how we can go to Walmart and Costco and buy our groceries."

Lisa took another sip of wine. "And you're enjoying the driving lessons?"

"Oh yes, very much so. I have an excellent instructor. Very patient, and he explains things well." She paused. "Oh, and tomorrow, I will have another instructor to help me practice." She pointed at Brian. "At the end of my driving lesson tomorrow morning, Brian has offered to practice driving with me in one of his parents' older cars. Thank you so much, Brian. Noon tomorrow, correct? The more practice I get the better."

"That's right," Brian said. "Tomorrow. Noon. I'll pick you up at the driving school. But right now, it's time for another episode of *Breaking Bad*. Chuck, buddy, can you get the lights and hit play? Let's find out how Walter White outmaneuvers everyone."

"Very good, Priya. Good job. Well done. You're controlling the car very well."

Brian was helping Priya with her driving in Las Cruces. Priya, driving Brian's parents' old Honda Civic for the first time, was practicing her city driving and the rules of the road. Like her weekly instructor, Mr. Ryan, she found Brian patient and his advice useful.

"Always give yourself some space from the car in front of you. At least so you can see the car's back tires entirely. Always use your blinkers and in advance. Taking a right on red is allowed unless the signs specifically say it's prohibited." Those were some of Brian's helpful pointers. Priya still had some questions regarding yielding the right of way, and she was finally getting the concept of merging, especially on highway exits. She was learning and getting better, and her confidence was improving too.

"Okay, Priya, nice. You took that last left turn a little too sharp. Take it wider the next time, but overall, nice job."

"Thank you, Brian."

"Hey, let's practice your highway driving now. Let's head east on I-10 toward El Paso."

"Okay," she said.

In five minutes, Priya was on I-10, correctly merging and maintaining the right speed. Soon, she was recognizing familiar sights: the Franklin Mountains to her left, the pecan farms to her right, and the smelly, massive cow pastures with all those poor black-and-white cows, all to her right.

"Great job, Priya. You're properly centering the car, always in the middle of the lane."

"Thank you, Brian."

Ten minutes passed, and then Brian said, "Take the next exit to the left, Priya, in about a quarter mile. See the sign?"

"Oh yes. Okay."

Priya shifted to the right lane and took the exit heading north, which meant the car traveled in a horseshoe pattern, encircling the Franklin Mountains that were always to her left.

"We'll take the third exit, Priya."

"Okay, but where are we going?"

"Got a surprise for you. You'll see."

"A surprise?" she asked. "What is it?"

"Like I said, you'll see. Besides, if I told you," Brian said, "it wouldn't be a surprise."

After Priya took the exit, Brian instructed her to follow the street heading toward the Franklin Mountains. Soon they were in a mixed residential and commercial area, traveling at around thirty miles per hour.

"Pull up to the parking lot to the right, Priya."

"At Tom's Bike Shop to the right?"

"Yes, that one."

"What is at this bike shop?"

"You'll see."

Priya parked the Honda Civic, and the two exited the car. They entered the bike shop.

"Is John here?" Brian asked the guy working the counter. Brian had gotten John Mays's name from a National Guard buddy two weeks ago. Armed with the name, Brian had actually phoned John Mays and inquired about a particular type of bike, and Mays had returned the call two days ago, saying the bike was in stock.

"Sure thing," said the guy at the counter. "John is in the back. May I ask your name, sir?"

"Yeah. Tell him Brian Robinson is here."

The counter guy headed toward the back of the shop and shortly reappeared. "John says to come on back."

Priya asked, "What is this all about, Brian? All these bicycles here. You know I don't know how to ride a bike."

"That's right," Brian said. During one of the intermissions at the last viewing of *Breaking Bad* at his apartment, Deepika had talked about the young boy who was on a bicycle and ended up killing one of the street drug dealers. Deepika had said she and her sisters didn't know how to ride a bicycle.

"Yes, Priya, I understand you and your sisters don't know

how to ride a bike, but you will see what I have in store for you."
Brian walked between two technicians, and Priya followed him.

"Where's John Mays?" Brian asked the technician to the
right.

"Dude right there," the technician replied, pointing to a
short, heavyset young guy no more than thirty years old who was
some thirty feet away, pumping air into a bike tire.

"Hi, John. I'm Brian Robinson."

Mays turned around. "Hello there, Brian. Always nice to put
a face to a name."

"And this is Priya."

"Hello, Priya. I'm John, the manager here." Mays walked to
some shelving and wiped his hands clean. "Got exactly what you
were looking for, Brian. Took a while. Came in this week from
Dallas. Follow me please."

Mays took them to an adjacent small warehouse in the rear
of the shop. "There she is, Brian, just like you ordered. I know
the color didn't matter to you. It came in candy-apple red. Hope
you like it."

"Awesome," Brian said. "Exactly what I was looking for."

Priya, looking at the shiny bike, said, "You ordered this bike,
Brian?"

"Yes. But look at it. It's a special type of bike. It's a two-seater
bicycle."

"I see," Priya said, her tone unexcited. "And you bought this
bike?"

"No, I'm renting it."

John Mays chimed in with, "That's right. Twenty bucks per
hour. And if you're renting it consistently, your rental payments
go toward the purchase price if you guys decide to buy it down
the road."

"Awesome," Brian said. He then turned to Priya. "Let's take
it for a spin. There are trails here to the north heading to the
mountains."

"But I've never ridden a bicycle, Brian."

"I know, Priya, I know. That's why it's a two-seater. I'll take the lead. I'll be in the front seat. Just do what I do. Just pedal basically. I'll pedal and steer."

Five minutes later, Brian and Priya were in the parking lot with the bike. "Okay, Priya. Great that you're wearing jeans and sneakers. Perfect. Just get on the bike by sitting on the second seat."

"Okay," she said, a bit nervous. Brian was holding the bike steady. Priya stepped over with her right leg, then got on the back seat.

"Yikes," she said. "I will fall, Brian."

"No. No you won't. I've got it. I'm holding the bike steady." Brian now had both hands on the bike. "Just put your feet on the bike pedals, Priya."

"Oh. I'm going to fall."

"No, you won't. The bike is swaying just a bit. I'm holding it steady though. I'm going to get on the front seat, and I'm going to start pedaling right away. You won't fall. Just pedal when I do."

"Okay, okay," she said nervously. "But we're going to fall, Brian. Hurry please."

Brian noticed Priya was perspiring a bit. It was a warm day in late February, the windy season in the Southwest. The temperature was near seventy degrees Fahrenheit with a nice, steady breeze. The past week saw the temperatures in the forties, with heavy winds, but later in the week, the temperatures climbed into the fifties, and the winds subsided.

Brian held the front handlebars and quickly occupied the front seat, his feet both firmly planted on the parking lot asphalt. He again told Priya to have her feet on the pedals, and she said okay and did as directed. The bike was a bit wobbly, but Brian felt in control. He suddenly saw their nearby parked Honda Civic, and he started to laugh.

"What is so funny, Brian? Hurry, let us ride, as we must. Otherwise, we're going to fall."

Brian kept laughing. "Seeing the car reminds me that you know how to drive a car, but you don't know how to ride a bike. I just find it funny."

"Well, we didn't have these things, these bicycles, in Chennai growing up. People walk and have motorcycles. Not these pedal bikes."

Just then, John Mays came out of the store and was walking toward them. "Dude, I almost forgot. I saw you guys from the store and realized y'all didn't have any helmets. I figured your sizes. It's the law. Gotta have helmets. Gotta charge both of you for this. How about a ten-dollar rental for both headsets?"

"Sounds fair," Brian said. "Man, it's been ages since I last rode a bicycle. Fifteen years or so. Forgot about the whole helmet thing." He instructed Priya, "Okay, Priya, you can get off the seat, but stay over the bike. Just have your feet on the ground. Like I'm doing."

"Okay," she said.

"Thanks for the helmets, John," Brian said, and he proceeded to fit the large helmet to his head and handed Priya the medium-size helmet. "Just fit it to your head like I did."

"Okay," she said nervously. "Is this a dangerous sport? Why do we have to wear helmets? It's the law for some reason, I presume."

"Yes, Priya, it's the law. It's for protection—protecting one's head."

"So this is dangerous? Brian, I do not want to fall. I want to go back home. Driving a car is easy compared to this."

"Don't worry, Priya. You're gonna love it."

And she did. Oh, how she loved the afternoon. Helmets on, the pair headed out of the parking lot, rode through a residential area, and soon found themselves on an asphalt trail heading up the Franklin Mountains. At first, the bicycle was fishtailing some because of its novice second rider, but she soon found a rhythm and realized it was by pedaling that the bike stayed up and steady. And the warm wind blowing in her face, the pedaling, the scenery—Priya absolutely loved it all. It was a great, warm spring day, the air having a certain scent of freshness, and this machine, this bicycle, she loved how one could actually feel the bike maneuver in union with the riders. *Man and machine working in unison. How wonderful. And great exercise too. This is better than driving a car,* she thought after ten minutes of riding.

The trail eventually turned into a dirt road, but it was a hard and relatively smooth dirt road, a path really, beaten down by walkers, joggers, and bicyclists. Priya, in the back seat, pedaling in unison with Brian, was all smiles. *What a gorgeous pastime, this bicycling.*

The bike ride lasted ninety minutes. And once they had reached the parking lot of Tom's Bike Shop, Brian paid for the bike and helmet rental and told John, "We'll probably be back for some more rides. Priya here really enjoyed it."

"Cool," Mays said. "I just need a day's advance notice in case some other couple wants to rent the two-seater. And let me know if you want to buy the bike down the road."

"Will do," Brian said.

Later that evening, Priya told her sisters all about her wonderful day of cycling. She finished the day by taking a warm bath, in part to massage her sore feet and legs, and right before she went to bed, she took out her personal notebook and wrote: "Rode a bicycle this afternoon with Brian. Most enjoyable. Splendid. Truly splendid."

Sunday night, February 3, and the Kumar sisters were at Brian and Chuck's apartment for Super Bowl LIII pitting the New England

Patriots against the Los Angeles Rams. Chuck's girlfriend, Lisa, was also in attendance, setting up a huge bowl of chips with assorted salsa and dips. Though no one was a Patriots or Rams fan (Brian's team was the Denver Broncos while Chuck always rooted for the Arizona Cardinals), Brian insisted on hosting a Super Bowl party at his apartment for tradition's sake.

The Kumar sisters weren't sure what to make of the invite at first ("We know little about American football," they'd said, "just what we briefly learned watching the game on Thanksgiving"), but when Brian explained that football was close to being a religion in America and that the sport was ingrained in American culture, well, that did it for the inquisitive Priya, and her sisters tagged along with her. Insisting "Just bring your hungry appetites; no need to bring any food," Brian had ordered a variety of pizzas, wings, chips, and favorites from Bombay Palace, consisting of samosas, rice dishes, chicken curry, and chicken tikka marsala. There was wine for Lisa, beer for Chuck and Brian, and hot tea for the Kumar trio. For dessert, Brian figured he couldn't go wrong with chocolate chip cookies, popcorn, and peanut butter cups. Rani, despite Brian's insistence, felt the need to bring some food to this most American of sport festivities and, after researching the Super Bowl, quickly discovered the most popular food for this annual celebration was an American staple—pizza. Armed with this research, she undertook to make two homemade cheese pizzas, using naan bread as the dough.

Like two months prior at Thanksgiving, the Kumar sisters kept asking questions during the eating and game watching, and Brian and Chuck fielded them in order:

Rani: "Who is the guy throwing the ball?"
Chuck: "That's the quarterback."
Deepika: "Why is he called the quarterback?"
Chuck: "I don't know."
Priya: "Why doesn't the quarterback always throw the ball?"

Brian: "It's good to run the ball to keep the other team's defense guessing as to whether they'll throw or run the ball."

Deepika: "What are these downs?"

Chuck: "Just think of them as attempts.'

Rani: "Oh, okay. So four attempts to advance the ball ten yards."

Chuck: "Exactly."

Priya: "Why is there so much kicking in this game?"

Brian: "Well, it's a low-scoring game, and the teams don't want the other team to have good field position."

Priya: "So just kicking the ball is a point correct, but if the kicker kicks the ball between the two yellow posts, that's three points?"

Brian: "Yes. Kicking the ball in the uprights is worth three points but only one point after a touchdown."

Deepika: "And a touchdown is worth how many points again?"

Brian: "Six."

Rani: "This game is a lot more complicated than cricket."

After the game, the sisters thanked Brian and Chuck for the food and the instructions on American football.

"We should be thanking Rani, because your naan pizzas are absolutely mouthwatering," Brian said. "Much better than the ones I bought." Chuck and Lisa agreed.

Rani drove herself and her sisters back to their apartment that night, and before Priya fell asleep, she wrote the following in her personal notebook:

> Watched an American football game for the second time. The Super Bowl championship. It's a complicated sport played by big, fast men who run after each other and shove one another to the ground. Sports is huge in America, and there are so many of them. NMSU is filled with sports too—college sports. Tocqueville— equality of condition; there's a big push for equality in

the United States. Sports are not just for men but also for women. I found the halftime show for this Super Bowl to be interesting. Singers singing songs I did not recognize. Light shows, a ball of fire exploding, bare chests, and lots of tattoos. Many people in America have tattoos. I believe this is so because individuality is huge in America, as is creativity, and tattoos are an expression of both of these deeply held values. I enjoyed the commercials very much. Here too, very creative. There were many beer commercials as beer/alcohol is a big business in America and seems to be part of the culture of viewing sports. One commercial—I believe it was a beer commercial— had a *Game of Thrones* reference in it. I have heard of this popular show, *Game of Thrones*, and Brian said he would like to start viewing it once we have completed the viewing of the *Breaking Bad* episodes.

On Sunday, February 10, Brian was at his apartment doing some online research on Gandhi when he took a break and decided to get himself a beer. As he walked to the refrigerator, he held his iPhone in his right hand. He was checking for any new emails or text messages, but he had none. He opened the refrigerator, popped open a bottle of Corona, and then decided to check the latest news by pressing the news icon on his iPhone.

"Trump to Visit El Paso Tomorrow" read the headline.

Whoa, Brian thought. *Cool. POTUS here tomorrow. Sweet.* He texted Chuck, who was at Lisa's apartment, to inform him of this news, and then he texted Priya: "Tocqueville. Guess what? I just read President Trump is visiting El Paso tomorrow. Gates to open at 3:00 p.m. Do you and your sisters want to go?"

Brian and the Kumar sisters were in the parking lot of the El Paso Coliseum, with Brian texting Chuck about where they were standing among the huge and growing crowd.

"There. I see him and Lisa," Rani said, pointing.

Brian said, "Oh yeah, I see them too," and he started waving. Chuck, after a few seconds, made eye contact with Brian, and he and Lisa started heading that way.

"Hey, gang, what a scene," Chuck said when they hooked up. "Place is packed. Do you think we'll get in?"

"Don't know," Brian said. "Let's get in line and see how it shakes out."

It was five thirty in the afternoon, the earliest Brian and the Kumar sisters could get there after classes, then the driving and parking, which took forever. Getting in line with the packed crowd, Lisa said, "I hate Trump. I think he sucks. Make America great again. We are great, and not because of him."

"Well, at least we'll get to see him," Chuck said. "Plus, you gotta hand it to him—the dude's got balls, man. He wants a wall, and where does he go to talk about it and sell it? Right here in good old El Paso, right on the border with Mexico. That's balls, man."

Lisa replied, "That's stupidity."

The line kept getting closer to the entranceway. Priya, like the others, was inching her way forward. She was behind Brian and ahead of Rani, tucked in between them. All types of people surrounded her: men, women, youngsters, seniors, people with signs praising Trump. Lisa, standing behind Chuck, said, "Gang, I'm not trying to be negative here, but this coliseum can only fit so many people. If we get turned away, there is a rally not far from here by Beto O'Rourke. I think it's more for the anti-Trump crowd. Frankly, I think that's a more important message."

"Who's Beto O'Rourke?" Deepika asked, standing behind Rani.

"He's a politician from El Paso," Lisa said. "And a good one.

He just lost his Senate bid against Ted Cruz. Narrowly, I might add. O'Rourke really gave Cruz a run for his money. Some say he might run for president against Trump in 2020." She looked at Chuck, smiling. "Trump wants to exclude, and O'Rourke wants to include. I think it's the better message."

The six of them inched up the line for another forty minutes, and sure enough, when they got close to the large entrance, an announcement was made that the coliseum was packed to capacity and could no longer take any more folks.

"Plan B, gang," Brian said. "Lisa's got a great one. Let's attend the O'Rourke rally, or counterrally, whatever it's called."

Thirty minutes later, the six stood and listened to the young O'Rourke and his arguments. Signs of "Viva Beto" were everywhere, the local son getting strong support. One sign drew laughs from Brian, Chuck, and Lisa. It read: "Elect a Clown, Expect a Circus. Any Functioning Adult, 2020."

Priya was enjoying it all—American politics at its core and at the retail level. "Walls do not save lives; walls end lives," O'Rourke said during his rally. "We stand against walls."

Shouts of "Beto, Beto, Beto!" often interrupted the passionate speaker.

Priya loved listening to the tall young politician who was wearing a white shirt and blue jeans, his shirtsleeves rolled up, his voice loud and clear and amplified by a handheld microphone.

Tonight I will watch and listen to the Trump rally; it must be on YouTube. That will give me the other perspective. Trump and this Mr. O'Rourke; how interesting. And Brian says they may face off against each other in the next presidential election.

Priya was at the Starbucks next to her apartment. It was mid-March, and she had just finished another driving lesson with Joe Ryan. Sipping Earl Grey tea, her plan was to review her semester coursework, especially work on her Memoir Chapter Workshop.

Thinking of her coursework, she first thought of her Applied Statistics class, which was going well in her opinion. She had taken statistics back in college in Chennai, and the material was coming back to her. Only once had she felt the need to text Brian and ask for his assistance on a homework assignment. As for her Operations Management class, that too was going well. It was a course that used the case study method and didn't require too much of her time.

Regarding her Independent Study paper, she never tired of reading Tocqueville and his observations on America. How true and relevant and prescient those many observations were, even though the French aristocrat wrote them eighteen decades ago. Lately, her notes about Tocqueville and his great two-volume series focused on law and lawyers in America.

Sipping her tea that bright, sunny Saturday afternoon, a weekend where Brian had one of his monthly weekend National Guard drills, Priya reviewed her recent Tocqueville entries in her ever-expanding notebook and also the digital file she had created on her laptop before her. She maneuvered her mouse to hover the cursor over the file, double-clicked it, and reviewed her latest notes.

Tocqueville:

In America, it may be said that no one renders obedience to man, but to justice and the law.

No nation ever constituted so great a judicial power as the Americans.

America is, at the present day, the country in the world where law lasts the shortest time.

Armed with the power of declaring the law to be unconstitutional, the American magistrate perpetually interferes in political affairs.

And next to that last entry, Priya, doing her own research on the modern American judiciary, had typed: "70 percent of the lawyers in the world live in the United States, even though the United States represents 5 percent of the world's population."

She sipped some more hot tea and reverted to thinking about her remaining courses.

Long-form narrative journalism. The course was taught by Professor Linda Cortez, a young, energetic Latina originally from Southern California, who was constantly telling her students to be great listeners and observers. "Interview people and always let them do the talking," she would remind her students. The course involved studying the writing styles of Tom Wolfe, Joan Didion, Gay Talese, Truman Capote, and Norman Mailer and then writing a twenty-page paper about a real story using the writing techniques of these greats. Priya was unfamiliar with these American writers, but in having to read some of their works, she soon became a fan, especially portions of Tom Wolfe's *The Bonfire of the Vanities* and Truman Capote's *In Cold Blood* and his feature piece on Marlon Brando for the *New Yorker. What detail, what dialogue. The characters were so alive, especially the way Capote wordsmithed his sentences.*

For her project, she had decided to write about the Patel family that owned a hotel in Las Cruces. She had interviewed the husband-and-wife team for nearly two hours and had already typed fourteen pages. The Patels, at first skeptical and reluctant, opened up to Priya later during the interview and answered all her questions.

Question: Where are you from?
Answer: The State of Gujarati.
Question: Why did you immigrate to the United States?
Answer: We came here to make money.
Question: Why did you settle in Las Cruces, New Mexico?
Answer: We first started in California with Mr. Patel's brother, but we found Southern California expensive. We wanted a college town, and Las Cruces has that. Plus, it is more affordable.

Question: When did you start the hotel?

Answer: In the fall of 1989.

Question: What do you like about the hotel industry?

Answer: It's not too complicated. Our son is in the business. We also own a hotel in Texas and plan to own another hotel in Albuquerque soon. Basically, we're in the real estate business.

Question: Is the restaurant, which is located in the hotel, a big part of your business?

Answer: We don't make money on food, but it is necessary to bring in the clients. The money in America is in alcohol. We make our money on alcohol and real estate appreciation.

And on it went like that, Priya interviewing the couple, firing away questions, and the Patels answering in a straightforward manner. The only subject the Patels were not forthright about was money. They would not reveal how much money they made or how much the hotel and restaurant had cost them in 1989. All they answered on the subject of money was that they pooled their money with family members and did not borrow from banks.

Priya's last class for that spring semester—the Memoir Chapter Workshop—was also taught by a relatively young, energetic professor, one Professor Mary Sanders, a thirty-two-year-old, tall blonde from Ohio who insisted her students call her Mary and who also required her students to write a twenty-page paper, either about themselves or someone they knew very well.

It was Priya's topic for her Longform Narrative Journalism class—writing about the Patels and their hotel/restaurant—that had provided the insight and idea for her memoir chapter, because by observing the hardworking couple, she couldn't help but think about her father.

Father too is in the hotel business, a high-level accountant at a major hotel in Abu Dhabi. Most of father's career has been in the Middle East, at times in Malaysia, and a small tenure in Japan, but mostly in the Middle East. Such a common story of many Indian men, ex-pats, working abroad and sending most of their wages back home to provide for the family. With Mother and four daughters, Father has worked very hard and sacrificed so much. Father also would have been successful in the hotel business here like the Patels. He too would have eventually owned a couple of hotels and maybe a restaurant. The American dream, the pursuit of happiness, these things are very real, and Father would have thrived in this equality of condition environment.

She looked outside the Starbucks window and observed the sunny, cloudless afternoon sky.

I will write about Father for my Memoir Chapter Workshop, how he provided for us and still does, how he bought a small apartment complex in Chennai to help us with expenses, how he accomplished his duties and obligations and still does to this day. But I will end with my thoughts on what could have been. What if Father—and all of us—had immigrated to the United States twenty years ago?

"Formation in thirty mikes, Lieutenant Robinson."

"Roger, sir."

"We'll be going over vehicle inspections. Ensure everyone has their paperwork squared away."

"Roger, sir."

Brian was in the small office space of the battalion headquarters at White Sands Missile Range. It was drill weekend, and the unit had just finished their afternoon lunch. While Priya was at the Starbucks going over her coursework and what she'd write for her Memoir Chapter Workshop, Brian, during some downtime, was reading about Gandhi for the Independent Study class, and he didn't like what he was reading. In South Africa, a country where Gandhi had resided for so many years, his statue was coming down. Same in Ghana. And why? Because it was discovered that Gandhi didn't want Indians in those countries to be compared to blacks—didn't want Indians lumped in with blacks and treated the same way. As written in the October 22, 2018, *New Yorker,*

Gandhi was an "unlikely symbol of racial arrogance." Gandhi was also harsh toward his sons and dismissive toward his wife, stating she was a simple, unlettered woman. And when she was dying, he denied her penicillin.

The more Brian researched and read about Gandhi, the more he realized just how complicated this seemingly simple man was.

Spring break, March 2019. Brian was putting in some extra time with Junk King to make some extra money, and Chuck, in his spare time, was scouring the internet for listings with good flipping potential. He was ready to buy such a property, a three-bedroom fixer-upper within walking distance of NMSU, but Brian emphasized there was no rush. "Keep looking, but we shouldn't buy anything until I graduate in August. There's always a good buyer's market in August for all the homes that didn't sell in the spring."

Brian had thought of taking a short vacation with Chuck, Lisa, and the Kumar sisters, maybe to the Texas Gulf coast or Vegas or San Diego, to celebrate his last spring break, but everyone was busy. The Kumar sisters were busy with schoolwork, and Priya, coupled with her homework, was dutifully practicing her driving, mainly with Rani. Then there was Lisa, who was in Boston, consoling a childhood friend of hers about a recent boyfriend breakup.

The only social event during the two-week spring break was a movie night at Brian and Chuck's apartment, a Friday night where the Kumar sisters (Lisa was still in Boston) showed up to watch three episodes of *Breaking Bad*. Friendly bets were placed on whether Jesse would actually kill the seasoned chemist who worked alongside Walt. The Kumar sisters, with the exception of Deepika, thought there was no way Jesse would do it. Brian was on the fence, and Chuck, like Rani, figured Jesse would pull the trigger. In the end, Brian sided with Priya and Rani, and they were wrong, which meant they were responsible for the food and drinks for next week's *Breaking Bad* Friday-night gathering.

It was a Thursday night in late March, and Brian was at his apartment researching prospective fixer-upper homes with Chuck when he received a text from Priya: "Hello, Gandhi. I have something to discuss with you if you should have the time. Something happened today, and I want to talk to you about it. Can I call you? If so, what would be an appropriate time to call?"

Brian texted her back: "Tocqueville, call me anytime. Now works. Best. Gandhi." Two minutes later, his iPhone rang.

"Brian, thank you for allowing me to call and taking the time to hear what I have to say."

"Sure, Priya. Anytime. What's up?"

"Well, this afternoon, this I tell you, my sisters and I had quite a unique experience."

"Oh, what happened?" Brian asked as he was sitting comfortably on the couch, flipping mute channels.

"Around five o'clock this afternoon, my sisters and I were all at our apartment, working on our studies and preparing dinner, when the doorbell rang. We asked who it was, and a lady's voice answered, saying, 'We are from the local House of Christ mission with an important message from Jesus.'"

Brian chuckled and said, "Oh, I see. Yeah, that can happen. They are good people. Religious folks can be a bit bothersome at times though." He stopped the channel at the *Flip or Flop—Nashville* show with Page Turner and DeRon Jenkins. "Wait, let me guess. And they left a Bible or some brochures for you all to read."

"Yes, that is true. They left a brochure and a flyer, which explains their mission of spreading the Good News of Jesus."

"Yes, well, as you know, Priya, there's a lot of religion in America, and some members want others to join their church."

"Yes, I see that now. I did open the door and spoke to the lady and her young daughter. Her daughter seemed to be around twenty years old. They both wore long dresses. Rani and Deepika did not speak with them, as they were busy in the kitchen. The lady asked me if I was a Christian, and I said I wasn't, that I'm a Hindu. She said that I need to discover the ways of Christ and that she and her daughter will be praying for me, my sisters, and my family in India so that we may 'find the light,' as how she put it."

"I see," Brian said.

"Yes, this is what happened, Brian. But I must say, the lady and her daughter were polite. They seemed genuine to me."

Brian's telephone conversation with Priya lasted another ten minutes, with the subjects eventually switching to coursework and how the driving lessons were going. Priya ended the conversation by saying, "And yes, Brian, back to this afternoon and the Christian lady and her daughter that I met, it makes me think of Tocqueville and his observations about this country. Did you know that Tocqueville said equality of condition is big in America because Christianity is big in America, and in Christianity, all are equal in the eyes of God? This explains the big push for equality in this country."

Tuesday, April 9, four o'clock in the afternoon. Brian had just entered his apartment after completing his last class of the day. He turned on the big-screen TV and headed to the kitchen to get a refrigerated bottle of water. Just as he was twisting off the bottle's cap, Chuck entered through the apartment's front door.

"Dude, I'm so freaking sorry," he said. "You thought I'd forgotten, but I didn't."

"What are you talking about?"

"You know what I'm talking about," Chuck said as he entered the kitchen. "You thought you'd keep it all low-key and I'd forget, but I didn't."

"What?"

"Dude. April 9. It's your freaking birthday, man. Twenty-five years old." They bumped chests. "Happy birthday, man. We got to celebrate."

"Nah, dude. I'm beat. It's a day like any other." There was a pause. "Mom and Dad called me earlier today, as did Anne-Marie. And you just wished me a happy birthday, man. That'll do."

"Au contraire. We need to celebrate. I say we invite Lisa and the Asian sensations over. Make it like a Friday. Movie night. We'll watch *Breaking Bad*. I'll get a cake at Walmart or at Paco's Bakery. What you say, birthday boy?"

"I don't know, Chuck. Again, I'm pretty beat. Plus I gotta prepare for tomorrow's classes. Maybe we can do something on Friday."

Chuck got himself a bottle of Corona out of the refrigerator. "Listen, Brian. Let me call Lisa and see if she's up for anything. You call the Kumar sisters and see if they're game. That'll help you with your decision-making. Fair enough?"

"Agreed," Brian said. "Fair enough."

Chuck headed to the living room, pulled out his cell phone, and dialed Lisa's number. Brian, still in the kitchen, decided to text Priya: "Hello, Tocqueville. How are you? How are your sisters? Hope you are all well. I had a busy day today. Just checking on you all. By the way, today's my birthday. 25 years old. It goes by fast. Would you guys want to come over here for cake and watch some episodes of *Breaking Bad*? Making an early movie night? Let me know. Gandhi."

Two minutes later, his phone rang. It was Priya. Just as he was about to answer the phone, Chuck said, "Lisa can't make it tonight, but she's up for Friday."

"Hello, Priya."

"Well, happy birthday, Gandhi. You should have told us about this most auspicious day. By the way, I have you on speakerphone."

"Hello, Brian, and happy anniversary," Rani and Deepika said.

Brian and the Kumar sisters spoke for the next ten minutes, about his birthday, their classes, how the house-flipping market looked, when his next National Guard drill weekend was, how the weather in the warm eighty-degree range was pleasant, and how the sisters' family back in India was doing. Brian did his best to sell the idea of a birthday party for that evening, but the sisters stated they had a full day of classes lined up for tomorrow, which prevented their going out. In the end, their counterargument was "We will celebrate your twenty-fifth anniversary this Friday at your apartment. Special treats on us. A most auspicious moment must be properly celebrated and at the right time, and it will be this Friday."

"Will Rani make her delicious naan pizzas?" Chuck asked, as Brian had his iPhone on the speakerphone option.

"Most definitely," Rani said.

"Well, okay then. As long as Rani will make her delicious pizzas, then Friday it is," Brian said.

"One, two, three. Happy birthday, Brian!" the Kumar sisters, Chuck, and Lisa said loudly in unison as Lisa placed a large carrot cake (Brian's favorite) in front of him at the small dinner table. The round cake with thick white frosting and twenty-five lit, dark blue candles occupied what seemed like a quarter of the table's surface.

"Make a wish now, bud," Chuck directed. "Gotta keep up with traditions." He sipped from his Corona. "Not that it's my call to make a wish, but I would think of something real estate related for a wish."

Brian, seated right in front of the cake, said, "Sounds like a plan." He closed his eyes and asked for good luck in the house-flipping business. Then he suddenly took a deep breath and blew out all the candles, except for two in the top right-hand corner that he extinguished with a second blow.

"Yeah!" everyone said, and they started clapping. Nachos, wings, chips and salsa, and Rani's popular pizzas were eaten that celebratory Friday night at Brian and Chuck's apartment, and then Deepika, with Priya's assistance, cut the cake and handed everyone a thick slice. After the dessert festivities were topped off with more beer, coffee, and hot tea, the six settled in for a night of three *Breaking Bad* episodes. Friendly bets were placed as to who would kill whom first: Walt gets Gus, or will it be the other way around? But first, it was Jesse accompanying Gus to Mexico. What was that all about? They would soon discover Gus was consolidating his power and controlling not just distribution but now even more meth production.

"Okay. Well hello, everyone," Professor Martin said as he entered the classroom five minutes late. "Our final class for the spring 2019 semester. We're almost there, gang. One summer session and our Independent Study course will be over. We're definitely in the homestretch now."

He placed his briefcase at the top left corner of his desk and took a seat on the opposite top right corner. Wearing blue jeans, a light blue shirt, and a light brown sports coat with elbow patches, he then said, "Your papers are really coming together, but before we go over them, I have an important announcement to make." He cleared his throat. "I am pleased to announce an important addition to the Martin family. Last evening, my wife and I welcomed into our home yet another of man's best friends. That's right. Our family has a new dog to be buddies with our great German shepherd, Cooper. We have a new Belgian Malinois, and we are naming him after our great, recently deceased Rocky, only this great dog is named Rocky II."

A few students clapped, and still more said their congratulations.

Then the next thirty minutes were spent with Martin leading a discussion about his newest best friend—how much Rocky II cost, his certified pedigree and breeding papers, details about the canine's strict diet, his age, his expected lifetime, his sleeping arrangement and exercise regiment, and how he was getting along with "good ole Cooper."

"Well, enough about Rocky II," Martin finally said. He stood up, opened his briefcase, and started handing out the graded papers (the grades were on the top right corner of the second page). Brian was the last to receive his paper, and once Martin handed him the paper, he turned around and walked to the head of the class.

"Okay. Well, I must say I'm pleased with everyone's papers. I really am. Let me go down my list of notes here." He was holding a three-by-five note card.

"Bob, great work on 'The Suck Called Vietnam.' Excellent work on the characters. I especially liked your section on race relations between the white and black soldiers. When the game is on and the bullets start flying, 'Ain't no atheists in foxholes; ain't no racists either.' I really like those quotes. I also liked your narrative discussion about the relationship between the few officers and the numerous enlisted soldiers. Great dynamics, great work. Keep it up."

Martin went back to sitting on top of his desk, then he looked down at his note card.

"By the way, gang. Some of you all are nearing the fifty-page limit, and that's a good thing. You will still have a lot of editing and rewriting to do, and that will obviously take place during the upcoming summer session. Remember, gang, the writing tips we discussed throughout this course: write what you know and know what you write; go where the pain is; conversely, go where the pleasure is. Good writing involves a lot of rewriting. And always remember to edit and edit and edit some more."

The next hour included Martin conversing about the students' papers and encouraging fellow students to also comment on their colleagues' work. For Carlos and how he was planning to beat Bobby Flay, a lengthy discussion ensued as to whether he should go with cod or salmon or mahi mahi, or maybe catfish for his fish tacos. He actually insisted on tilapia, but Brenda, the former pastry chef and Anthony Bourdain chronicler, argued for cod and also for a reduction in Carlos's planned two teaspoons of chili powder and generous use of heavy sour cream.

As for Geneva and her "Geneva Moves to Hollywood" paper, Martin gave her excellent marks for writing about her eager lover—also an aspiring actor—and their shotgun wedding in Las Vegas. For Jose and "How Muskia Will Save the World," Martin wanted him to expand on Elon Musk's arrangement with the United States, Israel, and South Africa to use artificial intelligence to dominate the market in precious energy crystals from Africa before the Chinese and Russians do. Thus far, only a consortium of Japanese banks were willing to finance the Muskian plan.

For Brenda and her account of the deceased Anthony Bourdain, Martin commented her paper was "near completion ... an excellent work ... and perhaps of publishable quality."

Tony's take on the cult-followed *Breaking Bad* series drew the most comments. Having Walt and Jesse tag team to eliminate Gus was plausible, and having the duo control the meth market in California and the rest of the Southwest was also reasonable. But having Hank promoted to the number two position at the DEA and then becoming a political donor to the Trump reelection committee, and having numerous pages of the paper discussing how a revitalization of the War on Drugs brought down the Walt-Jesse team, was too much of a fantasy ploy for some of the students to stomach. Bob commented, "You're making it too political, Tony. Keep Hank at his important ground level, not at the presidential 'We're Building the Wall' campaign."

Brian received an A-minus for the semester, and Martin wrote below that red ink grade: "Solid writing. Readers can tell you did a lot of research for this paper. I didn't know Gandhi was as controversial as some scholars and revisionist historians are pointing out."

And lastly, Martin especially liked Priya's argument, "The hustle and bustle of the American way of life produces a lot of good in the form of creativity, innovation, and prosperity, but not all will achieve success or share in it equally. Indeed, many find failure at the end of their many efforts, and such failure leads to the high rate of mental illnesses in America, such as stress, anxiety, frustration, and depression." A-minus was Priya's semester grade.

It was late May, and the Las Cruces temperatures had already hit the century mark. Brian, sitting on a heavy box of ammunition, was on his two-week National Guard Annual Training (AT) with his unit in nearby Fort Bliss, Texas. In one week, the summer NMSU session would begin, something he wasn't too concerned about because he only had three classes to take: Business Writing for Managers; Applied Case Study Management, where he had to write a ten-page paper about a local business; and the Independent Study class, where he was putting the final touches to his "Gandhi and Why He Matters" paper. One week of AT had already come and gone, his days filled with overseeing the loading of ammo boxes onto Humvees, cleaning warehouses, standard vehicle maintenance, directing forklifts to stack up pallets, and filling out inventory hand receipts. Meals were thrice a day at a huge tent in the middle of the desert while sleep took place in smaller adjacent tents filled with cots (*three hots and a cot*, as the saying goes). The upcoming final week of AT had all indications of being a repeat of the first, with temperatures hovering around one hundred degrees Fahrenheit. Water tanks, called water buffaloes, were omnipresent, and if a soldier—including an officer—was ever caught not drinking at the designated times, then the punishment was fifty push-ups and writing a four-page paper, with each line reading "A good soldier always drinks water during water time. I am a good soldier. I will drink water at water time."

In Brian's spare time, which took place in the evenings on his assigned cot one hour before lights out, he would go over emails from Chuck outlining prospective house-flipping opportunities, or he would edit his Gandhi paper, or he would text Priya to inquire how she was doing.

And each night, before retiring, he made it a point to go outside and catch the sights to the west, sunsets with their shades of rose and then purple off the jagged mountains, and while taking in those fading sunsets, he thought of the upcoming end of his academic years and moving on with his life by flipping houses with Chuck and progressing within his National Guard unit.

Priya was busy, always occupied with additions to her Tocqueville paper, but nothing took up more of her time than practicing her driving. Practice, practice, practice. Laser focused, she was determined to obtain that coveted driver's license. Once, during a lunch break at Bombay Palace with her sisters and Brian, she had heard Brian say, "Failure is not an option," in the context of one of his National Guard drill missions, a mission where he and his platoon were doing all the necessary work to pass a graded inventory inspection of their vehicles, supplies, weapons, and ammunition. "We fail, we are hosed," Brian had told his team the day before the crucial inspection, now relaying the story to the Kumar sisters. "Thank God we passed," he had said, "because I don't think we could have lived with the consequences of failure. It was a failure-is-not-an-option mission."

Now on those hot summer nights when Priya retired to bed, she inevitably thought of and eventually dreamed of Rani saying, "This is a no-failure mission; failure is not an option; you and I have practiced so much. You will get your driver's license."

Periodically, her thoughts shifted to her academic assignments, her final semester, and her future plans. But most of her thoughts were filled with practice, practice, practice—getting that all-important American driver's license.

It was Tuesday, July 2, right at 11:00 a.m. The temperature was ninety-seven degrees Fahrenheit. (By 5:00 p.m., the hottest part of the day—something Priya was still getting used to, having the hottest part of the day in the late afternoon—it would reach 104 degrees). Priya, at the Starbucks adjacent to her apartment, ordered an Earl Grey tea. She was surprisingly calm, given the earlier events of the morning. Eventually, she sat down at an unoccupied table, took a few sips of her tea, and decided to text Brian: "Gandhi. Please come visit my sisters and me tonight at our apartment at 7:00 p.m. Also, please invite Chuck and Lisa. Do not bring food. Your presence is important. I cannot reveal more at this time. Please confirm you will come. Thanks. Tocqueville."

Brian, just getting out of his Business Writing for Managers class, read the text and texted back: "Sure. Cool … What's this about? It better be good … Just kidding. Looking forward to it—whatever it is. Gandhi."

Brian and Chuck arrived at Priya's apartment at 7:00 p.m. sharp (Lisa wasn't able to attend). As soon as Brian knocked on the door, Deepika, wearing a shiny purple sari, opened it and said, "Oh great. Please come in, Brian and Chuck. Take off your shoes, and do make yourselves at home."

Brian and Chuck entered the incense-smelling apartment and took off their shoes. Rani, also wearing a sari, a dark green one, was in the kitchen, busy moving around, looking like she was putting the finishing touches on a dish. She quickly washed her hands at the sink.

"Hi, Brian. Hi Chuck. Thanks for coming. I'm almost done with the pizzas."

"Great," Brian said. "We sure love your pizzas."

"Please, help yourselves to the dinner table," Deepika said, directing the roommates that way. "Do you guys want anything to drink? Rani, in an historic first, bought beer today. Coronas. Do you guys want beer?"

"No way," Brian said, stunned. "Beer? You guys don't drink. What's this about?"

"You'll soon find out," Deepika said, smiling.

Chuck said, "Corona beers. That's awesome. I'll have one please."

"Great," Deepika said.

Brian asked, "Where's Priya, by the way?"

"Oh, she's in her room," Rani said, smiling. "I'm heading there right now; putting on saris is not easy, you know. Oh, and, Chuck, please help yourself to the beer in the refrigerator."

Chuck headed to the kitchen and said, "Dude, you want beer?"

"Sure," Brian said.

Chuck retrieved two Coronas from the refrigerator.

"Say, Deepika, where's your bottle opener?"

"Bottle opener?" she said, perplexed as she sat next to Brian at the dinner table. "What is a bottle opener? I don't know if we have one."

"You know. A bottle opener," Chuck said. "A handle with the metal edge to it or a metal lip to open bottles, especially beer bottles."

Deepika couldn't picture it.

Chuck asked, "Can I look where you all keep your cooking utensils? It might be there."

"Sure," Deepika said. "That drawer there." She pointed to the right of the sink.

"This one?"

"Yes. That one, Chuck."

Chuck pulled the drawer out, looked carefully in it, and didn't see a bottle opener. "Hey, no worries, man." He placed one of the bottles on the counter next to the sink and the other bottle against his belt buckle. He held that bottle and started pushing down. "There ... almost got it ..." He pushed some more, and the cap finally popped off. "One down, one to go." He did the same for the other Corona bottle.

As Chuck was carrying the Coronas to the dinner table, Rani appeared in the hallway, and behind her was Priya, smiling and wearing a shiny, light blue sari.

"Introducing Ms. Priya," Rani said as she and Priya took seats at the dinner table. Chuck handed Brian an open beer bottle and took a seat next to Deepika.

"Hello, everyone," Priya said, smiling.

Brian and Chuck said hello.

"So why are you all decked out in those beautiful, long dresses?" Brian asked.

"Well, Ms. Priya will explain that," Rani said, and she stood up and headed toward the kitchen. "I'll get the pizzas."

Priya cleared her throat. "Well, today is a most auspicious day, thus my sisters and I decided to wear our saris."

"Cool," Chuck said.

"And the reason this is a most auspicious day is, as you Americans like to say ... drumroll please ..." Brian immediately started tapping rapidly on the dinner table. "Today's my birthday!"

"Yes!" yelled Rani and Deepika in unison. Brian and Chuck smiled and started clapping.

"Cool," Chuck said. "Happy birthday."

Brian said, "Yeah, absolutely. Congrats, Priya. That's awesome. Happy birthday. And thanks for inviting us over."

Rani placed three of her homemade pizzas at the center of the dinner table and said, "Plates for the pizza coming right up.

Later, we will partake in Priya's birthday cake and also the peanut butter cups."

"Is that what was in the bag in the refrigerator?" Chuck asked. "When I pulled out the beers, I thought it might be a cake, but I wasn't sure on account of the bag covering it."

"Yes, that's the cake," Rani said. "It's a chocolate cake with a bit of frosting and two thin layers of raspberry jam within the cake itself."

"Sounds yummy," Brian said. "Priya, there's no need to be secretive about your birthday, at least in my opinion. You should've told me earlier in the day. At least I would have brought you a birthday gift."

"Oh, Brian, we Indians like to keep quiet about certain things and then build suspense." She started laughing.

"I see," Brian said. "Well, that's great, Priya. Happy birthday once again."

"Thank you," she said. "Oh, and there's one more thing why this is a most auspicious day."

Brian and Chuck both looked at Priya inquisitively. "Well, what else do you have for us, Priya?" Brian asked.

"Drumroll please," Priya said, smiling, and Brian once again started tapping rapidly on the dinner table.

Priya said, "I wish to thank every one of you for coming this evening to celebrate my anniversary." She cleared her throat. "And to also inform you that today the state of New Mexico has one more licensed driver."

Brian and Chuck stayed at Priya's apartment until close to midnight. Over pizzas, chocolate cake, peanut butter cups, and Corona beer for the guys, the conversation was dominated by Priya, explaining how many hours she practiced driving in the last couple of months, how she and Rani visited the temple the last five Saturdays in a row, praying to the gods and making offerings to them (dollar bills, an occasional coconut, many bananas), how Priya chose her twenty-sixth birthday ("a most auspicious day") for her driver's test, and how nervous she was, especially the past week and this morning.

Three days later, when the same quintet met at Brian's apartment for food and watching three episodes of *Breaking Bad*, Brian presented Priya with a birthday card that simply read: "To Tocqueville, Happy Birthday. Wishing you good health and happiness always. Namaste, Gandhi."

And inside the card was a twenty-dollar Starbucks gift card.

Sunny, hot weather, steady schoolwork, and Friday viewings of *Breaking Bad* episodes at Brian's apartment filled the month of July and August for Priya, but a description of those summer months wouldn't be accurate without the addition of the word *anxiety*, for it was that word, and the feelings and meaning behind it, that occupied so much of Priya's time. Nervousness, worry, and concern were constant, worse than her time preparing for the driver's license test.

There was always the chance that her plan would fall through, and nobody likes failure, including Priya Kumar. That explained her anxiety but only part of it. It paled in comparison to the main cause of her constant concern—her parents and, related to her parents, her upbringing and her culture.

Parental expectations, traditions, the Eastern importance of conformity and a sense of duty—these were the very things that kept racing in Priya's mind, twirling around, filling her with worry. She was determined, but was determination enough to succeed against the well-entrenched expectations of her mother and father, who both had sacrificed so much for their children? Priya, Rani, and Deepika dutifully called their parents and sister, Jani, once a week, always on a Sunday. In these weekly talks, Priya at no time mentioned her plan, let alone hinted at it, but she knew that with the rapidly approaching end of her American college experience, time wasn't on her side; eventually she would have to inform them of her intentions. How would they react? What would they think? What would they do? Such were her constant worries. Even Rani and Deepika didn't know of her plans, but that didn't concern Priya, for she knew they would understand and accommodate and support her in the end. But her parents? That was a big unknown, and as is often the case, it is the unknown that most worries us.

The latest from back home was that her father, Govin Kumar, had decided to move back to Chennai for good and take a position as the chief financial officer of a four-star hotel. Like so many Indian men, his working life took him to places overseas, in his case Abu Dhabi, the United Arab Emirates, Kuwait, and then short stints in Japan and Africa, all for greater prosperity to better provide for his family. Duty and obligation, that was the meaning of life, and Mr. Kumar dutifully performed his duties. But after nearly four decades of the expatriate life, with just the one annual visit to his family, Mr. Kumar was ready to perform his duties in the very city where his family resided. In less than a week, he would be working at his new job, and he also had that small apartment complex of his to oversee and manage.

To help clear her mind of the inevitable declaration, Priya immersed herself in her three summer courses, and she visited the Hindu temple in El Paso with her sisters every other week on Saturday mornings. The temple visits, the weekly Friday movie nights, and her academic work provided a welcomed reprise from her otherwise constant worry, but Priya knew that just up around the corner, her final academic session was coming to an end, and with that came the necessity of declaring her plan. Game day, Saturday, August 24. It would kick off at 11:00 a.m. at Lorenzo's restaurant, with the reading of the Independent Study papers. Priya was preparing for the most important day of her life.

The reading started at 11:00 a.m. sharp. Chicken wings, breadsticks, and various types of pizza (pepperoni, meat lovers, pineapple and ham, feta with spinach, and four cheese) were all paid for by Professor Martin. The students had to pay for their own drinks, including alcoholic ones (they were all of age to consume alcohol). Brian and Bob split a pitcher of Bud Light, Brenda ordered a glass of chardonnay, Professor Martin went with a gin and tonic, Tony opted for a lager from a local brewery, Bosque Brewing, and Geneva and Carlos, who had both recently turned twenty-one, opted for bottled Yuengling beer.

"Gang, help yourselves to the culinary comforts. The staff here will bring more food as needed to ensure we're not eating cold food," Martin told the eight students. "I want to thank you all for a great year and some fine papers." He started walking around the table and placed graded papers—facedown—before their respective authors. "It's thanks to fine students like you all that make my job worthwhile and this course fun. So relax and enjoy yourselves today by reading your papers. Everyone did well. Indeed, these are some of the finest papers I've ever read for this course; you guys rock. And there is no particular order in reading your papers. You guys figure it out among yourselves."

The students were casually dressed—jeans and T-shirts, except for Brenda (she wore a light white blouse and dress pants) and Priya, who opted to go with a light red salwar kameez with gold trim. Professor Martin, wearing designer jeans and a blue polo shirt, took a seat at the front of the eight-chair, square table (an adjacent table was filled with the food items) and sipped from his gin and tonic.

"Really informal, gang. Get up anytime, get some wings and pizza slices using the paper plates, and help yourselves to your drinks. You can read your paper sitting down or standing up, whichever you prefer. Oh, and I'm thinking we break every ninety minutes for comfort breaks. If you need an individual bathroom break, just politely and quietly do your thing. Okay, with that, who's going to bat leadoff and kick this off?"

Carlos and Geneva both raised their hands, then looked at each other. "Well, ladies first, Geneva. You win," Carlos said, smiling. "You go first."

Priya, alternating between sips of water from a glass and sips of hot tea from a teacup, was a bundle of nerves. Earlier in the morning, she woke up after a near sleepless night with the worst case of diarrhea, a condition she experienced when under extreme stress, like right before qualifying exams back in India or after she had applied for a foreign student visa to the United States. Four hours ago, she had confided her plan to Rani and how it would be launched today. Minutes later, she had relayed her plans to Deepika, and the trio of sisters soon found themselves sitting next to the makeshift puja display in Deepika's room, praying to the gods for Priya's plan to come to fruition.

Geneva read her paper sitting down, her bottle of Yuengling to her right. Her paper was filled with plot twists, taking place first in Los Angeles, then Vegas, then some acting in New York City, where she fell in love with a Shakespearean-trained actor named Ian. Then the story shifted back to Hollywood, with Geneva doing a bit of modeling, Ian being a parking valet, and the young lovers both taking acting classes together. Priya's facade seemed attentive, but her mind was elsewhere. *This is the most important day in my life*, she thought as she sipped some hot tea. *This is so important. More so than national exams in India, or waiting to hear about student visas to the United States, or even my recent driver's license exam. Those were all big moments, but they pale in comparison.*

Twenty minutes into Geneva's reading, Priya quietly and politely stood up and headed to the bathroom to handle her nerves.

By two o'clock in the afternoon, Geneva, Carlos, and Bob had read their papers. Geneva's ended with her engagement to Ian, with the two struggling actors landing parts with a touring group in San Francisco. The young, soon-to-be married couple gave themselves five years to make it into the movie business. "If success is not ours, we'll move to Vermont, open up a bed-and-breakfast, and start an acting studio on the side."

As for Carlos, he read his paper fast and loudly. He breezed through his first cookoff opponent, where the mystery cooking ingredient was tomatoes (he won with a southwestern-style tomato bisque), and then he faced off with the one and only Bobby Flay. His selected signature dish was fish tacos.

Carlos's reading kept Priya's interest for the most part, as she enjoyed learning about ingredients, chopping and slicing techniques, heat temperatures, and the reaction of the fictional onlooking and cheering crowd. The judges for the final competition were none other than the famous Martha Stewart, Washington, DC, celebrity chef José Andres, and local El Pasoan turned famous food expert and television personality Aaron Sanchez. Carlos ended by standing before his classmates, a bottle of Yuengling in his raised right hand, yelling, "I am Carlos Gonzalez, and I just beat Bobby Flay!"

But it was Bob's paper that was Priya's favorite thus far. Wearing a black Stetson, sporting a handlebar gray mustache, his bulky chest encircled by a tight black T-shirt with the saying "Don't Say I Wish—Say I Will," Bob read his paper sitting down and sipping his beer. His reading—like his writing—was blunt and also vulgar at times. Plenty of F bombs were thrown around, and the protagonist's R&R, which took place in parts of Australia, featured plenty of weed smoking and terms like "getting paid to get laid; mighty fine pussy in the Land Down Under." Priya knew Bob read and wrote from the heart, and she also knew his paper was really a memoir. At times, the subject matter of the paper made her think about America's role in the world.

Priya realized the soldier's account of the war fought a half century ago represented something important to America and its people, namely victory. Bob was big and strong and had a direct manner, a soldier fighting in combat, but was the war being won? Racial tensions were not only back in the homeland but among the American troops doing the fighting in Vietnam. America is a big, strong country, a superpower, one that represents certain values, but this war in Southeast Asia wasn't going so well, at least not in Bob's paper, especially after the Tet Offensive. Americans hate losing, and when losing comes their way, well, it's a tough pill to swallow, isn't it? America loves victory; America wants victory; America demands victory; America expects victory.

Priya thought, *Americans are not short on confidence. "You can be anything you want; the American dream; we're number one." All these are sayings Americans know quite well, for they learn them at an early age. Only in America will you find bumper stickers on the back of cars that read Proud Parent of an Honor Roll Student. Achievement, making something of oneself, victory, getting the job done in a competitive environment—all these are important to Americans, and informing everyone else about their successes is also important to Americans.*

Everyone knew that Bob modeled the young John Clark after himself, the young and tough soldier who landed in Vietnam with thoughts of beating the bad guys, just like his forefathers had done in World War II and in Korea (at least Uncle Sam kept the line and helped South Korea stay in the Western fold). That was a victory, one that is still being played out on the present-day Korean Peninsula. But the young Clark returns from his Vietnam War experiences, he's back in the States, and he's wondering, *Are we gonna win this war?* When 1975 rolls around and Saigon falls to the Communists, the answer to his question is an obvious no. John Clark, in a sad, alcoholic daze, finds himself asking, "How did we lose?"

"How did we lose?" That was the last line of Bob's paper. It's not a phrase Americans are used to asking themselves, but it was powerful the way Bob read it, and Priya applauded loudly when Bob said, "Thank you, all. This paper forced me to think long and hard about what my military service meant to me."

"Thank you, Bob," Professor Martin said as he stood up. "Truly excellent. And with that, how about we all take a comfort break for ten minutes. There's plenty of food too. Let me know if I need to tell the staff to warm up the pizzas or breadsticks or make new ones."

The students got up to stretch and hit the restroom. Priya was sipping hot tea and nibbling on a breadstick. She wanted to talk to Brian, but she noticed he and Bob were chitchatting near the bathroom's entrance, their conversation about the Vietnam War. She started debating when exactly she should read her paper. She started getting nervous again, so she paid a visit to the ladies' room.

"I'll go next," Tony said when the readings resumed. In no time, he was reading his paper, a fictional account of the popular *Breaking Bad* series with made-up plot twists. During the reading, Priya occasionally glanced at Brian, who was sitting directly across from her. He glanced back, smiling, sometimes shaking his head disapprovingly when he didn't agree with Tony's narrative. Priya would smile back, and she too wasn't in full agreement with Tony's take on *Breaking Bad*. Walt and Jesse conspiring to kill Gus? No, that wouldn't work, because the very tension between these two was central to the show's success. And Gus sensing the heat from his two cookers and maneuvering his way to having an affair with Skyler to get the goods on Walt? Nah, that wouldn't happen. Gus was much more intelligent, much more sophisticated than that.

But disagreements aside, Tony's work kept everyone's interest. When Gus is indicted by none other than the law-and-order good guy Hank (who got an anonymous tip from—who else?—Walt),

Walt and Jesse, seeing opportunity, take a little trip down south to meet with the one and only El Chapo himself, Mr. Guzman. Priya liked that twist, and when the big money starts rolling in, well, that's when Walt and Jesse and Skyler open more and more carwashes, a clever way to hide dirty money.

Priya loved how Tony ended his paper: El Chapo extradited to the United States, prosecuted, found guilty, and now sitting in a federal penitentiary. In the end, readers and listeners learn this all happened: It's Walt and Jesse, mostly Walt, who worked the American and Mexican governments to place the kingpin behind bars. And for Walt, Skylar, and Jesse, now that they have more and more carwashes, a couple of trucking companies, and more than one hundred pizzerias (also used to launder money), they become newly minted members of the annual Forbes 400 list of richest Americans. The end.

"Great work, Tony," Martin said. "Very creative. And with that, who wants to read their paper next?"

"I will," Brenda said. She took a quick sip of chardonnay from her glass and then began reading her paper.

Right off the bat, listeners discovered Anthony Bourdain's life was not just about food but also about culture and history and language and people and their relationships and their lifestyles. Bourdain came to prominence later in life, a late bloomer, and he sure paid his dues prior to any notoriety coming his way. He started from the ground up, learning all the jobs there were in a restaurant kitchen. "I never saw a white guy looking to start out as a dishwasher," he once said, a comment that summed up part of his views on America's immigration debate.

Knowledgeable and always respectful, those were two words Brenda highlighted in her paper, for Bourdain didn't have an ounce of arrogance in him, at least not on the television screen. Confident, yes. Always. But not arrogant. Never the big, loud, boastful American critical of someone else's food but rather the cool, calm, deep-thinking food connoisseur whose every remark—including criticism—contained a respectful tone.

As a younger man, he dabbled in writing crime fiction. He also loved martial arts, but he'll always be best remembered for his show about food and travel.

Brenda didn't pull back on anything, and she didn't make any value judgments on Bourdain, even when the topic turned to his substance abuse struggles. Why the depression? Why take one's own life? "We may never know," Brenda read, and Priya couldn't agree more, for she didn't know what to think about these matters. *A famous man, a hit show, a beautiful woman as a partner to share life with. Bourdain seemed to have it all. And yet this man had substance abuse problems, and he suffered from depression, and he kills himself? Strange indeed,* Priya thought. She couldn't help but conclude, *These mental health issues seem to be the problem of rich white people.*

"He may have left this world too soon under circumstances we can't explain," Brenda read in a clear, soft voice, "but the footprint he left gave us many lessons to ponder. True, he will be best remembered for recognizing what foods we eat, how we prepare such foods, and how we eat them. A people and their culture. Indeed, in the end, we should always be ready and willing to learn more from others. That way, we learn more about ourselves, and, in the process, we recognize that we're all sharing this planet of ours, and we're not all that different from one another. Good food, good drink, good friendships, good conversations, good experiences. Anthony Bourdain brought these to our television and laptop screens and also into our very lives. And for that, we should always be grateful. May he rest in peace."

"Very well done, Brenda. Thank you so much," Martin said. "And next up, judging by an excited raised arm, we have Jose Valenzuela, who will tell us all about Muskia."

"Thank you, sir," Jose said. His paper began by describing Elon Musk's childhood in South Africa, his eventual move to

Canada, and his entrepreneurial pursuits in the United States. Fast-forward to 2027, and Musk becomes increasingly politically active, raises not only capital but ardent followers, and successfully establishes a colony on Mars called Muskia.

"At first, the colony has one hundred settlers, but in two years, that number grows sixfold as more people on earth become increasingly frustrated with the constant state of warfare—overwhelmingly cyber warfare—between the Order Block, which consists of China, Russia, Iran, North Korea, Venezuela, Cuba, and some Middle Eastern and African countries, and the Freedom Bloc that includes the United States, Canada, Mexico Central and South America, the Western European nations, Israel, Australia, New Zealand, India, South Africa, South Korea, and Japan."

Filled with geopolitical considerations and discussions about energy and food resources, Jose's reading kept Priya's interest but only intermittently, for she reminded herself that soon she'd be the one reading to the class. How would it all turn out? As Jose was reading his paper, she prayed to the gods—mostly Ganesha and Vishnu—for good luck.

"And so it was, in the year 2033, when Musk and a group of his Muskian friends successfully landed in Brazil, then in Russia's Ural Mountains, and then in Madagascar, all to obtain ample quantities of quartz crystals to develop a new energy source to conquer Earth and bring peace and law and order. The Order Block and the Freedom Bloc didn't interest the world's first trillionaire, because in his way of seeing it, both blocs would have to be defeated to make Earth live up to its potential and possibilities."

"Thank you, Jose. That was very creative," Martin said. "How about we all take a ten-minute break, and then we'll hear the two final papers from Priya and Brian. And help yourselves to more pizza and breadsticks. There's plenty left."

Priya's nerves were acting up again, which meant another

restroom run. When she left the ladies' room, she ran into Brian, who was standing near the table filled with the food items.

"Good luck, Gandhi," she said, smiling.

"Oh, thank you, Priya. I mean, thank you, Tocqueville. It will all be done soon, won't it? A year to write a paper, and here we are, reading it—all of it—for the last time. It went by fast, didn't it?"

"Yes, yes it did, Brian." She took her seat.

Brian began by saying, "The young Gandhi was born in 1869 to a lower-middle-class family. Married at the age of thirteen to his fourteen-year-old wife, it was through a family friend that the young Gandhi was encouraged to pursue legal studies in London. Only when he made a vow to abstain from meat, women, and alcohol did his wife and mother permit him to go through with his plan. England did tempt him, but he stayed loyal to his vow during his London studies. Four years later, at the age of twenty-two, he returned to India.

"Soon thereafter, an Indian Muslim businessman with a large shipping business in South Africa—a country that was also part of the British Empire—had a cousin who needed a lawyer in that faraway land, and Gandhi was that lawyer. He would spend the next two decades in South Africa, not only applying his legal skills in matters of labor, commerce, and contracts, but also in the fields of civil rights and politics....

"Gandhi disliked and disagreed with the apartheid system he witnessed firsthand, and he soon took the cause of fighting for his people's rights. As a couple of scholars have pointed out, Gandhi's legacy has been reinvented since his passing, viewed as if he was always a saint. The reality is his life was complex, and his views evolved over time....

"In 1906, when the British declared war against the Zulu kingdom of Natal, Gandhi sympathized with the Zulus and encouraged Indians and black South Africans to treat *both* the injured British *and* Zulu soldiers....

"It was in 1915 that Gandhi returned to his native India to begin his career in politics and promote his message of change through nonviolence....

"Gandhi was dismissive toward his wife, and he was not a devoted father to his four children. The problem, in my [Brian's] view, was that Gandhi was a purist, dedicated to pacifism and nonviolence to a fault. He didn't eat meat, and when doctors informed him meat would assist in the curing of his ailing wife, he refused the granting of this remedy. He was opposed to close friendships, saying that they were dangerous, that friends would react on one another in destructive ways. Alcohol and tobacco were also never to be taken, as was sex—Gandhi believed sexual intercourse was solely to have children, and once that was accomplished, then celibacy was in order.

"Gandhi was the real deal, not only talking the talk but also walking the walk. A practitioner of celibacy once he hit his midthirties, Gandhi advocated not only complete chastity but the elimination of sexual desire. To live the part, Gandhi, once his wife had passed away, slept naked with his grandniece and two other female helpers too, all to 'cure himself of any lingering lust,' as the journalists Ferdinand Mount wrote.

"Social change through nonviolent means is a great message, but what about when the facts change and violence comes your way? For Gandhi, ever the purist, the equation did not change. When informed the Nazis were slaughtering Jews, Gandhi replied the Jews should commit mass suicide themselves. Informed that the Japanese may expand westward and invade India, Gandhi was okay with losing millions of his own people. For Gandhi, life was about purity and self-sufficiency, all in order to advance the cause of India's independence from the colonial British. Instead of buying cloth from the colonial power, Indians should spin and weave their own. Capitalism and trade were, in the eyes of Gandhi, bad, while living a simple life was to be cherished....

"The beauty and genius of Gandhi was his ability to see the good in everyone, even oppressors, and, more specifically, Gandhi was great at pointing out the sins of the oppressors based on the oppressors' very own values and rules. A devoted reader of the Bible, Gandhi, in the eyes of one pope, was 'more Christian than many Christians.' Indeed, Gandhi was using 'Christian acts as a weapon against men with Christian beliefs.' Gandhi's 'Truth Force' was a politics of embarrassment, used to shame the oppressive officials into 'behaving as their moral and religious codes instructed them to behave.'...

"At first accepting of the ban on intermarriage among the different castes, Gandhi came to reject the caste system altogether and fought against untouchability. From the writer John Ruskin, he learned and agreed with the notion that the noblest form of work is to farm and to make something with one's hands.

"Gandhi felt all religions basically taught the same fundamental values, and though he set the example of self-sacrifice over self-interest, individual obligations over individual rights, and dying over killing, plenty of Westerners agreed with his views and actions....

"It was an assassin's bullet that ended his life (an ultra-Hindu nationalist fired that bullet), and today, Gandhi's legacy of sit-ins, boycotts, hunger strikes, and social change through nonviolence lives on in the form of peaceful marches."

At the end of his reading, Brian mentioned the best writing on Gandhi was from the great novelist and essayist George Orwell, who wrote a piece about the civil rights pioneer back in 1949 titled *Reflections on Gandhi*. Brian ended his paper quoting Orwell:

> One may feel, as I do, a sort of aesthetic distaste for Gandhi, one may reject the claims of sainthood made on his behalf (he never made any such claim

himself, by the way), one may also reject sainthood as an ideal and therefore feel that Gandhi's basic aims were antihuman and reactionary: but regarded simply as a politician, and compared with the other leading political figures of our time, how clean a smell he has managed to leave behind!

Priya was surprisingly calm when she began reading her paper. Maybe going last and having listened to all the day's readings had something to do with that. Her paper was structured in the form of emphasizing Tocqueville's main themes and observations about the young democratic country, and then determining if those themes and observations were still in force and relevant today, 185 years later. Interwoven in these determinations were her own observations.

"Tocqueville's arguments about the equality of condition, the commercial orientation of Americans, and a high degree of Christian religiosity in this young country, how true and loud these themes still ring today. Americans, including perfect strangers who just recently met, will refer to one another by their first names. Even some professors in America insist their students refer to them not as professor but by their first names." She looked at Professor Martin, who was smiling, as were many of the students.

Martin, while still smiling, said, "Touché."

"Such a push for equality in the elimination of social distinctions is ubiquitous in the United States, but it is hard to imagine, and even grasp, for someone who comes from a country with a well-entrenched class system."

The next fifteen pages of her paper dealt with the commercialization and business orientation of Americans. "Stores and establishments open all day, twenty-four hours, seven days a week, drive-through options, no-hassle return policies, delivery to one's home—it is America that brought these business practices to capitalism and to other parts of the world. 'The client is king.' 'The customer is always right.' These are sayings very few other nations are familiar with, let alone practice. And what tremendous efficiency one experiences in America." She mentioned a few examples. "Need to scan a document and send it to someone? No worries, because FedEx-Kinko's is often open around the clock. Need your groceries done? Order online and have them delivered to your door. In the mood for Thai food, but your friend wants hamburgers? No problem, for you can get them both and delivered to your home or apartment through companies like Grub Hub or Doordash. And you need a cab? Whip out your smartphone and get on Uber or Lyft.

"It is no wonder why Jeff Bezos, the founder of Amazon, is worth something like a hundred and fifty billion dollars. Indeed, Mr. Bezos has brought so many efficiencies to the marketplace. And with self-publishing on the rise, budding authors such as myself now at least have a platform to market their books. I myself am giving serious consideration to self-publishing my novel *Money Matters* through Amazon.

"The degree of entrepreneurship and the high standing of the self-made person are both cherished American values. Even American television programs showcase the importance of business matters. *Shark Tank*, *Wall Street Week*, various house-flipping shows, and *Blue-Collar Millionaires* are examples.

"Tocqueville wrote, 'The passion of wealth takes the place of ambition,' and 'the pursuit of wealth generally diverts men of great talents and of great passions from the pursuit of power.'

"Related to commercialism and the heart of *the customer is king* edict is consumerism, and it is tremendously prevailing here in America. With milk, there is 1 percent milk, and 2 percent milk, and fat-free milk, and almond milk, and half-and-half milk, and soy milk, and skim milk. Just so many choices. Choices and choices and even more choices. Same with cheeses and coffees and toppings for pizza—so many choices to choose from, so many selections to make. Buying a car? Will that be a two-door or four-door? Sunroof? Bucket seats? Leather seats? And a vehicle's color? So many different shades of gray or silver or blue or red, just so many colors in different shades. And television? It seems having five hundred channels is the norm in America. And American television programs are quite unique. Reality TV is big here in the United States. And everything seems to be commercialized in the United States. Comedy, religion, consumerism, and sports, of course—all are on television. But twenty-four-hour sports coverage, that's an American pleasure called ESPN. There's the golf channel and the racing channel, just so much specificity. Take fishing, for example. We all understand the fishing industry and the need to eat. But it is Americans who have turned fishing into a competitive sport with championships and point systems and trophies and money prizes. Just the other evening, I saw a show on ESPN that showcased a fishing tournament. Trophies and titles for the biggest fish. The show consisted of professional competitive fishermen who are like celebrated athletes. Only in America will you see fishing turn into a competitive sport with rankings and points and money prizes.

"And to take part in this massive consumerism, what is it that one needs? Why, that would be money, and that too is available twenty-four seven in America with its ATM machines spread out everywhere in this large country. This I tell you: it is tremendously true to refer to America as the land of plenty."

Priya's reading shifted to exactly what can explain this widespread commercialization and consumerism. The answer, she said in her reading, is quite simple: "America has a well-developed legal system.

"This is truly a nation of laws. Contracts are honored, and property rights are valued and defended. An employer doesn't pay a wage-earning employee (as opposed to a salaried employee) time and a half for overtime? Well, there will be a lawsuit because time-and-a-half pay is the law. A homeowner doesn't pay a contractor for the agreed-upon price of fifteen thousand dollars for the remodeled kitchen? Well, that contractor can and will file a lawsuit or place a lien on the very house in question. And good luck selling your house with a lien on it.

"No wonder there are more lawyers in the United States than in all the other countries combined. Laws and rules and regulations are most plentiful here, and by and large, the people follow the rules because there are legal consequences for not doing so. As a further example, there are quite a few countries that have a hard time collecting taxes from their citizenry. That's not the case here in the United States, as the taxes are taken up front from payroll checks every two weeks. And if taxpayers or even companies somehow forget to pay their taxes or don't pay the right amount of taxes, they will get their wages garnished or pay hefty fines. The upshot is the government will get its tax revenue."

Priya took a quick sip of tea. "As a foreigner and foreign student here, it is only logical that at some point in observing all this abundance, all this consumerism, all these big homes and big cars, one wonders, *How is all this possible?* The answer is credit.

"So many things in this country are purchased on credit. Home loans, car loans, student loans, credit for furniture, credit for everything, actually. Virtually all merchants, and also doctors and dentists and lawyers—they all accept credit cards.

"In my country, we do not know, let alone understand, the concept of student loans. And in my country, when you go to buy a car, it is probably a small car, and maybe it sells for three thousand dollars, and you will not hear the dealer say, 'Let us run a credit check on you to see how much you can finance.' No, one must have all the money up front. And so, it is obvious that the extension of credit in America is only possible because of America's strong legal and banking systems. This explains America's continued success at creating wealth. People trust the system. Indeed, creditors believe the debtors—the very consumers—will pay them, because the whole system depends on credit.

"And Tocqueville was such a keen observer of these issues that he saw yet another key ingredient to America's growth and commercial orientation. This too can be explained in one word, and that word is failure. As Tocqueville observed, this concept finds itself on both sides of the consequence's equation.

"Americans do not have a fear of failure, which is a good thing, particularly in business affairs. Tocqueville wrote: 'In America, there is no law against fraudulent bankruptcies, not because they are few, but because there are a great number of bank processes.' This is so true, because business matters can be complicated and difficult, filled with tough competition, price fluctuations, changes in consumer preferences—all of which can at times contribute to a high degree of failure. The fact is many businesses do fail. A short list of businesses that have failed includes Borders Bookstore, Blockbuster Video, and Toys R Us. They are gone. Sears has also filed for bankruptcy, but they are reorganizing. General Motors too is giving it another go. And think of all the small businesses that fail. But the point is that these failures are accepted; they are accepted as a cost of doing business. As much as Americans have a difficult time with the very concept of failure, such difficulty does not translate to business matters, for, in that arena, failure is acceptable. When a small business is failing in India, the owner cannot just walk away and declare bankruptcy, because his creditors will be after him forever to get their money back. But not here in America, for the legal system protects the entrepreneur against his creditors, and his outstanding debts are forgotten, a thing of the past.

"One incredible discovery I have made during my yearlong studies here in America is the fact that people, regular people and not businessowners but workers and employees and common people, can file for personal bankruptcy. This is frankly mind-boggling. At a certain level, one can understand bankruptcy protections for businesses, but for individual people? For consumers? People can actually file for personal bankruptcy; it's absolutely incredible. Yes, filing for bankruptcy will affect one's credit for seven years, but nonetheless, such folks can simply walk away from their debts. This shows that Americans are not afraid to take on credit, to take on debts, for that is the system. Again, so many products and services are purchased on credit, including education and sometimes health care. So if you want the house and the car and the furniture and the swimming pool and a college education, then you get these things on credit, you take on debt. But to be able to walk away from these debts through the legal system, through personal bankruptcy, is quite unique. Perhaps it is through no fault of one's doing. For example, perhaps the person lost his job, or maybe a child's medical bills ballooned to one hundred thousand dollars. The monetary numbers are incredible in America, but what is equally incredible is being able to walk away from financial obligations legally.

"The desire of Americans to augment their material comforts, the ease of obtaining credit, a legal system bent on protecting property rights—these all contribute to two things, namely economic growth and pride. On these issues, Tocqueville wrote, 'He [the American] takes pride in the glory of his nation; he boasts of its success, to which he conceives himself to have contributed … Nothing is more embarrassing in the ordinary intercourse of life than this irritable patriotism of the Americans.'

"So Americans own a lot of things, a lot of these things are bought on credit, bankruptcy laws are lenient or permissible, and this all helps the economy, and the nation prospers. But then comes the other version of failure, the one that Americans don't like and don't accept, and this is the concept of pure failure, the failure of not having succeeded. To quote Tocqueville, 'The lower orders are agitated by the chance of success, they are irritated by its uncertainty; and they pass from the enthusiasm of pursuit to the exhaustion of ill success, and lastly to the acrimony of disappointment.'

"So the material well-being is plentiful in America, but the reality is not everyone will achieve it. For these folks, failure and disappointment unfortunately take hold. In my opinion, it is not enough to say Americans are hardworking. What explains it better is that Americans have to work hard because so much of what they own is on borrowed money. They want more—ambitious they are—and they work hard to pay the bills, and all this inevitably brings a lot of stress. And sometimes it brings failure. I find many Americans to be stressed. In America, everyone wants to be rich. It's about them. It's about the individual. And trying to achieve success can be very stressful.

"Science tells us that stress can be related to mental illness," Priya read. "On this issue, I think Americans, compared to other nationalities, suffer a lot from mental illness. Indeed, so many Americans are on medications for these illnesses, mainly for anxiety and depression. This pressure to succeed, this ambition to be number one, this drive to be the person you want to be is incredibly stressful, and it starts at a young age in America. From a foreigner's point of view, I think it explains school shootings, where a young student is frustrated about not being accepted and cool. In March of this year, we learned about the lengths parents will undertake to see that their child gets into an elite college. Paying bribes, getting records forged, even taking a child to a psychologist and paying that psychologist a lot of money to get a disability diagnosis for the child so that the child will get more time allotted to take exams. These are all measures, unfair ones at that, to ensure the child succeeds. In short, the pressure to succeed in America is enormous, and it helps explain America's high rate of entrepreneurship, economic growth, and wealth creation, but it also explains America's high rate of mental illness, drug use, medications, and crime. Here's a fact to emphasize the point: how many nations actually have schools and offices practice active-shooter scenarios to ensure students or workplace employees know what to do if there is a shooting? Answer: you'll only find this sort of training in America. That says a lot about this country."

Priya took a quick sip of hot tea, and then her paper shifted to the importance of Christianity in America.

"Central to Christianity is the belief that all people are equal and that it is the people who are the source of power. Tocqueville saw slavery firsthand in 1830's America, and he predicted it would end at some point in time, for Christianity would not allow it. He also predicted Texas would separate from Mexico and that, in the future, the United States and Russia would be two world powers with different ideas of governance, two rivals who would battle it out. And he was right of course.

"America is truly a religious country. For example, it seems so many politicians running for office in America cannot end a speech without saying, 'And God bless you all, and God bless America,' as if America and its people have been given a special status by God and that God blesses them but not the other nationalities."

Priya read some more about religion, about television evangelists spreading their messages, about Christianity's push to convert non-Christians, and how Americans' drive for wealth and wealth creation has a religious dimension in what is commonly called the prosperity gospel.

"And it seems religion is not only about saving one's soul but also about making money. Billboards and bumper stickers with sayings like 'Where are you going—heaven or hell?' 'Call 1-800 at Jesus' are popular in this country. It's about saving souls, but it's also about becoming the person you want to be, and for many, that's about becoming rich and successful. Tocqueville wrote: 'The people are the legitimate source of power,' and I agree. For example, my sister once told me about a certain college business course at New Mexico State University where the students circulated a petition requesting the firing of a certain professor. Students here have a lot of power in the United States. And Americans, in my opinion, have a voice if they unite and organize and raise money. If such facts materialize, politicians and institutions will no doubt have to listen and legislate accordingly. In the example I just gave, the professor was fired. To have students gather together and petition the university to fire a professor is unheard of in most countries."

She then gave another example of the people as the source of power in America. "In this country, for certain court trials, it is a jury made up of the regular people who decide the fate of the accused. This is incredibly unique. Tocqueville was amazed at the jury system, and he saw it as Americans being very civic minded, as the people taking part in government affairs and doing their civic duty."

Priya's paper then focused on the current American president. "While researching for this paper, it dawned on me that America's president, Mr. Trump, so exemplifies many of the themes and arguments Tocqueville put forward nearly two centuries ago. Political views aside, I think Mr. Trump is very representative of America, at least from a foreigner's perspective. At six foot three and some 250 pounds, he is big, as are a lot of things in America. He is very wealthy, and though he was born rich, it is clear that most of his wealth was self-made. Though successful, he has had a number of business failures and bankruptcies, the latter allowing him to reorganize and give it another go. This goes to the ability of Americans to reinvent themselves. And Mr. Trump is on his third marriage, again showing Americans' ability to deal with failure and bounce back. In many parts of the world, including my home country, divorce is extremely rare, for, in many respects, it is not an option because of the enormous stigma associated with it. Also, all indications are that Mr. Trump is very litigious, and so too is America. He's not afraid to sue people in court or to sue other businesses that go up against him. It seems that in this country, anybody can sue anybody in court. Currently, the president is facing numerous lawsuits for his political, business, and personal matters. And finally, Mr. Trump comes across as a bully, demanding things be done his way. Many foreigners believe America itself can at times be a bully.

"Maybe some fifteen years ago, the Bush government did say, in no uncertain terms, that the invasion/liberation of Iraq—whatever you want to call it—was based on 'regime change.' Today, a big news story in America is about the possibility of Russia interfering with the elections here while your very own country, the United States, actually has the audacity to say we are invading a country to change its regime. The big bully doesn't waste time with elections; it simply changes another country's government. This is all to say that America, in the past, has not always operated with clean hands.

"Nonetheless, even with her faults, America, I maintain as a foreign observer, stands for incredibly beautiful and powerful and, yes, difficult values: freedom, liberty, individualism, and the responsibilities that come with it, the rule of law, and opportunity. Though she may have not always lived up to such values, the very idea that she stands for them says a lot.

"Decades ago, during the Tiananmen Square protests, what symbol did the protestors select for their cause? It was your very own Statue of Liberty that proudly stands in New York Harbor, a symbol for millions that America, despite her faults, is good and welcoming. And as we read our papers today, in that same country, China, protestors in Hong Kong, fighting for fair elections and a fair judicial system, are singing your national anthem, 'The Star-Spangled Banner,' as a symbol for their important and just cause."

Priya paused and sipped some water. "Personally, I think my lasting impression of this country, the thing I will remember the most, is the ability of Americans to reinvent themselves, to do everything they can to live the life they desire to live. To be older than thirty and go to college is not possible in India. Also, the idea of borrowing money in the form of student loans to pursue higher education is just not an option. Here in America, people can reinvent themselves. The marriage is not going well? Then get a divorce. You started a business that unfortunately fails, then declare bankruptcy. You're fifty years old, and you want to go to law school, then go to law school, and if you can't afford it, borrow money to pay for it. In this country, it is all about you as an individual trying to live the life you want to live. It is even in your founding document, the saying 'life, liberty, and the pursuit of happiness.' Personally, I think a fair number of Americans have tattoos because of the importance of individuality in America. I believe tattoos are about an attitude, a statement, 'I matter. This is me. This is an expression of me.' Individuality is huge in America.

"As the conservative writer and filmmaker Dinesh D'Souza, a fellow Indian American, has said on a number of occasions during his talks on American college campuses, 'America allows one to write the script of one's own life.' In many other countries, as Mr. D'Souza correctly points out, many decisions are already determined for the individuals: issues of where to live, what career to pursue, who to love, who to marry, what religion to practice. Such important things in life are determined by birth and blood, by the country you were born in, and by your parents. And, often, one does not get a second chance at things. Your marriage is not working, but there is no divorce; your business is failing, but there is no bankruptcy—you just keep paying your creditors. As a student, you don't do so well at a national exam? That's it. That is your score, and you have to live with it. Too bad. That's why some students commit suicide once they get their exam results, because they are faced with the notion that they cannot become the person they had hoped to be because of their exam score. But here in America, you can take the exam again, and a third time and a fourth time if necessary. You can switch your major. Or you might take five years to graduate from a four-year college. You can take different classes. Try things and maybe see where your talents and where your interests lie. Such options do not exist in many other countries."

Priya paused. She was nervous, and she took a sip of water. Then she thought to herself, *Walter White. Fearless.*

"With all this, dear classmates, Tocqueville was an incredible observer and commentator about America, and his conclusion still rings very true to this day: the equality of condition, religion and its push for equality, the emphasis on individuality, the ability to fail and try again, the ability to reinvent one's self, the pursuit of happiness, and the ability to write the script of your own life are all very appealing. Which is why, this I tell you, to all of you, that I have decided to extend my stay here in America. My student visa runs out in a month, but I have applied for a work visa with the Department of Business Administration at New Mexico State University. Hopefully, this work visa will come through. This last year has been a very pleasant and enjoyable year, and it is thanks to classes like these and students like you who have enriched my educational experience and allowed me to learn about your great country.

"And, and ..." she said nervously, feeling her lower lip quivering a bit, "this country is not perfect. The degree of crime is high, and your opioid crisis is truly a crisis. I realize this, my fellow classmates, that failure is possible, that it may be the end result of pursuing one's happiness. Nonetheless, I have decided to give it a go. I want to get my novel, *Money Matters*, published here in the United States, and if I am not successful, I will publish it myself. Self-publishing is truly on the rise, especially in this country. I accept America as she is, with all her greatness and with all her faults, and I have chosen to give it a go here—to write the script of my own life. Thank you."

Professor Martin stood up, smiled, and started clapping, and Priya's classmates also started clapping. Priya smiled. "Thank you. It has been a great year for me, and this has been my most enjoyable class."

"Well, gang, that wraps up our final semester and our course," Professor Martin said. "To quote from our last reader, Priya, I too thank you all for the great papers and the great year. Hope you all enjoyed it, and help yourselves to the food. There's plenty of pizza and breadsticks left. Bring some home if you wish. I was happy to pay for all this, gang, and if you were pleased with the food and with the service, please tip the waitresses accordingly. Thank you, all. Oh, and, Priya, can I see you for a moment please?"

The students started gathering their things, and Priya said, "Yes, sir," and walked up to Professor Martin.

"After one year, and you're still calling me sir, Priya," he said, smiling. "Anyway, that was a great paper, very heartfelt."

"Thank you, sir. Uh, I mean Mark."

"Can you hand me your paper please, Priya?"

"Sure," she said, and she handed him her paper.

Professor Martin took the paper with his left hand, and he pulled out a pen from his shirt pocket with his right hand. He set the paper on the table, turned to the second page, and crossed out the A grade in the top right-hand corner and wrote A-plus. He handed the paper back to Priya.

"Great job, Priya, and best of luck with that novel of yours. I hope you find a publisher, and I wish you much success."

"Thank you, Mark," she said.

Professor Martin turned and thanked the Lorenzo waitstaff that was busily cleaning up. Priya turned to her left and saw that Brian was picking up his bookbag. He turned and looked at her and said, "That was an excellent paper, Priya. And a great reading."

She started walking toward him. "Thanks," she said nervously. She was standing right next to him, holding her paper in her left hand, her right hand nestled in her right front pocket of her jeans. She had her right index and middle finger secretly crossed as she said, "Brian, can I see you this evening at your convenience? How about the Starbucks next to my apartment?"

Brian looked at his watch. "Sure. It's almost six o'clock. How about now? Can I see you, say, in fifteen minutes? What's up?"

"I'll see you in fifteen minutes, and we'll discuss it then."

Priya was sitting in a far corner table at the Starbucks when Brian entered. He saw her and walked toward her, noticing she hadn't ordered anything. Not one to frequent an establishment without buying anything from it, he said, "Can I get you anything, Priya? A hot tea? I want to get myself a bottle of water."

Priya, nervous, quietly said, "Okay. I'll have an Earl Grey hot tea. Short please. Low-fat milk and sugar."

"Coming right up."

The Starbucks wasn't too busy, just two other patrons sitting near the counter, far from Priya. Brian placed his order, paid for it, and then went to the station with the milk and the napkins and the wooden coffee stirrers. He placed a bit of the low-fat milk in Priya's tea and then met her at her table.

"So what's up, Priya? Again, great job today with the paper. And hey, that's awesome that you're staying here longer." He opened his bottle of water and took a sip.

"Yes, thank you, Brian." She opened up the sugar packet and stirred it into her tea.

Brian said, "So what do you want to discuss?"

Priya took a deep breath. "Well, Brian, today when I read my paper, I was not 100 percent truthful."

"Oh really?"

"Well, you see, the NMSU Business Department has made it very clear to me that there are no guarantees that my extension will go through. They did assure me they will do everything they can to offer me a small administrative job and support my efforts to extend my student visa or somehow stay in this country legally, but they made it very clear there are no guarantees. They also told me the process for these papers takes time, that dealing with the federal government is not easy. Doing it in a month is a tight schedule."

"I see."

Priya, her right hand in her right pocket, crossed her fingers. Nervous, she thought of Walter White in the *Breaking Bad* series. *Fearless. Take chances. Go for it.* She took a deep breath and then said, "I want to be your wife, Brian. Will you marry me?"

Brian, stunned, said, "Excuse me?"

Inexplicably suddenly confident, Priya replied, "You heard me. I want to be your wife. Will you marry me?"

Shocked, Brian straightened his back and inadvertently let go of his water bottle, which caused water to gush out on the table. Somehow, he recovered quickly and placed the bottle upright.

"Sorry. I'll get some napkins."

He started to stand up, but Priya said, "Don't worry about the water. Answer me, Brian. Will you marry me?" She took another deep breath. "And please do not think that I am interested in you just because of your nationality. I could have easily applied for a PhD program here and extended my foreign student visa that way, but that is not the life I choose to live. I have been thinking a lot this year, and I've made choices. I have chosen to stay here and to become the person I want to be. It is enough that my parents and my sisters have assisted me financially to pursue my master's degree here. I did a bit of editing work during the year, but that was not enough to live on. I do not wish to be an academic. I wish to be your wife and a novelist." She was relieved. "And I will help you and also Chuck to be very successful in real estate. In your house-flipping business. I have good taste for decorating." She nodded her head up and down.

Brian smiled. "You're not bluffing, are you?"

"What is bluffing?"

"In poker, it's playing a weak hand in a strong way. Being deceitful. Faking."

"No, I am not bluffing."

"So you're serious."

"Yes. Very much so. I would not be asking you to marry me if I did not want you to marry me. You have been very nice to me during this past year. And I remember the first day I met you, in our Independent Study class, that you at first wanted to write about Afghanistan, but then you changed your subject to India, to Gandhi, all because you were interested in me. I can make logical deductions and reasonable inferences." She removed her hand from her pocket, and she took a sip of tea. She smiled confidently. "Am I not correct, Mr. Robinson? You wrote about Gandhi because you wanted to impress me. This I tell you—our interests are aligned. Now I want to be your wife."

All off guard, Brian said, "Can I get some napkins to clean up the spilled water?"

"Yes, you may, of course." She was smiling.

Brian stood up, walked to the condiment station, and got a handful of napkins. He returned to the table and started wiping it up. "Priya, you're a very nice girl, but we don't know each other. We haven't even dated and—"

"That is not so important, Brian. You have known me for a year, and I want to be your wife."

Finished with the wiping, Brian sat down. "Well, I have to think this through, Priya. I need some time, you know. It's a big decision and—"

"How much time do you need to make your choices?"

Brian thought for a moment. "I don't know, maybe a month or so if—"

"That is too much time. I'm sorry. I am not one to press things, but there is the visa issue here."

"Well, how about a week. That way I can—"

"That is still too much time, Brian. Again, I am truly sorry. How about a day? Twenty-four hours. Can you tell me your choice by tomorrow?"

"Well, I don't know. Maybe if—"

She cut him off. "Brian, do you like me?"

"Yes," he said.

"Well, what is the problem then? If you like me, then I should be your wife."

"It's not that easy, Priya. I mean, marriage is a big decision."

"Yes, well, we have a timeline here. Twenty-four hours."

Brian, uncomfortable, simply said, "Okay."

Priya stood up, as did Brian. She walked up to him and gently hugged him.

"Good luck with your choices," she said. "This I tell you: I would be a good and faithful wife to you."

Brian entered his apartment and went straight to the refrigerator. He popped open a Corona and joined Chuck in the small living room. A baseball game was on, Dodgers versus Diamondbacks. He placed his bookbag on the sofa to his left.

"How goes it, dude?" Chuck asked. He was also working on a Corona. "How was the reading? Hey, by the way, I always meant to ask you. Is it true that Gandhi used to drink his own piss and sleep next to naked young girls?"

"Dude, you'll never believe what just happened to me."

"Reading didn't go so well?"

"Nah, nothing like that. By the way, the answer is yes. Gandhi did on occasion drink his own urine, and he slept naked next to young women."

"Man, that's gross. I mean the urine part. The sleeping naked thing, that's damn good discipline. Anyway, so what's going on?"

"It's Priya," Brian said. "She—"

"How's the Asian sensation anyway?"

"Well. the Asian sensation is doing quite well actually. Reserved and always polite and a bit shy, she just asked me to marry her."

"No fucking way!" Chuck said. He popped up from the sofa.

"Way."

"You gotta be kidding. Priya asked you to tie the knot?"

"Yep."

"Wow, dude. Massive." Chuck looked directly at his roommate. "Well, what did you tell her?"

"I told her I needed some time to chew on it, to digest it, to think it over."

"Fair enough."

"Yeah, and get this: she gave me twenty-four hours to decide."

"Twenty-four hours? A day? Man, she doesn't waste time, does she."

"Nope. Just twenty-four hours. Just a day to probably make the most important decision in my life."

Chuck laughed. "This is crazy, dude."

"You don't say."

The roommates drank and talked for nearly an hour about Brian's big impending decision. At one point, the conversation turned to Chuck asking, "What brought this about? Does she just want to hook up with an American to further her stay here? You know, sort of like the mail-order bride thing. Chick just wants to live in the good old US of A."

"Na. Nothing like that. At least I don't think so. She insists it's not that," Brian said.

"And you know, dude, when I think about it, I never saw you two huggy-huggy, kissy-kissy. Know what I mean? You guys never dated, right? Just the platonic friend thing."

"Correct. We never dated."

"Didn't get a chance to check out the plumbing, hey?"

"Right." Brian took a sip of beer. He was staring at the television.

"Dude, that's like buying a house to flip without doing your due diligence."

"Agreed."

"Have you told your folks? I was just thinking—"

"Nope. I haven't informed them at all. Only you know about this."

Brian retreated to his room at 9:30 p.m. with two freshly opened Coronas. Wearing boxers and an NMSU T-shirt, he clicked open the television, placed it on mute (it was on Fox Sports 1 with UFC highlights), lay down on his bed, and reached to the small bedside table, ensuring his cell phone was charging. He stared at the television screen, his mind racing.

Maybe the most important decision in my life, and I now have less than twenty-four hours to make it. Should I marry her? Can such a marriage work? Can I ask Priya for more time? She'll understand. No, she won't. She was adamant. Should I get some guidance from someone? Maybe Chuck some more? No, we already discussed things. My parents? I don't know. This is crazy. She's Indian. I thought they had arranged marriages. I forgot to ask Priya about this. Will her parents approve of me? Did she consult with her parents?

Suddenly his iPhone buzzed. He reached over and grabbed it. It was a text from Priya.

"Gandhi, this I tell you: I will do everything within my power to be a good wife for you. I am a good cook. I don't eat beef or pork, but I can cook it—I'm sure I can. I can learn to make pizzas like Rani. I will clean our home. You don't have to do the cleaning. I will be a good mother to our children. On religion, we can both practice our traditions. I enjoy our bike rides a lot. As a married couple, we can go on bike rides together. I will support you with your house-flipping business. I am good with numbers, and I have good decorating taste. Here are a few links to some Las Cruces properties that I think have good potential." She ended with "What time tomorrow will you notify me whether I will be your wife?"

Overwhelmed, Brian mustered the following text: "I will let you know tomorrow at noon at the Starbucks next to your apartment. Best. Brian."

Fifteen seconds later, his iPhone buzzed again. Another text from Priya: "How about we make it 2:00 p.m.? I don't want too many people at Starbucks for this most important and auspicious moment. The crowd dies down after 1:00 p.m. Best. Hopefully your future wife, Priya."

Brian fell asleep after one o'clock. He dreamed of Priya, his parents, her parents, playing poker in Vegas, and riding the two-seater bicycle with Priya. For some reason, San Diego kept popping up in his dreams.

He woke up at nine the next morning. He made himself a cup of coffee in the kitchen and noticed Chuck had left a Post-it Note on the refrigerator: "Good luck today, dude. I've got a Junk King run this morning, then I'm checking out the property on S. Locust Street. Later, C."

Brian went for a six-mile jog. He then showered and ate two bagels with cream cheese. After eating, he decided to go for a walk on the NMSU campus. He drove to the campus, parked his car, and then started walking with no particular destination in mind. At one point, he stopped at the Barnes & Noble bookstore on campus and read the *New York Times*. He then ate two tacos at the food court, walked back to his car, and headed to the Starbucks.

He arrived at the Starbucks early, at 1:45 p.m., and as soon as he entered the coffee shop, he saw Priya, sitting at a corner table, next to a large window. She was wearing a blouse, rose in color, and dark blue jeans. A paper cup filled with hot tea was to her left, an untouched newspaper in front of her. She was looking down and hadn't noticed him yet.

He stood in line—three patrons were ahead of him—and when it was his turn to order, he selected a bottle of water, paid for it, and headed to Priya's table.

Priya had noticed Brian waiting in line. She placed her newspaper next to her tea, and now she placed her right hand in her right front jean pocket, crossing her fingers. She was nervous and hadn't slept well the night before. *Were my texts as to how I would be a good wife appropriate?* This morning, she had a bout with diarrhea, a further sign of just how nervous she was. She, Rani, and Deepika spent most of the morning next to the makeshift puja, praying to the gods for wishes on this most important of days.

As Brian approached her table, Priya managed a smile, and Brian said, "Hello, Priya," in a calm voice.

"Hello, Brian."

He took a seat opposite hers. He twisted the cap off his water bottle and took a sip. Then he placed his water bottle next to her teacup.

"Well, I thought this over, your proposal of marriage, and—"

"Before you begin, Brian," Priya said in a hurried, nervous tone without directly looking at him, "I want to reiterate my desires and abilities at being a good wife for you. I want to emphasize that should you answer yes to my request to be your wife, then I promise you—this I tell you—that you will not be disappointed in, as you Americans say, what I bring to the table. I am a good financial manager, which will not only be good for our family budget but also translates well for your house-flipping business. And I am—"

"Yes," Brian said, smiling.

Priya, looking slightly to the left and down at the table, continued with, "I am a hard worker. I can help you with your business affairs. As outlined in my text to you yesterday evening, I have excellent decorating tastes, so you will not have to hire a decorator. And I—"

"Yes," Brian said, louder this time.

Priya looked at him briefly and continued, "I am a good cook and can properly prepare dishes of your choosing, including meat recipes, even if I do not partake in such meat dishes. Additionally, along with—"

"Yes," Brian said, even louder this time.

But Priya, not looking at him, kept going with her sales pitch. "These skills that I have translate well to not only our family life, but to work-career goals as well. I believe I can get a part-time job at New Mexico State University, whether an administrative job or perhaps in the creative writing program. Also, if I cannot find a traditional publisher for my novel, *Money Matters,* then for a reasonable fee, I will self-publish it, and it will earn royalties, which will contribute to our finances so that—"

"Yes!" Brian exclaimed, his loud proclamation causing a Starbucks employee who was tidying up the condiment table to stop dead in her tracks. Priya, with eyes wide open, looked at Brian, and Brian, seeing that he had her attention, calmly said, "I will marry you. I want you to be my wife."

She stared at him for what seemed an eternity but was in reality five seconds. A combination of relief and energy overtook her, and she sprung up off her chair and yelled, "Yes!" causing the Starbucks employee to drop a few wooden coffee stirrers. She started clapping her hands rapidly, and she said, "He said yes. He said yes!"

With a beaming smile, she suddenly stopped clapping, and it was then she realized that in her excitement of standing up and clapping and yelling "Yes," she inadvertently had pushed against the table a bit, causing her teacup to spill.

Brian calmly said, "Let me get some napkins."

"I will get napkins with you, dear husband," Priya said, still smiling.

Brian replied, "Okay, okay, future Mrs. Robinson."

She smiled even wider, and she walked up to him. "I like the sound of that, Mrs. Robinson."

When they reached the milk, coffee stirrers, and napkin station, Brian said, "I only have one request."

"Yes, what is it, dear husband? I mean dear future husband." Her smile still beamed as she and Brian were gathering napkins.

"Can you make some pizzas for us tonight?"

"Yes, yes, but of course. Anything. Come to my apartment for dinner this evening. Say six thirty. My sisters will be excited to see you, their future brother-in-law. We'll have homemade pizzas. Chuck can come too, and Lisa as well if she's available."

Brian's drive back to his apartment took ten minutes, and during the drive, his mind was racing.

I just made the biggest decision in my life. This marriage will work. I will make it work. I am attracted to her, and she will be a good wife. I haven't told anybody about this, except Chuck. I haven't even bought a ring yet. Not exactly your traditional marriage proposal. I want her to choose her ring anyway. What will Mom and Dad think? What will they say? I think Mom will be cool with it all. I'm guessing Dad always wanted me to marry a Catholic girl. I'll call Mom and Dad tonight with the news; I have forty-two thousand dollars in the bank. Thank God for that poker score. We haven't discussed the wedding day. And will Priya be allowed to marry in the Catholic Church?

So many questions … so many unknowns. But he was happy.

CELEBRATION

Brian and the Kumar sisters (Chuck and Lisa had other plans) had a lovely dinner of pizza topped off with a dessert of mango yogurt and peanut butter cups. The upcoming wedding dominated the conversation, with a date not yet selected. "But it must be before September 30 because that's when my foreign student visa expires," Priya stressed.

After dessert, Rani, sipping a hot tea, asked, "Well, Brian, who have you informed about this most auspicious of occasions?"

"Just Chuck, about two hours ago," he said. "I plan on telling my folks this evening."

"I see," Rani said. Then she followed with, "We are planning to call our parents and our oldest sister this evening as well."

"Cool," Brian said.

"Maybe you call your parents now, Brian," Rani said.

Brian, who figured now was as good a time as any to inform his folks about his marital decision, said, "Okay, sure," and he whipped out his iPhone. He looked at Priya, and she was all smiles, relaxed, enjoying her hot tea.

After three rings, Brian's mother picked up.

"Hello, dear. How are you?" Her tone was enthusiastic.

"Fine, Mom. Everything's fine. How's Dad? And how are Curly and Fritz?"

"Oh, everyone's fine, dear. Your father had a busy day with the property management issues. He oversaw a crew installing a new roof on one of our apartment buildings today. Big job that took nearly a week. The new roof should last a long time. And Curly and Fritz are fine. They had their scheduled shots this morning. Everyone sends their hellos."

"That's great," Brian said. He cleared his throat and looked at Priya briefly. "Mom, there's something I want to share with you."

"Oh, okay. What is it, dear?"

"Me and Priya have decided to get married."

Silence on the other end for a full five seconds.

"Dear, did I hear you correctly? Did you say you're getting married?"

"Yes, Mom. You heard me right. Priya and I are getting married." He looked at Priya, who was looking at him with a beaming smile. She was clapping her hands silently, not producing noise.

"Well, this is ... how lovely. This is so exciting. Let me tell your father." She yelled, "John, Brian's getting married to one of the Indian girls."

She got back on the telephone. "Now, which one is Priya? Those sisters are all pretty. And so well mannered. They all look alike. Which one is Priya, dear?"

Brian answered, "She's the one who sat next to me during last year's Thanksgiving dinner. The writer."

"I'm not sure if I remember, dear, but this is so exciting. Even Curly and Fritz are all excited. Aren't you, Curly and Fritz? Yes you are, yes you are. So when will the wedding be, dear?"

Brian, caught off guard, said, "We don't know yet, but I'll let you know as soon as we figure a date."

"Well, this is so exciting. Here's your father."

Brian cleared his throat again. "Hello, Dad?"

"I'm listening." It was a firm voice.

"Dad, I've decided to marry Priya."

"I see," he said, firm but calm. "Have you thought this through, son? You know marriage is the most important decision you make in your life. I wouldn't be here today if it wasn't for your mother, who stuck with me through thick and thin. When we were starting out in business, we decided to forfeit having an apartment, and we lived in one of our trucks. We would shower and use the bathrooms of the nearby truck stops. Did I ever tell you that, son?"

"Yes, Dad. I know the story, and yes, I thought this through. And she's the woman for me. And she'll help me and Chuck with our house-flipping business."

"Okay," said the elder Robinson. Then he got right to the point. "Now, you guys are going to have a Catholic wedding, right? And you will have kids, and you will raise those grandkids of ours Catholic, right?"

"We've thought this over, Dad." Then he winged it. "Everything will work out. You and Mom will be happy with everything."

"Very well," Mr. Robinson said. "So when will the wedding take place?"

"We're not sure yet, Dad, but again, you and Mom will be pleased."

"Here in Albuquerque, right? At the Church of the Risen Savior. With Father O'Leary officiating."

Dad, you and Mom will be happy," Brian reiterated. "It will all work out."

"Son, have you thought of all these things? These important issues?"

"Yes, Dad. As we set the date, we will inform you and Mom of everything. It will be a nice wedding in Albuquerque."

"Very well. Okay then. Now, which of the Indian sisters are you marrying? You know you could have come to our home and introduced her to us."

"Well, we had the Thanksgiving dinner, and Priya was there with her sisters and—"

"Which one is Priya? The sisters all looked alike."

"The one who sat next to me during Thanksgiving dinner."

"I think two of the sisters sat next to you, Brian."

"Well, I'll send photos later tonight to Mom's iPhone."

"Well, okay. That's a good idea. And get with Father O'Leary with your plans."

"Yes, Dad. I will." The call ended.

"That sounded good," Rani said. "Congrats, Brian. Now we must call home to India with this most wonderful news."

"Cool," Brian said, relieved his phone call to his parents had gone as well as could be expected. He made a mental note to contact the Church of the Risen Savior Parish to discuss preparations with Father O'Leary.

"Oh, Brian," Rani said. "You like beer, correct?"

"Yes," Brian responded. "Of course. Goes well with pizza, by the way."

"Sorry we don't have beer," Priya said. "Next time, I will have beer here for my future husband."

Brian smiled at her and said, "Cool."

"Oh, Brian, why don't you go get some beer?" Rani politely suggested. "We'll call Chennai, India, and when you come back, you can talk to our parents."

"Oh, that's okay," Brian said. "I like beer, but there's no need for a beer run."

Rani shifted gears. "Dear future brother-in-law, Brian. Please go get some beer so my sisters and I can have some privacy while we discuss issues with our parents."

"Oh, okay. Got it. Privacy first. But before I do my beer run, I have one request. Let me take a photo of you all and then a photo of me with my future bride. My parents want to know which of the Kumar sisters I'm marrying."

Brian took the photos, including a selfie with Priya, and then headed out of the apartment.

"How long should my beer run last?" he asked as he opened the apartment door.

"Give us thirty minutes," Rani said. "Be here in thirty minutes. Our parents will want to speak to you."

Seconds later, Deepika made the call to Chennai, where it was already the next day, given the eleven-and-a-half-hour time difference. Her mother answered, and they spoke briefly in their native tongue, Telugu, mixed in with English. Then Deepika handed the phone to Rani, who spoke briefly with her older sister, Janni, then with her parents for fifteen minutes. All the while, Priya was nearby listening in, making out the discussions, which at times were heated. Inevitably, she would have to face the music. She had made her choices, and she was determined to be steadfast in defending them. She thought, *Walter White time. I'm doing it.* Rani handed her the phone.

"Father?"

"I'm listening," Mr. Kumar said firmly. "I'm not sure if I should be listening, but the gods know I am listening."

"Father, I have decided to extend my stay here in the United States and—"

"Yes, your sister Rani has already informed me of this new development. This extension, on the surface, does not concern me. It would be great if you were telling your mother and I and older sister that you have decided to pursue further advanced studies, like the good examples of your sisters Rani and Deepika, and pursue a doctorate degree. Instead, I hear you have somehow found it in yourself to marry an American, and I might add, without first informing your dear parents of these so-called plans."

Priya remained silent, knowing it was best not to interrupt. After a slight pause, Mr. Kumar continued. "Young lady, do you know what sacrifices your mother and I have made to support you and your sisters? Do you know why exactly it is that I no longer live and work in the United Arab Emirates and have focused the need to return to Chennai? It is because of the small apartment complex of ours here that we have saved for so long to purchase and that we also live in. It is only slightly profitable. It is what has helped put you and Rani and Deepika in graduate studies in America. Your dear sister here, Janni, may the gods protect her, works very hard in helping us with the maintenance and management of this small housing complex of ours. Your mother and I are currently looking for a good suitor to marry dear Janni, and now I hear that you have decided to get married, without our say and approval, without you having a job, and of all things, marrying a foreign man. You should follow the example of your oldest sister, Janni, and keep with our traditions."

"Father, I—"

"Silence. I am your father, who has sacrificed so much for you, and I am speaking. Your mother and I could have found a nice Indian man for you to marry, even in America. There are plenty of Hindus in America, foreign students such as you. Maybe a medical student at Harvard, or an engineer from that great American school, MIT, or Caltech of Stanford. Even a good Indian man graduating from where you and your sisters are pursuing your advanced degrees, at New Mexico State University. But an American? And who in the name of the gods made you think briefly that it was your decision as to who you would marry? How can I explain this? How is it that the first child of mine who marries—who happens to be the youngest child— decides to marry a foreigner? Can you explain this, young lady?"

"Dear father. I appreciate everything you and mother have done for me and our family. I truly do. But I have made my choice, and my future husband will be Brian Robinson. And—"

"And why is it that you think it is somehow your decision to choose who to marry? Do you not know your own culture, your own traditions? It is the parents—of both the bride and the groom—who choose the pairing. It is not a matter of your choosing. I have information that the family next door has a son studying for a PhD in computer science from Cornell University in the United States, in New York. Your mother and I have discussed this, and we think this could possibly be a good match. It is very easy for me to speak to this family and—"

"Father, I have made my choice. I have learned a lot in the last year, not only about America but about myself, and I have chosen to marry Brian Robinson."

Mr. Kumar said, "How strange it is you say you have learned about yourself. Do you not understand you have duties and obligations, duties and obligations to your family?"

"I have made my choice, dear father. I have learned a lot about freedom and free will, and I have chosen to marry Brian Robinson."

There was an awkward silence. "If your mother and I had known you would have ended up poisoned by these ideas of freedom and so-called free will, we would not have supported your studies in the United States."

"Father, I respect you and Mother of course, and our family, but I have made my choice and—"

"Doesn't duty and obligation trump this idea of free will, young lady? Think about the ramifications."

"I have given this a lot of thought, Father, and have chosen to stay here in America and marry Brian. Perhaps down the road I will pursue an advanced degree like Rani and Deepika, and Brian and I will be sure to visit you and Mother and Janni as much as possible. It is not that I am rejecting tradition. It is simply that I have made a choice."

Mr. Kumar, shaking his head, said, "In life, there are decisions that are irreversible. Marriage is one such decision. Once you make this decision, you must live with the consequences. You know the Americans have such a high divorce rate, don't you? Their movies are full of it. They don't seem to understand the concepts of duties and obligations."

There was silence, then Mr. Kumar said, "Let me speak to this Brian. Is he available on the phone?"

"Not just yet, Father, but he will be shortly." Priya and her father carried on a discussion about tradition and family, a conversation the elder Kumar dominated. Finally, Brian rang the doorbell, and Deepika got the door, reminding him to take off his shoes and briefing him about the current phone call to Chennai.

Priya handed the phone to Rani, and the conversation changed into the Telugu/English mix. Priya, with a determined demeanor, walked up to Brian and said, "Brian, my parents will now speak to you. Mostly my father, but my mother will say her greetings. Just answer my father's questions, okay?"

"Okay," Brian said as Deepika took the Corona six-pack of beer from him and headed to the kitchen. "And if you're stuck, just repeat the question so I can hear it," Priya said. "That way, I can be of assistance to you. I'll help you answer the questions."

"Okay," Brian said.

Rani, holding the phone, looked over at Brian and asked, "Ready?" Brian nodded, and she handed the receiver to him. "Say hi to my father, Brian."

Brian held the receiver and said, "Hello, Mr. Kumar. I am Brian Robinson, and I—"

"Hello, Mr. Brian" Mr. Kumar said loudly, cutting him off. "My wife will now state her greetings."

Brian heard the exchange of the phone on the other end, but he didn't hear any words. He decided to start the conversation, thinking that Mrs. Kumar was on the other end.

"Hello, Mrs. Kumar."

"Hello, Brian," he heard.

"Oh, great to hear your voice, Mrs. Kumar. How are you?"

"Hello, Brian."

"Yes, hello, Mrs. Kumar. Hello from Las Cruces, New Mexico. I am with three of your daughters. How are you?"

"Hello, Brian," she said, and then there was the exchange of the phone to Mr. Kumar.

"Hello, Mr. Brian," Mr. Kumar said. "My wife does not speak a lot of English. She knows how to say hello."

"Oh, I see, sir," Brian said.

Mr. Kumar got right to the point. "Mr. Brian, when were you born?"

Brian thought this was an odd question, but he went ahead with his answer. "Sir, I was born on April 9 in 1994."

"I see," said Mr. Kumar. "And what time of the day were you born, Mr. Brian?"

"Sir, I was born at ten in the morning." Brian's mother had told him his time of birth on a few occasions, so he knew the answer.

"I see," said Mr. Kumar, writing the information down on a small notepad. "And what is it that you do for a job, Mr. Brian?"

"Oh, well sir, for a job, I'm actually in the process of—"

"Stop," Priya said softly. She was standing four feet from him, waving her arms in a crisscross pattern to reiterate pausing the conversation for now. She whispered quickly, "Tell him you're a real estate developer. Father does not know what house flipping is."

"Sir, I am a real estate developer," Brian said into the receiver.

"I see," said Mr. Kumar. "Very good. You are a property developer. And, Mr. Brian, how much money do you make on an annual basis?"

Brian, caught off guard, repeated, "How much money do I make?"

"Yes," said Mr. Kumar.

Priya chimed in with a whisper, "Tell him you make a hundred thousand dollars per year."

"But Chuck and I haven't completed our first flip yet," Brian said quietly. "The typical flip profit is between 10 and 20 percent. It'll take us a while before we—"

"Just tell him you make a hundred thousand dollars per year, Brian."

"Uh, Mr. Kumar. I make a hundred thousand dollars a year."

"Very good," Mr. Kumar said. "This is very good."

Three hours after receiving the news that his son had planned to marry, John Robinson was kneeling before the king-size bed in the master bedroom of his home, saying his evening prayers.

Dear God and holy Mary, I thank you both for the news of our son deciding to marry. I ask and pray that you keep him and his bride safe, that they have beautiful and healthy children, and that my grandkids will be raised Catholic. I thank you also for our dear daughter, Anne-Marie. We love her and accept her as she is, and it is my prayer that though her sexuality is not in line with church teachings, perhaps this will all evolve in the future. We are all God's children. Amen.

At the same time John Robinson was on his knees praying

to his Christian God and the Virgin Mary, Govin Kumar was a world away, in a narrow city street in a commercial district two miles from his apartment complex home. A two-seat cart hooked up to and powered by a small motorcycle had taxied him to this busy district filled with heavy pedestrian traffic. Mr. Kumar paid his fare, then scanned the area. Half a dozen men, most of them older than sixty, but some being middle aged, sat on small stools, peddling their proclaimed abilities of seeing the future. Mr. Kumar was looking for one particular astrologer, Babu, an older, thin man he had encountered last year while he was on vacation, an occasion where the accountant and financial manager had asked Babu whether he should stay in Abu Dhabi or return here to Chennai for good to focus on his rented-out apartment complex.

Walking past a couple of goats and around a sitting cow, Mr. Kumar came to the middle of the street and noticed Babu sitting exactly where he had met him fourteen months earlier.

"Greetings to you, fine sir," Babu said in a kind, strong voice when he noticed Mr. Kumar approaching. Barefoot and bare chested, Babu wore a white linen garment wrapped around his waist that pulled down close to his knees. He was sipping hot tea from a large, ceramic cup, and he recognized Mr. Kumar right away. He knew to speak to the accountant in English, as Mr. Kumar was strong in English and in Telugu but only so-so in Tamil, Babu's first tongue. "I remember you, sir, from long ago. The financial manager working in the Middle East. I told you that you would return to Chennai." Babu pulled up a wooden stool for his newest customer to sit on.

"This is true," Mr. Kumar said as he sat down. He was wearing loose-fitting beige pants and a kurta, and on his feet were his well-worn brown sandals. He pushed up his thick-framed glasses on his nose as he took a seat across from Babu.

"I have returned, Mr. Babu, for yet another inquiry, another request, this one of a different sort." Mr. Kumar adjusted his seat on the soft brown earth next to the old asphalt road.

"I see," said the sixty-seven-year-old astrologer. "Is it money? I believe your apartment complex gives you headaches, but it is a good investment. Or is it your health?"

"Actually," Mr. Kumar said, "it is a family matter."

"Oh, family," Babu said. "Family, as you know, is the measure of life. Such duties. Such obligations."

"Yes, well, sir, it is one of my daughters. She has plans of marrying a Westerner. An American actually. A real estate developer in the state of New Mexico."

"I see," Babu said as he sipped some tea. "Well, my fine sir. As this is not your first reading, I shall give you a discount. Normally, such a reading is a thousand rupees, but for you, dear, fine sir, I give price discount, so it is eight hundred."

"Thank you," said Mr. Kumar, and he reached in his loose right pocket and handed Babu the money.

"For the reading of the stars, as you know, fine sir, I will need the names, date of birth, and time of birth for both persons."

"Yes, of course," Mr. Kumar said. "My daughter is Priya Kumar, and she was born on July 2 in the year 1993. She was born in the afternoon, at four thirty, in Bombay. I was working there in Mumbai at the time, as a chartered accountant."

"I see," said Babu. "And the Westerner? The American? When and at what time did he enter this earth?"

"His name is Mr. Brian Robinson. He was born on April 9 in 1994. He is one year younger than my daughter, this real estate developer. I do not know where he was born—I presume in America. But I know he was born at ten hours in the morning."

"I see," Babu said. "It is of no consequence that you do not know this American's place of birth." He looked up to the sky, then at the ground. He noticed two goats skirting away behind Mr. Kumar. "Your daughter. She is the first to marry of your children, is it not so?"

"Yes," Mr. Kumar said enthusiastically. "That is true. She is my fourth and youngest child. All daughters, my children are.

So unfortunate, as my wife and I wanted a son—keep the family name living."

Babu squinted. "That is the way of the stars, kind sir. We do not always receive what it is we want to receive. Perhaps the Buddhists are correct in believing all life is suffering, and it is we humans who are the cause of our suffering because of our desires. But not to worry. Your daughters have brought you and your wife great joy. Also great responsibility, which is only fitting, as many joys come with great responsibilities."

"I see," said Mr. Kumar.

"For some reason—unexplained, I might add—I see two weddings in the near future, so this would mean two of your four daughters will soon marry, say in about eighteen months or so. It is a bit difficult for me to decipher, if you will, which wedding is which. I of course recommend you save your money, dear sir, for you, as the honorable father, have duties and responsibilities when it comes to weddings. You need not worry, however. Your apartment complex is doing as well as to be expected. I do not sense financial hardships for you and for your family."

"Two weddings?" Mr. Kumar said, perplexed.

"Yes," Babu said. "This is what the stars tell me. And I must say, it is most difficult to decipher, to determine which is which."

There was silence, except for the occasional *beep, beep, beep* of small motorcycles and scooters passing by on the adjacent narrow street.

"Unfortunately, kind sir, given the situation, I must humbly and most respectfully request an addition to my already discounted fee. The skies are cloudy; it is more time that is necessary, and as a chartered accountant and property owner, you are most aware that time does mean an enhancement of fees. For proper service, of course."

Mr. Kumar frowned. "What is the additional fee you require?"

"Four hundred rupees. This amount, I should remind you, kind sir, will allow me proper time to read the stars."

"Very well," Mr. Kumar said, and he reached into his pocket and handed Babu the requested addition.

"Thank you most kindly," Babu said, placing the money in a small metal bowl next to his large teacup. He looked at Mr. Kumar. "Your youngest daughter, born in the afternoon of July 2 a generation ago, is a cancer of the zodiac signs. Cancer is a great sign, this I tell you. One of my favorites, quite honestly. Your daughter, as a cancer, is both charming and cunning. It is rare that cancers do not receive what it is that they seek to receive. She is a water sign, and water signs tend to like being around other water signs, the Scorpios and the Pisces." Babu looked down at the soft earth next to his bare feet. With his right hand, he brushed back the gray hair on his sides, for the center of his head was bald. Mr. Kumar, at sixty years of age, still retained some color in his thinning hair. He had a receding hairline, which meant a high forehead. With the passing morning hours and a rising sun, he and Babu were no longer covered by the shade of the street's four-story buildings. Mr. Kumar was looking at and listening to Babu attentively and adjusted his sitting posture on the small stool.

"Cancers' bright star is that of Beta Cancri," Babu said, his eyes shut, his facial look one of concentration. "Your daughter is disciplined, a bit irritable at times but disciplined. She is a thinker. These are the traits of cancers. She is slow to express affection, and she wants to make others happy. Beautiful traits, as you can see. This I tell you, fine sir, cancers are an interesting and good lot."

"But what of her plans to marry?" Mr. Kumar asked. "Is such a marriage feasible?"

"Let me see," Babu said, his eyes still closed. "I am sorry to reveal to you, dear sir, that the skies are cloudy. Quite cloudy. It is with great humbleness that I request a small enhanced fee once more to derive insights as to this most important inquiry."

"How much of an enhanced fee?" Mr. Kumar said sternly.

"Another four hundred rupees, dear sir. Most humbly."

Mr. Kumar reached into his right pocket and handed Babu another four hundred rupees.

"Thank you most kindly, dear sir. The stars are most appreciative." Babu shut his eyes. "The American, as his anniversary is April 9, he is an Aries. Not a water sign but a fire sign. This I tell you, the American has a lot of direction. He is a busy man. His property business keeps him occupied—tremendously so. His sign is very masculine, and he does not lack in self-esteem. Most Americans are not lacking in the department of self-esteem. It is their nature, rooted in their culture. But Aries have a lot of self-esteem to begin with, so this relatively young lad is quite confident. Which, by the way, as you are most aware, is an excellent trait in business, because money can be made and, conversely, also lost in business affairs. Markets, and with them prices, go up and down. It is not every individual who can stomach such price fluctuations. But this young man—like you, kind sir, in your current years—is quite comfortable working for himself, and he has the ability to take chances, to take risks."

"The American told me he makes one hundred thousand dollars annually," Mr. Kumar said. "At least I have the comfort of knowing that he can take care of my daughter and future grandchildren."

"Your daughter and the American are not the most compatible, but it is, nevertheless, a union that will work. I see the marriage taking place and—"

"Yes, but the Americans have such a high divorce rate," Mr. Kumar said. "They have no quarrels with letting things go. Look at their president—his third marriage. Failed businesses. It seems every month or so he is firing someone. Is it not true Americans have no concept of duties and obligations? My daughter marrying a Westerner concerns me."

"The stars understand your concerns, my dear sir," Babu said, his brown eyes open and fixated on his client. "Not to worry, however. The marriage will last. Your daughter is adaptable. This

I tell you, your daughter's discipline and selflessness coupled with the American's ambition and direction make for a productive union."

"Thank you," Mr. Kumar said, smiling. He stood up and repeated, "Thank you." He turned and began walking down the narrow street, ready to flag a small motorcycle-cart taxi.

Babu took a sip of tea and then said, "My pleasure, dear sir. And remember, the stars informed me of two marriages in the near future. Save your money, sir, for this I tell you: it is not one but two marriage celebrations that await you in the not-so-distant future."

The three-and-a-half-hour drive from Las Cruces to Albuquerque seemed to have taken half that time, at least from Brian's point of view. Driving the old hand-me-down pickup truck with his fiancée in the front passenger seat, the soon-to-be newlyweds were to meet with Father James O'Leary, a semiretired Catholic priest who had baptized Brian twenty-five years earlier in Albuquerque. The meeting, arranged by Brian's father, was to inform the young couple about the requirements of getting married according to the Catholic faith.

What helped make the time fly by was the wonderful phone call that came around the halfway mark of the northern trek, a phone call from Brian's dad, John Robinson, the self-made multimillionaire. He said, "Your mother and I have decided to pay for your wedding, son. That's the tradition, and we're going to follow it."

Brian, actually not expecting such news, had placed the call on speakerphone and proclaimed, "Wow, thanks so much, Dad."

Priya had added, "Yes, thank you, Mr. and Mrs. Robinson, for the—"

Before she could express her excitement and gratitude, the elder Robinson revealed an even greater development: "And,

Priya, my soon-to-be daughter-in-law, my wife and I will pay for your parents and sister who are back in India to attend your wedding here in the States."

Mrs. Robinson added, "That's only fair, dear. The more, the merrier."

And as if the awesome news couldn't be topped, Mr. Robinson announced another freebie: "And, Brian and Priya, my wife and I have always wanted to visit India. Given that you will be having a Catholic wedding here in the States, it is only fitting that Priya have a wedding of her faith, of her culture. So Mrs. Robinson and I insist you have a second wedding, in India. We will travel there, and we will pay for everything."

Brian and Priya were utterly speechless, and before they could get a word in to thank the Robinsons for their incredible generosity, Mrs. Robinson said, "It'll sure beat my wedding. Do you know your father and I drove to our wedding in one of our two trucks? We were starting our business, and we were so strapped for cash. No honeymoon, no big wedding. We had family and friends attend of course, and Father Morales spoke so well at the wedding Mass, but we sure were low budget out of necessity. Dinner was in a separate room at the Howard Johnson."

What a development—not just one wedding but now two weddings, and one of them overseas, a world away. For Brian, the drive to Albuquerque filled him with thoughts of just how fast things were moving. It was just a year ago that he had met Priya in the Independent Study class, and he had changed his paper topic from writing about Afghanistan to writing about India to impress her. Now they were getting married, and his parents were footing the bill, both here in the States and across the globe in Chennai, India. For Priya, her feelings were of joy and excitement, especially about the phone call she would make that night to inform her parents of Mr. and Mrs. Robinson's generosity.

During the ride up to Albuquerque, Priya sent a quick text

to Rani to inform her of the wonderful news, news so wonderful that Rani had texted back "Fabulous! The gods are with you. We will call Father and Mother this evening together."

Also during the northward ride, Priya had said, "On the topic of religion, Brian, do you think Father O'Leary will allow me, a Hindu, to marry you? I mean, will I have to convert to Christianity to marry you?"

Brian, behind the wheel, answered, "A fair question, and I honestly don't know, Priya. But what I do know is Father O'Leary is a very nice man, respectful of everyone and very approachable. I'm glad Dad set up the meeting with him."

"I must inform you, Brian," Priya said politely. "My studies here in America lead me to the conclusion that Christianity is quite strict and also narrow. Has it ever occurred to you that one can have multiple views on religion at the same time? The Eastern religions are more about one finding his or her way, his or her path to purpose and duty. But Christianity is about the need to so-called be saved. There seems to be a need to save non-Christians by converting them. You don't think I'll have to convert, do you? Father and Mother would have a problem with that."

"I don't know, Priya," Brian reiterated. "I don't know."

Father O'Leary greeted Brian and Priya with a warm smile when they rang the doorbell of the rectory of the Church of the Risen Savior.

"Come in, come in please. Such a nice beautiful Sunday, isn't it?"

"Yes, Father," Brian replied as he led Priya inside.

"You must be the wonderful Priya," Father O'Leary said as he shook hands with her. "Please come in. You can keep your shoes on. We'll meet in my office."

Father O'Leary led the young couple through a narrow

hallway. He entered his office and said, "Please have a seat and make yourselves comfortable."

Dressed in the traditional black pants, black, long-sleeved shirt, and white collar, Father O'Leary was seventy-four years old. Sitting behind his massive oak desk, he was surrounded by floor-to-ceiling wooden bookshelves, filled to the tilt with books on religion, history, languages, and philosophy. Priya was impressed by this medium-size wood-paneled office with photos of various popes and other religious figures, including Mother Teresa, who she recognized right away, given the saint had made her mark in Priya's native India. *And what is that great smell in this office? Certainly incense,* Priya thought, but there was another fragrance that was pleasing, a fragrance she wasn't familiar with. She leaned in to Brian's left ear and inquired about it, to which he whispered, "That smell is the combination of incense, the cedar wood paneling, and Father O'Leary's pipe tobacco, cherry flavor."

Originally from Boston, O'Leary was the first of four children of a bricklayer and a homemaker. When his grandfather arrived in the eastern port city in 1901, straight from Ireland, he was welcomed to the New World of America by the popular, ubiquitous signs of "NINA" posted in so many windows, its message of No Irish Need Apply loud and clear. Only "their own people" in the form of previous and settled Irish immigrants—and the Catholic Church—welcomed the nineteen-year-old Connor O'Leary. Soon after his arrival, a distant cousin found him work in the docks, and in a couple of years, Connor would wed one Ava Murphy, the daughter of a Boston police officer. Together they would raise six children, with Joseph, Father O'Leary's father, being the second child and second oldest son.

Bookish from a young age, James O'Leary heard the calling to become a Catholic priest at the tender age of fifteen. He attended Boston College and then seminary studies at Notre Dame. After a brief stint as a Catholic priest in Portland, Maine, Father O'Leary pursued further religious studies at Georgetown

University, earning his doctorate there. He then embarked on a largely academic career that took him to Catholic University in our nation's capital, the University of Saint Mary of the Lake in Mundelein, Illinois, Saint Charles Borromeo Seminary in Wynnewood, Pennsylvania, Peru, Brazil, the Philippines, a brief stint at the Vatican, and five years in Albuquerque, where he baptized Brian and thousands of newcomers to the church. Then came a long stint at the Athenaeum of Ohio in Cincinnati. Two years ago, Father O'Leary, in semiretirement, decided to settle in Santa Fe (he was a fan of the Southwest and its dry weather and split his time administrating the sacraments in parishes in Santa Fe and Albuquerque).

"Well, it's so nice to see you, Brian. I remember your baptism vividly," the Catholic priest said as he settled in his chair. "It was two weeks after your birth. Late April. A warm, cloudy day with spring showers. Delightful. So nice to know you're doing well and just completed your studies."

"Thank you, Father," Brian replied, thinking, *Father O'Leary looks the same, just more white hair now. He still looks like Phil Donahue, glasses and all.*

"And dear Priya. So well named. As you probably know, child, your name means *nice and beloved*. How fitting."

Priya, impressed, said, "Thank you, sir."

"Mr. Robinson informed me you are originally from Chennai. How interesting. Formerly Madras."

"Yes, sir, that is correct."

"Madras," Father O'Leary repeated. "There are reports the Italian explorer Marco Polo visited Madras on a return trip, but scholars still debate this. The Portuguese, however, certainly settled there for some time, erecting a lovely chapel in honor of Saint Thomas. So fitting for one of the great disciples and saints. I think we all have a little of Doubting Thomas in us, but seeing is believing, and faith itself is believing. I must tell you, dear Priya, the church in Madras as the resting place of Saint Thomas is one of the places on my bucket list. Given my advancing age, I should get going on my desires, don't you think?"

Brian said, "You have nice travel plans, Father."

"Yes, I've been quite fortunate with the traveling, both here in the States and globally. It's a small world but yet also a large world. Our heavenly Father has given us so much."

Father O'Leary quickly adjusted his gray swivel chair and asked, "Can I get you both something to drink? Water? Coffee? Tea? Priya, I know you must love tea, as all Indians seem to be tea drinkers. Such a great drink, tea is. I believe even more popular than coffee, although Starbucks in China may change that."

"I'm fine, Father," Brian said. "We drank water and tea during the drive here from Las Cruces." Priya simply nodded her head approvingly.

"Very well then," Father O'Leary said. "Well, I must say, Priya, not only is the resting place of Saint Thomas on my bucket list, but so is the Taj Mahal. What an architectural marvel that is. And Delhi, site of Saint Teresa, Mother Teresa, and her devoted works. Your country is quite fascinating, I must say. I'm also a fan of the great book, the Bhagavad Gita."

Priya's eyes lit up, and she smiled broadly.

"A great book indeed," Father O'Leary said. "So profound. Truth is eternal. The soul is eternal. These are such great beliefs. It confirms my experiences of studying and living abroad: there is so much we as a people have in common with other peoples. We are all part of the human race. Interfaith cooperation and understanding is a big interest of mine. There is a lot of work to be done, but we have come a long way.

"Well, on the subject of interfaith cooperation and understanding, I am looking at such a beautiful example of it right before my eyes. How lovely. On the issue of the church and its teachings, the church recognizes baptized Catholics sometimes feeling the call to marry someone outside the faith. The church does not require the non-Catholic to convert to Catholicism, but we do require that any child of the marriage be raised Catholic and eventually baptized Catholic. Any questions for me? And, importantly, are you both comfortable with these requirements?"

"Yes, Father, we are," Brian said.

Priya followed with "Yes, sir." The two had actually discussed the very topic during the ride to Albuquerque, and Priya made it clear any children of theirs would be raised and familiar with the two religious traditions of their parents; she saw nothing wrong or even unique with exposing or raising a child with two faiths.

"So you both agree to these requirements?"

"Yes we do, Father," Brian said.

"Very well," Father O'Leary said. "Now, Mr. Robinson informed me that you both desire the sacrament of holy matrimony prior to the end of this month, given your visa status, Priya."

"That is correct," Brian said.

Priya followed with "Yes, sir."

"Oh, the issue of church and state—they pop up on us from time to time, don't they? Such is the country we live in and the rules we play by. As our Lord so poignantly said, 'Grant to Caesar what is Caesar's, and grant to the Father what is the Father's.' Very well. Let me look at my calendar."

Brian, seeing Father O'Leary looking down at a large desk calendar, said, "We believe it is you who will be officiating and giving us the sacrament of marriage, Father."

"Yes, of course, Brian. Indeed. Your father insisted on such. He has already made a customary donation, and he has paid for one of our great talented organists, Paula Cantu." He looked at his calendar. "How does Saturday, September 28, sound? You can get a marriage license at the county office that is good for a month, which means your wedding must take place within thirty days. We sign the back side of the marriage license—which is the marriage certificate—at the wedding ceremony."

Like most premarital Indian women, Priya was a virgin. When she was thirteen, she was playing marbles with boys and girls of a similar age in one of the narrow alleyways behind the apartment complex where she and her family lived, the apartment complex her father, many years later, would purchase. When the marble game wrapped up shortly before dusk, she found herself alone with a twelve-year-old boy named Vijay, a boy of a lower caste, the Vaishyas (the Kumars were members of Hinduism's second of four castes, the Kshatriyas). The two were picking up marbles in a small crack in the soft earth next to some old, crumpled asphalt. The two reached for the same marble, and Priya, uncharacteristically, grabbed Vijay's left hand and placed it on her right breast. The shorter boy, stunned, turned to her in bewilderment, and she looked at him seriously and leaned toward his face. Their lips met for maybe five seconds. Then Priya pulled back but kept his hand on her breast. She leaned in again, and the second kiss—which she preferred—lasted twice as long. That was the extent of Priya's sexual experience: a few polite hugs from colleagues and friends during her college years, and the touch and kiss of the young Vijay.

That all changed on the weekend of September 7 and 8, for Brian, exhausted with the necessities of planning a wedding (tuxedo rentals, reserving a ballroom at the Albuquerque Hyatt, booking a DJ, selecting a photographer/videographer, reserving a limo, and selecting a cake with Priya), had the need for a well-deserved weekend getaway. For Brian, that meant three nights in his favorite city, San Diego. It was Brian who had chosen the destination, and the couple started their drive early Friday morning, both of them enjoying the wide-open spaces of New Mexico and Arizona. Ten hours later, they reached the Southern California city and the Coronado Hotel. That evening, with the bright sun still out and the temperatures in the low seventies, the couple took a stroll on the gorgeous beach, and it was then that Brian knelt down on one knee, pulled out a $2,700 ring he and

Priya had selected five days earlier at Costco, and said, "Priya, will you marry me?"

"Why, of course I will marry you," Priya said, smiling. "We have already decided this. But thank you. Thank you, dear husband, my dear future husband. This is so beautiful."

Brian placed the ring on her ring finger, and she stared at the jewelry piece. They hugged, and then they kissed.

Later that evening, they ate at an Indian restaurant in the Gaslamp District. Saturday was a fun-filled day at the zoo (Priya's favorite was the pair of huge polar bears in the small pool, playfully wrestling with each other), some shopping, including snacks for when her parents and sisters would arrive in the States, browsing through bookstores, and dinner once again in the Gaslamp District. Sunday was a repeat of Saturday, except Brian bought a large photo book of India as a gift for Father O'Leary, and the young couple took a nighttime stroll on the beach of Coronado Island.

Brian and Priya made love every night during their San Diego weekend, and during Monday's pleasant and conversation-filled ten-hour ride back to Las Cruces, Priya periodically thought, *I thank the gods for the beautiful city of San Diego and for Brian. I just had the best weekend of my life.*

Torino's at Home, an Albuquerque favorite and an Italian restaurant featured on Guy Fieri's popular *Diners, Drive-Ins and Dives* TV show, was the site of the rehearsal dinner on Friday, September 27. So much had happened in the three weeks since the lovely sojourn in San Diego: selecting a photographer, videographer, and DJ; ordering and sending out the invitation cards; renting a limo; renting tuxedos for the men in the wedding party and dresses for the ladies; paying for a five-layer chocolate cake with white frosting and four thin layers of raspberries, all baked to perfection by one Diane Hopkinson, a master baker originally from Liverpool but now making her home in Albuquerque; paying for flower arrangements; reserving the reception hall in the downtown Hyatt, Albuquerque's tallest building; and selecting a caterer. Priya and Brian decided to go with the Italian buffet selections from the Hyatt, coupled with Indian dishes from the local Curry Leaf restaurant. What Brian was most proud of pulling off in the incredible time crunch of twenty-one days was obtaining travel visas for the visiting Kumars. As for Priya's student visa, Carlos Guzman, the young couple's trusted immigration lawyer, assured the soon-to-be newlyweds that Priya's immigration status, now based on marriage, would be immediately filed, and a new government immigration clock would be reset and start ticking anew.

After the salads, bread, pastas, and individual orders came the amaretto Rosati, the tiramisu, the cannoli, and gelato, topped off by hot tea, cappuccinos, and more wine for the Robinsons. Everyone was in a relaxed and festive mood, except for Mrs. Kumar, who was enjoying her delicious cannoli all while attentively keeping a watchful eye on the Robinsons' two small dogs, Curly and Fritz (the co-owner of Torino's at Home was French and allowed dogs in his popular restaurant).

Chuck, unsurprisingly chosen as Brian's best man, was sitting to the left of Mr. Robinson, who had footed the bill for everything thus far, including visas, tuxedos, and dresses. (Brian had paid Mr. Guzman $3,000 up front and would owe the lawyer another three thousand on Monday once the final immigration packet—including a signed marriage certificate—was filed.) Nursing a Peroni beer and talking house flipping with Mr. Robinson, Chuck suddenly gave a short nod to the elder Robinson and started clinking a nearby wineglass with a dessert spoon.

"Speech, speech!" he said loudly, for all to hear, and within seconds, the sounds of clinking glasses and "Speech, speech!" were repeated.

Mr. Robinson wore beige khakis, a long-sleeve white shirt

with open collar, a blue blazer, and loafers. He was all smiles as he said, "I want to thank everyone for coming tonight. Sandra and I are so happy for our son, Brian, and soon-to-be daughter-in-law, Priya. We can't wait for tomorrow, and we are so anxious to continue the celebration in India next week. We are also extremely happy the entire Kumar family could make it. With that, I propose a toast. To Priya and Brian." He raised his wineglass. "May they find joy and happiness in their lives together and forever."

There were a few "yeahs" and much clapping, and everyone raised a wineglass, including the Kumars (theirs were quickly filled with water by Rani right before the toast).

Mr. Robinson, beaming with smiles and full of pride, sat down in his seat at the head of the combined tables, and it was then that Rani, sitting next to her dad, said, "Father, it is now your turn to give a short speech." She started clinking her dessert spoon against her water-filled wineglass to kick things off.

Mr. Kumar, sixty and standing just five feet, five inches in height, was bald with thin black hair on the sides that showed just an inkling of the graying process. He stood up.

"I want to thank all of you, particularly the Robinson family, for your kindness and generosity and for joining us in the celebration of our youngest daughter, Priya, getting married to Mr. Brian." Wearing a Western three-piece gray suit, Mr. Kumar spoke in a loud and confident voice. English was his strongest language, having attended a Jesuit university in Chennai as a young man. "My wife and I and our oldest daughter, Janni, want to thank you for being such great hosts during our short stay here in America. And yes, we are quite impressed with Costco and its wide aisles and floor-to-ceiling shelves stuffed with great products. And yes, we are devoted fans to the wonderful peanut butter cups. Delicious indeed." His last comment drew loud and long laughs.

Chuck, working on his fourth Peroni beer, said during the laughter, "That's awesome, Mr. K. You rock, man."

Mr. Kumar smiled. "My wife and I did not think it would be our youngest daughter who would marry first, but such is the way of the gods and the stars. To echo the fine previous speaker, may Mr. Brian and our daughter find prosperity and happiness, and may they be faithful to their duties and obligations. Thank you."

"Yeahs" and clapping ensued, and as Mr. Kumar was sitting down, Rani said, "That was most excellent, Father. Well done. But as the Robinsons have been so generous to pay for the round-trip airfare and hotel, I think it would only be fair that we pay for this rehearsal dinner."

Mr. Kumar nodded in approval. He immediately stood up, and Chuck and Uncle Ron, with their alcoholic buzzes, said in unison, "Encore! Encore!" Rani again tapped her dessert spoon to her wineglass, and the other guests did the same.

"I have another announcement," Mr. Kumar said proudly. "Let it be known, this I tell you, that it is only fair that I, as the father of the bride-to-be, am paying for this fine dinner this evening. If it has already been paid for, then I will reimburse the Robinsons for this fine meal. Thank you once again."

Mr. Kumar, as rehearsed yesterday, was escorting Priya up the center aisle. Rani, as the maid of honor, was to the left of Brian and Chuck, some ten feet to their left, dressed in a beautiful, long mauve dress rented from David's Bridal. In the pews to the right of Priya were guests of the Robinsons, and in the pews to the left was the Kumar party. In total, the Saturday-morning crowd at the Church of the Risen Savior numbered thirty-six. Ms. Cantu, behind the organ, was playing the traditional wedding entrance piece, Wagner's "Bridal Chorus," commonly known as "Here Comes the Bride." And Father O'Leary, smiling, stood in between Brian and Rani, directly facing the incoming bride.

Priya, with a thin veil covering her face, had her right arm in her father's left. The father-daughter duo slowly came up the church's widest aisle—the center aisle—their steps coordinated and in unison. Mr. Kumar, dressed in a navy blue suit with a fresh white carnation corsage on his lapel, walked erect and radiated pride. When he and Priya arrived at the end of the aisle, he stood next to Brian. He did not speak or hug his youngest daughter, but as rehearsed, he oversaw the exchange of her right arm in his left to Brian's left arm. "You now have duties and obligations," Mr. Kumar said during the exchange to Brian. He turned and sat down in the front left pew next to his wife, who was dressed in a beautiful green sari.

"We are gathered here today to witness the uniting of Priya Kumar and Brian Robinson," Father O'Leary said without the aid of a microphone. "Let us pray and ask that God bless them on this most important occasion."

Father O'Leary then turned and walked up the few steps to the altar and sat at the head chair behind it.

Ann-Marie, Brian's sister, dressed in a beautiful, light red dress with white trim, walked up to the podium to the right of the altar. She adjusted the microphone. "Today's reading is from 1 Corinthians 13." She read the following:

> If I speak in the tongue of men and angels, but have not love, I am only a resounding gong or a clanging cymbal. If I have the gift of prophecy and can fathom all mysteries and all knowledge, and if I have a faith that can move mountains, but have not love, I am nothing. If I give all I possess to the poor, and surrender my body to the flame, but have not love, I again have nothing. Love is patient, love is kind. It does not envy, it does not boast, it is not proud. It is not rude, it is not self-seeking, it is not easily angered, it keeps no record of wrongs. Love does not delight in evil, but rejoices with the truth. It always protects,

always trusts, always hopes, always perseveres. Love never fails. But where there are prophecies, they will cease; where there are tongues, they will be stilted; where there is knowledge, it will pass away. For we know in part and we prophecy in part, but when perfection comes, the imperfect disappears. When I was a child, I thought like a child, I reasoned like a child. When I became a man, I put childish ways behind me. Now we see but a poor reflection as in a mirror; then we shall see face-to-face. Now I know in part; then I shall know fully, even as I am fully known. And now these three remain: faith, hope and love. But the greatest of these is love.

Ann-Marie stepped down from the podium and returned to her front pew seat. Father O'Leary stood up and walked down the steps to stand next to Priya and Brian, who were off to the left, in their chairs. Chuck was to the right of Brian in his chair, and Rani was to the left of Priya, in her chair. Father O'Leary spoke about the reading, incorporating the theme of "love is patient, love is kind, love does not keep score," in his brief, five-minute wedding sermon. At the end of his remarks, he asked the official party to stand for the exchange of vows. Brian went first, his right hand holding Priya's left. He turned slightly to the left and faced Priya.

"I, Brian, take you, Priya, to be my wife. I promise to be true to you in good times and in bad, in sickness and in health. I will honor you and love you all the days of my life."

Priya, smiling through her thin veil, looked at Brian and said, "I, Priya, take you, Brian, to be my husband. I promise to be true to you in good times and in bad, in sickness and in health. I will honor you and love you all the days of my life."

The couple turned slightly to face Father O'Leary, who then asked, "And how do you wish to express your bond of marriage?"

"With rings," Priya and Brian said in unison, and Chuck reached in his right front pocket and handed Priya's ring to Brian.

Brian said, "Priya, take this ring as a sign of my love," and he proceeded to look at her directly and place the ring on her ring finger.

Seconds later, Rani, standing to the left of Priya, handed Priya Brian's ring. Priya took the ring and said, "Brian, take this ring as a sign of my love," and she proceeded to guide the ring around Brian's ring finger.

The couple then faced Father O'Leary, who then said softly while looking at Brian, "You may now kiss the bride."

Brian, gently lifting Priya's veil, kissed his bride. The newlyweds then turned and faced the guests. Father O'Leary proclaimed, "Ladies and gentlemen, I present to you Mr. and Mrs. Brian Robinson." The guests clapped and smiled.

Photos, photos, and more photos followed the wedding, all care of José Calderon, a well-known Albuquerque photographer. Numerous photos of the couple, both inside and outside the church, were taken. Then it was photos of the couple with the maid of honor and best man, followed by photos of the newlyweds with the Robinson family, then photos of the couple with the Kumar family. The videographer, Roger Phillips, stayed around to ply his trade, but he left after twenty minutes of filming because he needed time to set up at the Hyatt reception hall.

The downtown Hyatt is Albuquerque's tallest building, and on its fifth floor is where Mr. Robinson reserved a ballroom for his son's wedding. Two caterers split the buffet lunch duties—Torino's at Home (Mr. Robinson got a 30 percent discount for using the restaurant for both the rehearsal and reception) and Curry Leaf, an Indian favorite. When the head party—Priya, Brian, Rani, and Chuck—arrived at the ballroom at twelve thirty in the afternoon,

DJ John, behind the microphone, announced the grand entrance of the young couple to the applause of the enthusiastic guests.

Priya, Brian, Rani, and Chuck sat at the head table, the center of which was occupied by a five-layer chocolate cake covered with white frosting. Priya and Brian led the buffet line soon after sitting at the head table, and toward the tail end of lunch, Chuck rose and gave his spiel about his best friend and business partner. The funniest part of his remarks was retelling the story of how Priya once received a flyer in the mail notifying her she had won a brand-new car. The story drew long laughs and cheers. In proper form, Chuck ended his remarks by raising his champagne glass and saying, "To Priya and Brian. May they live happily ever after." He took a long gulp of champagne, then added, "Now let's enjoy ourselves today and then continue this party in Chennai, India, in a couple of days."

A break in the dancing came in the form of the traditional cutting of the cake. Brian and Priya, holding the cake knife together, sliced two small pieces from the cake's small fifth layer, and then Brian gently stuffed the piece he was holding into his bride's mouth at the same time Priya was placing her piece in her husband's mouth. More dancing followed the traditional cake cutting, and a good time was had by all. Ron, with plenty of alcohol in his tank, struck up some interesting conversations with Janni, and the two danced a couple of dances. Rani and Deepika also danced but only with Brian and only a few times. Mr. and Mrs. Kumar did not dance. They were unfamiliar with Western dancing and Western music, but they enjoyed the food and observing the people at an American wedding. And while enjoying the festivities, Mrs. Kumar was sure to keep a watchful eye on Curly and Fritz, who divided their time between Mrs. Robinson and Anne-Marie. Fearful of dogs, Mrs. Kumar was taken aback at how such animals could be allowed inside such a nice building.

At 3:30 p.m., Anne-Marie stood up and said, "Mom, I need to go to the ladies' room. You got Curly and Fritz, right?"

"Sure, honey," her mother said.

Then Sheila got up and said, "I'll join you, as I gotta go too."

The couple held hands and headed to the restroom section of the reception ballroom. In no time, they were outside the ladies' room door, directly across from the men's room, and Mr. Kumar suddenly popped out from the men's room.

"Oh, hello, Mr. Kumar," Anne-Marie said, smiling. She and Sheila, who was also smiling, were still holding hands. "We haven't met formally, but I am Brian's sister, Anne-Marie. And this is my partner, Sheila."

"Please to meet both of you," said Mr. Kumar. They all shook hands. "You are partners. This is interesting. What business are you in? I happen to be in a similar business as your father—real estate. You are in real estate?"

Anne-Marie and Sheila both looked at each other, smiling.

"No, sir, we are not in the real estate business," Anne-Marie said, still smiling. "We are partners." She looked at Sheila. "Committed partners."

Mr. Kumar frowned, confused. "I see. Well, I wish you both much luck in your partnership," and he turned and headed to the reception hall.

In the late-afternoon hours, with the crowd fading and the Hyatt cleanup crew doing their thing, Brian walked over to Chuck, who was sitting on a chair next to the DJ table where the sound equipment was being packed. Both had their tuxedo coats off, their bow ties and collars loosened, and both were nursing Peroni beers.

"Congrats, stud," Chuck said as Brian pulled a chair next to his best man. "You did it. Tying the knot, man. Cool shit. Well done."

"Thanks, man." They both touched bottles, and then Chuck shifted gears.

"Listen, Brian. I might as well let you know now. There's a bit of a change of plans."

"Oh?" Brian said inquisitively. "What's up?"

"It's Lisa. We're in that on-again, off-again stage, and it's currently in the off-again department. Bottom line is she informed me today that she's not making the trip to India for the wedding there. Says she needs to think things over and that she needs her space. Go figure, man."

"Sorry to hear that, Chuck."

"Hell, maybe it's for the better."

There was a pause.

"Hey, but I'm still going. I wouldn't miss this trip and the wedding for the world."

"Thanks, Chuck."

"Yeah. Oh, and that reminds me. There's something else I gotta tell you."

"What's that?"

"Well, with you and Priya hooking up, you'll need the apartment. I'll move out and get my own digs."

"You sure?"

"Yeah, of course."

"Game plan was to move in with Lisa, but now that she's not going to India, things are all up in the air. Anyway, this might be a good thing. I want my space too. About time I get my own place."

"You sure?"

"Absolutely."

After an awkward pause, Chuck said, "Hey, by the way, that run-down bungalow outside the campus is still on the market. I spoke to your dad about it today. Lots of potential for our first flip. Going for forty K. We have what—something like seventy thousand dollars saved up. Twelve thousand is all we need to fix it up."

Chennai, India, is 9,300 miles from Albuquerque, New Mexico—that's if one is traveling the Pacific route. Over the Atlantic Ocean, the distance is a couple hundred miles short of eleven thousand. It was Mr. Robinson who was paying for the airfare of ten people—he and his wife, the newlywed couple, Anne-Marie and her partner, Sheila, brother Ron, the best man, Chuck, and two of the Kumar sisters, Rani and Deepika. Mr. and Mrs. Kumar insisted on paying their own fair, plus the fair of their oldest daughter, Janni.

Though the Atlantic passage adds 1,500 miles to the trek, the wind currents are favorable, so the trip takes about the same amount of time and, importantly, comes at a discounted fare, a savings of close to $200 per person, so it was a no-brainer the trek would be over the Atlantic, Europe, and the Middle East, specifically Albuquerque to Dulles Airport outside the US capital, Dulles to Heathrow Airport in London, then a straight shot from London to Chennai. Total airfare for the ten passengers: $27,500, round trip of course. The inclusion of Curly and Fritz normally came with a pet fee, but British Airways politely removed the charge, "given the number of fliers in your party." Departure time from Albuquerque was three in the afternoon on Tuesday, October 1, three days after Saturday's wedding. Estimated travel time was twenty-six hours.

Prior to the flight out, Priya so desperately wanted to show San Diego to her parents and her sisters, but there was no time. Instead, her days were spent receiving and organizing her bridal shower gifts from Macy's (her favorites were the rice cooker and set of Emeril Lagasse steak knives from Dr. Patel and his wife, neighbors of the Robinsons who had attended Saturday's wedding). When she had a bit of spare time, she drove her family to Santa Fe to do some sightseeing and to the Inn of the Mountain Gods Casino on the Apache reservation in Mescalero, New Mexico.

Mr. and Mrs. Kumar, Janni, and the Robinson party arrived at Chennai Airport in the early morning hours of Thursday, October 3. Upon his arrival, Mr. Robinson remarked to his wife, "This is a nice airport. Nice tile work, hey, honey? And lots of carvings too."

"Yes," she replied. "Very nice indeed."

The Robinsons walked through two hallways, and Priya explained that the intricately carved wooden statues on display were Ganeshas and Buddhas.

"Say, that's an elephant, right? That one," Mr. Robinson said, pointing. "But it's sitting Indian style, with two legs."

"Yes, that is correct," Priya said, hauling her luggage like the others. "God Ganesha has an elephant head on a human body. He is the master of intellect and wisdom."

"And he has forearms?" Mr. Robinson politely asked.

"That is correct, sir."

"You can call me John, Priya."

"Yes, John."

"And Buddha?" Mr. Robinson asked. "I thought India was a Hindu country."

"Buddhists are a small minority in India," Priya said. "Buddha was actually a Hindu. He was known as Siddhartha Gautama, a Hindu who was critical of the caste system, so he started a new way of thinking."

"Oh, I see," Mr. Robertson said.

His wife added, "That's a nice story."

The group continued to walk through the quiet airport until they came to the customs section, where a short line of patrons had formed.

"Honey, it's kind of stuffy in here, and Curly and Fritz must be in need of a stretch. I'm going to feed them while we wait in line."

"Sounds like a plan, Sandra."

Mrs. Robinson bent down and guided Curly and Fritz out of their dog carriers. She reached into her large purse and pulled out two dog treats. "Good dog, Curly. Good dog, Fritz. Here you go." The two dogs started wagging their tails as they enjoyed their snacks.

Priya suddenly said, "For us Indian citizens—my sisters and I— the line is over there," and she pointed to the right. "My sisters and I will go through that process. Then we will wait for you at the baggage claim. My parents and Janni will take a taxi to our home."

"Sounds like a plan, Priya," Mr. Robinson said. "The line here isn't too long. We'll see you all in a bit. I'm guessing twenty minutes or so."

Two hours later, the Robinson party finally hooked up with the Kumar sisters at the baggage claim. They were all sweaty and red-faced.

"God, Priya. Does the air-conditioning work in this airport?" Mrs. Robinson asked, wiping sweat off her brow. "We need water, not only for us but also for Curly and Fritz."

"Most sincere apologies, Mrs. Robinson, but—"

"You can call me Sandra, dear. Customs took so long. There was some hand scanner machine, but it broke down, so the customs officials started writing things down on paper. But then they ran out of paper and—"

"Apologies, Ms. Sandra. My sisters and I inquired about the lack of air-conditioning. The system broke down unfortunately. But we have a trolley for all your luggage."

Just then, Brian arrived with six bottles of water.

"Finally found some water bottles for sale. Here you go, guys."

"Thank you, dear," Mrs. Robinson said as she took a bottle. "Curly and Fritz are dying of thirst. I can tell."

Mr. Robinson took a bottle of water from his son. As he opened the bottle, he asked, "Say, can we change some money here?"

Priya said, "The money exchange is right around the corner. Let me take you there."

An hour and a half later, the Robinson party, with their luggage in tow, met up with the Kumar sisters outside the money exchange.

"Finally got that done," Mr. Robertson said. "More hiccups. Their machine broke down. Then there was tons of paperwork to fill out. I just wanted to convert five thousand US dollars to rupees. Do you know the exchange rate here is sixty-six rupees to the dollar? That's three hundred thirty thousand rupees. All on credit cards now, with fifty thousand rupees per card. That's six credit cards, with the rest in paper money."

"Very well," Priya said. "And sorry the money exchange took so long." She shifted gears. "It is this way to the taxis. My sisters and I will take a separate taxi to my parents' home. I believe two taxis will be sufficient to bring all of you to the hotel. We will meet you tonight at the hotel."

"Sounds like a plan," Mr. Robertson said.

Ten minutes later, John and his brother, Ron, were helping one of the taxi drivers, a middle-aged man named Devesh, place the luggage items in the trunk of the old taxi. John didn't recognize the model of this car, but all he could think of was some of the photos he had seen about Havana, Cuba. Cars like that—1950's America. Brian, Ann-Marie, and Sheila were in the other parked taxi behind them, all set to go in an old Volkswagen. Priya, Rani, and Deepika had taken a taxi to their parents' home five minutes ago.

Ron got into the back seat of the cab between Sandra and the dog carriers. It was hot and sunny out but cooler than the inside of the airport. John headed to the front passenger seat.

"Oh, dear sir," Devesh said. "The other seat is for you. I am your driver."

John, who had just opened the door, realized his mistake. "Sorry, Devesh, buddy," he said. "Not used to the driver on the front right side. In America, the driver position is in the front left seat."

John kept the door open for Devesh, and he walked around the front of the old black car and took his seat on the front left side. He got comfortable, and then he started fumbling with the seat belt.

"Whoa, wait a minute here," he said. He fumbled some more. "Devesh, buddy, I'm sorry to report the seat belt here ain't working."

"Same here, John," Ron said. "I can't seem to be able to stretch my seat belt."

"How about you, honey?" John asked his wife. "You good back there?"

"Negative," she said. "Like Ron, my seat belt isn't working. It stays stuck; can't pull it."

John opened the door and got out. His window was open, and he spoke through it. "Devesh, buddy, I'm sorry, but this is unacceptable. We can't ride in a taxi where the seat belts ain't working. I'll tip you for helping us with the luggage though. Frankly, I think your cabs are too old." He began flagging another cab, and then he noticed Brian stepping out of his taxi.

"Dad? Everything okay?" Brian yelled.

"Nah, it's just that none of the seat belts work in this here old cab. I'm getting another one."

"Dad, it's the same with us. We asked our driver, and he told us no seat belts."

The elder Robinson was puzzled. He looked at Devesh through his passenger-side window. Devesh, smiling, said, "No seat belt, sir."

"Well, ain't this the risk factor," John said as he reentered the cab. "Okay, Devesh. Just get us there safely. Regency Towers Hotel, please."

"Yes, sir," Devesh said, again smiling. He took his sandals off and pulled out of the line of taxis.

"AC working here, Devesh?" John immediately asked. He followed with, "Ron and honey, you guys comfortable back there?"

"We've got the windows down," Sandra said.

"How about it, Devesh? Any air-conditioning in this here old cab?"

"AC, sir?" he asked, puzzled.

"Yeah, you know, air-conditioning. To cool the inside of this taxi. See the knobs there?" He pointed to the front end of the console. "Looks like an AC control."

"No, sir. Not working. No air-conditioning," Devesh said, and John rolled his eyes.

The taxi moved slowly underneath a gray concrete underpass, then Devesh steered sharply to the right and started merging into a wide road. John's eyes suddenly focused ahead, and he placed both his hands on the dashboard. "Dear Lord!" he exclaimed, and Curly and Fritz both barked short barks. Devesh's taxi, traveling at an estimated twenty-five miles an hour, was entirely surrounded by small motorcycles and scooters traveling at a similar speed. Sandra looked to her left in amazement. Motorcycles and scooters were everywhere, and the passengers so close to her she could touch them if she wanted to. And the *beep, beep, beep* sounds of the motorcycles and scooters was constant. Just motorcycles and scooters moving and beeping, two, three, and even four passengers per motorcycle, sometimes three passengers on a small scooter.

"Can you believe this, John?" Ron said, keeping a watchful eye on the two-wheel traffic around the taxi.

"Amazing," John said. "Absolutely amazing."

"And I'm noticing there ain't any painted dividing lines on the roads," Ron said. "Where are the lanes, man? How do they know where to drive?"

The traffic suddenly slowed and then stopped altogether. "Honey, look back to see if you can see Brian's cab please," John said. Sandra looked back.

"Nope. Only motorcycles and scooters, honey. Completely filled with passengers. I don't see a taxi."

"Then text him," her husband said. Two weeks prior, John had asked Brian to ensure everyone's cell phone would work in India, including texting, and Brian found the answers to that mission in the form of WhatsApp and a Verizon data plan. "Are you guys okay?" Sandra texted to Brian.

She soon saw on her screen his text: "Crazy traffic and tons of motorcycles. Love you."

John observed his surroundings and was amazed as to how many people could fit on a motorcycle or scooter. A small kid sat on the gas tank, the dad sat on the seat, driving, and another kid was in between him and the mother, who, on a motorcycle, always sat at the end of the back seat and, because she was wearing a sari or the traditional salwar kameez, sat sidesaddle. Ron was equally amazed that so few of the riders and passengers wore helmets or shoes—all barefoot or sandals and often without a helmet.

The traffic started moving again, and with it came the constant *beep, beep, beep* sounds.

"Notice that many of the scooters are driven by ladies, but so rarely are women the drivers of the motorcycles."

"I see. That's right," Sandra said to her husband.

"And some of the ladies are all dressed in black, and their heads and parts of their faces are covered," Ron added.

"Those are Muslim women, sir," Devesh said as he gently tapped his horn. "Muslim women wear black."

"I see," Ron said. "Thanks, Devesh."

The cab came to a four-way intersection with no lights; instead, a thin police officer with a beige shirt and green pants blew a whistle and directed traffic with arm signals. Devesh continued driving straight at around fifteen miles an hour, occasionally beeping, always surrounded by motorcycles and scooters traveling at a similar speed. Thus far, John had only seen a few small cars and one tiny Toyota pickup truck, with a stack of twigs that measured about twelve feet in height in its payload. Otherwise, it was all motorcycles and scooters and the *beep, beep, beep* sound. Up ahead, there was more development, and with it more congestion. The traffic moved at a snail's pace. John, ever observant, noticed all the buildings were either white or gray, and sometimes there was asphalt or tile sidewalks, but sometimes a sidewalk was just hardened dirt. Plenty of pedestrians were walking the sidewalks, the women always wearing saris and the men in plain slacks and loose-fitting shirts. John noticed most people wore sandals, some were barefoot, and a few wore shoes.

"Dear Lord, no way," Sandra said loudly as she peered through the window. Curly and Fritz again gave short barks. "John, look to your left. Do you see that man on the street corner? He's actually urinating outside. In public. On a street corner."

"This is wild man," Ron said, laughing. He saw the man urinating, and then he saw a skinny white cow comfortably sitting, squatting down on the side of the road, next to the pissing man, motorcycles and scooters slowly maneuvering to the left to avoid hitting the animal.

"Amazing, man," Ron said, laughing some more. "But you got to hand it to these motorcycle and scooter drivers. I haven't seen an accident yet."

"Hey, y'all. Look to the left," John said. "A couple of goats."

Two goats were crossing a parallel street, motorcycle and scooters coming to a halt to let the animals pass.

"Sir, I am sorry to disturb you and your family," Devesh suddenly said to John. "But I must stop at the nearby gas station, for this vehicle is in need of fuel."

"Sure, Devesh, we understand," John said. "That's part of your job."

Minutes later, Devesh pulled into the gas station, Indian Oil, the national brand. He parked the car next to a pump, killed the motor, slipped on his sandals, and entered the gas station.

"This is wild," Ron said, smiling. "Totally wild."

"You got that right," his brother said.

Sandra gently opened up Curly and Fritz's carrier. "How are my little precious ones?" she said as she twisted the cap off a water bottle, cupped her left hand, and poured a bit of water into it. "Are you guys thirsty? Yes you are. Yes you both are." The canine duo, both wagging their tails, started drinking from her hand.

Devesh walked out of the gas station building and approached the car. He popped open the lid, pressed two buttons on the pump while holding the nozzle, and started pumping the gas. John, relaxing in his passenger seat with the window down, noticed there was only one other car at the gas station, an old Honda Civic; the other vehicles were either motorcycles (mostly Hondas but also of the brand Royal Enfield) or motor scooters.

Devesh finished pumping the gas and soon pulled into the main road, the *beep, beep, beep* sounds and sights of motorcycles and scooters everywhere, as well as occasional goats and cows, now familiar to the passengers. John, looking slightly to his left, saw a tiny white Toyota pickup with dark brown twigs stacked maybe twelve feet high in the truck's bed. He had seen a similar truck minutes ago. "What exactly are those wooden twigs or branches, Devesh? See the white pickup truck?"

"Yes, sir. Most definitely," Devesh said. "The truck is carrying sugarcane to market, sir. Quite popular, sir."

"Oh, I see," John said. "Nice."

Suddenly, a three-wheel cart powered by a motorcycle and sporting a covered two-seat bench passed their cab to the left. John caught a glimpse of the back cover of the cart; it was a picture of Jesus.

"Hey, gang, did you see that? The cart," he said.

"Sure did," Ron said. "Cool stuff."

Sandra said, "Interesting to see a picture of Jesus."

Devesh, maneuvering the steering wheel, shifting the standard shift when necessary, and doing his fair share of *beep, beep, beeping,* remarked, "We have Christians here in Chennai. The rickshaw carts are popular taxis. Competition for us, really. Many of them have pictures of Jesus. It is important to find your way in life."

"Very well said, Devesh, buddy," John said. "Very well said. So true."

Ten minutes later, Devesh pulled into the short, hilly driveway of the Regency Hotel. Two security guards met the taxi at the beginning of the driveway, the guard on the left signaling for Devesh to stop.

"Everything okay, Devesh?" John asked, concerned.

"Yes, sir. All is well. Standard procedure."

The security guard to the right walked to the back of the taxi, carrying a five-foot pole with a mirror attached at the end of it. The security guard tapped the back trunk, and it was then that Devesh, with the taxi parked, slipped on his sandals, turned off the engine, and said, "Just one moment, sir."

He got out of the taxi and opened the trunk for the guard to see and check its contents. The trunk was nothing but luggage, and the guard instructed Devesh to shut the trunk. Devesh then headed back to the driver seat, and while doing so, the guard maneuvered the pole so he could see and check the taxi's underside. The guard started walking around the cab, looking down at his angled mirror.

"Cool stuff," Ron said as he observed the security guard. "Good security here, heh, John?"

"Yep, I'm seeing that. They seem to know what they're doing."

The guard with the mirror walked to the back end of the cab and tapped the trunk twice, the signal for Devesh to move. Devesh put the cab in gear and accelerated up an inclined asphalt driveway. The huge yellow-beige Regency Hotel was to the right, and next to the horseshoe entrance was the cab with Brian, Chuck, Anne-Marie, and Sheila. The four were exiting the cab with their luggage.

Devesh pulled up behind the parked taxi, and John, Ron, and Sandra got out, Sandra carrying the dog carriers by their handles.

"Have you all ever seen so many motorcycles?" Ron asked as he made eye contact with Brian and Chuck.

"Totally wild, man," Chuck said. "Packed like sardines, but we didn't see any accidents."

"Same here," Ron said. "Pretty amazing stuff."

Devesh and Ron placed the luggage on the sidewalk, and immediately, without their asking, a bellhop dressed in cream-colored pants, a long, cream-colored, collared shirt, a wide, bright red belt around his waist, and a red top hat affixed to his head, approached them with a gold-plated luggage pushcart. As the bellhop faced Ron, he maneuvered his right arm across his chest at a forty-five-degree angle and bowed his head slightly forward. After this respectful greeting, this short, middle-aged man began loading the pushcart with the luggage.

Anne-Marie and Sheila, standing in front of their cab, were greeted by an older and taller bellhop. Identically dressed and giving the two ladies the identical forty-five-degree arm cross and slight forward bow, the bellhop instructed the two to place their purses and personal items, including cell phones, on a nearby conveyor belt next to the hotel's entrance. At the center of the conveyor belt was a metal box—the x-ray apparatus, similar to those found at American airports. Anne-Marie and Sheila did as instructed and placed their personal items on the conveyor belt.

John approached Devesh. "How much do I owe you, buddy? And by the way, great driving. 'Em motorcycles sure don't leave much room for error."

"Thank you kindly, sir. The fair is two hundred and fifty rupees," Devesh said, slightly bowing his head as he revealed the charges.

John reached for his wallet and started trying to figure out what two hundred and fifty rupees meant in dollars.

"Oh, Devesh, buddy, I got these here credit cards for rupees. Do you take American dollars? How about twenty dollars?"

"Yes, sir. Yes, dollars are accepted. Of course. Thank you. Thank you so much, sir."

John handed Devesh a twenty-dollar bill, and Devesh's face lit up and beamed with a wide smile. "Thank you once again, dear sir, for your kind generosity."

Sandra, holding Curly and Fritz in both arms, suddenly approached her husband from behind.

"John, I've just been informed by one of the bellhops that they do not allow dogs here. Didn't you plan for this when you made the reservations?"

"Well, I guess I didn't think about that at the time."

"Well, what do we do now?"

"Let me talk to them."

John walked to the older bellhop, and the man bowed in greeting. John stuck out his hand to shake his. "Name's John Robinson. Albuquerque, New Mexico, United States of America. And who do I have the pleasure of meeting?"

The bellhop, awkwardly shaking John's hand, said, "I am Ajith, dear sir."

"Yes, well, nice to meet you, Ajith. We're all the way here for my son's wedding; he's marrying a local girl.

Silence.

"Well, I understand rules are rules. We're law-abiding folks, you know. I can tell you this: our dogs—their names are Curly and Fritz—are well behaved and won't cause any trouble."

Again, silence and a blank stare from Ajith.

"We don't want anything for free, Ajith. Back in the States, hotels charge a pet fee. I'm thinking twenty US dollars a day is a fair pet fee. I'm a bit low on twenties right now. How about I cover the fee for five days? John reached into his wallet and pulled out a crisp Ben Franklin hundred-dollar bill and handed it to Ajith.

"Thank you most kindly, sir," Ajith said, smiling. "I am the head bellhop here at the Regency. I will inform management of your two small dogs and your generous pay for their stay here."

"Ah, thank you, Ajith, buddy. A great hotel like this is well served by a fine leader like you."

Ten minutes later, after having their personal items scanned through the x-ray machine, the Robinson party, including Curly and Fritz, were inside the hotel, checking in at the front desk.

"Man, the air-conditioning feels real nice inside here," Ron said as he entered the hotel and started heading to the massive front desk.

"Right you are, Ron," Sandra said as she walked toward the front desk, Curly and Fritz in tow. She noticed a few patrons—an Asian couple, two Indian families, and an elderly British woman based on the way she spoke English. The Indians looked strangely at Sandra and her canine companions, but Sandra politely smiled and kept walking to the front desk. She noticed Ajith walk around the long front counter and speak to the concierge, who was eyeing the small animals. The Regency Hotel was truly spectacular, with its polished marble floors and columns, modern concierge section, and upscale gift shop.

John stepped up to the front desk and was kindly greeted about his reservations and planned stay. He paid for the four rooms (he and Sandra, Brian and Chuck, and Anne-Marie and Sheila would all share rooms while Ron would have his own room) for the weeklong stay with his American Express card. While paying, he was politely told the bar and restaurant were downstairs at the ground level, the outdoor swimming pool was on the back side of the hotel, the dry-cleaning services were available daily, and their four rooms were all adjacent to one another on the seventh floor.

"We hope you enjoy your stay here with us, sir," said the

pretty front desk clerk as she handed Mr. Robinson four room keys resembling magnetic stripe credit cards. "Please call this front desk at any time should you have any questions."

"You betcha," Mr. Robinson replied. Then he proceeded to hand out the keys and directed three bellhops to assist with the luggage.

The Robinson party unpacked and settled into their respective rooms. All were impressed with the accommodations of modern flat-screen televisions, good Wi-Fi connectivity, and adequate storage space. The beds were a bit on the small side, and the mattresses seemed thinner, but they were firm, and, most important of all, the air-conditioning worked, soundly and quietly. The game plan, devised by John, was for everyone to meet downstairs near the front desk in forty-five minutes to discuss the afternoon plans. When that meeting took place, Brian and Chuck said they wanted to head downstairs and check out the bar, Anne-Marie and Sheila expressed their interest in checking out the pool, and Ron said, "I'm exhausted, gang. Jet lag is kicking in. I think I'll head back to my room for a nap." John and Sandra said they too were truly tired and preferred to catch up on sleep.

"Okay, team. Everyone's on the Verizon plan on their cell phones, right?" John asked in a confident tone, for he knew the answer to his question. "Okay, good. Y'all are on your own today. If jet lag hasn't hit you yet, it probably will soon. You can always call or text so we know where everyone is. Everyone has some dollars and rupees and those credit card rupees, so we're all good," he said. "Tomorrow, Janni wants to show us a few sites here in Chennai. Wedding's in three days. Let's plan to meet back here tomorrow morning at nine."

When Brian and Chuck were nursing their Kingfisher beers (India's most popular) at the hotel's bar at ten thirty that first night, they noticed most of the hotel's patrons were Orientals (Chinese, Japanese, Koreans) and Europeans, either tourists or folks on business; there were just a few Indian couples. Bon Jovi and George Michael songs seemed to dominate the music selection, and everyone was having a good time.

"Cheers, my best man," Brian said, raising his Kingfisher beer bottle. "Our first day in India."

"Cheers," Chuck said. They touched bottles. "How's Priya?"

"Fine," Brian said as he gulped some beer. "Busy with the wedding preparations. She just texted me and said her family says hello."

"Cool," Chuck said. "I'm happy for you, man."

What Priya had failed to inform Brian about in that latest text of hers was the following discussion she had had with her father three hours earlier:

"Father, I request your permission to stay the night with my husband, Brian, at the Regency Hotel, for we are a married couple—"

"Absolutely not, young lady."

"But we are married, Father, and I know it will not be a problem for best man Chuck to stay with Mr. Ron. There is a lot I want to discuss with my husband about our Hindu wedding."

"Absolutely not. You are not married, not yet. You are married in the Western tradition but not in ours. This is India. When in India, do as the Indians. You'll be married soon enough. Your request is denied; permission not granted."

At nine o'clock the next morning, the Robinson party and Priya and Janni met as planned near the hotel's front entrance, and then they all proceeded to take the elevators to the ground floor for the large buffet. Breakfast included American staples such as scrambled eggs, toast, muffins, biscuits, oatmeal, home fries, coffee, tea, and orange juice. There were sausage links, but they were of the chicken variety—no beef or pork—and also absent were pancakes, waffles, and French toast. Indian favorites were also part of the breakfast options, including various naans, rice dishes, and mango juice. Mr. Robinson insisted on paying for everything, but a young male waiter, dressed in a long-sleeve white shirt, black slacks, and a black vest, politely informed the elder Robinson that breakfast was included in their hotel fare.

"Well that's awesome, buddy," Mr. Robinson replied upon hearing the welcomed news. "Well, in that case, let me tip y'all's fine waitstaff here." He proceeded to place a twenty-dollar American bill on the table as everyone was wrapping up their breakfasts.

"Oh, kind sir, thank you for your generosity," the young waiter replied as he was gathering empty coffee cups. "However, I must inform you we are prevented from accepting tips."

"You don't say?"

"Yes," the young waiter said shyly, just as a short, bald Indian man approached Mr. Robinson.

The man greeted Mr. Robinson with the traditional arm cross and slight head bow. "We are most appreciative of you and your family's stay here, sir," the man said. Like the bellhops, he was wearing the cream-colored shirt and pants with the thick red belt around his waist. "But it is true, we have a no-tipping policy here. This I tell you."

"Well, why's that?" Mr. Robinson asked, befuddled. "Service was great this morning. Last night, my wife and I ate in our rooms. We ordered room service, and it was great." He quickly decided not to reveal he had tipped the staff person last evening for bringing the food to his room. "So why this no-tipping policy?"

"Kind sir," the man said matter-of-factly, "it is quite simple. There is no tipping, for we cannot have waiters making more money than the management employees."

Ten minutes later, everyone (Curly and Fritz included) squeezed into two taxis. Destination: the site where Saint Thomas preached two millennia ago. Mr. Robinson sat in the front passenger seat of the lead taxi, a repeat of yesterday in that the air-conditioning and seat belts weren't working. And just like Devesh, the taxi driver also wore sandals, ensuring he slipped them off to go barefoot and better feel the accelerator, clutch, and brake pedals.

The drive to the site took roughly half an hour. They witnessed basically a repeat of yesterday's taxi rides from the airport: heavy motorcycle, scooter, and autorickshaw traffic, roads with no dividing lines, cows squatting on the sides of the streets, stray dogs, plenty of goats, women in saris on motorcycles, pedestrians walking about—many with cell phones but few wearing shoes—and the constant beeping of the two-wheeled vehicles. The irritation of the beeping noises and the shock of having so many vehicles surround the taxis had worn off, not bothering them as much, certainly not as much as yesterday.

"We have to walk from here," Priya said when everyone got out of the taxis.

Mr. Robinson paid both fares—plus tips—and said, "What a gorgeous day for sightseeing. How long is the walk to the site?"

"I think it will take us twenty to thirty minutes, Mr. Robinson," Priya said. "About the same time as our cab rides."

"Okay," Mr. Robertson said, looking up at an asphalt road that led to the site. "And you can call me John."

Priya was wearing jeans and a blouse while Janni wore a salwar kameez, but both were wearing sneakers. Priya led the way, Brian to her side. Mrs. Robinson was in jeans and comfortable shoes, as were Anne-Marie and Sheila. The young female couple held the leashes, guiding Curly and Fritz, who were trotting about and smelling their new environment.

Five minutes into the upward walk, the Robinson party saw

an elderly, small lady dressed in a light blue sari, bent over and sweeping away goat excrement. Her short broom was nothing more than a series of twigs tied in a bundle. The sight made the elder Robinson think of the nice, large push brooms on sale at Home Depot or Lowe's.

As the group continued walking uphill, goats, usually brown in color but a few white ones, could now be seen in packs of two to four on both sides of the asphalt trail. Stray dogs, all light brown and skinny, also roamed around the adjacent fields. Brian couldn't help but notice that the dogs, numbering a half dozen, never barked, and Curly and Fritz, walking about and sniffing away, barely noticed them.

"I now see the statue of Thomas," Priya said, leading the group. After more uphill walking, one hundred feet behind her, Janni and Ron, the last two of the party, looked up to Priya to see what she was pointing at.

"The statue of Thomas," she repeated. She walked another twenty yards to be at the base of the statue. "We should take photos," she suggested.

Everyone gathered at the base of the eight-foot-tall statue of painted stone.

"I read somewhere that Saint Thomas resembled Jesus, and I can see that now," Mr. Robinson said as he sipped some water. "The clothes, the long brown hair, the beard, especially the beard. He really did look like Jesus. At least the way we understand Jesus to have looked."

Priya and Brian took photos from their cell phones, as did Anne-Marie, Sheila, and Mrs. Robinson. Minutes later, Priya once again led the group on the uphill path, and soon the trail, on both sides, now had short concrete walls that featured framed sculptures of the fourteen stations of the cross. Mr. Robinson photographed each station, crossing himself each time he passed a station.

Ten minutes later, Priya, with Brian at her side, waved her

arms and yelled, "We have reached the site." Janni and Ron were now at least seventy yards behind the newlyweds, walking slowly uphill. It took them more than five minutes to reach Priya and Brian.

"What incredible views," Mrs. Robinson said when she stood next to her son. She looked to her left and saw the large, twig-thatched-roof hut, a replica of where Saint Thomas preached. She then scanned the panoramic view of Chennai. She was seeing its many white buildings and, farther out, the choppy waters of the Bay of Bengal.

"We have arrived at Saint Thomas Mount," Priya said enthusiastically. To her right was the chapel the Portuguese had built in the sixteenth century to commemorate the site. Brian noticed a pack of brown stray dogs lying on a patch of dirt next to the hut. They were sleeping, soaking up the sun. There were also a few other visitors—an Indian couple and some white tourists—next to the chapel. Everyone gathered around Priya and Brian and took photos of the white chapel.

"I have to see the inside of this chapel," Mr. Robertson said purposefully.

"Most certainly," Priya replied. "The chapel is open to the public for viewing, but photos are not allowed inside."

Priya and Brian entered the chapel first, and the rest of the Robinson party followed. Patrons, all Indians, were kneeling in prayer next to the dark, wooden pews. The altar was at the head of the chapel, the stations of the cross prominently displayed on the walls. Stone statues of various saints were everywhere, but none were more prominent than the bearded Saint Thomas himself, patron saint of India.

When the group exited the chapel, they exited from the side and came upon a small building with a sign that read "Orphanage." A picture of Mother Teresa, Saint Teresa, featured prominently on the sign. To the left of the closed orphanage were concrete steps heading down a small hill, and at the base of that hill was a snack bar. Priya and Brian led the group down the solid stairs, and once at the snack bar, the Kumar sisters ordered tea while the Robinsons bought and drank from water bottles.

After the brief respite at the snack bar, the group followed a walkway down the side of the hill that reached a plateau. Small trees were to the left, as was a prominent black iron bench that was a small shrine. From a distance, it looked like someone was sleeping on the bench. Curious, Priya and Brian decided to walk to the bench, and the group followed. Priya and Brian reached the bench and read a plaque next to it: "Homeless Jesus." Curly and Fritz were walking around the bench, enjoying the grass and soft dirt. Chuck, standing next to Janni and Ron, stared at the statue of Jesus sleeping on the bench for what seemed like a full minute. He took a photo of what he was staring at, then he noticed the group moving to the right, where a prominent statue of Pope John II was situated, commemorating this religious mount. Chuck stayed next to the bench for another three minutes before he caught up with the others.

The walk down Saint Thomas Mount was much faster than its climb up, and once everyone reached the base of the wide asphalt walkway, they noticed a line of taxis and autorickshaws hungry for business.

"Allow me to be in the lead taxi once again," Priya told the group, "before we visit the Saint Thomas Cathedral near the Bay of Bengal. There is another church I want all of us to see."

"Which one is that?" Brian asked as he gulped down what remained in his water bottle.

"It's a surprise. Follow the taxi I'm in."

Everyone, including Curly and Fritz, got in a taxi, and in a few minutes, Priya instructed the taxi driver to park in an adjacent parking lot. To the left of the parking lot was a large white church, and before getting out of the cab, Priya instructed the driver,

"Stay here, for we will need taxis for the ride to the Saint Thomas Cathedral." Everyone exited the two taxis.

"This is a church dedicated to Saint Patrick," Priya said loudly.

"How interesting," Mrs. Robinson said. "Such a nice church."

"Wow, the patron saint of Ireland has a church here in Chennai," Ron said as he was walking next to Janni. "Cool stuff. Say, Priya, do you know why this church is here in Chennai?"

"I'm afraid I don't. I can look it up. We have a lot of Christians here in Chennai. Perhaps this is one of their holy places."

The group walked to the front of the church and took photos. It was much larger than the Saint Thomas chapel and more modern. Brian noticed the adjacent parking lot was empty, except for the two taxis waiting for them, and when he climbed the church's front steps and attempted to open the large wooden front doors, he realized they were locked.

"I guess we can't visit inside. Locked doors."

The group stayed around for ten minutes, taking photos of the church, and Curly and Fritz sniffed around.

Situated near the shores of the Bay of Bengal, Saint Thomas Cathedral is the site where Doubting Thomas is interred. Some twenty minutes after leaving the Saint Patrick Cathedral, the taxis with the Robinson party and Kumar sisters parked in a large church parking lot adjacent to a long line of stationary motorcycles and scooters.

"Great sea breeze," John Robinson said as he got out of the cab and started paying for both taxi fares. "Nice and cool. I always love being close to the ocean."

"Me too," Ron said as he stretched his legs once out of the small taxi. Everyone started heading toward the large cathedral, with Mrs. Robinson carrying Curly while Anne-Marie carried Fritz.

Inside, the cathedral featured high ceilings and rows and

rows of wooden pews. Patrons could be seen walking about or lighting candles to offer Masses for desired causes or deceased loved ones. The familiar stations of the cross and a large statue of Saint Thomas couldn't be missed, for they were much larger than other walled hangings and statues. No one seemed to care that Mrs. Robinson and Anne-Marie were holding two small dogs; patrons kept walking around, marveling at the statues and the large stained glass works.

Toward the back of the cathedral was a small sign that advertised the downstairs tour where Saint Thomas was interned. Mr. Robinson said he wanted this experience and insisted he pay for everyone's one-hundred-rupees entry fee. Everyone agreed to follow his lead to the lower level of the large cathedral. After paying the fees, Mr. Robinson picked up a small brochure about the cathedral and then followed the directional arrows. Everyone followed him.

After passing through a few narrow hallways, Mr. Robinson came upon a small chapel with dark, wooden benches. To the left of the benches was a large, glass case featuring a man-size plastic replica of the patron saint of India. There were a few Indians in the pews, kneeling and praying, and Mr. Robinson decided to sit behind them. The Robinson party took up the last two pews.

Mr. Robinson, sitting in the pew, pulled out his brochure and quickly discovered Saint Thomas was actually interred directly below this chapel, below the plastic replica to the left. He then kneeled and bowed his head in prayer for the next five minutes.

After visiting Saint Thomas Cathedral, the group decided to check out Chennai Beach, a short taxi ride that took less than ten minutes. Mr. Robinson observed rows and rows of motorcycles and scooters lined up at the edge of where the asphalt road met the dark gray sand of the beach. He had never seen such a large beach; the distance from the edge of the road to where the water ended had to be an eighth of a mile, maybe more. A massive beach with soft gray sand.

The Robinson party started walking on the beach. They noticed only a few young men were swimming, all of them in shorts, some bare chested but most wearing T-shirts while they swam. There were couples walking the beach as well, the women all in saris or salwar kameezzes—no bikinis—and the men wore pants and loose-fitting shirts. Only young children—both girls and boys—wore shorts like the few swimmers.

After some thirty minutes of walking on the beach, the rest of the afternoon was spent back at the Regency Hotel where folks were on their own. Brian and Chuck decided to check the pool out, Priya and Janni returned to their parents' home to help with the wedding planning, Anne-Marie and Sheila decided to check out the small shops surrounding the hotel, and Ron, John, and Sandra decided to nap back in their rooms. What was new for the Robinsons was the relatively quick six-fifteen sundown, after which it was pitch black with little traffic. Chennai, situated near the equator, quiets down and slows down in its dark evenings.

The next day, the Robinson party found itself in two taxis heading south—their destination the World Heritage Sites at Mahabalipuram, roughly a two-hour drive from Chennai. Priya and Janni hired two taxi drivers for the day and accompanied the Robinsons while Rani and Deepika stayed back for wedding preparations.

The two taxis departed the Regency Hotel in unison, and for the next twenty minutes made their way through Chennai's undivided streets, congested with mostly two-wheeled traffic and its beeping noises. Such congestion waned toward the city's outskirts, and the Robinsons noticed the replacement of three-story white buildings with taller glass ones, hosting IT centers and medical research facilities, the latter mostly for diabetes. And to their left was a modern subway train with tracks supported by huge concrete supports. The two taxis, following each other as best they could, made it out of the city, and soon they would follow each other on a four-lane highway (two lanes heading south, the other two lanes heading back into Chennai).

"Finally!" Ron exclaimed upon seeing the highway. "Painted dividing lines to make out lanes. 'Bout time." Then some ten minutes into the drive, as he was sitting next to Janni in the back seat of the lead taxi, he said, "Now, this is nice. Very different from the city."

"Yes, it is nice, Mr. Ron," Janni replied.

"Nice green fields, some traffic, but no congestion. Palm trees and the occasional white cows on the side of the road or in the fields. Pretty nice, hey, John?"

"Absolutely," his brother said. John occupied the front passenger seat. "Very nice green fields. And the beautiful ocean to our left." He noticed his wife taking photos with her cell phone.

Halfway along the trip to Mahabalipuram, Ron noticed a cricket game going on in a large field to his right. Janni explained, "Cricket is our national sport. That game is a young boys' league. In our professional leagues, particularly our national team, the players get paid very well."

Then, about fifteen minutes later, with the taxis reaching speeds equivalent to sixty miles per hour, Ron noticed more palm trees and then what looked like white sand.

"Is that the beach over there?" he asked Janni.

"No, Mr. Ron. That is a salt field. We have lots of salt around here."

"I see. Very interesting." He took photos with his cell phone.

Close to two hours after departing the Regency Hotel, the lead taxi took a left into a large parking lot that was filled with motorcycles, a few small cars, and numerous tourist buses resembling Greyhound buses, except their exteriors were red.

"Welcome to Mahabalipuram," Janni said as she exited the taxi. The second taxi, transporting Priya, Brian, and the others, parked next to the first taxi.

Janni spoke Tamil to the first taxi driver, instructing him to stay put, that he was their driver for the day, and she and these foreign guests would be visiting the historic sites here for probably the next three hours or so. She walked over to the second taxi driver and told him the same. Then she gave both drivers sufficient rupees for their lunches.

Wearing a red sari, Janni turned to Ron and said, "Mr. Ron, would it be possible, as to you being so kind, to give me rupees so I can pay the entrance fees for all of us?"

She smiled, and he said, "Sure. Of course. How much does it cost?"

"Let's see." She looked around. "We are a party of nine. The authorities will not charge for the two dogs of Ms. Sandra. I believe it is ten rupees for Indians and two hundred and fifty rupees for foreign nationals."

Ron, puzzled, said, "They charge foreigners more?"

"Yes," she said, embarrassed.

Ron shook his head, reached into his wallet, and handed her two thousand rupees.

"That should cover it," he said.

With a bright sun and the temperature in the nineties, John Robinson saw various hats for sale at a gift shop next to the ticket counter. "I don't know about you all, but I'm getting a hat for some cover," he said. "Who's joining me?"

Anne-Marie and Sheila both said they were okay, that they loved the sun, but Anne-Marie added, "We're thirsty though. We could use some more water bottles."

"Good idea," Mr. Robinson said. "I'll get more water, plus the hat," and that was when Brian, Chuck, and Ron said they'd join him to buy hats. Sandra, at first undecided, also chose to get a hat, and then Priya and Janni—not used to wearing hats—figured it was best to do as the Robinsons.

The purchases were made, including the admission tickets, and once Janni handed out the tickets and everyone had their water bottles and head covers (except for Anne-Marie and Sheila), Priya, wearing loose pants, comfortable sneakers, and a short-sleeve blouse, led the group on a long trail that had numerous turns and eventually reached a raised plateau on the edge of the Bay of Bengal. The trail was filled with visitors like them (there were many foreign tourists) and also young school-aged children who were all wearing school uniforms (red shorts, red socks, and beige shirts). Priya kept reminding the group, "We are coming up on Shore Temple, which is temples carved out of granite, all in the seventh century. This is a World Heritage Site, as designated by the United Nations."

She kept leading the group on the trail while Anne-Marie and Sheila dutifully held the leashes of Curly and Fritz. Some twenty yards away, there was yet another turn, heading to the right, and directly at the point of curvature was an old, skinny lady squatting down on the ground, her legs bent Indian style, her right arm and hand out, her stomach visible, as were her skinny legs. Mrs. Robinson let out a quick, "Oh my."

Her husband said, "Sandy, we too have beggars in Albuquerque, honey. Nothing new. Although a good portion of our beggars are druggies. This poor lady here, she's so frail."

As the group started passing the lady, John said, "I got this," and he handed the beggar a water bottle and a one-hundred-rupee bill. Chuck, who was the last person in the group, couldn't help himself. He too stopped and handed the lady his water bottle and an American five-dollar bill.

The trail ended after another one hundred yards of walking,

and the group came upon a carved wall of granite decorated with animals resembling goats.

"Oh, how beautiful," Mrs. Robinson said. "How intricate. John, look at the detail in the stone carvings," she said, addressing her husband but wanting the others to hear. "And to think this was carved fourteen centuries ago. The Spanish weren't even in Santa Fe back then, but here, look at these works."

"They are beautiful," her husband said. He stared at the base of the carvings. "Some of these animals are bigger than I am. Imagine how long it took to do these detailed works."

"That I don't know," Priya said, "but I recommend we all walk around these walls and temples for the next ... shall we say forty minutes? Then we can all meet over there." She pointed to a large, dark gray temple to the far right.

"Sounds like a plan," John said.

Brian and Chuck started taking tons of cell phone photos, especially of the small temples that resembled pyramids, except they were so much more detailed than pyramids, with their intricate carvings of people and animals.

"The coolest part about these temples," Chuck said when he was observing his third such structure, "is that you can actually walk inside them. Not much room, but two to three people fit comfortably. I feel like I'm Indiana Jones in the *Raiders of the Lost Ark*, like I'm searching for a buried treasure or something."

As planned, the entire group met at the designated temple nearly an hour later. Priya once more took the lead and said, "Follow me." She led them all on another trail, away from the ocean, heading back to the large parking lot where all the tour buses were parked. But before they reached the parking lot, the trail curved to the left, and the entire group stayed on the trail for a solid fifteen minutes. The trail finally ended in an open field filled with carvings of animals and small temples.

"Oh, this is so beautiful," Anne-Marie said. "The animals look so real. Look at that elephant carved in granite."

"Sure is," Ron said as he walked forward. "And look at this one. A full-size elephant. Just like it was alive." He started taking photos with his cell phone.

"I recommend we stay in this area, for there's lots to see," Priya said, smiling. "How about we take photos and check out the temples and carvings for the next hour. Then we can meet at the edge of the parking lot. My watch reads 11:40 a.m."

John once again agreed to Priya's plan, as did the entire group. He said, "Edge of the parking lot next to that souvenir stand at 10:40. Enjoy."

The next hour was spent taking photos of temples and animals—both small and large—all made of granite. Brian and Priya were walking behind Brian's parents, enjoying the carvings.

"Do you like the carvings, Gandhi?" Priya asked.

"Yes, very much, Tocqueville."

She smiled. "And tomorrow afternoon, we will get married, the Hindu celebration. Are you happy?"

"Yes, very much so," he replied earnestly. "We're already married, but I'm looking forward to the Hindu wedding. I'm as happy as I've ever been." He looked to the edge of the parking lot where a large bus had just parked. Filing out of the bus were more young Indian schoolchildren, all dressed in their school uniforms.

"Do all Indian grade schools require school uniforms?" he asked.

"No," Priya replied. "It depends on the school. The Western-style schools, where English is taught, are sought after, and some require uniforms. Some non-English schools also require uniforms."

As the young couple walked behind Brian's parents, Brian observed a large pig lounging on his belly, resting directly in front of one of the large buses where the students were debarking.

And some ten feet from the pig were two brown goats chewing on grass.

Modernity in the form of a large, bright bus, Brian thought. *All next to free-roaming animals, and in the background, beyond the bus, an intricate temple carved in granite, a temple that is fifteen hundred years old. What an incredible mix.*

"We have one more stop here at Mahabalipuram before we head south to Pondicherry for lunch," Priya said as the group met as designated. "But before we get into our taxis, I recommend we try the coconut water." She pointed to an older, thin lady wearing a yellow sari and sitting Indian style next to where the water bottles were being sold. She was selling coconut water to patrons.

Brian counted seven people in line for the drink. "I love coconut. Let's do it," he said.

Everyone got in line, and Priya insisted, "I'm paying for all of us."

"Oh, you don't have to, dear," Mrs. Robinson said, but Priya was adamant.

Brian observed the old lady executing her craft. There was definitely a system—a rhythm actually—to what she was doing. Pick up green coconut from pile of coconuts to her left; hold coconut with left hand; with right hand, hold a two-foot-long machete; strike coconut once or twice at its tip to create an opening for patrons to drink from out of a straw; place straw in opening; hand coconut to patron; get money from patron; repeat the process. Her business was brisk, and the line was moving steadily, and when Mrs. Robinson got her coconut and took a sip of its water, she said, "This is the real thing. The best coconut water I've ever had, hands down."

"I know you must all be hungry, but we have a special luncheon plan in Pondicherry," Priya told the group as everyone was enjoying the coconut water. "Pondicherry is a former French city in India. It is a ninety-minute drive from here. The coconut water should keep us full just in time for a nice lunch. But before we head south, there's one more site to visit. It is only five minutes from here."

Priya spoke Tamil to the two hired taxi drivers, and everyone squeezed into the taxis. Five minutes later, the taxis parked in a small parking lot. Brian was in awe at what he was seeing.

"Welcome to Krishna's Butter Ball," Priya said enthusiastically as they exited the cabs. She was smiling and pointing to the large boulder. Brian quickly estimated the stone was at least twenty feet in height and maybe thirty feet wide. "Legend has it that this boulder is a chunk of stolen butter dropped by the gods," Priya said.

"Man oh man, how can that huge boulder not roll down the rocky slope?" Ron asked, bewildered. "It's gotta be a forty-five-degree slope. What's keeping it from rolling?"

"That is the mystery, my dear sir," Janni said. "The gods are keeping it from rolling."

Brian noticed children sliding on their behinds down the smooth, rocky surface directly adjacent to the huge boulder, the path black in color from the many years of patrons sliding away. He started taking photos, and everyone started walking toward the immense boulder. Chuck, Anne-Marie, and Sheila decided to try their luck at the nature-made slide, and they all laughed as they slowly descended the steep slope mixed in with Indian schoolchildren.

Fifteen minutes later, the Robinson party was back in their taxis, heading south for lunch. Just before he got into his designated cab, John Robinson noticed an old lady sitting Indian style next to yet another souvenir shop. She was begging, and he walked over to her and placed a five-dollar bill in her outstretched hand. And just as previously witnessed, as if an earlier event would repeat itself, Chuck saw what took place and did as he earlier had, following in the footsteps of Mr. Robinson, also giving American money to the begging lady.

Sipping his coconut water during the southward drive, Brian decided to Google *Pondicherry* and find out what he could about the former French colony-city. Unable to get a connection, he said to Priya, "So tell me about Pondicherry. I thought the British ruled India for so many years. At least that's what my research showed when I was looking into Gandhi. But the French were here too?"

"Yes, dear husband. That is correct. As were the Dutch and the Portuguese."

"Why were they here?" Chuck asked as he looked at the bright green fields and palm trees off the highway.

"Money and religion," Priya said. "Tea, salt, spices, other foodstuffs. The European nations were big on trade. India was providing a lot of the raw materials, especially cotton. There were also a lot of missionaries converting Indians to Christianity. Islam too made its way to India. I guess you could say it was about capitalism, Christianity, and some Islam."

It was a late lunch at an outdoor section of a large luxury hotel in Pondicherry. Packed with European tourists, the waiters—all Indian men wearing white shirts and black pants—were bringing dishes of Indian favorites like samosas, chicken tandoori, chicken curry, an assortment of naans, and various rice and lentil dishes to the patrons. Priya, who insisted on paying for everything, happily proclaimed, when everyone was shown to the two reserved tables, "This is the prewedding rehearsal dinner for tomorrow as Brian and I get married."

Water—with no ice—was served, and the menus were handed out. Looking at the menu, Brian noticed a large selection of beers and wines. "Uncle Ron, would you believe they have Budweiser here?"

"You don't say. That's what I'm talking about. All I need is my good buddy wiser. How about we get a pitcher?"

"Sounds good," Brian said, but to his disappointment, when the waiter returned to take the drink orders and appetizer selections (Priya chose two orders of chicken samosas and one order of vegetarian samosas), the waiter politely said, "My apologies, sir, but we do not sell pitchers of beer, only bottles."

"Then make it four bottles of Budweiser please."

"And two glasses of your house white wine," Anne-Marie added.

The late lunch / reception dinner lasted two hours, and everyone marveled at the beautiful palm trees and cream-colored hotel built in the French colonial style. The meal (the Kumar sisters stuck with vegetarian biryani while the Robinsons, Chuck, and Sheila selected different chicken dishes) was topped off with delicious slices of crème brûlée, numerous individual pieces of macaron, and, to the delight of Mrs. Robinson, "The best coffee I've ever tasted." And for the first time, the Robinsons weren't the only people with a dog or two at a restaurant, for four tables from John and Sandra, there sat a middle-aged French couple with two poodles by their feet.

Just five minutes after leaving the hotel restaurant, Priya instructed the lead taxi to stop and park in front of a large, old, French, three-story colonial building, also cream-colored and even larger than the hotel where they lunched. Tall palm trees lined the streets, as did countless parked motorcycles.

She led everyone into the huge six-aisles bookstore that sported a gray concrete floor and countless wooden shelves. Only the first floor comprised the bookstore, as the other two floors housed administrative agencies or office suites.

Browsing through the book aisles, Brian noticed most of the books were old and in English. A few were in Hindi, and even fewer were in French. He bought an old David Baldacci paperback (Priya paid for it in rupees), and after a half hour of book browsing, the group was back in the respective taxis, cruising along a stretch of a seaside road overlooking the Bay of Bengal.

"Dear husband," Priya said cheerfully. "Notice the beach here in Pondicherry. What do you think?"

"Well, I can see it's not a beach at all, honey. It's these huge, shiny black boulders," Brian replied as the lead taxi driver navigated the road slowly behind a couple of motorcycles.

"Yes, that is true. There was a natural erosion, and then there was the contraction of a harbor that also brought erosion. But there is dredging now in an effort to bring back the sand."

Minutes later, Priya said something in Tamil to the lead driver, and he slowly parked the cab to the right. The second taxi parked behind them.

"Let us get out," Priya said. "It is a nice afternoon for a walk. Besides, I have something to show you."

Everyone got out of the taxis and followed Priya along the seaside road, and in just a few minutes, she pointed to what looked like a large gazebo with a statue inside. She kept walking, the others right behind her.

"What is it?" Brian asked as they kept approaching the gazebo. He noticed a small crowd of patrons—mostly Indians but some whites—observing the statue. They kept walking forward, and at around sixty yards from the gazebo, Brian could now make out the statue. "It's Gandhi!" he exclaimed.

"Right you are, dear husband."

"I can tell by the bald head, the skinny bare legs, his sandals, his skimpy clothing, and the thin glasses over his eyes."

"Correct. We are at the Gandhi statue at Gilbert Avenue, Beach Road," Priya said.

The Robinson group stood along with the rest of the gathered crowd and took many photos.

"Didn't you write a paper on Mr. Gandhi, dear?" Mrs. Robinson asked her son as she was focusing her cell phone.

"Sure did, Mom. He was an interesting person to write about."

"Dear husband, I must take a photo of you with the Gandhi statue," Priya said as she took a few such shots with her cell phone. Brian had an idea.

"Priya, let's take a selfie. Better yet, you and me, with Gandhi in the background." She agreed, and the young couple took a few of those shots.

As the group headed back to the taxis, Brian thought about the paper he had read not too long ago describing how Gandhi had fallen into disrepute in certain African countries, to the point where his statue in parts of the African continent was coming down, because, as a young man in South Africa, Gandhi had told the white ruling class not to compare blacks to Indians, that the blacks were below Indians such as himself.

But his statue is not coming down here, Brian thought. *He remains quite popular, based on the crowds.*

Just as he was about to enter the taxi, he heard a slight beep on his cell phone. He got in the cab and touched his text icon. It was a text from Priya with one of her versions of the selfie photos of the couple with the Gandhi statue in the background. It read: "To my Gandhi, Brian Robinson, one day before our Hindu wedding. Pondicherry, India. Wife forever, Priya."

Sitting next to her, he looked at Priya and squeezed her hand gently. "Thank you," he said. "It's been a wonderful day. These will be great memories."

Just as the taxis were reaching the outskirts of Pondicherry, Priya, sitting in the lead taxi's front passenger seat, noticed a big crowd gathered down a narrow street to the right. To the left of the crowd, she caught the glimpse of a large elephant. In Tamil, she told the driver to take a right and to park the cab. The second taxi did the same.

"An elephant," Priya said as she exited the taxi. She waved to the others to follow her.

Sitting atop the large elephant's head and neck region was a young, thin man, and behind the animal's right hind leg was another young, thin man, sitting on a small chair and holding a short stick, a stick used to tap the beast's right hind leg. A wide, U-shaped curve of patrons directly faced the elephant, who seemed to enjoy moving his trunk up and down and left to right, then right to left, the man atop of him feeding him peanuts every few seconds.

"Wow. This is incredible," Mrs. Robinson said as she started taking photos with her cell phone. The group was four rows back from the frontline U-shaped curve. "Look, John. The elephant keeps moving his trunk right up to people's foreheads."

"I see that," her husband said. "Pretty cool. I guess those two guys know how to direct that beautiful animal."

"The elephant is moving his trunk to people's foreheads for good luck," Priya said matter-of-factly. "Elephants are a sign of good luck, and having an elephant touch you with his trunk is even more good luck. See how people are leaving a few rupees in the large basket?" she said, pointing to the basket on the dirt floor next to the front line of patrons. "That is to help feed the big elephant."

"He sure is big," Chuck said as he took some photos. "Look at the size of those legs. And the feet. Lord, they're huge."

"Would anyone desire to have photos taken with the elephant?" Priya asked. "I think it would be wonderful to have one's photo with this most auspicious of animals."

"Yes, yes," Janni said energetically. "Mr. Ron, would you like the elephant to give you blessings by placing his trunk on your forehead? I will capture such a moment on my cell phone camera."

"Only if I had the pleasure of having you in the photo, Janni."

Janni smiled and then nodded approvingly, and the two kept moving up the crowd to find a place in the front curved row. It was Priya who took the photo of Janni and Ron together, the elephant's trunk between the top of their heads. In the end, everyone had their photo taken, some as couples—Priya and Brian; Mr. and Mrs. Robinson; Mrs. Robinson with Curly and Fritz, who surprisingly didn't react to the huge beast behind them; Anne-Marie and Sheila; and the two taxi drivers.

Later, during the four-hour drive back to Chennai, Janni explained to Mr. Robinson, "It frankly would be unimaginable for any Indian to pass on the opportunity of having one's photo taken with the good luck of an elephant."

At 6:30 p.m., the two taxis had reached the beginnings of the outer city limits of Chennai.

"Man, I get a kick out of the sun setting so early," Chuck said as he looked at the pitch-black sky.

Mr. Robinson agreed. Then he changed topics with, "Say, Janni. How much longer to your parents' home and then to the hotel?"

"I would say another forty minutes or so, sir," she said politely.

"I see. Well, hey, I don't know about y'all, but I've got a case of the munchies. That lunch was great at Pondicherry, especially the crème brûlée, but I've worked up an appetite. I know there's a McDonald's in Chennai because I Googled it. How about we do takeout and bring the food to your place, Janni?"

"Oh, great blessings to you, sir, for such a kind gesture, but I must politely decline on account that my parents are busy putting the final touches to the apartment for tomorrow's great wedding celebration. But your idea is a good one, sir," she said. "We can have the food at the hotel, and I will bring some McDonald's food items to my parents."

"Okay then. Great. How does that sound, gang?" Mr. Robinson asked loudly, for all to hear.

All were in agreement, and Curly and Fritz both barked when Ron loudly said, "That's what I'm talking about. The sandwiches at the hotel ain't bad, but I'm in the mood for my favorite American staple, the Big Mac. How great it is we can have McDonald's here so far away from the USA. Sandra, text the others in the cab behind us and tell them the game plan."

A half hour after the late dinner plans were agreed to, the two cabs transporting the Robinson party pulled into an underground parking lot of a well-lit shopping mall. Minutes later, everyone— except for the taxicab drivers—was in the mall, following Priya's lead to the McDonald's.

"Oh dear," Mrs. Robinson said to Deepika as she was carrying both Curly and Fritz. "Just curiosity on my part, but why is it that the taxi drivers don't join us for dinner? They must be hungry too. Did they eat at all today?"

"Yes, they ate, madame," Deepika said as she kept walking in the lead position. "I gave them some rupees for their meals, and they did have coconut water. I will bring them something to eat."

"Why don't they eat with us?"

"Well, Mrs. Robinson, the drivers stay with their vehicles; they don't mix with the travelers."

Brian was walking behind Priya and observing his surroundings. He noticed modern stores with modern lighting, mostly clothing stores and cell phone shops. He also noticed younger Indian women in pants, mostly blue jeans.

The McDonald's was the last establishment on the right at the end of an aisle, and directly across it was a Subway franchise.

Everyone was up for McDonald's except for Anne-Marie and Sheila, who both decided to try out Subway.

Priya entered the small McDonald's, which featured no booths but a dozen or so small tables. Six patrons occupied three of the tables. Ron, with Janni behind him, was the first to order.

"All right. That's what I'm talking about. A nice slice of Americana right here in India." He looked at the cashier, a young, short Indian girl who couldn't be more than twenty years old. She had her long black hair in a bun tucked under a McDonald's cap.

"Sweetie, I'll have me a Big Mac with a large fry and a large Coke."

The cashier was puzzled. "A Big Mac, sir?"

"Yeah, Big Mac. Your number one seller. That with a large fry and a Coke."

"My most sincere apologies, sir, but we do not have Big Mac."

"What's that?"

"Sorry, but we do not have Big Mac."

"Ah, man. Well ain't that a shame. I was really in the mood for a Big Mac. Well, let's see. Let's make it a quarter pounder with cheese. That's my second favorite, by the way."

The short cashier, her face barely clearing the cash register, shyly said, "Apologies once again, dear sir, but we do not have quarter pounder with cheese."

Ron did a double take. "Well, what do y'all have here?"

She extended her short arm and pointed to the brightly lit menu hoisted above her. Ron looked up.

"Kind sir, if it is a sandwich you desire for this evening's meal, we have the plain McAloo Tiki sandwich, the Mexican McAloo Tiki sandwich, and the Lebanese McAloo Tiki sandwich. We also have a fish sandwich, a big spicy paneer wrap, the veg Maharajah Mac, and our bestseller, the Maharajah Mac." The cashier was smiling.

Ron, frustrated, asked, "Well, what's the Maharajah Mac?"

"Dear sir, it is a sandwich made with chicken patties. Very delicious. Our best seller, sir."

"Well, I guess I'll have that … the Maharajah Mac. My brother—who is at the end of the line—is paying for everything. We're all together here. Make it to go please."

"To go, sir?"

"Yeah, to go. We're heading back to the hotel. We'll snack there with our Indian Mickey D's food. A new experience. It's all cool."

"Oh no, sir. The food will not be cool. It will be served warm, as it should be. And you mean to take away, correct?"

"Yeah to take out. Take away, I guess. Whatever."

"Absolutely, sir. Your food will be ready shortly to take away to the hotel."

"Cool," Ron said, as the cashier looked at him strangely.

Everyone got their to-go/takeaway food and met Anne-Marie and Sheila directly outside the Subway (both were holding vegetarian subs in clear plastic bags). Then the group descended two flights of stairs and walked to the taxis. Janni, who had ordered McAloo Tiki sandwiches for the two drivers, handed them their bagged orders, and everyone started getting into the cabs. Ron, holding his white paper bag with his order, was standing next to Janni, who was holding her order. With his free hand, Ron opened the right rear passenger door and said, "Ladies first."

Janni entered the cab, and Ron followed. He cleared his throat and went for it. "Say, Janni, how about you stay over at the hotel tonight? There's twin beds in my room and good television. We can hang out and enjoy our food together. Good AC. Great bathroom too. And the bar downstairs has drinks and decent wings. They play a lot of Bon Jovi hits. Sinatra too. What you say?"

Janni matter-of-factly said, "That would not be appropriate,

Mr. Ron. Mother and Father—especially Father—would not approve. The wedding starts at two o'clock tomorrow. You can have breakfast tomorrow but not lunch, as there will be plenty of food at the wedding. I will see you around one o'clock with the taxi."

Rani and Deepika, both decked out in shiny blue saris with gold trim, arrived at the Regency Hotel at 1:00 p.m. sharp. The Robinsons, waiting for them in the large, air-conditioned lobby, were dressed in Western attire: business suits and ties for the men, dresses or dress pants with blouses for the women.

Rani and Deepika instructed the taxi driver to wait for them while they got the other guests, and when they entered the lobby and exchanged their greetings, Deepika spoke to the head bellhop, Rajesh, and instructed him to call a taxi, as two (the one waiting for them and another one) would be needed for the trip to her parents' home. "Most certainly," Rajesh said as he bowed slightly to Deepika. "Yes, I will call for a taxi right away."

He walked to the main counter to instruct a receptionist to make the call, and then he smiled and bowed as he made eye contact with Mrs. Robinson, who was holding Curly and Fritz's leashes.

"Good early afternoon, Mrs. Robinson. And how are the two lovely dogs today?"

"Hi, Rajesh, and thank you for asking. Curly and Fritz are fine, and they send their greetings. Don't you, Curly and Fritz? Good dogs ... yes you are ... say hello to Rajesh."

Mrs. Robinson petted her two dogs, and she then said, "And, Rajesh, I must tell you. This hotel is great, and we especially like the dry-cleaning service. So organized and structured, so efficient. Such great service. All of us use the dry-cleaning service here every day. This dress of mine was dry-cleaned here. Thank you so much."

"Pleasure to be of service to you, madame," he said, and minutes later, when the second taxi arrived, he opened and closed the door for Mrs. Robinson.

The Robinson wedding party arrived at the Kumar residence twenty-five minutes after getting into the cabs at the Hyatt Regency. Mr. Robinson paid both drivers, and all guests followed Rani and Deepika inside the three-story white apartment building.

Brian, walking slowly behind his parents and his uncle Ron, looked both to the left and right of the street. There was no traffic on this apartment-complex-lined, narrow street. To the left, he noticed three children, two boys and a girl, no more than ten years old each, kicking a red ball. To the right, he noticed a thin cow with brown hide, walking slowly, foraging for some food scraps.

"Welcome, dear guests," Janni said loudly when the Robinsons were near the front-door entrance. Like Rani and Deepika, she too was dressed in a blue sari with gold trim, and in her hands was a gold plate containing some flammable liquid. A short flame was at the center of the plate, emitting the slightest of black smoke. She was guiding the plate in small circles, telling the wedding party guests that this small fire was to ward off evil energy. "Please. Welcome. Enter."

Mr. and Mrs. Robinson were the first to enter the home. Prior to the taxi ride from the hotel, Brian had instructed, "When entering the Kumar residence, be sure to take off your shoes. Priya and her sisters are always big on that with their apartment back in Las Cruces."

Mrs. Robinson, with Curly and Fritz behind her on their leashes, took off her shoes. She noticed Mr. and Mrs. Kumar stood erect, some seven feet inside their home. Mrs. Kumar, like her daughters, was wearing a blue sari while her husband wore a silk beige kurta with matching silk pants. Both were barefoot, and both didn't like the idea of live animals, in the form of two small dogs, in their home, but out of politeness, they let it go.

"Welcome," Mrs. Kumar said as the guests kept filing in.

Mr. Kumar said, "Blessing to you all." To his left was a large couch, and to his right were plain metal chairs. Priya, dressed in a shiny maroon sari, stood behind her parents.

The guests sat in the couch and in the chairs, with Brian sitting in a chair next to his bride. Rani and Janni offered tea, and all the guests, including Ron, agreed to have some.

When Janni presented Ron his cup of tea, Ron leaned to his left and quietly asked Brian, "Do they have iced tea here? Kinda hot in here. I was hoping for iced tea."

Brian, looking at him, said sternly, "No, they don't. Be polite and drink your hot tea like I'm doing. Remember, when in Rome, do as the Romans."

Ron smiled, said, "Okay, boss," and took a sip of tea.

Minutes after the tea offering, Rani welcomed everyone to a table inside the small kitchen, where numerous plates and bowls displayed various food selections. There was naan, three different types of rice (white, fried, and lemon), vegetable and chicken samosas, pickles, various chutneys, two biryanis (chicken and vegetarian), a fish dish, tandoori chicken, and a mango curd dessert. At the end of the table was a stack of empty dishes.

"Please help yourselves to the food," Mr. Kumar said, holding his white tea cup with his left hand. "There is plenty to eat."

The guests served themselves and ate on the chairs or couch. On the back wall was a large television screen showing an old Bollywood movie, the sound on mute. Polite small talk occupied the late-afternoon wedding luncheon.

At 4:00 p.m., Cha Cha Gi, a short, barefoot, bare-chested Hindu priest of sixty years of age, entered the Kumar home, the inside of his hands touching each other for the traditional namaste greeting, which he gave to everyone. Brian noticed the priest was bald, except for a long, thin ponytail that straddled the priest's back, the hair source being the back center of the priest's head. *Just like the hair of the Hindu priest back in El Paso*, he thought.

Cha Cha Gi went straight to the small puja display of the home, which, per Mr. Kumar's guidance, was in the bedroom directly to the left of the front entrance. As he passed Mrs. Robinson, he saw Curly and Fritz, and bent down next to her. He stared at the dogs momentarily, frowning, then continued walking to the puja room. Everyone filed behind Mr. Kumar, who was behind the short priest. Once inside the bedroom, the guests formed a U-shaped semicircle behind Cha Cha Gi. The puja consisted of a tray with small bowls containing clean water, bananas, mangos, bright flowers, incense, and a candle, the latter directly at the foot of a small Ganesha statue no more than eight inches in height.

Cha Cha Gi sat Indian style before the puja display. He picked up a handful of the flowers, dipped them in the water, then flicked the flowers at the small Ganesha, giving it some water droplets. Next, he placed the flowers on the tray, grabbed a small white cloth, and proceeded to dry the half-man, half-elephant statue and place a tiny necklace of flowers around it. He said a few hymns, unrecognizable to the Westerners. Then, in a soft voice, he said, "Ganesha is the remover of obstacles, the god of wisdom, and the god of beginnings. May the unison of the groom and the bride be a great beginning." He then instructed, "Everyone but the newlyweds, first bow, then kneel, and then touch your head to the floor to honor Ganesha." After everyone completed this ritual, Cha Cha Gi picked up a short stick of prelit incense, held it, and made three clockwise circles with the stick, all before Ganesha. He then chanted in Sanskrit for five minutes.

After the Ganesha pooja, more tea was served in the living room, and the guests engaged in polite conversation. Cha Cha Gi stayed for about an hour, drinking tea and wishing the newlyweds many blessing and much wealth. He occasionally looked at the two small white dogs strangely.

At 6:30 p.m., with the sun down and the skies pitch-black, Mr. Kumar announced, "Dinner is now ready in the kitchen. Please help yourselves."

The food dishes were similar to the earlier luncheon. There were just more of them—more rice dishes, more vegetable dishes, more chicken selections, and more fish. Dinner lasted two hours, during which there was more polite conversation, especially between Mr. Kumar and Mr. Robinson. The two spoke a lot about real estate investments and business matters. Mr. Kumar was impressed with Mr. Robinson's direct style of talking. ("In the United States, real estate usually returns .08 to 1.2 percent of monthly rent revenue, so a one-hundred-thousand-dollar house will usually rent out for eight hundred to twelve hundred dollars.") When the topic turned to Chennai's current water problems (the city of four-and-a-half million was running out of it), Mr. Robinson said, "Man will find a way. Water is not a problem; there's plenty of it. The Israelis have been very successful with desalination plants. Oceans are full of water. Take the salt out, and there you have it. Y'all be good to go."

At 9:00 p.m., with the Robinson party ready to call it a night and head back to the hotel, Ron, who was close to finishing his third cup of hot tea, said, "This has been a very enjoyable wedding. Well done. Just the family. That's the way it should be. And right here in the bride's home. None of the big powwow stuff we have back in the States. People back home sure blow a lot of money on weddings. This quiet stuff is much better."

Janni, sitting next to Ron and sipping from a hot tea cup, said, "Dear Mr. Ron. Thank you for those most gracious and polite comments. However, this is just the first day of the wedding."

He did a double take. "The first day? How many days are there in an Indian wedding?"

She smiled. "Three days, Mr. Ron."

The Robinsons returned to the Hyatt Regency and had drinks at the bar in celebration of Brian's wedding. Breaking protocol, Chuck insisted that he, especially as the best man, pay for all the drinks, and Mr. Robinson finally caved on that issue.

Sitting at the tables with the back wall featuring framed posters of Elvis and Humphrey Bogart in Casablanca, and with a mix of Bon Jovi, George Michael, and Sinatra tunes playing, the Robinson party, all drinking Kingfisher beer, gave toast after toast to the young Brian Robinson.

A large rented banquet room, guests numbering around one hundred, a row of tables filled with food plates, the tile floor barely visible because of the countless flower pedals covering it—that was the scene of day two of the Hindu wedding.

The newlyweds occupied the rug to the left of Cha Cha Gi, who was officiating. And though Mr. Robinson had insisted on paying for all the wedding expenses, including the rent for this hall in the Chennai outskirts, he was overruled by the bride's father, Mr. Kumar, who made it clear Mr. Robinson's generosity was "thoughtful and nice but not necessary, for expenses were already paid for."

The day had started at 10:00 a.m. for Brian and his extended family; it was at that time that Deepika and Janni, both decked out in beautiful, shiny, red satin saris with gold trim, arrived at the Regency Hotel to deliver the clothes the Robinson party was to wear. With help from two taxi drivers and Brian and Chuck, the clothes and shoes and Brian's turban, packed in boxes, were carried upstairs to Ron's room for disbursement. Once the boxes containing the women's saris and sandals were transferred to Mrs. Robinson's room, Deepika and Janni stayed back and assisted Mrs. Robinson, Anne-Marie, and Sheila with unfolding and properly wearing a sari.

Noticing the intricate brown designs on the sisters' hands and feet, Mrs. Robinson had to ask, "What exactly are those patterns, Deepika?"

"Dear madame, these are henna," she said. "It is a colored paste from the henna plant."

"So lovely," Mrs. Robinson said in wonderment. "So detailed. It must have taken you a long time to place such designs on your hands and feet."

"Yes. Of course, madame," Deepika said. "Many hours last night. Janni and I want our sister to look lovely for this most auspicious of occasions."

Back in Ron's hotel room, the four men—groom, best man, the Robinson brothers—had no difficulty figuring out how to wear their maroon sherwanis (long top shirt and loose-fitting pajamalike pants) and brown sandals. There was only one turban, also maroon in color, and it was for the groom, Brian, who upon checking himself out in the mirror once he fitted it to his head, asked, "What do you guys think?"

Chuck, sitting on one of the beds and aiming his cell phone to take a photo, said, "Dude, groovy stuff. Gimme a thumbs-up," and he proceeded to snap a photo of the smiling groom.

"Real nice, son," his father replied while tying his string belt for his pants. "Interesting hat, that's for sure. I'm sure glad Janni got extra-extra-large shirts and pants for yours truly and Ron here. Clothing's still tight, but it'll do. How's your clothes holding up, Ron?"

Ron, squinting while squeezing into his pants, said, "Tight, but I'll manage."

Two hours after Deepika and Priya's arrival at the hotel with the clothes, the Robinsons and the pair of Kumar sisters found themselves at the wedding hall, the bride, her parents, and Rani already there and waiting in a separate adjacent room within the large hall.

"Brian and Chuck, please both wait here," Janni said, leaving the pair at the entrance of the hallway. "But first, please remove your sandals and place them in the corner. Everyone else, also, please remove your sandals. Then follow me."

Janni led John, Ron, Sandra, Anne-Marie, and Sheila to the front of the hall, directly in front of where the bare-chested Cha Cha Gi was sitting Indian style on a wide beige carpet completely covered with red flower pedals. While following Janni's lead, Mrs. Robinson noticed a few stares, as she was carrying both Curly and Fritz, their leashes neatly tucked into her purse that was hugging Fritz.

Brian, standing at the hall entrance, looked ahead and saw what had to be at least one hundred people, all sitting in white plastic chairs, the men dressed similarly to him, except for his turban. The women were all wearing saris. Everyone was barefoot or in sandals, and everyone was looking at him. He looked straight ahead and saw his parents, sister, Ron, and Sheila occupy the first row of seats.

"Decent-size crowd," Chuck said.

"Yeah, sure is."

Suddenly, to the left of the large beige carpet, a side door opened, and out came Mr. and Mrs. Kumar, walking slowly forward toward some empty front-row chairs. Behind the couple, he could see Priya and Rani, both in red saris, similar to their mother's sari.

The Kumars took their seats to the left of the Robinsons. Looking straight ahead, Brian noticed Cha Cha Gi lighting incense sticks. Then came the sound of a beating drum, not too loud and fast, just a slow and steady rhythmic beat. He couldn't make out where the drum sound was coming from. He didn't see any drummer and figured it was recorded music from a built-in sound system within the hall. He noticed Rani standing up and walking toward him and Chuck. She was carrying a small gold dish.

"Hello, Brian. Hello, Chuck," she said, smiling. "Please follow me, gentlemen."

She led the groom and best man to their seats next to Brian's parents. Cha Cha Gi then started singing a few chants, and the music started to play faster and louder.

"Stay in your seat, Brian," Rani said. "I will begin applying the *haldi* to you."

"What is haldi?" Brian asked.

"Turmeric paste." She dipped her right hand in the dish and applied the red-orange paste to Brian's forehead and then his cheeks.

"I see Deepika is doing the same to Priya," Chuck said, smiling. "Applying the paste to Priya's face."

"Yes, that is correct, Chuck," Rani said as she applied more of the haldi.

"And I now see it's your mother who's applying the paste to Priya."

"Yes, Chuck, my whole family will take turns applying the haldi to Priya," Rani said. "Not only on her forehead and face but also her neck, arms, and feet. And so will you guys. Here you go, Mr. Best Man. Apply the haldi to the groom-to-be."

Chuck reached into the dish with his right hand and said, "Okay, dude, here it goes. Let me get some of this on your neck."

Brian, smiling, said, "Thanks, dude. Steady hand now. You're a carpenter by trade. Don't mess this up."

"And what is this paste, Rani?" Mrs. Robinson asked, holding the alert Curly and Fritz in her two arms. The dogs were trying to smell the paste on Chuck's right hand.

"Dear madame, the haldi possesses healing, purifying, and beautification properties. Please, come and apply some to your dear son, my future brother-in-law."

The recorded music steadily got louder and faster and included high-pitched female singing. All the Robinson party took turns applying the haldi on Brian, and to their left, the Kumars were doing the same to the bride, who, when the finishing touches of the haldi were completely applied, stood up and started dancing, moving her arms in L-shaped patterns and shaking her hips. With that, the guests—men and women and children—all stood up, and they too started dancing, moving about, dancing in their individual styles.

Rani said, "C'mon, brother-in-law, Chuck, Anne-Marie, and Sheila. Everyone—Mr. and Mrs. Robinson, you too, Ron— this is a wedding. One must dance." She placed the gold dish containing the haldi underneath Brian's chair. Then she gently grabbed his left hand and guided him to stand and dance.

"Well, this isn't exactly music I'm familiar with, but here goes," Brian said as he started bending his knees and shaking his torso. He looked over at Priya, who was maybe ten yards from him. Their eyes met, she smiled at him, and he started mimicking her arm movements.

"Dude, you got the hang of this," Chuck said, laughing. He too was dancing about.

Priya and her sisters danced together in a coordinated fashion, moving in slow circles. Mr. and Mrs. Kumar just moved their heads and torsos up and down, their feet moving slowly in circles next to their daughters. They did not move their arms, and they both sported broad smiles on their happy faces.

As for Mr. and Mrs. Robinson, they were slowly bouncing up and down and taking short steps, unsure of themselves but having fun and smiling. And Curly and Fritz, forced to move with Mrs. Robinson, were enjoying the ride, based on their energetic, short yaps.

After nearly an hour of dancing, Priya, her parents, and her sisters took a break and got themselves some food from the long tables. Other guests followed their lead, but there was no system to it, as some guests stayed near their seats, dancing to the music that kept playing.

"Well, I've worked me some appetite," Ron said, perspiration covering his forehead and cheeks. "Time for a time-out. I'm gonna grab me some grub."

"I'm right behind ya," Chuck said, also sweating. The two headed toward the food line, and then Brian and the rest of the Robison party decided to do the same.

Priya and her family sat at their seats, their paper plates, napkins, and plastic utensils on their laps, their mango lassis in foam cups either in their hands or on the floor next to their chair. Brian and his family walked past them while heading to the food line.

"My apologies for now," Mr. Kumar said as he stood up. "I have some men bringing in long tables for us to eat our meals. They should be coming here shortly."

"Sure, no problem," Mr. Robinson said. "It's all good. This is a lot of fun."

Mrs. Kumar smiled at Mr. Robinson, and then she looked curiously at Curly and Fritz.

"Hello, wife," Brian said to Priya as he walked by her. She smiled at him reassuringly and gave him a thumbs-up.

She softly said, "Can't really talk now; tomorrow's the main ceremony."

The Robinsons got their food and started heading back to their seats, and as Brian was about ready to start eating, he noticed a half dozen men carrying long brown tables. With the music playing and some guests still dancing, Mr. Kumar stood up and started directing traffic, instructing the men to set up the tables near the food tables.

A few minutes later, Mr. Kumar stood up and waved to Ms. Robinson. "Please. Come. Join us. The tables are set," he said. "Your family is to sit to the left of us. Please. Come."

The Robinson party stood up and sat at one of the long

tables as directed. They started eating their selected food items, a combination of Indian and American favorites. Ron, always a hearty eater, had selected two slices of Domino's pizza, two pieces of KFC chicken, one slice of naan, one vegetable samosa, and a couple of fritters he was unfamiliar with but later learned were called pakora. He tried every item he had placed on his plate and washed it down with water from a plastic bottle.

"Too bad there's no iced tea or beer," he said, turning to Chuck. "But the KFC is close to what we have back home. No original recipe, but the crispy style is the same. Pizza is so-so. No pepperoni. I can tell they use goat cheese here, so it tastes different. These fritters are pretty good."

"Cool," Chuck said. "Grub's pretty good. I like this lentil dish—good with garlic naan. Like you, I'm not a fan of goat cheese."

Brian was eating a chicken samosa and gave just a tiny morsel of it to Fritz, who ate it quickly.

"Dear, you know the rule: if you give a piece to one of my cuties, you must also give it to the other cutie."

"Yes, Mother, of course." He cut out a small piece of his samosa and handed it to Curly.

The Hindi music, wherever it was coming from, kept playing, and the crowd of dancing guests thinned down as more and more people filed to get food. Brian looked to his right to catch a glimpse of his bride. She was eating, and then she caught a glimpse of her husband. She smiled and gave him a thumbs-up.

Brian smiled back and reciprocated with a thumbs-up of his own, and then, out of the corner of his left eye, he saw a man dressed in a light beige robe. He looked squarely at the man. It couldn't be … Yes it was! Father O'Leary! Unmistakably. The white hair, the small, dark brown, wooden cross around his neck. It was Father O'Leary. What a surprise. He stood up and started walking toward the Catholic priest.

"Father O'Leary, gang. He's here!" he said as he passed members of his family.

Father O'Leary approached the groom, and they shook hands and hugged.

"What a surprise, Father. You coming all the way to celebrate with us. So nice to see you! How did you know where to come for the wedding?"

"Likewise, my child. Glad I could make it. Technology and your father are the answers. Your father told me the dates, and I didn't want to miss it. Aren't smartphones a great invention? As you know, I always wanted to visit India. In a couple of days, I'll be in Delhi to visit where Saint Teresa practiced the faith."

The two walked over to the table where the Robinsons were sitting, but before Father O'Leary got himself a seat, he made it a point to introduce himself to the Kumars. They all remembered him from the wedding in Albuquerque, and Priya was especially thankful for his visit and presence, saying, "Oh, thank you so much, kind sir, for attending our wedding."

"The pleasure is mine, dear child. As you know, I always wanted to visit your home country, and yesterday I spent the entire day visiting where Saint Thomas preached the good word."

Father O'Leary took a seat next to Brian and Chuck. Just as he was about to stand up to get food, Brian said, "Dad, you never told me Father O'Leary was coming."

His father replied, "I wanted to keep it a surprise, son. Congratulations on your wedding."

The Hindi music continued to play for the rest of the afternoon, and there was more dancing. Around four o'clock, servers, all males dressed in white shirts, black pants, and black vests, brought out more trays of food and replenished the long food tables. Father O'Leary made it a point to eat only Indian food and no meat while in India.

Then at six o'clock, Cha Cha Gi stood up before the Kumar-Robinson guest tables and said, "Thank you for this celebration.

Today has been the *sangreet*, the introduction of the couple. Bride and groom, please join me here for the introduction."

Priya and Brian both stood up and walked up to Cha Cha Gi. They turned to face the crowd.

"Tomorrow, this beautiful couple will have their third and final day of their wedding. Please join me in applauding them."

Everyone stood up and started clapping. Curly and Fritz both barked short barks, and Mrs. Robinson said, "Shush. Priya and Brian are getting married."

Once the applause faded, Cha Cha Gi said, "Thank you for this celebration. Stay as you wish. Tomorrow's festivities and celebration will be here, starting at noon."

Guests stayed for another hour or so, and then the crowd started thinning. Mr. Kumar, carrying a box of envelopes, approached Brian, who was sitting next to Chuck and Father O'Leary. Rani was behind her father.

"These are the gifts for your celebration, Mr. Brian. You should open them. Rani will help you."

"Yes, sir, absolutely," Brian said. He stood up, and Mr. Kumar spread the numerous envelops—dozens and dozens of them—on the table before him.

"Dear brother-in-law," Rani said, smiling. "Notice wedding gifts here are all money gifts."

"I see that," Brian said as he opened the envelope and kept finding rupee bills.

"Yes, that is the tradition," she said. "And the monetary value must always end in a one—51 or 101 or 301 rupees, something like that. Always the money ends in the number one."

"Why's that?" Brian asked.

"For good luck," she said, smiling.

"Yes, good luck for this most auspicious of days," Mr. Kumar added. "We will count the money, and Rani will keep it for you and Priya's behalf."

"Okay," Brian said.

Noon the next day at the same rented hall. Mr. Kumar had wanted to have the baraat where the groom arrives on a white horse, but finding a white horse proved to be too difficult, cumbersome, and expensive (one hundred thousand rupees), not to mention he wasn't sure if Mr. Brian, though a military man, knew how to ride a horse. With that expense saved, he decided to buy more food for the wedding.

Brian, dressed like he was yesterday, turban and all, was standing next to his parents and Chuck at the front entrance. To the left were the Kumars. The way they were standing, he couldn't see his bride because the Kumars had encircled her. He looked out in front of him. It seemed it was the same guests as yesterday, perhaps a few more. He looked out for Father O'Leary and found him to be sitting toward the right front portion of the seats. Like yesterday, he was wearing a brown robe, brown sandals, and a wooden cross around his neck. And also like yesterday, the long food tables were to the left, as were the honored guests' tables for the Kumars and the Robinsons.

Brian noticed Cha Cha Gi sitting Indian style on a large carpet in front of where the seats ended. Cha Cha Gi was bare chested again and lighting some incense sticks. Brian noticed there were more trays and flowers on the carpet next to Cha Cha Gi.

Rani approached Brian carrying a gold dish. Brian figured she was carrying the turmeric paste once again, just like yesterday, and he was correct, because Rani, once she stood directly in front of Brian, began applying the paste on his forehead—just his forehead this time.

As Rani was putting the final touches, a young, thin man, wearing a beige kurta with white pajamalike pants and beige sandals, and carrying a huge seashell, walked toward Brian. Standing next to Brian, he brought the seashell opening to his mouth and blew in strongly, producing a loud horn sound. He repeated the blowing, emanating two more loud horn sounds, and all the guests stood up. Then the Kumar family, with Priya in the middle, started walking up the middle aisle to where Cha Cha Gi was standing.

"Kind in-laws, do follow our family to Cha Cha Gi," Rani told Mr. and Mrs. Robison and Brian, and the trio followed behind the Kumars.

Cha Cha Gi stood up and greeted both families by combining his hands in prayerlike fashion beyond his bare and hairy chest, bowing down slightly forward, and saying "Namaste."

The Kumars returned in likewise fashion with "Namaste."

The Robinsons, slow on the uptake, eventually followed the custom and said, "Namaste."

Cha Cha Gi instructed the Robinson party, except for Brian, to take their front-row seats and for the Kumar sisters, except for the bride, to do the same. Brian got a good view of his bride for the first time on this third and last day of their Hindu wedding. *Unrecognizable* was the word that came to his mind, for Priya truly was unrecognizable. A gold headpiece covered the top and sides of her head. A chain, also made of gold, hung from the left side of her head to the edge of her left nostril. Gold necklaces covered her neck, and gold bangles covered her forearms.

Cha Cha Gi gestured for Mr. and Mrs. Kumar to stand next to the bride. They did as instructed, and then Cha Cha Gi presented a large red-and-white garland of flowers to Brian and said, "Place it around the neck of your bride."

Brian did so. Then Cha Cha Gi gave a similar garland for Priya to place around Brian's neck. She did so with difficulty, as Brian, at six feet, was considerably taller than Priya. To add to the challenge, he was wearing the tall turban. His forward bow helped his bride accomplish her task. The couple was now facing the guests.

Cha Cha Gi, barefoot and bare chested for all three days of the wedding festivities, nodded at Mr. Kumar, and then he loudly said for all guests to hear, "We will now do the *kanya daan* where the bride's parents give her away."

Mr. Kumar took Priya's left hand and placed it in Brian's right hand. "Mr. Brian," he said, looking directly at his son-in-law, "as I informed you last week in your country, you now have duties and obligations concerning my daughter, your wife."

There was an awkward pause, and then Brian managed to say, "Yes, sir."

Cha Cha Gi turned around and sat Indian-style on the red carpet behind him. He instructed the couple to still hold hands but to sit like he was. He started placing small wooden pieces and tiny twigs into a sizable clay bowl that resembled a large wok. He lit some wooden matches and also some more incense sticks. He placed the incense sticks to his left and added more tiny twigs to the clay bowl fire he had started.

"This fire is called an *agni*," Cha Cha Gi said as fine gray smoke billowed from the clay bowl. He quickly stood up and instructed the bride and groom to do the same and face him. He then bent down and picked up a sturdy white cloth, tying one end around Brian's waist and the other end around Priya's. After putting the final touches to the knot around Priya's midsection, he started singing high-pitched Hindi hymns in Sanskrit that had a lot of "oh" and "umm" sounds. While still singing, he reached down and placed a small green coconut within the slack portion of the cloth separating the bride and groom. He told the couple to join hands.

With the small fire producing a steady stream of smoke, Cha Cha Gi said, "The couple will now do the *manghalphera*." He instructed the couple to each take four steps around the agni, "Slowly, and ensure the coconut between you does not become dislodged." He pointed at Brian, instructing him to lead the way. Brian took four steps, a full rotation around the agni fire, and Priya followed while keeping a watchful eye on the balancing coconut.

"The agni symbolizes the highest degree of a witness," Cha Cha Gi said loudly. "The four steps around the agni symbolize dharma, which is moral duty, *artha*, which is prosperity, *kama*, which is the pursuit of earthly pleasures, and *moksha*, which is spiritual salvation."

Ron leaned over to Chuck and softly whispered, "This is pretty cool. I just hope that coconut stays on board." Chuck smiled and nodded approvingly.

Cha Cha Gi sang some more Hindi hymns for about a minute, then he said, "We will now do the *saptapadi*." After more hymns, he said, "The saptapadi is a vow to support each other. The groom will lead for the first four rotations. Then the bride will lead for the final three." He looked at the newlyweds. "Be sure to take seven steps around the agni."

Brian did as instructed in a clockwise fashion, going slowly, careful not to make any sudden shifts.

"The first of the saptapadi rotations symbolizes respect for one another," Cha Cha Gi said as the couple completed their first rotation. "The second rotation reminds us to develop mental, physical, and spiritual balance in our lives. ... The third of the saptapadi tells the couple to prosper together and acquire wealth to share in their lives." Once Brian and Priya started their fourth rotation, Cha Cha Gi said, "The fourth of the saptapadi reminds the couple to acquire happiness and harmony and knowledge."

Once Brian and Priya completed their fourth agni rotation, Cha Cha Gi explained, "Now the bride will lead the saptapadi. Simply turn around and walk around the agni, counterclockwise now."

Brian turned around, and then Priya did the same. She started taking small steps around the agni. Brian did the same, fixating his eyes on the green coconut between them.

"The fifth of the saptapadi reminds the new couple to raise strong and virtuous children," Cha Cha Gi said. Shortly thereafter, he said to the crowd, "And to live in perfect harmony—that is what the sixth of the saptapadi tells us. It is this sixth of the saptapadi that, in my humble opinion, is the most important of all lessons." He chanted in Sanskrit and watched the young couple walk slowly. The agni's flames were small but of the sturdy quality, and the smell of incense was pungent, emitting steady smoke.

"And the last of the saptapadi reminds the new couple to be the best of lifelong friends."

More hymns from Cha Cha Gi, and then he instructed the couple to sit on the carpet Indian style. He removed the coconut between Priya and Brian, placed it on the carpet, sang more chants, washed his hands, and instructed the newlyweds to wash theirs. "Now apply this red powder on your bride's forehead," he told Brian, handing him a small gold plate holding the dry scarlet paste. "Just a small mark. A dot will do."

Brian dipped his right index finger in the paste and gently pressed his fingertip to the center of Priya's forehead. Cha Cha Gi nodded in a satisfied way and then said, "After wiping your hand, tie this black necklace around her neck." He handed Brian a white cloth for the first task and then handed him the thin beaded necklace.

Brian tied the necklace around Priya's neck, and then Cha Cha Gi said, "Now it is time for this new couple to eat a piece of cake." He handed each a small morsel of cake that, to Brian, resembled and tasted like a soft piece of vanilla fudge. After eating their cake portions (they had eaten the small samples out of their hands), Cha Cha Gi said, "Stand, hold hands, and walk down the middle aisle." Applause and cell phone photos followed the newlyweds as they walked past the crowd.

Brian was sitting next to Priya at the head guest table. Chicken biryani, pakoras, a slice of Domino's pizza, and two pieces of KFC chicken filled his plate. Chuck was to his left, eating from a similar plate, while Priya was to his right, working on a samosa and some vegetable biryani. Just as he was about to try a pakora, he noticed an older man—a man he didn't recognize—approaching the head table. He quickly turned to Priya to see if she knew this man, but she was talking to Rani.

"Namaste," the man said, bowing in front of Brian.

Hearing the greeting, Priya immediately turned around and said, "Oh, Mr. Mehta. So nice to see you. Thank you most kindly for attending our wedding."

"It is my pleasure to do so," he replied, and he gave her the namaste greeting. "Such a lovely ceremony. And you both did so well. You are a lovely couple. I would not miss this most auspicious of ceremonies." He handed her a small white envelope. "Something for you both. It is a money gift, as is the tradition here. And the amount ends with one. For good luck." He smiled.

Priya opened the envelope and counted 501 rupees. She smiled.

"Mr. Brian, I understand that in your country, the tradition is to give gifts often in the form of kitchenware. I studied in Canada and in the United States many years ago, and I had the honor of attending a wedding in the state of Delaware. It was very nice. But here in India, the tradition is to give money gifts." He smiled.

Brian smiled back, saying, "Thank you."

"And, Priya, your father told me you will live in America and work with your husband as a real estate developer. How exciting."

"Yes, it is true, Mr. Mehta. Brian and his roommate, Mr. Chuck, are very knowledgeable about the real estate business, as is Brian's father. We are excited. Please visit us if you can."

"Thank you so kindly," Mr. Mehta said, smiling once more. He correctly deduced the man sitting next to Mr. Brian, a man who was politely looking at him, was Mr. Chuck, and he proceeded to give this Mr. Chuck the namaste greeting of left and right hands together, opposing palms and fingers perfectly lined up and touching, as if the person was praying. Chuck returned the greeting in kind.

"Most exciting indeed," Mr. Mehta said. He was barefoot and wearing loose-fitting pants and a tunic, both off-white in color, the tunic a slightly darker shade, almost beige. "And I must tell you, dear Priya, now the Ms. Brian, that should you desire to once again write for the *Chennai Times*, I will definitely find an opportunity for you. In fact, this I tell you, I already have one such opportunity."

"Is it true?" Priya asked.

"Yes. You can work for us while you live in the United States. Yes, I am certain of this."

"You think so, Mr. Mehta?"

"Yes. Technology today is so advanced, thanks to the gods. You could be a freelance writer, writing a weekly or biweekly column for our newspaper. I even have the name of the column in mind. *Notes from America.* I have already spoken about this to management, and this I tell you—they approved my idea."

"Truly?" Priya asked, thrilled and excited.

"Yes. They are on board, as the Americans say."

Brian smiled and said, "You should do it, honey. It's right up your alley."

"This is a most welcomed opportunity, Mr. Mehta. Yes, yes indeed," Priya said joyfully. She blurted, "I accept this writing job." (Later that evening, she realized she accepted the employment without discussing compensation, but the truth is she would have taken the job even if it was uncompensated, which it wasn't. It would pay one thousand rupees—fifteen dollars—per article). A writer with a byline—that was worth something.

"Wonderful. We will keep in contact, Ms. Brian. Electronic mail is such a wonderful invention. Blessings to you both."

After their meals, Priya and Brian stayed at the head table and discussed various topics: their upcoming honeymoon in New York City (Priya's choice, "No way can I live in America without experiencing its biggest city), Las Cruces real estate, the subject of her first *Notes from America* column (McDonald's: An American and Indian Comparison).

"Oh, what a lovely ceremony. What a lovely three days it has been," Mrs. Robinson said as she took a photo of Brian and Priya at the head table. "So colorful. The flowers—look at those beautiful garlands around your neck. And the saris—you look so lovely, Priya. A beautiful bride. I love this sari I'm wearing. So exciting, so different, so pleasant. And, son, your turban, that is something special. It looks great on you."

"Thank you, Mom. And thank you and Dad for paying for our wedding."

"Oh, it is our pleasure, dear. Believe you me. This is so exciting. And the Hindu priest did such a lovely job. I love the smell of incense. How lovely." She kept taking photos of the folks at the head table.

"And your father and I can't wait to visit the Taj Mahal, Brian. We leave tomorrow, as you know."

"Yes, Mom."

"Uncle Ron will join us. I think Janni is coming too. And Anne-Marie and Sheila, they just informed me and your father that their plans have changed. You know they were supposed to fly with you and Priya to London, and they wanted to backpack Europe and—"

"They changed their plans?"

"Yes, dear. That's what I'm saying. They already decided to take the fall semester off from school, as you know. That would have given them the time to backpack Europe. Now they want to join us for the trip to the Taj Mahal, and then they want to backpack India. They like it here."

"Well, that's cool," Brian said. "Good for them."

"Yes, it is most exciting," Priya added. "I have seen the Taj Mahal once, when I was a little girl. You will not be disappointed, Mrs. Robinson. This I tell you. And we are happy for your daughter and Sheila."

Curly and Fritz were on their four legs, sniffing the floor and Mrs. Robinson's feet (she was wearing thin brown sandals that exposed her feet). She said, "Oh, thank you, dear. Again, such a lovely wedding. And we will send you photos from the Taj Mahal."

Priya and Brian kept eating their dishes while Chuck, Anne-Marie, and Sheila engaged in conversation with Mr. and Mrs. Robinson. Ron and Janni sat together while eating, with Ron periodically feeding small morsels of food (mostly tiny bits of KFC chicken) to Curly and Fritz.

"Here, you try it, Janni," he said. "Feed Curly and Fritz. They love this chicken."

"No, no, Mr. Ron. The dogs are lovely, but I am nonetheless scared of them."

"No need to be scared. See? Watch me." The canine duo ate from his hand. "See? It's easy. And see how happy Curly and Fritz are now that they're fed? They're wagging their tails. That's a sign they're happy."

Janni still resisted, but Ron insisted, and she finally caved, allowing Curly and Fritz to eat out of her right hand. She started laughing as the dogs' licking tickled her. "See? They're happy," Ron said, smiling. "Good job. They like you. Don't you, Curly and Fritz? You like Janni. Yes, you both do." He sat back in his chair and stretched his back. "This is a nice wedding. Real nice. And I like the drum music once we started eating. Nice rhythm."

"It is called the *dhol*," Janni said. "It played softly during the saptapadi, but it was difficult to hear, especially when the priest spoke. Now we hear it well."

To the left, they saw Father O'Leary coming to the head table. Like yesterday, he was in his brown robe and brown sandals, and he sported a beaming smile. He started shaking hands and talking with Mr. and Mrs. Robinson. Then he made his way leftward, smiling and greeting Ron, Janni, Chuck, Anne-Marie, and Sheila.

"And the newlyweds. Mr. and Mrs. Brian Robinson. Brian and Priya. What a lovely wedding for you both. Namaste," he said, his hands in prayer formation, his smile wide and confident and sincere. "Congratulations to you both."

"Thank you, Father," Brian said.

"Namaste to you, sir," Priya added.

"A wonderful ceremony indeed," Father O'Leary reiterated. "Great symbolism, great meaning. The walking around the fire— how nice to stress the importance of respect, balance, happiness, knowledge, friendship. Very impressive."

"Yes it was, Father," Brian said. "So nice of you to come all the way to India to celebrate our wedding."

"Oh, as we've discussed, Brian and Priya, the pleasure is mine, I assure you."

Priya asked, "Have you eaten, kind sir? There is plenty to eat."

"Oh I have. Great food. The samosas and curries are wonderful."

"That is good to hear," Priya said. She then asked, "We return to the States in less than two days. How long will your stay in India be, sir?"

"Kind of you to ask, dear child. I always wanted to visit Delhi, and my flight leaves tomorrow for that city. No definite plans, but I imagine I will return stateside in a week or two."

Brian and Chuck were at the hotel's swimming pool. It was the next day, the day after the final wedding day. Earlier in the morning, Brian had said thank you and goodbyes to his parents, sister, and Sheila at the airport before their flight to Agra to experience the Taj Mahal. Priya was at her parents' home, along with her sisters, to do some final packing and say her goodbyes, as her (and Brian's and Chuck's) flight to London was early tomorrow morning. Ron too was at the Kumar home, passing up on the Agra trip in order to hang out with Janni and take care of

Curly and Fritz. (Janni was starting to like the canine duo, and Mrs. Robinson wasn't sure if dogs were allowed around and inside the Taj Mahal. "Why risk it?").

The roommates and business partners were chilling, sipping Kingfisher beers, enjoying the sun. They hadn't checked out the water yet but had plans to do so later.

"Bud, there's something I've been meaning to tell ya."

"Oh? Okay. What's up."

"I'm not on that plane with you and Priya tomorrow."

"No way."

"Way."

"Why?"

"I like it here. I belong here—at least for now."

"You're serious?"

"Yep. I've made up my mind. My relationship with Lisa is shot. She didn't want to come here, and I kind of figured that was really the end. Plus, I like it here. The people—they just do their thing and leave you alone. Plus, I like the fact that it's dark at six thirty at night. There's traffic during the day, but at night it's quiet. People are in their homes, and they are quiet. I like quiet."

Brian straightened up from his chair. "So no house flipping with me and Priya?"

"I'm afraid not. At least not for six months. Or a year. I'm not sure how long I'll stay here. I'll see how it goes."

"What will you do?"

"Well, there's always a demand for a carpenter out there. Who knows. Maybe I'll do house flipping here."

"You serious about this?"

"Dead serious. I need some time to chill, and this is a good place for that. People are calm here. I like calm."

Brian thought for a moment. "You like it that much here, huh? When did your idea of staying here kick in?"

"You know what it was, dude? It was one of those first days, when we were visiting where Saint Thomas preached. Seeing that sight, seeing the Homeless Jesus Bench. It all got me thinking. What do I want to do with my life? And where do I want to do it? I can do a lot of good here in India, help people with my carpentry skills."

The two sipped from their beers.

"Well, I guess I owe you some money. You fronted half of the buy-in fee for that New Year's poker tournament."

Chuck was quiet. Then he managed a shy "Yeah."

"When I get back to Las Cruces, I'll wire you the money."

"Thanks, Brian. I know you will. I know this is all late in the game. I wanted to tell you sooner, but with the wedding and all, it would have been awkward. It's just that I've been thinking this is the place for me. At least for now."

"Understood, man. And you gotta do what's right for you. And I have to ask you, you good on money for a while? As you know, our honeymoon's in New York City. It's for three days. Heck, I've got National Guard drill in eleven days. Hey, if need be, I can wire you the money from the Big Apple. Just set up an account here in Chennai."

"That won't be necessary. I'm good for a while. Send me the money once you get back in Las Cruces. I've got a bit more than one thousand bucks right now. It's not expensive here. I'll lay low until you wire me my share of the money."

"Okay. Text me if you need it sooner."

"Agreed," Chuck said. "I think you and Priya will do great, really. Just move my stuff over and place it in storage if you need to at the U-Haul station. I'll reimburse you. You can use my pickup if you need it. Or Priya can use it. Who knows? Maybe I'm back in Las Cruces in six months. I'll send you a power of attorney if need be."

"Cool," Brian said.

"You'll have about forty-five thousand bucks. That's enough to start house flipping. That small house on Lomas is still for sale for just that amount. I bet you can talk down the sellers another five K."

"Yeah. It'll work out," Brian said reassuringly. "Like I said, you gotta do what's right for you. Priya and I will be okay."

While Brian and Chuck were sipping beers poolside and discussing Chuck's stay in India, Ron, over at the Kumar home—a forty-five-minute drive away—was showing Janni and her mother how to feed Curly and Fritz. At first fearful of the two small dogs, Janni and Mrs. Kumar were getting the hang of feeding the dogs small bites from their hands. They were petting the dogs too, enjoying the animals' pleasant and relaxed disposition when they were petted.

Janni and Ron, both on the couch with Curly and Fritz (Mrs. Kumar sat on a chair next to them), engaged in conversation while feeding and petting the dogs. Janni was sipping her hot tea while Ron, who had difficulty finding a store that sold beer or liquor in Chennai, just drank bottled water. As for Priya, Rani, and Deepika, they were packing their clothes in a separate room. Tomorrow, Rani and Deepika would join Priya and Brian at the airport, but their itinerary was not westward to London and then New York City but rather eastward, specifically Chennai to Singapore to Los Angeles and then to El Paso.

"Thank you so much, Mr. Ron, for showing us the way to handle Curly and Fritz," Janni said, smiling, as Mrs. Kumar was petting the two dogs. "They are quite lovely and well behaved. I would not have thought it possible to have dogs in our home."

"Sure, nothing to it," Ron said. "Once a dog gets to know you, it'll be your friend and protector forever. See, they like you and your mother."

Mr. Kumar was having tea at the dinner table, observing the petting of the dogs and listening in on the conversation.

"Yes, thank you, Mr. Ron, for showing my daughter and

wife the ways with these dogs. The animals seem quite content to be here."

"Absolutely, Mr. Kumar. Like I said, there's nothing to it really."

Mr. Kumar took a sip of tea. He rubbed his chin and asked, "Mr. Ron, what do you do in your country? How much money do you make?"

Ron, taken aback by the question, straightened himself from the couch. He looked at Mr. Kumar and saw that this man was looking directly at him and serious about his question.

"Well, I do odd jobs, sir," he said. "I work for a lawn-maintenance company when they need me. I also work as a janitor a couple of days a week. Night shift. And right before the wedding here, I got a call from a Grubhub manager who told me they'll probably have a job for me in a couple of weeks."

"What is Grubhub?"

"Food delivery."

"How much does it pay?"

"I'll be making about ten to twelve dollars an hour there."

"I see," Mr. Kumar said, quickly doing the math (around seven hundred rupees).

"And I also draw disability from the Social Security Administration."

"Oh?" Mr. Kumar said. "And how much money is that?"

"Well, sir, that's about nine hundred dollars per month. I'm still allowed to work with my disability. I try to make three thousand dollars a month. I make that most months."

Mr. Kumar's eyes widened, and his neck seemed to spring up. *Three thousand times about seventy rupees to the dollar is … two hundred ten thousand rupees per month.* He took a sip of tea and looked at his daughter Janni. Then he looked at Ron. "Mr. Ron, tell me, when is your anniversary? When were you born and at what time of the day were you born?"

Janni smiled.

Earlier in the morning, the entire crew—the Kumar family, Ron, and Chuck—bid farewell to the newlyweds, and Rani and Deepika.

Brian and Chuck bear-hugged before Brian and Priya entered the airport to check in their luggage.

"Take care of yourself, buddy. I'll wire you the money as soon as I can."

"Thanks, Brian. Best to you and Priya," Chuck said. "And good luck with everything. I just need some time here to chill and do some good works. And remember—that house on Lomas is still on the market."

"Absolutely," Brian said.

Chuck ended by saying to his best friend, "Namaste."

Brian replied, "Namaste to you too, buddy."

The young couple waved to everyone. Brian, now getting ready to push the luggage on a trolley, had a hard time grasping what he was seeing. Mrs. Kumar was holding Curly in her arms while Janni had Fritz in hers. *Amazing.*

"Visit us in New Mexico," Priya said loudly as she waved at her parents.

The flight to London took eleven hours. Once at Heathrow Airport, Brian and Priya had a five-hour layover before their flight to Newark Liberty International Airport. Both were tired but excited about their upcoming honeymoon in America's largest city.

Once the Wi-Fi kicked in at Heathrow, Brian received a ton of texts with images: photos of Mom and Dad and Anne-Marie and Sheila enjoying themselves at the Taj Mahal. From his mother: "The trip of a lifetime. We send our best wishes. Anne-Marie and Sheila are anxious to start backpacking this beautiful country."

From Ron, photos of him with the Kumars, then Mrs. Kumar and Janni feeding Curly and Fritz, and Mr. Kumar sipping tea.

"Safe travels from us in Chennai. Curly and Fritz enjoying their new temporary home. I'm thinking of staying here in Chennai for some time. Wishing you both a blast in the Big Apple."

And from Father O'Leary, who, on the last day of the Hindu wedding, had the phone number of the Robinsons and Brian (through WhatsApp): "Enjoying Delhi. I feel a calling from the Lord to stay here and continue the great and important works of Saint Teresa." Behind him, in the background, was a clear photo of the patron saint of doubters herself, then a text below that photo: "I have decided to retire in Delhi, teach English, and continue the example of Mother Teresa. May our Lord bless you both. In God's name, Father O'Leary."

Brian and Priya hung out at Heathrow. When they were hungry, they hit a food court—Priya ate vegetarian Indian food while Brian settled on fish 'n' chips. Afterward, they settled at one of the many cafés; Priya had her tea and read a magazine while Brian had coffee and caught up on sports scores and news from his recharging iPhone. (He thankfully brought a converter charger.)

The flight from Heathrow to Newark was slated to take eight hours. Priya was sound asleep soon after takeoff, but Brian was wide awake. India had been so much: new, different, old, pleasant, shocking at times, busy, slow, noisy, and quiet. Everything and with extremes. Big contrasts and so many of them. The wedding had gone off well, but there was so little time to relax and digest it all. He started reflecting: *A great wedding, but Priya never had the chance to stay with me at the hotel, and I couldn't stay over at her home. New York will be great; at least it will be time spent together, some time to have sex. I miss sex. I miss nachos and cheese. I miss Corona beer.*

He pressed the photo selection on his iPhone and started going over the photos of the past year: he and Priya in Professor Martin's Independent Study course; the buffet line at Bombay Palace in Las Cruces where he, Priya, Rani, and Deepika had eaten lunch; photos at the Inn of the Mountain Gods Casino—the Native American beauty pageant winner; Priya and her sisters with dead animals mounted on the walls; Thanksgiving at his mom and dad's; Vegas with Chuck after the deep poker finish; snowshoeing around Albuquerque; a Friday movie night with Priya and her sisters—Chuck with a Corona, Priya working on a Reese's peanut butter cup; paired up with Priya on a two-seater bike; him with Priya at Lorenzo's before the reading of the papers; and the newlyweds with Father O'Leary at the Church of the Risen Savior. Then came the tons of photos from India: traffic in Chennai surrounding the taxi—tons of motorcycles and motor scooters; the Saint Thomas chapel; a photo of Chuck next to the Homeless Jesus Bench; the many animal granite carvings and temples at Mahabalipuram; him and Priya with the Gandhi statue in Pondicherry; Hindu wedding day one at the Kumars; day two, with turban and all; Priya and the henna on her hands and feet; day three with Priya, him, his mom and dad, and Ron; him and Priya with the Kumars; Ron and Janni with Curly and Fritz; Priya and him with Father O'Leary.

He kept looking at the many photos. Then he started reading an issue of *Time* magazine. Twenty minutes into his reading, he started to doze off.

An announcement came on the airline: "Please fasten your seat belts. Estimated time to land at Newark Airport is twenty-five minutes."

Brian woke up at the sound of the announcement. He glanced to his left and saw that Priya was still sleeping soundly, her seat belt fastened. Looking down, he saw the *Time* magazine next to his feet and his open carry-on bag. Protruding out of his carry-on was an old copy of the *New Yorker* with a yellow Post-it marking the article he had read months before. This was such an old issue—the January 7, 2019, issue. It had started with Chuck, for it was his roommate who had come across the issue and the article during the holidays. "Dude, I saw this magazine at a house I was working on. Maybe it can help you for your Gandhi paper," he had said a week or two after the Vegas poker tournament. "I told the homeowner about your school project, and he said I could keep the issue."

Brian remembered reading the article and highlighting the parts that had interested him. He had brought this *New Yorker* issue with him to Chennai to gain a certain perspective about India. He had forgotten about the article this past busy week. He removed the issue from his carry-on duffel.

"A Critic at Large. A Passage from India. Ruth Prawer Jhabvala and the Art of Ambivalence." That was the title of the article. He started reading the portions he had previously highlighted:

> But Jhabvala was her married name; Ruth was not Indian, a point she later took pains to stress …
>
> Ruth Prawer was born in Cologne in 1927 into a bourgeois, assimilated Jewish family …
>
> Jhabvala's work scrutinizes societies never quite her own. "Once you're a refugee," she said, "I guess you're always a refugee." …
>
> Candid to a fault, "Myself in India" loses its pungency when Jhabvala posits that "most Indians" ignore poverty because of "their belief in reincarnation" …
>
> "If you don't say that India is simply paradise on earth, and the extended Hindu family the most perfect way of organizing, you're anti-Indian," she told a *Times* interviewer in 1983 …
>
> Jhabvala's clipped social satire belongs to a world entirely different from the sprawling canvases and the linguistic innovation of Roy, Rushdie, Amitav Ghosh, and Vikram Seth.

Reading the highlighted passages made Brian ponder why he hadn't discussed this article with Priya when they were both working on their papers for Professor Martin's class, but then it came back to him.

It's too sensitive, he thought. *It's a critique. Ambivalent to beggars and poverty because of a belief in reincarnation. I didn't know how to approach this subject with Priya.*

The article had left his radar screen only to resurface when Priya asked him to marry her, and the next thing he knew, part of his wedding would take place in India. Now married, he felt better about broaching the article's critical arguments. Originally, he had planned to discuss the article in India, but the schedule was so tight, and he had so little time alone with his bride. He promised to discuss the article during their honeymoon.

He glanced at his comfortably sleeping bride.

It's been a great year, he thought. *Largely thanks to her.*

The article made him further reflect on the past week. India: he had been concerned about drinking the water, but there was bottled water everywhere. *Sure they were beggars, but as Dad said, "Albuquerque has its beggars too." India did something for so many—Anne-Marie and Sheila changing their plans, Mom and Dad having the trip of their lifetime, Father O'Leary deciding to retire there, Ron too extending his stay. And most of all, Chuck staying back in India to chill, do some good, and figure things out.*

In the background, with the window shade open behind his bride, he could make out New York Harbor and the Statue of Liberty, small but visible nonetheless on this clear day. Priya had insisted that they visit this cherished site during their honeymoon.

Brian gave her a couple of gentle nods. "Priya, Priya. Wake up," he said softly. His face was close to hers. "Wake up, Priya. We're about to land. And the Statue of Liberty is visible."

She slowly opened her eyes, then she stretched her shoulders. "The statue is visible?" She turned to see through the window. "Oh, thank you, dear husband. This is most wonderful. We will visit it, won't we?"

"Yes, Priya. Absolutely. Most definitely."

She had planned for this moment, and here she was, now confronted with it, now living it. During her research for the Independent Study paper, she had come across many readings, some including the immigrant story of America. So much of it took place here in New York Harbor and Ellis Island, the statute representing liberty, a theme so central to the immigrant story itself.

It was Priya who had chosen New York City as the honeymoon destination, largely because of the many who had landed there to start their lives anew. She was fascinated by it, especially when she read about the American philosopher Ayn Rand who, as a young girl emigrating from the recently formed Soviet Union, actually wept when she first saw the New York City skyline. Now Priya was about to experience this great city. True to form, she was sticking to her plan. She reached inside her purse, which was tucked snugly between her and her husband, and pulled out the poem she had read for her research paper, promising herself she would read it again if she were ever to see the Statue of Liberty.

"Whatcha got there?" Brian asked.

"A poem. It's from a page I read during my research paper for Professor Martin's class."

Brian saw a serious look in Priya and decided to not ask any questions, at least not now. She looked at the statue through the small window, and then she started reading the poem she was holding in her hands, Emma Lazarus's "The New Colossus":

> Not like the brazen giant of Greek fame,
> With conquering limbs astride from land to land;
> Here at our sea-washed, sunset gates shall stand
> A mighty woman with a torch, whose flame
> Is the imprisoned lightning, and her name
> Mother of Exiles. From her beacon-hand
> Glows world-wide welcome; her mild eyes command
> The air-bridged harbor that twin cities frame.
> "Keep, ancient lands, your storied pomp!" cries she

With silent lips. "Give me your tired, your poor,
Your huddled masses yearning to breathe free,
The wretched refuse of your teeming shore.
Send these, the homeless, tempest-tossed to me,
I lift my lamp beside the golden door!"

Priya refolded the poem and placed it in her purse. She looked at Brian, and he smiled at her.

So much had happened to her in this last year. She had made choices: to study here, to learn here, to ask Brian to marry her, and to live and make her life here in the United States. She was happy with her choices, happy the way things turned out—*fell into place*, as the Americans like to say. She was excited about New York City, about living with Brian, about their house-flipping business, about writing that *Notes from America* column for the *Chennai Times*, about trying to get her novel, *Money Matters*, published. She reflected on the many choices she had made, realizing a big one—the biggest one of them all—was the man sitting next to her. Brian. She chose to marry him, and he had said yes. And yes meant her life would change forever. She couldn't have been happier with her choice.

ABOUT THE AUTHOR

Paul Bouchard is the author of Enlistment, The Boy Who Wanted To Be A Man, A Package at Gitmo, A Catholic Marries a Hindu, Having It Good Downrange, and many others. A retired Army reporter and JAG officer, he practices law in Washington, D.C. For more on Paul Bouchard visit paulbouchard.com.

ABOUT THE BOOK

Nine thousand miles separate Chennai, India, from Las Cruces, New Mexico, the distance Priya Kumar, 25, travels to join two of her sisters for a one year graduate program at New Mexico State University. Busy with school work and learning all she can about the United States, it's in Professor Martin's year-long Independent Studies course where her comparison-culture learning is put to the forefront, for she must write a 50-page paper about Alexis de Tocqueville's classic Democracy in America and whether it still rings true nearly two centuries after its first publication. The American Story is often best told from a foreigner's perspective, and it's in writing this paper that Priya not only learns about her host country, but more so about herself and the choices she's faced with. One choice stands above all the others, and it changes her life forever.

Printed in the United States
By Bookmasters